Outstanding praise for M. V. Byrne and
Meet Isabel Puddles!

"I was very happy to meet Isabel Puddles and I'm sure
readers will enjoy making her acquaintance, too.
M. V. Byrne's small-town sleuth with a big heart sees
the *possible* in impossible, whether she's cooking up
a delicious pot roast or solving a devious crime."
—Leslie Meier, author of *Irish Parade Murder*

"When you meet the delightfully witty and no-nonsense
Isabel Puddles, you'll never want her to leave."
—Lee Hollis, author of *Poppy Harmon and the Hung Jury*

"I've met Isabel Puddles and I love her. She's a smart, funny
AARPster who can whip up a mean pot roast while solving
a diabolical murder. I eagerly turned the pages of this
charming, action-packed whodunit. What a fun read!"
—Laura Levine, author of *Death of a Gigolo*

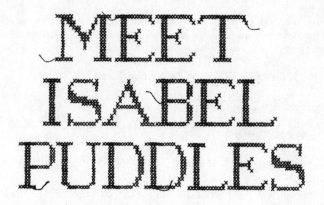

MEET ISABEL PUDDLES

M.V. BYRNE

KENSINGTON BOOKS
www.kensingtonbooks.com

KENSINGTON BOOKS are published by

Kensington Publishing Corp.
119 West 40th Street
New York, NY 10018

ISBN-13: 978-1-4967-2832-6 (ebook)
ISBN-10: 1-4967-2832-7 (ebook)

ISBN-13: 978-1-4967-2831-9
ISBN-10: 1-4967-2831-9
First Kensington Trade Paperback Printing: December 2020

10 9 8 7 6 5 4 3 2 1

Printed in the United States of America

For Aunt Isabel . . . who taught me
everything I know about funny

Chapter 1

Isabel Puddles was no hero. At least she didn't think so. But if you asked anybody in her hometown of Gull Harbor, Michigan, a charming harborside hamlet tucked into the stoic, tree-lined shores of Lake Michigan, Isabel—Iz or Izzy to her family and friends—was the biggest thing to come out of Michigan since Gerald Ford, Henry Ford, and the Ford Mustang combined.

"Yep . . . she's a regular Miss Marple," Kayla, the waitress at Isabel's favorite breakfast haunt, was fond of saying whenever the topic of her sleuthing skills came up.

Frances Spitler, another breakfast regular, had a slightly less demure take on the crime-solving abilities of the woman who had been her best friend since kindergarten. "More like Sherlock Holmes with a C cup." Frances was famous in her own right for saying pretty much whatever popped into her head.

Isabel and Frances started meeting for breakfast at the Land's End nearly a decade before when the breakfast special was just $2.99. It was now up to $6.99. But in the summertime, when rich Chicagoans and Milwaukeeans sailed across the "Big Lake" to Gull Harbor to summer on their yachts; and well-heeled Detroiters, Hoosiers, and Buckeyes drove north to open their summer homes for the season, Gull Harbor's population soared. And so did the price of the Land's End breakfast special, which, from Memorial Day to Labor Day, skyrocketed to $9.99. But for regulars like Isabel and Frances, the price stayed fixed at $6.99. And for Isabel, that included a couple of extra rashers of bacon, which usually found their way onto her plate if Chet Morris was working. He had had a crush on Isabel since junior high social studies, but, sadly for Chet, his unrequited love could now be expressed only through slices of thick-cut maple-smoked bacon.

Spending nearly ten dollars, including tip, on breakfast was still pricey for Isabel Puddles, but despite her overburdened checking account and her innately frugal nature, and because she had never in her life been able to cook an over-easy egg the way she liked it, Isabel still had breakfast at the Land's End with Frances almost every morning.

The last time Isabel had cooked a proper breakfast at home was the morning her husband died, but she was always quick to point out that these events were unrelated. Like the good wife and mother she had always tried to be, Isabel had eaten scrambled eggs the way Carl liked them, and the only way her kids would eat them. For more than twenty years she never let on, or even admitted to herself, that she really didn't care for scrambled eggs at all. She liked her eggs over easy and basted with butter the way *her* mother cooked them. Isabel Puddles was known to be an exceptionally good home cook, but she was no match for her late mother Helen's kitchen wizardry. . . . Over-easy eggs remained her blind spot.

It was around the time that Isabel had become a widow that Frances decided it was time to retire. After twenty years working as a secretary at a local canning factory where her husband, Hank, was a first-shift foreman, Frances decided her shift was up. Daily breakfast for Hank ended the day after she retired. "The only way you're getting breakfast out of me at six thirty in the morning anymore is if I get a job at the McDonald's drive-through!" she ranted defiantly after Hank objected to his wife's revised breakfast policy. Frances was late to embrace feminism, but she got up to speed pretty fast once she figured it out.

"Poor Hank," Isabel once remarked to Frances. "He married Harriet Nelson and ended up living with Gloria Steinem."

And so the Land's End Breakfast Club was born—two independent, middle-aged women finally enjoying breakfast on their own terms, and with no dishes to do.

Isabel and Frances were as close, and as different, as two people could be. Frances was brash and to the point; Isabel, circumspect and thoughtful. Frances was brutally honest; Isabel, cautious and diplomatic. Frances was excitable and high strung; Isabel, calm and measured. But these were guidelines, not rules, and on occasion, if the circumstances called for it, they flipped the script. What never changed after forty-plus years of friendship was their unconditional love for each other and a fierce loyalty, going back to the first day of kindergarten, when Jacqueline Klinger bullied Isabel out of her chocolate milk. Thanks to Frances's intervention—after finding her new classmate Isabel sitting on a swing and crying—Jacqueline Klinger ended up wearing that same chocolate milk all over her head, and all over her crisp white, Raggedy Ann pinafore . . . and Frances ended up in the principal's office.

Isabel returned the favor the following year, when their first-grade teacher, a mean old battle-ax named Miss Marlin, came up behind Frances and flicked her ear so hard, it made her cry, just for whispering to Isabel during morning announcements. Miss Marlin returned from lunch that afternoon to find several thumbtacks planted on her chair, waiting to greet her rather large posterior. Their occasional recollection of the shriek that came out of Miss Marlin made them laugh out loud to this day. Theirs was an unbreakable bond, and although it had been strained a time or two over the years, it was a bond that always held fast.

Unlike Frances, Isabel was shy by nature, and not somebody who wanted or needed the sort of attention that had been recently visited upon her, so playing the role of local hero was more a burden than anything else. Her snowballing notoriety as a small-town crime fighter was becoming more and more difficult to deflect, but it would appear she was stuck with it, at least for the time being. Her reluctant celebrity began a few years after her husband, Carl, died, very suddenly, following a heart attack. Carl's modest life insurance policy covered his funeral expenses and paid off some bills, but that was about it. Both her kids were out of college, so there wasn't that expense, but if she was going to survive, Isabel knew she had to go back to work. But doing what? She had long ago given up her "career" as a hairdresser, which was a job she enjoyed about as much as she did scrambled eggs, but as a middle-aged widow with no college degree, Isabel didn't have much choice. The Michigan economy was a mess, and jobs were hard to come by, so eventually she started doing hair again, converting the mother-in-law apartment attached to her garage to a hair salon. She also managed to toggle together a handful of other part-time ventures—enough to keep the lights and the heat on, and keep herself and the dog fed. But in the years of widowhood that followed, she never really felt she was ever in the clear financially. There always seemed to be an accumulation of bills and an assortment of other expenses looming, along with the occasional big-ticket surprise expense, so she was continuously on the lookout for new revenue streams to fish. She was open to any and all possibilities. Provided she was physically able, and it was legal, Isabel was game. . . . Which was how she ended up accepting a job doing hair and makeup at a local funeral home.

It was not a job she particularly relished taking on, and she wasn't anxious to meet the person who would, but it was more money than she could pass up for an afternoon's work, so she braced herself and decided to at least give it a try. Not only would she be helping out her bank account but she would also be helping out a dear old friend who was in a bind, and who happened to be the owner of the funeral home. Little did Isabel Puddles know how fateful this decision would be or where it would eventually take her. . . .

Although she never finished college, Isabel did graduate from the Whitehall Beauty Academy, with honors. But putting her skills to work on the newly departed was not something that had ever occurred to her—and why would it? Still, when it came to postmortem makeovers, she was not a complete novice. Isabel had in fact provided this slightly cringeworthy service once before, not for money but purely out of love and a sense of duty. And it was just her luck that she seemed to have a flair for it. This unexpected addition to her résumé happened after her favorite high school teacher, Gladys DeLong, passed away.

For more than half a century, Miss DeLong had been a pillar of the community, a beloved high school teacher, and a revered figure in Gull Harbor. Gladys came from a prominent Grand Rapids family that for many years owned an impressive summer home on Lake Michigan. Her father had made a fortune in office furniture but died penniless, and their stately summer home was now an elegant, very pricey bed-and-breakfast. Gambling was rumored to be the cause of Raymond DeLong's downfall, although nobody ever knew for sure. But while the getting was good, Gladys was sent east to Miss Porter's School and went on to Smith College. When she decided to become a teacher, she returned to the place that brought back her happiest childhood memories:

Gull Harbor, Michigan. Although Gladys DeLong's pedigree was highly unusual for such a small town, she was anything but pretentious, never exhibiting any hint of snobbery, unlike many of the summer people who paraded around town with their noses in the air, and with far less to be snobbish about.

Isabel had Miss DeLong for both her junior and senior years, first for English lit, and then for American lit. Later in life—long after Isabel Peabody had become Isabel Puddles and raised a family, and after Miss DeLong had retired, the two became close friends when Gladys began volunteering at the Gull Harbor Library a few days a week. Isabel, who was an avid reader, thanks in large part to Miss DeLong's influence, was a library regular. For years they had been chatting at the front desk in hushed tones, mostly about books, gardening, the weather, Isabel's kids, and recipes they had recently tried or wanted to try, all of it peppered with a healthy dose of local gossip, along with Gladys DeLong's dry, but razor-sharp wit. Every few weeks, the two would get together for lunch, and Gladys always came to Isabel's annual Christmas Eve party with her famous curried shrimp dip and mango chutney, an appetizer as exotic for Gull Harbor as it was delicious. Isabel was convinced that some of her guests came only for the shrimp dip.

Gladys was a handsome woman of Dutch descent—a staunch, no-frills, midwestern matron. In Isabel's memory she never wore much, if any, makeup, and her long, thick salt-and-pepper hair was worn in a bun that always looked about ready to come undone. Round tortoiseshell glasses completed her professorial look. No slave to fashion—but then who needed to be in Gull Harbor, Michigan?—Miss DeLong owned a half dozen or so classic knit suits, with skirts that fell just below the knee. The suits came in various shades of beiges, grays, and blues, some patterned, some not, and looked to have been purchased sometime in the late 1950s, probably in some posh New York City department store. Her impeccably made suits were always accessorized with a smart print scarf—of which she seemed to have many—along with an impressive collection of simple but elegant gold brooches, always worn on her left lapel. Isabel could still hear her revered teacher clicking through the halls of Swift Lather High School, always in a hurry, her plain black purse hooked around her elbow, an armful of books or loose papers, and wearing the same pair of sensible black heels. In retirement, Miss DeLong segued seamlessly from schoolmarm to librarian with no costume change required, although she had taken to wearing shoes that looked slightly more orthopedic, and she had done away with the scarves and the brooches. The suits gradually became a little snug over the years, but she once admitted to Isabel why she had more or less maintained her weight all these years. "I'm Dutch . . . I'm too frugal to buy new ones." Isabel could relate—if she couldn't find something she liked that fit her on the clearance rack, then she was done shopping.

Isabel last saw Miss DeLong at the library in August of that summer, just a week or so before she passed, when Isabel came in to return a book, rather sheepishly. It was the latest James Patterson novel, and she wasn't at all sure that the woman who had introduced her to William Faulkner, Flannery O'Connor, Jane Austen, and Charles Dickens was going to approve of her former student reading anything so commercial. Gladys took the book and winked at her, then leaned over the desk and quietly confessed, "I've read everything John Grisham has ever written." Isabel laughed. So had she.

That particular day they chatted about who had the best sweet corn that season and who had the juiciest tomatoes (the battle of the farm stands was an ongoing one in Kentwater County), and Gladys lamented about how the wisteria she had planted when she bought her house in 1966, although beautiful to look at, had become so prolific that it was overtaking her garage and making it almost impossible to get her car in and out anymore. Isabel then checked out a book by a new author Gladys thought she might like, and they made plans to get together for lunch again before the Labor Day weekend. She never dreamed it would be the last time she ever saw Gladys DeLong again . . . alive.

After hearing at breakfast just a few days later that Gladys had dropped dead trimming that out-of-control wisteria *herself*, Isabel was devastated by the news. At eighty-six, on a stepladder, with garden shears in hand, it was a fittingly noble way to go, but the despair Isabel felt losing someone who had been so much a part of her life for so long was hard for her to take in. Without Gladys, the town instantly felt different to her, and she was going to miss her teacher and friend terribly. Isabel feared she was reaching that age where good-byes were going to start becoming more common than hellos.

Later on that dismal day, Isabel drove by Miss DeLong's neatly kept Cape Cod cottage on Westbury Road and saw her equally well-kept, twenty-five-year-old light blue Buick still parked in the driveway. She slowed to a stop and stared at the wisteria, blooming victoriously, fondly remembering her friend until she was struck by another crashing wave of sadness, and slowly pulled away. Isabel continued on her way to the Cook Funeral Home in Hartley—a little town about five miles southeast of Gull Harbor—where a viewing was scheduled for that afternoon. With a year-round population of only about 750, Gull Harbor wasn't large enough to support a funeral home of its own, nor were any of the other surrounding villages and hamlets in the county, and the summer people seemed to prefer dying at home, so if you were a local who died in Kentwater County, Cook's was probably where you were going to end up.

Isabel was a Gull Harbor girl, but Hartley was her parents' hometown, as well as her grandparents' and great-grandparents', on both sides, before them. The Peabodys had been in Hartley ever since Great-Grandfather Manchester—"Chester"—Peabody arrived from England in the late 1800s. Chester escaped a childhood of abject poverty in London to seek his fame and fortune in the Michigan lumber industry . . . but failed. He did, however, manage to convince the town's most beautiful girl, Zelda Gerber, a doctor's daughter, to marry him. Ironically, he did end up in the lumber business, managing a lumberyard. The couple lived modestly on Chester's salary, and along with a small inheritance from Zelda's father, they were able to send all three of their kids to college, which was quite a feat at the turn of the twentieth century. Chester and Zelda's offspring managed to do pretty well for themselves. Their two girls, Madeline and Marjorie, both gifted with their mother's beauty, married well and moved to the East Coast, never to return to Hartley. Their son, Isabel's grandfather, Charlie Peabody, moved back to Hartley after college and, being a shrewd investor, eventually became a local land baron of sorts, owning an entire city block in Hartley known as the "Peabody block." Isabel's grandmother, Hazel, was a MacGregor, another prominent family in Hartley, who owned a furniture store in town, and another in nearby Wellington. But after the Great Crash of 1929, both families found themselves in "diminished circumstances," as her grandmother Hazel used to say.

Hartley was the county seat, and although it was about five times the size of Gull Harbor, it was still a very small town. But because it had the only traffic light in the county, was home to the county fairgrounds, and had its own highway off-ramp, it was practically a metropolis by comparison. With a timeless stateliness, less beachy and casual than Gull Harbor, Hartley was a dignified old town with beautiful old homes—some in better shape than others—lining either side of the main drag, State Street, with its canopy of hundred-year-old maples. A few of the grandest old homes hugged Hartley Lake, a man-made lake Charlie Peabody had helped develop in the 1930s, and where he later built the family home. The old Peabody home was not as grand as some of the others on Hartley Lake, but it was a handsome old Queen Anne revival with a wide, sloping lawn and a sweeping view of the lake and the town beyond it. Isabel had very fond memories of her grandparents' house on Hartley Lake, and in fact every holiday season she was invited to a Christmas party hosted by the "new" owners, Robert and Bonnie Bagley, who purchased the home after Grandmother Peabody died. The Bagleys were convinced Hazel Peabody, known as the consummate hostess, was still there with them, but given the eerie, unidentifiable racket they heard in the attic from time to time, Hazel Peabody was not as gracious in spirit as she had been in life.

So although Gull Harbor was home, Isabel also felt very much at home in Hartley. She still had family there, she did her grocery shopping there, she went to church there, and she worked part time at her cousin Freddie Peabody's hardware store, also in Hartley.

After parking her old minivan on State Street, just up from the Cook Funeral Home, she sat back and took a moment to reflect on what lay ahead. She had been to Cook's more times than she cared to remember, but knowing Miss DeLong was in there now was especially unsettling for Isabel. She hoped she would find her old friend Gil inside to help her get through this. Gil Cook was now a third-generation funeral director, and the two went back many years.

Hartley and Gull Harbor kids all went to the same high school back in those days—Swift Lather High School—named after a wealthy and eccentric lawyer who gained fame, and a fair amount of fury, for being a card-carrying, FDR-loving Democrat in a staunchly Republican county. There was no stauncher Republican in Kentwater County than Isabel's grandfather Charlie, but surprisingly he and Swift Lather were great friends and had been for decades, despite Charlie's overt contempt for President Roosevelt, and Swift's similar feelings toward Herbert Hoover. Swift was a true philanthropist, giving money away anonymously wherever he saw a need, and defending anybody in the county who needed defending, whether or not they could afford it. He was a small-town hero in Kentwater County, revered despite his "radical" politics. Charlie Peabody had done his fair share of service to his community, too, but in the end, it was Swift Lather who had the high school named after him and not Charlie Peabody. "I'm sure the Roosevelts were behind that decision," Charlie snorted to his wife when he heard the news.

It was the start of their freshman year at Swift Lather when Isabel Peabody and Gil Cook first met, and Gil asked Isabel to the homecoming dance. She accepted, and although they enjoyed each other's company, nothing romantic ever developed. When she met Carl Puddles in the fall of their sophomore year, the handsome new transfer student from Wisconsin, she was immediately smitten by the boy from that mysterious land of cheese across Lake Michigan. But despite being jilted, Gil Cook still adored Isabel, and vice versa, so the two had remained the best of friends all these years. Frances was sure Gil was still carrying a torch for her, a suggestion Isabel dismissed as nonsense.

Carl, a star athlete, and Isabel, a cheerleader, dated for the remainder of high school. When they became the Asparagus King and Queen in the spring of their senior year— Kentwater County was, after all, the asparagus capital of Michigan—it was as if the Fates had deemed them Kentwater County royalty, destined to one day marry, raise a family, and reign happily ever after. But that plan went south the following fall when they went off to Michigan State, where Isabel excelled and Carl struggled. When she got pregnant eighteen months later, they married quickly before anybody could do the math, left college, and moved back to Gull Harbor. The plan was to return to school together after the baby got a little older, or at least that was Isabel's plan. She was determined to go back and finish her two remaining years and get her teaching degree. But in the meantime, she was happy to stay home with the baby, while Carl went to work for the County Road Commission. He eventually got his degree in civil engineering by going to night school at a nearby college, which the county paid for. In exchange, he committed to working as the county engineer, which he did . . . for the rest of his life. But Isabel remained a stay-at-home mom, first with their daughter, Carly—not named after Carl, as he liked people to think, but after Carly Simon, her favorite singer at the time— and a year and a half later, a son, Charlie, named after Isabel's grandfather, joined the family. She never intended to give her children rhyming names, and she was still apologizing to them for it today. Sadly, Isabel's dream of going back to school and one day becoming a teacher like Miss DeLong was one that faded away over the years. Not finishing college was one of her biggest regrets in life, although there had been times when marrying Carl Puddles was pretty high on the list, too.

Chapter 2

Isabel took a few moments more to collect herself before heading into Cook's. According to the paper, Gladys De-Long's viewing was to begin at 3:00 p.m., and although it was already 3:15, the place looked empty. But it was a weekday, so most people wouldn't be arriving until after work. She thought about coming back later herself, but then decided to go in and have some alone time to quietly reflect on her friend without having to engage in a lot of conversation.

She finally made her way up the cobblestone path and to the front door, took a deep breath, and entered the impressive carved-wood foyer, where she was immediately greeted by a young woman she had never seen before in her life. Over her shoulder was a young man in a suit, also a complete stranger. The woman approached her with a friendly smile. "Hello . . . Thank you for coming." She took Isabel's hand with both of hers. "I'm Elise Phillips." The young man slowly approached, barely managing enough interest to shake Isabel's hand and mumble a hello. "And this is my brother Stephen DeLong. . . . Gladys was our father's sister." Stephen was looking down at his phone before the introduction was even over. "We live in

California. We haven't really seen our aunt in . . . how many years has it been, Stephen?"

He shrugged. "Ten? Twenty?"

Elise continued, "I'm afraid our father is not in very good health and just too frail to travel. He asked us to come on his behalf and see to everything." Isabel remembered the never-married Gladys DeLong talking about a younger brother in San Diego, as well as a nephew and niece, but never with any overwhelming fondness or attachment.

Somewhere in their mid-thirties, the two were very attractive, well dressed, suntanned, and both had very white, perfect teeth. She then remembered Gladys telling her that her brother was a dentist. Isabel found the niece quite pleasant, but the nephew's slightly surly attitude began to work her nerves almost immediately. She knew the type. Many of the summer people had that same condescending attitude toward the locals, treating them like a collective of hayseeds unable to comprehend the sophisticated, citified world they hailed from. The contempt many locals had for the summer people was far better disguised, because, snobby or not, they were the bread and butter that would get many of them through another long Michigan winter without starving.

Isabel had mixed feelings about the summer people. She was a fair-minded woman and didn't like to paint with too broad a brush, but she could see why many of the locals were less than enamored of them. She had limited interaction, but by and large, she felt that they were agreeable enough, although she had met some real doozies. But rather than focus on the bad apples, she counted her blessings instead, feeling a little sorry for these summer folks who could spend only a few weeks out of the year in what she considered to be the most beautiful place on Earth. They were stuck in places like Chicago or Detroit or Milwaukee—cities she had visited and couldn't wait to leave— so she could understand why living in places like that might tend to make some of them a little unpleasant. Isabel Peabody Puddles was a small-town girl and proud of it. She wouldn't leave Gull Harbor for anything in the world.

As kids Isabel and the other local children always made "summer friends," but those friendships were not only fleeting, they were not friendships the parents of their summer friends encouraged very much. Most of them considered the local children not quite good enough for *their* children. Isabel never forgot overhearing the mother of a boy from Bloomfield Hills, an upscale Detroit suburb, sitting on the back porch with her friends, drinking gin-and-tonics, in broad daylight, and referring to Isabel as a "pretty girl, but she's a bit down-market." Isabel and the woman's son, Drew, were on their way to see a matinee together, but they had stopped in the kitchen for cookies and lemonade, which was when she overheard the remark. The family's housekeeper, a lovely African American woman named Lucy, was standing at the sink and also heard the slight. Lucy just shook her head slowly in response. Isabel wasn't exactly sure what "down-market" meant, so later that evening at the dinner table she asked her mother. Helen Peabody tried to convince her fourteen-year-old daughter that it was meant as a compliment, but Isabel could tell from the steam coming from her mother's ears that it definitely was not. Regardless of where she fell on Drew's mother's "market scale," the first time young Isabel Peabody ever took a puff of a cigarette, had a sip of beer, or on one occasion became an unwitting accomplice to shoplifting, there was a summer kid spearheading the crime. And the first time any boy ever tried to cop a feel, it was that presumably "up-market" boy from Bloomfield Hills . . . in the middle of a matinee.

Frances was far less tolerant of the summer people. When a Chicago woman at the Land's End sitting a few tables over scoffed at the toast she was served with her breakfast, proclaiming to Kayla that "no restaurant in *Chicago* would ever

dare serve such cheap white bread for toast!" Frances spoke
right up, and in a voice loud enough for everybody to hear,
offered to drive the woman down to Lake Michigan so she
could "swim home in time for breakfast tomorrow morning!"

After offering her condolences to Gladys's niece and
nephew, Isabel approached the casket in the somber fashion
one does, but as she got closer, she was helpless in prevent-
ing her jaw from literally dropping open. At first glance it
appeared that whoever had been assigned to do Gladys De-
Long's hair and makeup either had a very inappropriate sense
of humor or had at some point worked for Barnum & Bailey.
The second glance was not any better. Isabel slowly turned to
the niece and nephew, her jaw still open, wearing a pained
expression. The niece looked concerned as well, but only
managed to shrug her shoulders. Her brother was texting.

As "The Old Rugged Cross"—one of the Cook Funeral
Home's hit parade of hymns—wafted through the funeral
parlor, Isabel took Gladys's family aside. Speaking in a hushed
tone, as if she didn't want Gladys to hear, she shared her concerns. "I'm sorry . . . but this just isn't the Gladys DeLong I
knew—or *anybody* knew, for that matter."

The nephew managed to look up from his phone and
chime in, "It's like *What Ever Happened to Baby Jane?* meets
The Golden Girls."

"Stephen, stop it," his sister scolded.

Isabel looked at Gladys again. "I do remember that gray
suit . . . and the earrings." She recalled Miss DeLong talking
about buying the pearl cluster earrings on a trip to Paris after
college.

The niece smiled. "She had the suit hanging in the closet
with a note. I remember the earrings, too. I don't know that
she ever took them off. They're going with her, of course."

Stephen looked up from his phone again, this time with

an expression that indicated he wasn't necessarily in favor of burying expensive jewelry. He then offered his take on matters. "Well, obviously I haven't seen her for a while . . . but what I remember was a spinster English teacher sent straight from central casting. This look is more, I don't know, *Mrs. Doubtfire* meets—"

"Stephen, do not!" Elise had clearly had enough. He forced a smile, shrugged, and sat down, turning his attention back to his phone, while Elise tried to explain her brother's behavior.

"My brother works in television. Doing *what* exactly, I don't know. Everything is a movie or a television reference with him. It's *very* tedious."

Isabel lifted her eyebrows and gave the nephew a look best described as *unimpressed*, then turned back to the niece. "Miss DeLong loathed television. She never owned one, as far as I know."

"I don't believe she did," Elise recalled. Then, aside to Isabel under her breath, "She wasn't all that fond of my brother, either."

"Well, she always did have discriminating taste." Isabel extended her hand again to Elise. "I'm so sorry. . . . It just occurred to me that I never introduced myself. I'm just so overwhelmed to have to say good-bye to my old friend . . . and my very favorite teacher. I'm Isabel Puddles. I hope you know how beloved and admired a figure your aunt was in this community." Isabel lowered her voice, "But I'm afraid nobody coming to pay their respects is going to recognize her—she just never looked like this."

Stephen, still busy on his phone with one hand and fixing his wavy, blondish hair with the other, looked up. "Nobody looks like that . . . unless they're going trick-or-treating."

"Stephen, if you can't be respectful, you're welcome to leave. Please . . . just go back to the hotel."

"You mean *motel*?" Stephen said with a sneer.

Elise turned to Isabel. "Please forgive my brother." Then back to him. "He's *very* insensitive."

"Don't forget callous," her brother added, not looking up from his phone.

"Yes, that, too," she snapped. "And a few other things I won't mention."

Although Isabel didn't like the nephew—at all—she had to agree that his aunt's appearance was, to be kind, alarming. She looked back at Stephen, who was still texting and playing with his hair. "Your aunt carried herself with such elegance. She had such lovely manners. Shame you couldn't have spent more time with her." He ignored her not so veiled insult. Typically a very patient person, Isabel Puddles had now reached her limit with this one. "I don't know if you missed the sign in the lobby—Stephen, is it?—but cell phones are *not* permitted to be used inside this funeral home." The nephew stopped cold, looking up and glaring at Isabel, who glared right back, then turned to the niece. "You wouldn't think a sign would even be required, would you? But then you can't count on good taste *or* good manners dictating people's behavior. Not in this day and age."

Stephen stood up in a huff and headed for the door. After landing her comeuppance punch, Isabel took a smiling Elise by the arm and walked her back to the casket. "With your permission I'd like to see what we can do to fix this . . . well, this . . . situation. Let me talk to Mr. Cook. He's the funeral director here and an old friend of mine. Gil had Miss DeLong in high school, too. In fact, we were in the same class one year. I know he'd want to see this remedied."

Elise flushed with relief. "Yes . . . please do." She gave her new friend a hug.

With a side tilt of her head, Isabel signaled to J.T., the assistant funeral director, who was standing in the wings, looking on curiously. J.T. was a pale, gangly, but still oddly good-looking boy in his early twenties with jet-black hair and deep green eyes. Isabel had known him since he first came to work for Gil while he was still in high school. She grabbed him and pulled him by the sleeve into a side parlor. "J.T., who in the world did Miss DeLong's hair and makeup?" she asked with a reserved annoyance.

"Well, Judy usually takes care of this for us. You know Judy. She works down to the Hair Today salon over on Grant Street."

"Yes, of course I know Judy. But that's not what I asked you."

"Well, Judy had to go up north to help her daughter out with her grandkids this week."

"That's not what I asked you, either, J.T." He was hedging.

"Well, you know, Mrs. Puddles, none of the girls down at Hair Today were willing to help out. . . . People get squirrelly about this type of thing."

Isabel raised her eyebrows at J.T., then dipped her chin, her meaning quite clear. J.T. stumbled through his response. "Well . . . to answer your question . . . I didn't want to bother Mr. Cook, so . . ." Finally he blurted out, "So I just decided to handle it myself!"

"Oh, good Lord . . . You did this? Well, that solves the riddle, doesn't it?" Isabel took a deep breath. "I do not think this is your calling, J.T. Where's Gil?"

"Mr. Cook left for South Bend today . . . for a morticians' convention. I thought she looked pretty good. I never had her in school, but . . . well, I saw a picture of her, and—"

The look on Isabel's face stopped him midsentence. They both looked over at Gladys. "I'm sorry, J.T., I know you did your best, but . . ." Isabel let out a heavy sigh. "Here's what we're going to do. I want you to draw the curtain of the front parlor, turn off the music, and go stand at the door. Tell anybody who might show up to come back in an hour. Tell them there's been a short delay. Now I'm going to run over to the Rexall and pick up a few things. Bring whatever hair and makeup supplies you have from downstairs up here. Let's see if we can just tone down that makeup a little and bring her hair down a touch and do something with those eyebrows. I don't want poor Miss DeLong arriving at the Pearly Gates looking so, well, so surprised."

J.T. did as he was told, and Isabel went back into the lobby and suggested to Elise that she and Stephen, who was now on the front porch texting his little heart out, go down the street to Hobson's Choice bakery for coffee and a pastry while she handled things there. She told her to come back in an hour. Elise thanked her again profusely on her way out the front door. Isabel watched through the window as Elise grabbed her brother firmly by the arm and walked him off the front porch like a disobedient schoolboy.

After returning with some cold cream and facial wipes, Isabel went to work. She never could have imagined this particular task—a surreal experience at the very least—was going to be added to that day's to-do list, but her unease, coupled with her profound sadness, was overridden by her love and respect for Gladys DeLong. She was determined that her dear friend's final farewell to a community that also loved her would be in keeping with the dignified woman she was.

Taking control in a difficult situation was not at all out of character for Isabel Puddles. She was a problem solver. And like Gladys, she was a staunch character who was not easily daunted. If she had the time, and could figure out how to do it, she did the job herself. That meant, this week alone, repairing the stairs on her back deck, replacing her leaky kitchen faucet, scraping and repainting her garage door, regrouting the shower tile, and now, giving a posthumous makeover to the woman who taught her to love Jane Austen and the Brontë sisters.

When Gladys's niece and nephew returned, Isabel instructed J.T. to pull open the curtains and turn the music back on—Mozart's Requiem this time. She had found a DVD of classical music at the drugstore, which seemed more fitting than a collection of random, overwrought hymns. She then led them back to the cherrywood casket, where, lying elegantly in repose, was the Miss DeLong everyone would remember, her long gray hair softly swept back from her face and gathered into a loose-fitting bun, with some light powder, a hint of blush on her cheeks, a trace of lipstick, and finally her round tortoise-shell glasses grasped in her hands, which were folded across her chest. A beloved exemplar of dignity and distinction now awaited the community that admired her to pay its respects. Gladys DeLong looked peaceful . . . and somewhat relieved.

Elise gave Isabel a hug. "She looks just lovely. I cannot thank you enough, Isabel."

Even Stephen seemed impressed, and a little bit contrite. "Yes . . . she looks, well . . . much calmer. Thank you, Mrs. Puddles." He went back to his phone, but quickly stopped, looked up at Isabel, then slipped it back into his pocket. She still didn't like him, but he had redeemed himself slightly.

Elise looked back at the casket, then, turning to Isabel. "I don't remember the scarf."

Gladys's gray suit had been lovingly accessorized with a soft blue-and-gray paisley-patterned scarf, loosely tied around her neck and tucked smartly into her suit. Isabel smiled. "I had it in my purse. The colors were perfect. I'd like her to keep it."

Gil Cook returned from his morticians' convention in South Bend two days later. After J.T. told him what had happened, he called Isabel and thanked her for saving his reputation. He knew better than to offer payment for her services, as they pertained to Gladys DeLong, for what he knew had been the very definition of a labor of love, but he did try to hire her as his new full-time, on-call hair-and-makeup person. Isabel demurred. Yes, she was always open to earning extra money, but she made her position on this very clear. "Gil, if I ever decide to go back into hairdressing full-time, I would prefer to do it for clients sitting upright and with a pulse." When the conversation came to an end, and Gil's efforts had failed, Isabel closed with a simple request: "Promise me that when I go, you won't let J.T. anywhere near me."

After a long summer, Isabel was happy to see autumn arrive, despite the melancholy that lingered after losing her friend Gladys. Not only was fall a gorgeous time of year in this part of Michigan, with the crisp air and the fall colors slowly presenting themselves, but after having so many plates spinning that summer, she was worn out. Summers meant vacation time for most, but for Isabel Puddles, it was her busiest time of year.

In June, her famous bread-and-butter pickles took up a lot of time. What had started out as her putting a few jars on the counter of an old friend's farm stand a few years back, just for fun, had now become a commercial enterprise. The growing popularity among the summer people of Puddles Pickles was bringing in some serious revenue, at eight dollars a jar, although she couldn't really wrap her head around anybody paying eight dollars for a jar of pickles. "It's a rudimentary rule of retail economics," Cousin Freddie told her the previous summer, when she was deliberating over whether or not to raise the price of a jar from five dollars to eight dollars. "Charge whatever the market will bear! These summer people have more dollars than they have sense. They can bear it! And your pickles are the best I've ever tasted. I'd charge ten!"

Isabel always reserved several batches of pickles for family and friends, as was customary, and a few more to keep on hand just in case. If she was in a pinch to find a birthday gift, she went to her well-stocked pantry and pulled out a jar. Not only were her pickles coveted, they were sometimes even used for bartering. One spring, Freddie offered to put her dock in if she would add two more jars to his usual quota of four. Isabel agreed, and he had been doing it ever since. Her neighbors offered to take it out in the fall for two extra jars. When her van needed a new radiator, her mechanic, Kit Hopkins, offered to replace it for two jars. She gave him three, and out of sheer gratitude, he rotated her tires.

Through July and well into August, Isabel baked cherry and blueberry pies for a few of the local restaurants and a handful of farm stands. Her pies had become the stuff of legend in Kentwater County, and had consistently won blue ribbons at the county fair whenever she found the time to enter. And in the fall, her apple, pumpkin, and mince pies were a hot commodity with the locals, who ordered them in advance for the holidays. But everything she knew about baking pies she learned from her grandmother, Hazel Peabody, so she couldn't take credit for their excellence. In homage, she named her pie-making business the Peabody Pie Company.

There was also the booth she kept at Berta's Antique Barn, where she was still trying to unload her mother's antique collection, and where she also promoted her line of hand-knit scarves, caps, and mittens. Knitting had also become a fairly serious business. For Isabel, knitting started out as a hobby born of necessity. After her doctor convinced her to quit smoking twenty years earlier, she was desperate for something to do with her hands. She was determined not to become one of those people who ballooned up after quitting cigarettes and taking up snacking instead, so to ensure she maintained her weight within a range she liked to call "pleasingly plump," she joined Weight Watchers and took up knitting. She estimated that over the years she had knitted enough scarves to stretch to Chicago and back. Scarves by Isabel had become a big hit with locals and summer people alike, who ordered them in advance as gifts for the holidays. And these days, she was always on back order.

But Isabel's favorite job by far was working at her cousin Freddie's hardware store in Hartley. She loved Freddie, who had always been like a big brother to her, and she liked keeping up with the Hartley locals. She also liked her 25 percent employee discount when she needed supplies for home repairs and the like. Freddie had been encouraging his cousin to open a commercial kitchen, where she could make her pickles and bake her pies, and then hire people to help her out. He even offered to invest. But Isabel resisted. She didn't want to lose the personal touch. But she did agree to let Freddie put a double oven in the break room so that she could make her pies at home and then bake them while she was at work. But Freddie was no dummy. The smell of those pies baking brought people into the store all summer long, and it wasn't bad for Isabel's sales, either.

Whenever she could find the time, Isabel baked a few extra pies to bring to the county nursing home out on the edge of Hartley, a depressingly nondescript building known as *the facility*. Freddie's oldest sister, Cousin Maggie, who was suffering from dementia, had been at the facility for a few years now, so Isabel would always bring a special slice of pie especially for her. Poor Maggie didn't have a clue who Isabel was anymore, but seeing the joy that slice of pie brought to the cousin who used to take her to the fair when she was a little girl and buy her cotton candy was ample reward for her efforts.

Isabel also took her civic responsibilities seriously, something she had learned from her mother, Helen, who had always been an active member of her community. Doing volunteer work in Gull Harbor and elsewhere in the county was something Isabel was always ready, willing, and happy to do. She was a member of the Garden Club and had been elected to the steering committee for the Friends of the Gull Harbor Library, taking Gladys DeLong's place. She was a founding member of the Western Michigan Shoreline Preservation Society and a member of the Kentwater County Historical Society. Isabel Puddles loved being of service, and although she loved people, she trusted animals, especially dogs, a little bit more, so she spent whatever time she could at the local animal shelter, sometimes even fostering puppies or senior dogs at home. "You always know what you're getting with dogs," Isabel contended. "People? Not so much." This was a sentiment she often shared with prospective adopters at the shelter to help seal the deal.

It was at the shelter that she adopted her most devoted companion, aside from Frances, an adorable Jack Russell terrier she named Jackpot, who was brought into the shelter after being found as a puppy in a trash Dumpster. Although she was forever grateful, she still felt like getting her hands on whoever did that to her Jackpot. Because her friends and family knew how much she loved animals, whenever a dog or cat sitter was needed—or a potbellied pig sitter, if Barb and Al Farley had to go out of town and leave Montgomery behind—Isabel was the one they called, and she was only too happy to oblige.

So, Isabel Puddles was a very busy woman, and often a very tired woman. But no matter how tired she got, she continued to walk the walk, even if she got the occasional blister. Yet despite her hard work and tenacity, her commitment to her community, and her famously frugal nature, Isabel still lived in fear of one day becoming a burden to her children or to the county, winding up alone, elderly, and penniless, living out her days at *the facility*, eating pie with a stranger.

Chapter 3

It was in early October of that same fateful year after Gladys DeLong died that Isabel got a call from Gil Cook. The hair-and-makeup person he was forced to hire when Isabel turned him down had just quit without notice. He began his lobbying effort by asking if he could take her to lunch. Isabel accepted the invitation, knowing he likely had a favor to ask. Not only was she pretty sure she knew what the favor was going to be, she was also pretty sure she knew who it was going to involve. But she could hear the desperation in her old friend's voice, so she decided to pay him the courtesy of at least hearing him out over a turkey club.

It was that morning over breakfast at the Land's End—where folks got all their breaking local news—that the death of Earl Jonasson, a well-known and highly respected farmer, was the lead story. The panel discussion, held at the end of the old Formica counter, included Kayla (popping in between orders with random commentary), Caleb Baxter, who owned the Black Bear Tavern next door, Isabel, and of course Frances, just home from visiting her sister in Buffalo. Everybody knew, or knew *of*, Earl Jonasson and his wife, Ruth. Isabel had been good friends with their daughter Meg ever since third grade. As a kid, she spent a lot of time out at the Jonasson farm, but she never really knew Mr. and Mrs. Jonasson all that well. They were a lovely but reserved couple. After Meg graduated and moved away, Isabel might from time to time run into Earl or Ruth at the Kroger or maybe at the bank, but those encounters never went much beyond a friendly "hello" or "how about this weather?" Meg's parents were what Isabel's mother used to call "good country people." And although they didn't look it or act it, the Jonassons were also *rich* country people—asparagus and cherry growers, mostly, who owned about 2,500 acres of some of the most fertile land in Kentwater County, or in the whole state, for that matter. This was a county full of rich farmers, but Earl Jonasson was one of the richest. Ruth Jonasson, a friendly but demure woman known for her cherry preserves and the cherry print quilts, aprons, and potholders she made for her church rummage sale every year, had died just a couple years earlier, following a long and terrible illness. Isabel remembered bringing a chicken pot pie out to Meg and her family after she learned of Ruth's passing, but mostly she remembered how lost poor Mr. Jonasson looked after losing his wife of sixty-six years. Earl, the Land's End panel decided, had to be way up in his eighties by now, so his death was not exactly shocking. And there was a consensus that old men, especially farmers, didn't usually last long after losing their wives.

According to the initial reports, Earl died sitting on the front porch of the old family farmhouse with his cocker spaniel, Corky, curled up in his lap. Corky wouldn't let the ambulance attendants near Earl, so they had to call the local animal shelter to send someone to tranquilize her. There was a lot of panel discussion about it being a peaceful way to go. There was also a lot of feeling bad for poor Corky. Was she at the shelter or was the family going to keep her? Isabel said she would look into it. The touching scenario reminded her of how distraught her mother's beloved Chihuahua, Guapo, was after she died. Guapo was even older than her mother in dog years, and less than two weeks after her mother passed away, he passed away too, curled up in her mother's chair.

It was just after she went home to call her friend Meg to offer her condolences that Gil Cook called Isabel to ask her to lunch. They met at the Copper Kettle, an old diner overlooking Hartley Lake. After a few minutes of chatting, the kind of easy banter two people who have known each other forever engage in over lunch, Gil finally got to the point, "Iz . . . I need somebody to fix up Earl Jonasson." "Fix up" was how Gil always put it.

"I knew it! I knew that's why you invited me to lunch. Gil Cook, you are a very easy read. Always have been. So, is J.T. not available?" Isabel asked. "I'd love to see what he could do with old Earl."

"It's not a very big job, Izzy."

Isabel was resisting by way of silence and a stare, but she could tell he was in a pickle. Then, finally, "I don't know, Gil . . . I've got a very busy couple of days. It's my turn to host the Knit Wits—that's my knitting circle—so I have to plan a lunch menu and come up with a theme." She stopped and looked sternly at Gil. "Don't make a face. . . . We like to do themes sometimes. And I have to get busy on my Christmas scarves. I'm already behind on my orders. Before you know it, it'll be December. I think I'm going to hire Betty Hodges to help me out this year. That woman can knit circles around me."

Gil stared at her for a beat. "Just curious . . . what kind of *themes* do a group of lady knitters come up with?"

"Oh, holiday themes, seasonal themes, musical themes . . . Sometimes we have movie themes where we sit and knit and watch an old movie after lunch. Last month Myrtle Mayfield had a *Longest Yarn* theme, which was really just a good excuse for us to lay our eyes on Burt Reynolds again. . . . Sometimes you have to make your own fun around here, Gil. We don't all have a mortuary at our disposal to keep us entertained."

Gil laughed out loud. Ever since high school he thought Isabel Peabody was about the funniest person he ever knew. The waitress brought the check and Gil snapped it off the table. Isabel pulled her purse into her lap and began digging through it. "Let me leave the tip."

"I'll pay you three hundred cash," Gil said, pulling out his wallet.

Isabel snapped her head up. She didn't want to appear too anxious, but three hundred cash could very well be a game changer. "Three hundred dollars? Really?"

Gil knew he had sunk his hook. "Really. All the old boy needs is a little powder on his face and a haircut. It's a little on the wild side. And his beard could use a trim. Might want to bring your weed whacker."

"What time do you want me there?" Isabel asked with a sigh.

Gil smiled. "Can you come back with me now? We have three and a half hours . . . the viewing starts at five p.m."

"I have some errands to run. I'll be there in thirty minutes. Thank you for lunch, Gil." Isabel grabbed the to-go box with the other half of her club sandwich. That and a can of tomato soup would be dinner tonight. She stopped as they were going out the door. "Gil . . . You know my license expired years ago. The only hair appointments I do now are for friends and family who either barter or pay cash. Do I need a special license to do this work? I don't want us to get into any trouble."

Gil chuckled as he put a quarter into the bubble gum machine at the front door. "Izzy, nobody's going to know. And Earl won't spill the beans. But if you decide you want to do more of this work, we can look into a mortuary license." He cranked the knob on the gum machine, then looked down in disappointment. "Orange . . . I hate orange."

"I'll take it. I love orange. Thanks anyway, Gil, but I'm doing this as a favor to you, to Earl, and to Meg . . . and for three hundred dollars."

After leaving Gil at the diner, Isabel headed to the bank, pulling in just as Frances was pulling out. They put down their windows to have a quick chat. When she told Frances that Gil Cook had just hired her to give Earl Jonasson a haircut, Frances took it in stride. "If you told me you were joining the merchant marine next week or going to Spain to be a bullfighter, I wouldn't be a bit surprised. Everybody raved about how great Gladys DeLong looked, so I'm sure you'll have old Earl looking like a million bucks, too!"

Frances hadn't seen how great Gladys DeLong looked because she wouldn't attend the funeral, despite Isabel's urging. "The woman flunked me! Twice!" Frances huffed. "It's a beautiful summer day and I'm going to the beach. And you know what I'm *not* going to be doing? Reading Jane Austen!" Not that Frances Spitler was the kind of person to hold a grudge.

After her chat with Frances at the bank, Isabel made a quick stop at Berta's Antique Barn to check her sales, which she did every couple of weeks.

"Just sold your grandmother's clock, Izzy," Berta yelled from her office up in the rafters.

"Finally! Who bought it?"

"Oh, some summer gal from Milwaukee, I think. . . . Said it would be perfect on her mantel. Paid full price!" Berta said as she came down the stairs to say hello.

"Late in the season for summer buyers," Isabel casually observed as she straightened up around the booth and blew the dust off her assortment of collectibles.

Berta came over and gave her a hug. "Lots of people've been commenting on your scarves this season, Iz."

"That time of year, I guess . . . I've got fourteen on back order. I need to get busy on those! Never enough time in the day!" Isabel headed for the door.

"Bye, Iz. I'll have a check for you next week!" Berta yelled after her.

"Thanks!" Isabel yelled back as she passed the counter, grabbed a mint, and sailed out the door. She was pleased to know she could count on another $140 for the clock after Berta took her cut, but she couldn't help feeling a little sad, too. Grandmother Peabody wouldn't exactly be happy to know that one of her prized wedding gifts was sitting on a stranger's fireplace mantel in Milwaukee, but then she'd be less happy to learn her granddaughter was living in a storage unit with her dog.

Isabel parked on State Street again and walked up the stone path to the front door of Cook's. Gil opened the door and greeted her with a smile. She was already getting butterflies. *What had she gotten herself into?* The Cook Funeral Home was a stately old Frank Lloyd Wright–style structure built by Walter DeCamp, once the richest man in Hartley. Gil Cook's grandfather, a mortician from downstate, came to Hartley and bought it after Walter died, then converted it to a funeral parlor. The Cook family had always lived upstairs, which seemed perfectly normal at the time. A lot of people lived above their stores back in those days. But Gilbert Cook III couldn't wait to end that tradition, buying a big new Colonial on the golf course the day after his father retired and announced that he and Gil's mother were moving to Florida. "I spent my entire childhood with dead people living downstairs, and I *still* spend at least five days a week with them," Gil told Isabel after he had bought his new place, "I don't need to be spending evenings and weekends with them, too."

The Cook Funeral Home was a beautiful structure, and impeccably maintained, but for Isabel, it was hard to ignore its provenance. The place still gave her the creeps. She followed Gil into the basement and through the casket showroom, where as kids they used to play hide-and-seek. Long before they had even the slightest awareness of their own mortality, it all seemed like great fun. Today the sight of all those caskets was just downright depressing. Next they walked into a room adjacent to the embalming room, an area that Gil's father had always made clear was off-limits. Gil unlocked the door and they went in. There in the middle of the room was Earl Jonasson, lying peacefully on a gurney, already dressed in a black suit, a white shirt, and a maroon tie. Isabel froze. She wanted out. Gil, sensing her discomfort, knew he needed to get her busy before she hightailed it out of there, so he whipped out a barber's smock from a drawer and threw it over Earl's chest. "J.T. washed his hair after we embalmed him. Standard protocol. All you have to do is give him a haircut, trim that beard up, and then put a little color on his face. Whatever looks natural. Just make sure he doesn't look like he's been on a golf outing to Orlando. All the supplies are in that makeup box over there."

Isabel couldn't stop staring at this man she had known for so many years, now lying dead in front of her, a plain walnut casket waiting for him nearby. "He's so still," she said without even realizing what she was saying.

"Well, Iz, he's dead. . . . They're much easier to bury that way." Gil had a peculiar sense of humor for a mortician, but Isabel was too overwhelmed at the task ahead to even respond. "Just pretend he's taking a nap. No need to worry about waking him up, though." Chuckle, chuckle. Gil could tell she was getting more and more nervous. He hoped lightening things up might help. It didn't. "Now, J.T. is coming in a little later to help me get him into the casket and then upstairs in time for his bon voyage party. So, chop-chop!" Gil looked at Isabel to validate his accidental joke. Nothing. He shrugged and headed for a back staircase.

"Wait . . . you're leaving me here alone?" Isabel was not at all pleased with this development.

"You'll be fine. I've got some errands to run, and then I have an appointment with Dr. McKernan to have a filling replaced. I'm probably the only man in town people are less anxious to see than him!" Gil chuckled some more to himself as he bounced up the stairs, then yelled back, "I'll see you in a couple hours, Iz!"

Isabel had often told Gil Cook that he had to be the most cheerful mortician in America. But today that cheeriness had not been helpful. She took a deep breath and closed her eyes, trying to conjure up some fortitude. It helped to remember the three hundred dollars that would cover her car insurance that month, her electric bill, and the rest of what *she* owed Dr. McKernan herself for fixing the tooth she cracked eating popcorn two weeks before. There might even be enough left over to fill her tank with gas. What a luxury that would be, given that she had pulled into the Shell station that morning with eleven dollars' worth of change in a plastic cup.

As she approached the body, Isabel put on the latex gloves Gil had given her. She looked down at Earl and cautiously began to run her hands through his wild mane of thick gray hair. She took another deep breath, committed to the task now at hand, grabbed her scissors, and went to work, quickly realizing that Gil's suggestion of a weed whacker might not have been a bad idea.

Chapter 4

At first Isabel thought the little bump she was feeling on Earl's scalp was a tiny scab of some kind, maybe from an insect bite or a tick. But rather than ignoring whatever it was and just getting on with Earl's farewell haircut, she found herself parting his hair for a closer examination. Something seemed awfully strange. . . . It was too hard to be a tick. It actually felt more like a tiny piece of something embedded in his scalp. And the area around it seemed to be slightly swollen. No, something definitely wasn't right here. Isabel went for her purse, where she always kept a small magnifying glass among thirty or forty other items. She referred to her oversize leather purse/tote bag as her *"Let's Make a Deal* purse." Her chiropractor referred to it as the reason for her chronic lower back pain.

After digging out her pocket magnifier, she carefully parted Earl's hair with her fingers until she found the spot again. Squinting through the glass, whatever was there looked like something metal, almost like the tiny head of a nail. She looked up and around the room as though hoping the walls might provide some explanation. Squinting even harder now, she found the spot again and tapped it with the tip of her scissors. Maybe it wasn't a nail, but it was definitely something metal.

At that very moment, as she tried to digest her strange discovery, J.T. magically appeared in the basement. "How goes it, Mrs. Puddles?"

Isabel was so startled, her feet actually left the ground. She must have looked as if she had just been electrocuted. "*Good Lord*, J.T.!" Isabel snapped, trying to catch her breath. "What are you doing, sneaking up like that on a woman my age? In a funeral home, no less!" She leaned down and picked her scissors up from the floor. "Are you trying to drum up some new business?" Isabel put her hand on her chest to make sure her heart was still beating.

"Sorry, Mrs. Puddles . . . we're taught to walk very softly around here. Didn't mean to startle you. How's that haircut coming?"

Isabel decided she didn't need to get J.T. involved right now. "I need another half hour or so. Earl's hair is a bit of a challenge. . . . J.T., is there a phone down here I can use? I need to call Gil."

"Mr. Cook called me five minutes ago. He was just sitting down in the dentist's chair."

"Oh, that's right." Her wheels were turning. "Well, I have another call I need to make."

"You're welcome to use the phone. It's over there on the wall. Old school." J.T. turned to leave, then turned back, "You don't have a cell phone, Mrs. Puddles?"

"No, I do not, J.T. Apparently I'm the only person in this county other than the Dunkards and the Amish who *doesn't* own a cell phone . . . and by the way, I never *intend* to own a cell phone."

"They're very convenient," J.T. offered.

"Well, so are adult diapers, I suppose," Isabel blurted out, "but I still manage to find the time to go to the bathroom."

J.T. wasn't quite sure what to make of that comment, so he quietly made his way toward the stairs. Isabel wasn't quite sure why she said it, either. It was the kind of thing Frances would say and not think twice about it, but what Isabel did know about herself was that when she was under duress, she was never quite sure what might come out of her mouth. She waited until she heard J.T. close the door upstairs, then walked over to the phone and dialed her cousin Ginny, who happened to be the secretary for the Kentwater County sheriff, Grady Pemberton. She also happened to be his fiancée. Ginny answered on the first ring, "Sheriff's office."

"Ginny, it's me."

"Izzy? What's wrong?"

"Nothing's wrong."

"Something's wrong. You never call me at work."

"Ginny, nothing's wrong. . . . I just have a situation. I can't really go into it with you right now, but I would like to ask Grady for some advice." There were not many things Isabel couldn't tell her cousin Ginny, but this particular thing, at least at this point, she felt should be one of them.

"Isabel, have you been in an accident?! Are you in some kind of trouble?"

"Ginny, calm down. I'm fine. It's just something I need to ask Grady about."

"Well, he's out on patrol right now. I know he was going to swing by Cook's to pay his respects to Earl Jonasson later. . . . You know he died?"

"Yes, I did . . . very sad . . . such a sweet old man. Do you know how?" Isabel asked.

"I'm not sure. . . . I heard it might have been a stroke. . . . Sounds to me like he just died from being eighty-eight. That gets a lot of 'em. I don't think poor Earl ever really got over losing Ruth. Apparently, he passed away sitting on his porch with his dog in his lap . . . such a peaceful way to go."

Well, maybe it wasn't such a peaceful way to go, after all, Isabel thought. "Ginny, can you put me through to Grady over the phone? I'd really like to speak to him ASAP."

"Are you sure you're okay, Iz?"

"I'm fine. If you want to know the truth, I'm asking for a friend." Isabel looked over at her friend Earl lying across the room with a nail in his head.

"Hang on . . . I'll put you through," Ginny replied, not entirely convinced.

"Thanks, Gin. I'll see you Sunday at church."

"See ya Sunday, Izzy."

Ginny's father and Isabel's mother were brother and sister. Ginny grew up with four brothers, and Isabel was an only child, so she and Ginny, who were just one year apart, had grown up like sisters. They had been going to church together their entire lives, and they were still going today, every Sunday, usually followed by breakfast at Land's End. If it was a nice day, they might follow up breakfast with a walk along their favorite stretch of Lake Michigan beach or drive around looking for garage sales or drop in to visit other relatives who hadn't managed to get to church that morning.

In the summertime, they'd almost always end up back at Isabel's house, sitting at the end of her dock, enjoying a Bloody Mary or two. They had imposed a two–Bloody Mary limit after the day they went for a third and decided to put the canoe in the water. They swamped it a hundred yards out. Two teenagers on Jet Skis plucked them out of the water and returned them to Isabel's dock, where they stood fully clothed, dripping wet, half-bombed, and watching the canoe slowly sink.

In the winter they'd usually go back to Isabel's after breakfast, build a fire, make fudge, read, or maybe watch an old movie while Isabel knitted, and Ginny tried to. She had been working on a sweater for her cat for at least two years, although Isabel didn't remember Ginny's cat having two heads and three legs.

She loved her Sundays with Ginny, but when it came to church, Isabel Puddles wasn't really all that "churchy." She went mostly out of habit and to see her favorite cousin and other parishioners she had known for years. And where else did she have to be at ten o'clock on a Sunday morning? Plus, neither cousin thought it looked good for the family pew to be empty and have people think the Peabody-MacGregor clan had turned into a collection of heathens. Since her freshman year of Sunday school at age four, Isabel had been in attendance at the Hartley Congregational Church nearly every Sunday of her life, with rare exceptions. The birth of her son Charlie—after her water broke at a Saturday-night dance at the Moose Lodge—was one of those times. That Sunday virtually the entire congregation, including the late Reverend Curtis, came to the hospital to see her after church and meet their newest parishioner. But little Charlie Puddles's early introduction to Congregational fellowship didn't take. He was now a Buddhist.

Isabel's great-grandparents, Chester and Zelda Peabody, who helped found the church back in 1888; her grandparents on both sides; and her parents, Buddy and Helen, had all been devoted members of the church. The men had all been deacons, while the women, as usual, did all the real work, organizing rummage sales, holding bake sales and book drives, delivering meals to the homebound, and teaching Sunday school. Midge Usborne even mowed the lawn, trimmed the hedges, and shoveled the walkway in the winter. All the men did was show up on Sunday morning in a suit and tie and show people to their seats, which was pretty light lifting. The Hartley Congregational Church was where the Peabodys and the MacGregors were "married and buried," her father used to say. The impressive stone structure on State Street—right down from Cook's Funeral Home, in fact—was built, according to her grandmother, Hazel Peabody, as a testament to God's grace. According to her grandfather, Charlie Peabody, it was built to put the Methodists in their place.

"Boy, those Methodists really thought they were something before we came along and showed them what was what," she remembered Charlie saying. He also claimed that after construction was completed, more than a few Methodists decided to become Congregationalists because they no longer wanted to be seen, as Charlie told it, "in that little clapboard firetrap up the street."

By 1920, all the "best families" in the county, again, according to Grandfather Charlie, attended the Hartley Congregational Church. Isabel's always-diplomatic Grandmother Hazel, in a nod to Congregationalist-Methodist relations, always complimented the Methodists on their choir. To which her husband, the *never*-diplomatic Charlie, would snap, "Well, they have to do something to try to get the Lord's attention while He's down the street here with us!"

Ginny and Isabel sat in the same pew their families had sat along now for four generations. In fact, there was a bronze plaque at the end that gave THANKS AND PRAISE TO THE PEABODY AND MACGREGOR FAMILIES FOR THEIR TIRELESS DEVOTION AND GENEROSITY. Other members of the clans would show up at church from time to time, and there were still the weddings and funerals, but as a rule, it was just Isabel and Ginny representing the family before the congregation and—if He hadn't been distracted by the Methodist choir up the street—the good Lord Himself.

Isabel loved her family history with the church and the fellowship of it, but when it came to the actual existence of God, she would have to admit to being a devout agnostic. She was grateful when she learned the term existed while still in high school, because then she had something to call herself. Atheist seemed a bit severe, and not entirely accurate, because the truth was, she had always been open to being wooed by the Lord. And who was she to be so matter-of-fact that He *didn't* exist? It was just that, so far, after all these years, she was still not completely convinced. This ambivalence, however, was not something she ever felt comfortable sharing with others. It just wouldn't look good for a Peabody or a MacGregor or even a Puddles to be questioning the Congregationalist status quo. But if He was all-knowing and all-seeing, well, He had dropped the ball one too many times for Isabel to take very seriously. And if she ever did get to meet Him, she was going to have plenty of questions. . . .

Frances was a Catholic, but there weren't many of those in Kentwater County, which was made up mostly of Dutch Reform, Lutherans, Methodists, Congregationalists of course, and a smattering of Amish, Mennonites, and Dunkards. Frances considered herself to be a good Catholic, so she attended Mass fairly regularly, despite the fact that she didn't like the priest at her church, who she deemed dull. "I'd rather watch ants carry crumbs across my kitchen floor," she once said about his sermons. She also hated the physical structure itself. "I've been to Saint Peter's, Notre Dame, and to Saint Patrick's . . . three of the most beautiful cathedrals in the world. And then to come home to this monstrosity?"

The Catholics had torn down a quaint little stone church in the woods near the Big Lake north of town and replaced it with a modern-looking structure Frances absolutely hated. And she was pretty sure God shared her opinion. "It looks like a bus station," she said to Isabel when they first laid eyes on the new construction. "If I were God, I wouldn't be caught dead in there."

Isabel shared with Frances what she remembered about the battle between the Congregationalists and the Methodists, and her grandfather Charlie's obsession with building a church meant to impress. "Well, if there *is* a God," Isabel said, "I can't imagine architecture is a very high priority. . . . At least it shouldn't be."

Frances shot her a look. "What do you mean '*if* there is a God'?"

Oops . . . Isabel had never let her agnosticism slip like that before, not even with Frances. But it felt good to be honest on the topic for a change. "Well, Frances, I'm just going to say it—I'm not sure I believe in God."

Frances was slightly taken aback by her best friend's admission, but naturally she was only too happy to share her viewpoint on the topic. Frances loved to share her opinions, and even more so when she wasn't asked for them. "Well, here's what I believe," she declared, crossing herself. "You just make a decision that you *are* going to believe . . . that you are going to have faith. Even if you aren't quite there, you make that leap, if for no other reason than it helps shoulder the burdens life sends your way. What's the worst that can happen if it's all a big, fat hoax? Eternal slumber? But if you're wrong, you're going to be in some deep you-know-what! Me? I'm playing it safe. It's kind of like how I decided somewhere around 1986 that I wanted to be a redhead. I took a leap of faith. And I liked it! It suited me. So I've just kept it up. Going to church is like going to the beauty parlor—you keep doing it because it makes you feel better about yourself."

Isabel laughed, but the hair color analogy actually made some sense to her. She remembered Frances's conversion to red. She had originally asked Isabel to dye her hair. They could be the "Lucy and Ethel of Kentwater County," she said. But Isabel refused. She was not going to risk the fallout if it all went to "H-E-double hockey sticks," as her father used to say. If Frances didn't like it, Isabel would never hear the end of it.

Isabel then shared her take on things, in keeping with the hair color theme. "Well, I started getting gray fairly young, as you know. So I rinsed every few weeks to hide it. But I knew I was getting grayer by the day, and eventually I just got tired of pretending it wasn't happening—because it *was* happening. So I stopped. Who was I trying to fool? Myself? The world? And why does it matter? If I can't be comfortable with the real me, just as I am, gray as a storm cloud, then who *am* I? I'm not going to just keep rinsing and rinsing to try to erase reality." Isabel proudly shook, and then straightened her handsome gray bob cut, the same hairdo she'd had for well over a decade. Frances didn't really get the analogy. Isabel wasn't quite sure she did, either, but it seemed to hit the right notes. Her philosophy of life was a work in progress.

Ginny was just about to patch Isabel through to Grady when she stopped short. "Oh, wait . . . he just walked in the door, Iz." She put her hand over the receiver and signaled Grady to her desk. "Something funny is going on here. It's Isabel. She needs to talk to you."

Grady was a tall, ruggedly handsome man in his early fifties who reminded Isabel of one of her favorite TV detectives from the 1970s: Dennis Weaver as McCloud. Ginny, a former homecoming queen, was still a beauty, so they made a very fetching couple. Grady took the phone as he leaned over and gave his fiancée a kiss on the cheek.

"Hello there, Isabel . . . are you all right?"

"I'm fine, Grady . . . but I wonder if you could meet me over at Cook's."

"Cook's? What are you—oh, you're there for Earl Jonasson's viewing?"

"Yes and no. I'll explain when you get here."

Grady flashed Ginny a puzzled look. "Well, I was going to come by at five. Maybe I could meet you—"

Isabel interrupted. "If you could come over right away, Grady, I sure would appreciate it."

Grady looked at Ginny again with an even more puzzled expression, "All right, Iz . . . Give me ten minutes."

Isabel was outside waiting when Grady pulled into Cook's back parking lot, driving his official black-and-white Kentwater County Sheriff's SUV. He got out and gave her a big hug. Isabel was happy to see him. She adored Grady and was glad he would soon officially be part of the family. "Thank you for coming over, Grady. I didn't know who else to call. I just felt like it was my responsibility. Poor Ginny must wonder why I'm being so mysterious."

Grady smiled. "You know Ginny. She's a worrier."

After explaining what she was doing at Cook's in the first place, and how she happened to become Earl Jonasson's hairstylist, Isabel asked Grady to come downstairs with her. Just as they reached the back door that led down to the basement, Gil Cook pulled into the parking lot in his red VW Beetle convertible, top down, and tooted his horn. Gil knew driving a red VW Beetle convertible was about the last thing anybody would expect a mortician to drive, which was "exactly why I bought it," he would tell anybody who mentioned the obvious, adding, "I know where to get a black Cadillac when I need something more formal."

Gil jumped out and walked up to them with his usual bouncy step, also unusual for a mortician. But he had always walked like that, earning him the high school nickname "Bouncy Butt," which Isabel had given him. "Sheriff . . . Izzy . . . How about this weather?" Gil offered. Although it was the middle of October, it was the second day of a beautiful Indian summer. Gil was clearly wondering what was going on. Why was the sheriff in his parking lot? Was this just a friendly stopping-by or was somebody being arrested? He searched Isabel's eyes for an answer.

"Gil . . . it's about Earl," she said softly.

Gil turned to Grady. "I promise he was dead when he got

here, Sheriff." Grady chuckled. Isabel did not. She reached over and opened the back door.

"Can you two come with me, please?"

The three of them descended the stairs with Isabel in the lead. As she walked into the embalming room, there was J.T. again, standing silently next to Earl, and startling her a second time. "You are determined to put me into full cardiac arrest before this day is out, aren't you, J.T.? I'm going to be lying right there next to Earl if you keep this up!"

"I'm sorry, Mrs. Puddles," J.T. responded quietly.

All four reverently assembled next to Earl's body—Gil and J.T. on one side, Isabel and Grady on the other. She handed her magnifying glass to the sheriff, then leaned over and parted Earl's hair carefully until she found the spot. "Take a look here, Grady." She tapped the tiny spot again with the tip of her scissors, then handed them to Grady, who did the same.

Gil was confused. "Izzy . . . what exactly is going on?"

"I don't know, Gil, but I didn't know what else to do." Grady was concentrating hard with the magnifying glass. He tapped the spot himself again with the scissors.

Gil was still looking for answers. "Grady, what is this all about?"

Grady turned to Isabel. "Izzy, you did the right thing. Gil, we need to postpone this viewing. Do you have a copy of Earl's death certificate?"

"I do," J.T. replied quickly.

"What was the cause of death?" Grady asked as he went back for another look with the magnifying glass.

"It says cerebral hemorrhage—stroke," J.T. answered.

"Dr. Stratton signed that?" Grady asked.

"Yes, sir, he did."

Grady handed the scissors and the magnifying glass back to Isabel and got on his walkie-talkie. "Ginny, call Dr. Stratton and have him call my cell phone as soon as possible. And then call the medical examiner's office and have them send a van over to Cook's right away. Do you copy?"

"Copy that, sweetheart." Ginny's voice crackled. "Is Isabel okay?"

"Thank you. Yes, she's just fine, nothing to worry about."

Gil was now officially peeved. "Grady, what in the world is—"

"What in the world is Earl Jonasson doing with a nail in his head?" Grady said, interrupting. Gil and J.T. looked at each other, both stunned silent.

Isabel filled the quiet. "I found something that just didn't feel right when I was combing out his hair, Gil. I took a closer look and, well, I knew whatever it was didn't belong there. I had a hunch it was a nail. So, I thought it best to call Grady."

Gil took the magnifying glass and the scissors from Isabel, then turned to Grady. "May I?" Grady nodded.

J.T. was flummoxed. "But I washed his hair, Mr. Cook. . . . I promise I did. . . . And I didn't feel anything."

"Well, how could you with this mop? Like finding a nail in a cornfield." Gil was quick to stop J.T. from beating himself up over it. He was about as devoted an employee as Gil had ever had, and with three grown daughters who couldn't get far enough away from the funeral home business, J.T. was not only the son he never had but the young man he was grooming to one day, hopefully, take over the business. Gil tapped the nail with the scissors. "It does seem to be a nail. Well, that's a first. Do you think it might have been the nail that killed him, Sheriff?" Gil asked.

"Well, I can't imagine it did anything to help," Grady replied. "And it could certainly cause a cerebral hemorrhage. But that's what we need to find out, Gil."

"But why no blood, Sheriff?" J.T. asked in earnest. "Seems to me, if you put a nail in somebody's head, there would be blood and plenty of it."

"You would assume, but that will all be part of the investigation," Grady said, leaning in closer for another look with the magnifying glass.

Gil had an explanation. He had been a pre-med student briefly until he decided to go into the family business. He liked to say it was because it was less risky and *his* patients couldn't sue him. But he always liked to share what medical knowledge he had whenever he could. "Well, there are places in the head where an injury like this wouldn't cause much external bleeding, if any. And the nail could very well block the release of what blood there was." He took the magnifying glass from Grady and looked again. "There's some swelling and maybe a little bruising, too."

The sheriff was making some notes in a small leather-bound notebook, then looked up and rejoined the conversation. "In the meantime, this doesn't leave the room. Everybody understand?" All three nodded affirmatively as Grady continued, "I'm going upstairs and wait for Earl Jr. Is Meg here yet, Izzy?"

"She'll be up this evening. She was away on business," Isabel answered.

Grady put away his notebook. "Okay . . . so I'll explain to Junior that we have some dispute about cause of death and we need to get a coroner's report before there can be any funeral or burial, or even a visitation. Gil, you'll probably want to come up with me to calm any nerves. Iz, you should go on home. You've done your part."

Grady headed back up the stairs with J.T. right behind him, mumbling in disbelief that he had missed something as obvious as a nail. Gil walked over to Isabel, pulled out his wallet, and handed her three hundred-dollar bills. Isabel shook her head. "I didn't do anything, Gil. I can't accept that."

"You may have just uncovered—well, I can't even believe I'm saying this—but you may have just uncovered a murder,

Isabel. Nobody ends up with a nail in their head accidentally. . . . I mean, I'm sure it's happened, but not to some poor
old man sitting on his porch with his dog."

"Who in heaven's name would want to murder Earl
Jonasson? He was such a nice, harmless old man. There has
to be another explanation, Gil," Isabel said, looking back over
at Earl.

"He was set to be cremated tomorrow right after the funeral. If you hadn't discovered what you did, and had the
wherewithal to call Grady, we likely would never have known
it was anything other than a stroke."

Isabel shook her head. "It sure is a puzzle. It's just . . . I
mean, you would never think . . ." Her words trailed off as
the awfulness of the situation slowly sank in. Gil tried to give
her the money again but Isabel still refused to take it, so he
discreetly tucked it into her purse as she threw it over her
shoulder and headed for the stairs. Halfway up, she turned
around. "You know what, Gil? I think I'll wait here with Earl
until they come for him. Just doesn't feel right to leave him
alone." She pulled up a stool, laid her purse on the counter,
and stared back at the old man again. "Poor Earl."

About thirty minutes later, two men from the county
coroner's office came to collect Earl's body. Once they got
him out the door and into the van, Isabel headed for her van.
She could see Gil through the window talking to a handful
of Earl's friends and family inside. Grady was outside on the
porch, waiting for Earl Jr. As she climbed into her van, Isabel
saw Junior arrive, wearing what might have been the same
suit he wore to his high school prom. Grady walked down the
steps to greet him, then turned him around and steered him
back down the walkway and onto the sidewalk. She watched
the two of them walking down State Street, deep in conversation, with Earl Jr. shaking his head and looking confused.
Then something on the porch caught her attention—or *some-*

one. It was Earl's new girlfriend, Tammy Trudlow, lighting a cigarette.

Isabel had completely forgotten Meg telling her about this unhappy development the last time she was home. Tammy and Earl had been together for a few months before Meg knew about it; now she was mortified that they might be planning to marry. The Jonassons were a family of prominence, admired and respected by everybody in this part of Michigan. Theirs was certainly not a family tree that deserved the likes of Tammy Trudlow dangling from it like some cheap dollar store Christmas ornament. When Meg finally found out about the relationship, Earl Jr. told his sister he was in love with Tammy, and she with him. Meg didn't buy the latter half of that equation, not for a second. Neither did Isabel. Based on what little she knew about Tammy Trudlow, that girl was not a lover, she was a fighter. In fact, she had been arrested for it more than once, according to the local police blotter in the *Hartley Journal,* which Isabel read religiously. But Earl Jr.'s claiming to be in love with Tammy was no real shocker. It didn't take much, given that the boy's best friend and constant companion throughout most of his childhood was a goat named Oliver. As far as companionship, he would have been better off sticking with goats, as far as Meg and Isabel were concerned. Isabel had never had the misfortune of actually meeting Tammy, but she certainly knew of her, and knew she was not exactly popular around Kentwater County, or at least not popular with *respectable* people. Although Isabel didn't care for the term "white trash," if she *were* to use it, she couldn't think of anybody better to use it *on* than Tammy Trudlow. Anybody with a neck tattoo, an arrest record as long as her frizzy bleached-blond hair, and who thought it was acceptable to wear short shorts and a tube top to a funeral home—Indian summer or not—was not a gal you were going to find at a Betty Crocker bake-off.

Scrunched down slightly in her seat so as not to draw attention to herself, Isabel watched Tammy carefully as *she* watched Grady and her boyfriend walking along the sidewalk, still deep in conversation. But even more than concerned, Tammy looked agitated. Blowing smoke out of her nostrils like a Chinese dragon, she stayed fixated on them until they shook hands and said good-bye. She then angrily flicked her cigarette out onto the sidewalk and waited for Earl to come up onto the porch. When he did, she said something that didn't look terribly friendly, grabbed him by the arm, and marched him inside.

Isabel drove home lost in thought, wondering what other explanation there might be for a nail winding up in Earl Jonasson's head. Things certainly seemed to point to foul play, but could it have been some kind of freak accident? She knew Earl was a woodworker. Could this have happened in his workshop? It seemed highly unlikely that an eighty-eight-year-old man could somehow have taken a nail to the head, then gone to sit down in his rocking chair to pet his dog. So scratch that idea . . . Or maybe it wasn't a nail at all. Maybe it was a piece of metal that flew off some farm equipment or was turned up by a plow or a truck and then sent flying into poor Earl's skull. That was certainly possible, wasn't it? Possible, but not probable . . . So now the question Isabel couldn't stop asking herself was, If this was a murder, who could have wanted to kill Earl Jonasson? The man was eighty-eight years old. What was the hurry?

Chapter 5

Isabel Puddles was an avid reader and had always been a fan of mysteries, especially old-school English crime mysteries. Agatha Christie was the master, as far as she and Gladys De-Long were concerned. But as a kid, before she was introduced to Agatha, Isabel read every Nancy Drew mystery she could get her hands on, and as she got a little older, turned her attention to the Hardy Boys. Her favorite cartoon as a kid? Scooby-Doo, naturally. After her parents allowed her to watch "grown-up programs," as her mother called them, she became addicted to TV detective shows at a time when computers, high-tech forensics, and DNA didn't drive the plotlines. *Columbo, Mannix, Cannon, McCloud,* and *McMillan & Wife* were some of her favorites, but Jim Rockford was her *all-time* favorite. Isabel told her mother she planned to marry Jim Rockford one day, to which Helen replied, "Well, that's nice, dear. I'm sure you'll enjoy living at the beach—even if it is in a trailer."

But Isabel didn't watch much TV these days. Cable was not available at Gull Lake, and a dish was way too expensive, so she got by with the antenna Carl had put up on the roof twenty years before. She was able to get the local news out of Grand Rapids and Traverse City so that she could follow local goings-on and keep an eye on the weather, which was mostly fruitless, because it changed along the Big Lake about every fifteen minutes. She hadn't watched any national news since Dan Rather went off the air. The news today either depressed or angered her, or both, so she decided to stop doing that to herself. The only newspapers she read were the *Gull Harbor Gazette* and the *Hartley Journal*. And when it came to any talk of politics outside of local races, she was completely unengaged. In fact, the best way to get her to leave the room was to bring up politics. So, when it came to current events outside of western Michigan, Isabel Puddles lived in a bubble of sorts, and she knew it. Not only did she know it, she was perfectly fine with it.

She was also able to get the PBS stations out of Grand Rapids and Kalamazoo, and sometimes, weather permitting, she could pick up Chicago or Milwaukee. So, in addition to her local news, Isabel's limited television viewing consisted of nature shows, cooking shows, and the occasional documentary. And she did tune in to *Jeopardy!* and *Wheel of Fortune* from time to time. But what she looked forward to most were the British detective shows. Give Isabel Puddles a fire in the fireplace on a snowy night, a hot cup of tea (or a glass of wine, depending on the day she'd had), Jackpot curled up next to her on the sofa, knitting in her lap, and an episode of *Miss Marple*, and she was in heaven. It just didn't get any better than that for her. Although from time to time, she hoped maybe someday it might. . . .

Now, after so many years of being a devotee of murder mysteries, a real-life murder mystery—one she unwittingly uncovered—may have just visited itself upon her sleepy little community. If this was a murder, she trusted Grady and local investigators would get to the bottom of it. But she was afraid they might be faced with a challenge. Isabel had read or watched enough murder mysteries, both real and fictional, to know that when a rich old man is murdered, or dies under suspicious circumstances, there were usually some greedy, impatient relatives behind the crime, desperate to get their hands on the money. So, family was where detectives usually first turned their attention. But in this case, that formula didn't make any sense at all.

Earl Jonasson Sr. had just two heirs: Earl Jr. and his older sister, Isabel's dear old friend, Meg. Earl Jr. and his first wife, Brenda, had four boys together, so they were next in line. One day Brenda went off to the grocery store and never came back, having run off with a vending machine repairman she'd met at the bowling alley. "Classy gal," she remembers Frances saying to Meg at breakfast one morning when she told them what happened. Meg never liked Brenda, so in *her* book, her brother and her nephews were better off without her. Isabel agreed. Brenda was rude, mean spirited, and had never properly conjugated a verb as far as Isabel could remember.

After Brenda ditched her family, Earl Sr. bought his son and grandsons a manufactured home and plopped it down a few hundred yards from the old family farmhouse. Three generations of Jonassons all living together happily . . . until now.

Isabel liked Earl Jr. and had known him for many years. And although he was never the brightest lighthouse on the shoreline, she remembered Meg's kid brother as a shy boy with a gentle spirit. According to Meg, Junior, as he was known to many, had always been a loving son to his parents, a loyal brother to her, a good father to his boys, and a hard worker devoted to keeping the family farm running smoothly. The notion that he might have murdered his father was one Isabel could not even remotely imagine.

Meg was an even *less* likely suspect. Her family was very

important to her, and she loved her father dearly, always doting on him. Even though she lived a good three hours away and had a busy career, Meg was home as much as possible during her mother's illness, and had been visiting her dad at least two or three times a month ever since Ruth died. She adored her brother and her four nephews, too. Meg and her husband, Larry, had no children of their own, so as their only aunt, she once told Isabel, she felt as if she were filling the void left by the mother who had abandoned them. And Meg didn't have any money problems, so what could possibly be her motive to kill her father? She was a successful CPA, married to another successful CPA. They ran their own business and lived in a beautiful home, once owned by a Kellogg, in an upscale Battle Creek neighborhood. Plus, she was about the nicest person Isabel knew. Of course it made sense that Earl Jonasson's family would be the first ones investigated if his death was ruled a murder, but in the investigation Isabel Puddles had already launched in her head, she had cleared both his children of any culpability.

After pulling into her driveway, Isabel sat in her van for a moment and took in the view of Gull Lake, peaceful and mirrorlike. What a day this had been. What a *terrible* day this had been. She was ready to go inside and shut out the world. Seeing Jackpot appear at the front gate jumping for joy was just the cure she needed to help her out of her melancholy. She always loved getting home to her beloved Jack Russell, Jackpot, but tonight his wagging little stump of a tail was especially comforting.

As she opened the front gate, she heard a familiar car horn. It was Frances pulling into the driveway and, as usual, going way too fast. She let Jackpot out, but immediately bent down to pick him up to keep him out of harm's way. She walked over to greet Frances while Jackpot slathered her face with kisses. Frances got out of her car—a late-model burgundy Cadillac—and was, of course, already talking.

"Why you let that dog lick your face like that is beyond me. You know I've heard of people contracting diseases from letting dogs lick them. Diseases that *killed* them!"

Isabel was used to her friend's alarmist warnings by now. "A lot more people die from being run over by people like you driving around like maniacs. Why do you always drive like you've just knocked over a bank?"

"I've got places to be, Izzy. I can't be driving around at a snail's pace."

"But there are children on this road, Frances."

"Well, good! It'll keep 'em on their toes. Sooner they learn not to let their guard down in this world, the safer they'll be! Speaking of reckless drivers, I almost got into a head-on collision with that trashy Trudlow girl—the one with the tattoo on her neck. I can't ever remember her name. Are you going to invite me in or are we going to just stand here in the driveway?"

"*Tammy* Trudlow?" Isabel asked, suddenly engaged.

"That's it! Tammy . . . awful white trash. Well, that whole Trudlow family is trash." Frances headed for the front door. Isabel put Jackpot down and followed her in. Frances continued, "So, she comes roaring out of the Shell station driving some old rust bucket just as I was pulling in, and she's screaming into her cell phone. Never even saw me! I had to swerve to avoid her! She almost took out Pansy's little coffee wagon there on the corner, too. Put the fear of Jesus into poor Pansy . . . Then she just went on her merry way. Those Trudlows are nothing but trouble." Frances quickly surveyed the yard before opening the front door. "You need to trim these hedges."

Isabel's first instinct was to tell Frances about her day and her own Tammy Trudlow sighting, but she promised Grady she wouldn't say anything, and she knew if there was one person in the entire county most likely *not* to keep a secret, it was Frances Spitler. She might as well hire a skywriter.

Everything Frances ranted on about for the next five minutes had to do with her trip to Buffalo, a town she was apparently less than enamored of. But Isabel had tuned her out. The only thing on her mind was what Tammy Trudlow could have been so upset about when she almost crashed into Frances. Isabel walked into the laundry room, where she reached into a big jar and pulled out a doggie treat for Jackpot with Frances hot on her heels, and still talking. She bent over and opened the dryer, took out an armload of clothes, and began folding as Frances prattled on until she abruptly stopped. "Isabel Puddles, are you listening to a single word I'm saying?"

"Sure I am. I've just had a long day. . . . Have a lot on my mind."

"Well, I'll leave you to it, then. I might as well be talking to the dog. Just thought I'd stop by on my way to the Kroger and say hello. Didn't have a morsel of food in the house! You would think that husband of mine would pick up on the cue and take his wife out to dinner. But no, sir! He says he missed my home cooking while we were away. So you know what *home cooking* he's getting tonight? A store-bought roasted chicken, instant mashed potatoes, and a can of cream corn. And you know what? He'll love it. Man's got no taste. Except in women, of course! Okay, I'm off. I'll talk to you tomorrow, Izzy." And like a gust of wind that comes from nowhere, blows leaves all over your yard, and then disappears, Frances got back into her car and took off down the road, disappearing in a cloud of dust.

After she finished folding her laundry, Isabel made some chamomile tea and sat down at the kitchen counter to ponder over the day's bizarre events until she realized it was Jackpot's dinner hour. Every night at six, he sat politely next to his bowl and stared at her until she got the message. She could swear that dog could tell time. She dug the to-go box from lunch out of her purse, took the turkey-and-bacon out of her soggy club sandwich, and mixed it up with Jackpot's dry food. She didn't have much of an appetite tonight. A can of soup would be enough for her. After watching him devour his dinner, she walked out onto the deck facing the lake and made her way down to the dock. Jackpot followed, stopping for a drink of lake water before joining her on the bench at the end of the dock and curling up in her lap, just as Corky had probably done with old Earl.

As evening settled around the lake and the woods surrounding it began to darken, Isabel reflected on how lucky she was to live where she did. It was a state of mind she always tried to steer herself back to after a stressful day. A few lights appeared in the homes of some of her neighbors who, like her, were year-round residents, while the summer cottages remained shadowy outlines, lit by a lone porch light or a lamp inside.

Whatever the season, this was quiet time on Gull Lake. Even in the summer, by this hour, most water activities had ceased for the day and the lake got quiet and calm again. The waterlogged and sunburned summer people returned to their cottages to dry off, apply lotion, and get ready for dinner. The smell of barbecue grills and the campfires from a nearby campground soon filled the air, along with intermittent bursts of laughter and squealing children. But this time of year, it got quiet and stayed quiet. There was something magical about all lakes in this part of Michigan, but her lake, Gull Lake, was extra special. . . . At least it was to her.

Isabel always counted her blessings that her father, Buddy, had the foresight to buy the lots on either side of the house

when one could still afford to buy lakefront property in Kentwater County. And because all three parcels, thick with poplar trees, sat on the lake's highest point, above an inlet where
the lake was fed by a stream that cascaded over a small stone
waterfall, she felt removed from the rest of her neighbors. This
was Isabel Peabody Puddles's domain, her touchstone with the
past, and her hope for the future. But the property taxes on
three lakefront lots were killing her. And with two of them
empty, providing zero income, it was sometimes hard to jus-
tify hanging on to them. Although at times tempting, especially when her checking account dipped into triple figures,
she was still determined not to sell. Poplar Bluff—the name
her mother had given the place the day they moved in—
wouldn't be the same with next-door neighbors. Plus, given
the sizes of the houses the new summer people were building around the lake, she would most likely end up bookended
by two- or three-story behemoths, making her quaint little
clapboard-and-river-stone cottage look like a garden shed. She
looked back at the place. . . . It had always been white with
green shutters, but for the past few years she had been thinking about painting the shutters another color, just to spruce
the place up a little and surprise the kids. She still couldn't
decide on a color, though, so they would likely stay green for
the time being, and probably always. For Isabel, change always
looked good on paper, but not always in practice.

Whenever she fretted about money, her kids, Carly and
Charlie, were quick to point out that as long as she had Poplar
Bluff, and it was paid for, she would be just fine. She could
always sell off the lots or hold out and sell the entire property,
cottage included, although both kids agreed that to any new
buyer, the cottage would be considered a "teardown." She had
never heard the expression before, and she never wanted to
hear it again. The very idea that anybody would intentionally

tear down a perfectly good house—especially *her* house—and replace it with a new one made her bristle. And it only served to embolden her determination to hang on to her property.

"Most people would kill to have a nest egg like this all paid for," Charlie said to her on his last visit home. That might be true, but it was the "paid for" part neither of her kids knew about. It wasn't. Not anymore. After being hit with a barrage of unexpected expenses, including a new roof, another hike in property taxes, and four new crowns (even her dentist's "friends and family" rate set her back a few thousand dollars), Isabel was left with no choice but to take out a home equity loan. She never told her kids about it because she was too embarrassed. It was a fairly modest lien, but it still made her nervous to be in hock to the bank.

When Isabel went in to apply for the loan, the young man at the bank—a city transplant named Justin who had no idea with whom he was dealing—tried to get her to borrow about ten times the amount she needed after hearing about the collateral she was putting up. He suggested a new car, maybe a trip to Europe (Isabel had never been), college funds for her nonexistent grandchildren, or just some liquid security in case of a medical emergency, at one point even alluding to her age . . . Isabel was not impressed with the junior loan officer's aggressive, bordering-on-predatory sales pitch, and was just about to get up to leave when she smiled and waved across the lobby at somebody she knew. That somebody was Justin's boss, the bank president, Norm Sullivan, whom she had known since they were in fifth grade together. Norm came over and greeted her with a warm hug and some friendly chitchat, then asked her what she was there for. When she told him, somewhat sheepishly, he turned to Justin and said, "Send that application on over to me. Izzy, don't you worry about a thing. We'll have that money in your account first thing in the morning." Isabel thanked Norm and got up to leave, then turned back to Justin and gave him a wink. "Oh, and thank you, too."

Regardless of how modest the amount of the loan, Isabel had never been in any real debt, aside from having a small credit card balance from time to time. And all that talk of nest eggs and selling off lots was completely lost on her. What her children apparently didn't understand was that their mother had no intention of ever selling. This was not her nest egg, this was her nest. Her eggs had long ago hatched and flown away. Poplar Bluff was her home and, fingers crossed, it always would be.

What was once a ramshackle cottage her father bought from his elderly aunt Ida as a rental property became Isabel's childhood home when she was five. After the insurance agency Buddy Peabody worked for folded, the Peabody family fell on some difficult times. Their big Victorian home on Palmerston Street in Gull Harbor became too expensive to maintain, so Buddy sold it, and the cottage became home. Despite the close quarters, even for three people, they grew to love living on the lake. A few years passed, and after Buddy started his own agency and managed to get back on his feet, he came home excitedly one night to tell his wife and daughter that their old home was up for sale again. But he was not greeted with much enthusiasm. Both Isabel and her mother voted to stay put. And so they did. Improvements were made along the way: a new kitchen went in one year, and a new master bedroom and bath were added the year after that. Then Buddy bought the lots on either side. But for whatever improvements and incarnations Poplar Bluff had gone through over the years, the place never lost its rustic charm.

Both of Isabel's parents lived in the house right up until they died—her father, while napping next to the fireplace in his favorite old wingback chair, and her mother, a year later, in the same chair, doing needlepoint. Two weeks after that, her mother's Chihuahua, Guapo, died in it. Isabel eventually donated what had become known as "the chair of death" to the Salvation Army because nobody would sit in it. "It's like an electric chair done in toile," Charlie once remarked.

It made Isabel a little sad to know her kids didn't share her sentimental attachment to Poplar Bluff. Without their ever saying so, she knew she would most likely be the last of the Peabody-Puddles clan who would ever live there. So, with that in mind, her goal was to go out feetfirst, just as her mother and father had. Or four paws–first, as was the case with Guapo.

Mom and Dad were buried in Hartley, but Guapo was buried in the lot to the west, alongside Isabel's beloved English bulldog, Ernie, a pup some heartless summer people had abandoned and the Peabodys then adopted when Isabel was just eight years old. Ernie died the day after her sixteenth birthday and she cried for a week. Along with Guapo and Ernie, there were two family cats, Impy and Shoo, and next to them, a hamster named Colonel Mustard, a parakeet named Alfred—who had an unfortunate run-in with the ceiling fan—and a half dozen goldfish she had won at the county fair over the years.

But the most recent addition to the Poplar Bluff pet cemetery, as Charlie called it, was the kids' black Lab, Pepper, who died just after Charlie left to go to college in California. She and Carl might have bought Pepper for the kids, but he was really Isabel's third child. After Pepper died, she swore she would never have another pet. She could never go through that again. To this day, Isabel still choked up whenever she saw a black Lab. But then along came Jackpot. She joked to her kids that she hoped Jackpot outlived her, and if he did, she made them promise one of them would take him. But she wondered if she really was joking. Losing Jackpot was something she could not even fathom.

★   ★   ★

Isabel's peace and quiet were broken once again when another car pulled into her driveway and honked. She looked back from the dock to see Ginny parking her old station wagon. Knowing her cousin would likely be on the lake at this hour, Ginny came around the house, down the sloping lawn, and out onto the dock. Jackpot ran up to give her a friendly greeting. Ginny picked him up and gave him a smooch, then carried him down the dock. She sat down on the bench next to Isabel with him still in her lap. "Hi, Gin," Isabel said as she reached over and patted her arm.

"Hi, Iz . . . sure is a beautiful evening."

"It sure is." They both gazed out across the lake for a moment until Ginny put Jackpot down and turned to her cousin.

"So, who do you think killed Earl Jonasson?" she asked nonchalantly. Isabel looked at her with a puzzled expression. Ginny smiled. "Grady has a bad habit of leaving his walkie-talkie on. And I have a bad habit of listening in. I heard the whole thing at Cook's . . . you poor girl."

"It's just terrible, isn't it?" Isabel said, feeling relieved she could finally talk about it to somebody. "Do you think there could possibly be another explanation?"

"For how an eighty-eight-year-old man ends up with a nail in his head? There might be . . . but none of them are very likely," Ginny declared. "The question is, who would want Earl Jonasson dead?"

They stared out at the lake and mulled the question over for another moment until Isabel spoke up. "Ginny, I probably shouldn't say this, but I saw Tammy Trudlow, Earl Jr.'s new girlfriend, and possibly soon-to-be wife, standing out on the porch at Cook's while Grady was talking to Junior. And there was just something very peculiar about the way she was acting."

Ginny shrugged. "I did hear they were engaged or about to be. He's no grand prize, but he could certainly do bet-

ter than that. . . . I'm sure she's not after the money or anything. . . . So, you say she was acting peculiar?"

Isabel nodded knowingly. "Well, she didn't look at all
happy. Angry even. And then just thirty minutes ago Frances
stopped by here and told me Tammy almost crashed into her
pulling out of the gas station. Said she was screaming into her
cell phone and never even saw her. So, what in the world is
Tammy Trudlow all of a sudden so upset about?"

Ginny was mulling this new information over carefully.
"And right after she learns there is some uncertainty about
how her future father-in-law—her *rich* future father-in-law—
died. Hmmm . . . Yes, I'd say that qualifies as peculiar."

"I don't know about you, Gin, but I think if they were
planning to marry, maybe Tammy decided she didn't want to
wait to get her hands on Junior's inheritance. Who else would
have any motive to kill Earl?"

Ginny nodded, indicating they were on the same page.
"I think we ought to let Grady know what you just told me.
He may have a few questions for ol' Tammy." Ginny got out
her cell phone and placed the call to Grady. She briefly shared
Isabel's concerns about Tammy with him and then hung up.
"He'd like you to come by the office in the morning if you
have time."

"I'll make time," Isabel said.

Ginny stood up. "Okay, well, I just wanted to stop by and
make sure you were doing okay." Isabel walked her down the
dock and up to her car. Ginny gave her cousin a hug. "So, I'll
see you at the office in the morning, then?"

"I'll be in around nine."

"I'll have coffee and doughnuts waiting."

"Not on my account, Gin! Please . . . I have Weight
Watchers next week. And I haven't weighed in for two
months!"

Ginny laughed. "Honey, I have Grady and eight other

sheriff's deputies working out of my office. Without coffee and doughnuts in the morning, they wouldn't be able to find their way to their patrol cars. I don't know what it is about cops and doughnuts, but it's real. Bobby Hobson provides them free of charge. He tells me it's his way of serving the community. So I stop by and pick up a box every morning on my way in. They're day old, but my deputies wouldn't know the difference between day old and week old. You know Bobby always asks about you."

"Well, he can keep asking. The last thing I need is a boyfriend who owns a bakery. I'd be the size of a refrigerator! People would be asking if those were buttons on my blouse or magnets!"

Ginny laughed again. "You have never looked better. Whatever you're doing, you need to just keep on doing it. Okay, I'll see you tomorrow."

Isabel waved good-bye and called Jackpot into the house. It was time to settle in for the night.

Chapter 6

Isabel found it difficult to sleep that night. At about midnight, she finally drifted off, but then woke up just after four, thinking about poor Earl Jonasson lying in the medical examiner's office with a nail in his head. She thought about how awful it was going to be for Meg and Junior to discover their father had possibly, even likely, been murdered. Jackpot, who always slept at the foot of her bed, snored away while she tossed and turned for another couple hours, ruminating over who could do such a thing to such a nice old man. And why? Although she had a hunch Tammy Trudlow was up to something shady—because she usually was—she also knew it wasn't right to leap to any conclusions about somebody in a matter this serious. She might be a pretty unsavory character, but that didn't make her a murderer.

She finally turned on her bedside lamp to read, but after reading the same paragraph several times over—and retaining none of it—she gave up. By now it was getting light out, so she got up to go to the kitchen to make a pot of coffee. Jackpot looked up, breathed a heavy sigh, then plopped his head back down on the bed and went back to sleep. He liked his eight hours, and it was way too early for him to get up.

Isabel looked out onto the lake as it slowly emerged in the light of dawn. The weather report said they were in for another Indian summer day, but it wouldn't warm up until later. She put a heavy coat on over her flannels, then slipped into her duck boots and took her coffee out onto the dock. She thought about how much time she had logged sitting on that bench over the years. Carl built it for her on their twentieth anniversary. It was not exactly romantic by most wives' standards, but for Isabel it was perfect, especially when she and Carl needed a little distance. She sometimes wondered if maybe that was why he built it for her in the first place. Maybe it was an anniversary gift to himself.

Whenever she was up at this hour, weather permitting, Isabel liked to go out with her coffee and sit on her dock to watch the sun come up. Charlie called it her "moment of Zen." But this morning her moment ended abruptly when she remembered what she had to do that day. Although she was looking forward to talking to Grady, she was then going out to the farm to see Meg, something she was not looking forward to at all.

Isabel arrived at the sheriff's department at nine on the nose. Ginny and Grady were sitting in his glass-enclosed office inside the main office. The deputies were already out on patrol, so the only other person in the office, dressed in his jail clothes, was Roger, busy pulling a big plastic garbage can around and emptying the wastebaskets.

"Good morning, Mrs. Puddles," Roger said in his quiet, slightly timid manner of speaking.

"Good morning, Roger," Isabel said with a polite smile. Isabel had known Roger for years, but then everybody knew Roger. Nobody knew where he came from, or even knew his last name. He just kind of showed up in Hartley one day . . . drunk. As town drunks go, Roger was pretty harmless. He had always been polite and friendly to Isabel, so she always showed him that same respect in return. Roger was somewhere between forty and fifty, rail thin, and looked as if he might have been handsome at one time, but it was clear he had been through some rough times. His people were not Kentwater County people, so he had no family to fall back on. And he did a lot of falling. But as sad as his condition was, Roger was never belligerent or nasty, and he was always quick with a wave and a slurred hello to passersby as he pulled his old wagon around town filled with bottles and cans and other odds and ends. And he always seemed to be half singing and half humming tunes nobody could identify. One summer Roger pulled a large stuffed gorilla around in his wagon. He said he found it in the parking lot at the fairgrounds, where someone had either abandoned or forgotten it. But the gorilla seemed to be good company for Roger. They were even spotted in the park a time or two sitting together on a bench, deep in conversation. "Looks like Roger's putting together a ventriloquist act," Frances said to Isabel as they drove past them in the park one afternoon.

Most people just sort of felt sorry for Roger. His only source of income—that anybody could figure out, anyway—was collecting bottles and cans. Nobody knew where he lived, until it was discovered he didn't live anywhere. Roger constituted the entire homeless population of Hartley, Michigan, not counting a handful of feral cats. Grady, being a kindhearted soul, was usually able to find a reason to arrest him, so if it got too hot or too cold, he'd bring him in, give him free room and board, sober him up, and then put him to work. In the summer, Roger could be seen in his yellow jumpsuit behind the sheriff's office washing patrol cars, or out in front, mowing the lawn or pulling weeds. In the fall he would be raking leaves, and in the winter, shoveling snow. When his work was done, and he had paid his debt to society for his latest transgression, and the weather had either warmed up or cooled down, Grady would let him out. He called it his "catch and release" program. But a day later Roger would be drunk again.

Both Ginny and Grady spotted Isabel at the same time and waved her into the office. Grady opened the door as Ginny slipped out, patting her on the back as she passed. "Morning, Iz . . . I'm going to go get you a cup of coffee."

"Thanks . . . but no doughnut!" Grady pulled out a chair for her and got right to the point.

"Well, we haven't heard anything back from the coroner's office yet. . . . Hopefully in the next day or two. I'm going out to the farm here in a little bit to talk to Meg and Junior and let 'em know the funeral will have to be postponed." Ginny came back in with her coffee as Grady continued, "We also haven't yet confirmed that Earl was murdered, so you understand this is all very premature, but Ginny tells me you think maybe I should be talking to Tammy Trudlow?" Grady took a bite of his glazed doughnut. "Say that three times fast!"

"Even harder with your mouth full," Ginny scolded.

Grady smiled and wiped his mouth with a napkin. "So, tell me what you know, Iz."

Isabel was more than happy to share her concerns. "Grady, I just have a hunch. I watched her watch you and Junior yesterday outside Cook's after I got in my van. She looked agitated . . . and angry. Now, why would she be so concerned about what the two of you were talking about if she didn't have some idea about what you two might be talking about?"

So far Grady wasn't biting on anything but his glazed doughnut. "Okay . . . continue."

"Well . . . that's it. There was just something about the way she was watching you men, eyes glued, just like my Jack-

pot does after he trees a squirrel. It just gave me the creeps."
Grady nodded slowly as he mulled things over, but Isabel could
tell from the expression on his face that he didn't consider this
an earth-shattering development. Then Ginny chimed in.

"There's more. Tell him what Frances told you."

"Well, it was maybe two hours later that Frances came
by the house and said she had just missed a head-on collision
with Tammy at the Shell station. Said she was screaming at
somebody on her cell phone and driving like a maniac. Almost drove right into her."

Grady smiled. "Well, we all know Tammy Trudlow's one
terrible driver. I've got a whole file on her traffic citations
alone. And she's pretty well known for having a bad temper,
too, so screaming at somebody on her phone isn't anything
unusual."

Ginny chimed in again. "All those Trudlows are ill tem-
pered. They're like a pack of rabid hyenas."

Grady was looking more circumspect than convinced.
"Well, a bad temper doesn't translate to murder, which is
what I gather you two are getting at. And, like I said, we don't
know for sure that Earl was even murdered." Isabel stared at
him with her best poker face. Grady continued, "I'm starting to think there may be a reasonable explanation to this,
something other than cold-blooded murder. We shouldn't be
jumping to conclusions. Farm accidents happen all the time;
plows, harvesters, wood chippers—all very dangerous pieces
of machinery. More than a few times I've had to call the coroner to come out to so-and-so's farm and collect bodies that
were in a whole lot worse shape than Earl. . . . Ginny, do you
remember—"

"Please, spare us the details, Grady. It's early. And I'd like
to keep my fritter down." Ginny finished the last of her coffee and her last bite of apple fritter. Ginny could eat an entire

apple fritter, and did, almost every morning of her life, and never gain a pound. It was the only thing Isabel didn't like about her cousin.

Isabel obviously needed to bolster her case. "Don't you think it's a little coincidental that Tammy was coming unglued just hours after you came to the funeral home to tell her boyfriend you were doing an autopsy on his father? I'd sure like to know who she was screaming at and why. Wouldn't you?"

Grady got up to leave. "Well, it may eventually be something to look into . . . so thank you for bringing this to my attention, Isabel. Now I'm headed out to the farm. If Tammy's there, I'll talk to her, too. . . . Meanwhile, not a word of this to anybody." Isabel and Ginny nodded to each other and said their good-byes to Grady. Ginny's good-bye included a kiss. As soon as he closed the door behind him, Isabel stood up.

"Ginny . . . I don't know about you, but I think if we can find out more about Tammy's comings and goings on the day Earl died, and maybe figure who she was screaming at over the phone, we'll know a little bit more about how Earl Jonasson ended up with a nail in his head."

"I tend to believe your hunches, Iz, but you know Grady's right. Until we hear from the coroner, we shouldn't jump to conclusions. I guess this *could* be some kind of freak accident. Maybe that nail had been there a while." Isabel gave her the raised-eyebrow look as Ginny stood up. "Okay, I have to get to work. It's getting toward the end of the month and I need to make sure we're hitting our quotas."

Isabel shot her a look. Ginny smiled. "I'm kidding." She knew her cousin was still steaming about a ticket she had recently received from a new deputy for what he called a "rolling stop." Isabel's father used to call them "Michigan stops." Buddy saw no point in coming to a complete halt at a stop sign if there was no traffic coming in either direction, and neither did his daughter. Waste of time and gas. But she accepted the ticket as gracefully as she could, and without playing the "my cousin is engaged to the sheriff" card. Grady offered to take care of it, but Isabel refused, although that didn't mean she wasn't plenty perturbed about writing that fifty-five-dollar check.

Isabel's next stop was the Jonasson farm, but she decided to stop at home first and pick up a couple of jars of pickles to take with her. Meg always raved about Isabel's pickles, but then so did everybody. She pulled the jars from her pantry and turned around to see Jackpot looking at her with those pleading eyes, so she decided to take him along with her. He could run around the farm a little while she visited with Meg. He loved going for rides almost as much as he loved chasing squirrels. When they got to the van, Jackpot jumped into the passenger seat with a big smile and waited for her to crack the window enough for him to stick his head out.

Having skipped dinner the night before, and missing breakfast that morning so she could meet with Grady, Isabel was starving. And now that she had postponed her Weight Watchers weigh-in again, she figured it was safe to stop for a quick lunch at the Dog and Suds, where she had been eating chili dogs since she was a kid, along with the best onion rings on the planet, and their creamy homemade root beer served in a frosted mug. The Dog and Suds was an old-fashioned drive-in—the last of its kind in this part of Michigan—so Isabel and Jackpot could have lunch together in the van. The minute they pulled in, he began to get excited. Isabel had her usual, and Jackpot had his; one plain hot dog. Just as the carhop—a new girl she didn't recognize—brought out their lunch, Isabel looked over to see who other than Tammy Trudlow pulling in next to her. "Just my luck," she said to Jackpot. Tammy sure was getting around lately.

What was noticeably out of the ordinary, though, was that she was driving a brand-new silver pickup truck. She usually drove around town in cars that looked like they had just been towed off a salvage lot, so this was very peculiar. Also odd was that she was with a man Isabel didn't recognize somewhere in his twenties, with long hair, with sunglasses on, and wearing a baseball cap turned backward. He was a sketchy-looking character, but just the kind of company you would expect Tammy Trudlow to keep. Isabel and Jackpot finished their lunch quickly and she pressed the button to alert the carhop to come back for their tray. Tammy and her friend seemed to be deep in conversation, so she was able to back out without their noticing her.

Jackpot had his head out the window the whole way to the Jonasson farm. A hot dog followed by an open car window, and he was about as happy as any dog could be. Not a care in the world. Isabel only wished she could experience that kind of bliss someday. As she turned down the private dirt road leading to the Jonasson farm, she saw Grady coming toward her in his SUV, leaving a long cloud of dust in his wake. They both slowed to a stop and rolled down their windows. "You tailing me?" Grady asked.

"I forgot you said you were headed out here. . . . I came out to check on Meg and Junior."

"Meg's there with the boys, but Junior's not home. He went to Wellington for some tractor parts. I'm coming back a little later so I can talk to them both. Remember, not a word about anything. Meg only knows there's been an autopsy and that we're waiting for the results. They don't know any specifics, and we need to keep it that way for now."

"I know, I know. Not a word . . . I'm just going to see how they're doing and bring them some of my pickles."

"She seems to be holding up. She's making lunch for her

nephews right now. Did you say you were bringing her pickles? We just finished our last jar." Grady was clearly dropping a hint.

"Well, I'll see if I can maybe find another jar for you and bring it by the office."

"And in return I'll make sure my deputies go easy on you the next time they catch you doing one of your Michigan stops."

Isabel stared at him deadpan for a beat. "Too soon, Grady . . . too soon."

Grady laughed as Isabel raised her window and pulled away.

When she drove up to the beautiful old Jonasson farmhouse, Meg and her nephews were sitting at a picnic bench under an old sycamore tree. She tooted her horn and got out with pickle jars in each hand, followed by Jackpot, who immediately started doing laps around the yard, then ran over to say hello to the boys. Meg came to greet her while the boys finished their lunch. "Hi, honey," Isabel said softly, giving Meg a big hug.

"Hi, Izzy. I've been meaning to call you. . . . I'm sorry . . . I've just had so much to do today."

"Don't you worry about that. How are you holding up?"

Meg looked at her in earnest. "Well, you know one minute I'm fine, and then the next minute I'm falling apart. Just hard to believe Mama and Daddy are both gone now. . . . But I like to think they're having a happy reunion somewhere right now." Meg looked at the jars of pickles Isabel was handing her. "And I know they'd both be sorry to be missing your bread-and-butter pickles!" Isabel handed the jars to her with a smile. "Thank you, Iz. That was so thoughtful. . . . You just missed Sheriff Pemberton."

"I know. I met him down the road," Isabel said, waving at the boys. She then looked over at the house and spotted a sad-looking Corky coming down the porch steps, her ears swinging slowly back and forth. *That poor dog,* she thought.

"I don't really know what to make of all this," Meg continued, "but yesterday the sheriff told my brother they needed to do an autopsy on Daddy. For the life of me, I can't figure out why, and he wouldn't tell me. The paramedics told Junior it looked like a stroke. If that's all they're trying to determine, it doesn't really matter to us. Stroke? Heart attack? He's gone, either way." Isabel just listened and let her talk. "Sheriff Pemberton is coming back later to talk to us, so I'm hoping he can provide some answers. I'm very confused."

Isabel hated knowing more than she was able to let on to a dear old friend grieving the loss of her dad, but she had promised Grady to stay mum. She only hoped Meg would forgive her when she eventually found out that she was the one who had put all this into motion and then didn't say anything to her about it. "Well, I'm sure Grady will have some answers very soon. But I know this can't make things any easier for you."

They both looked over and saw Corky and Jackpot playing on the lawn together. "Well, look at that," Meg said with surprise. "That dog has barely left the porch since Daddy died. She won't eat, she won't come inside. She just sits next to his old rocker, looking lost and lonely. But look! Her tail's even wagging."

Isabel was touched, and proud that Jackpot was such a friendly dog. Corky suddenly rolled over on her back with her legs in the air while Jackpot licked her face. "Well, Corky, that's not very ladylike, is it?" Meg said with a chuckle. "I don't know what we're going to do with her, Iz. . . . Daddy loved that dog to death. Literally, to death. But two of Earl's boys are allergic, and Larry's not a dog person. If I came home with that dog, I think he'd divorce me. Are you still volunteering at the shelter, Iz?"

"I am . . . but you're not thinking about taking her to the shelter, are you?"

"Well, I'm sure somebody would love to adopt her. She's a pretty girl, and very friendly. I mean I hate to, but I just don't know what else to do."

At that very moment Corky came over to Isabel and jumped up on her leg, followed by Jackpot, who jumped up on the other one. She reached down to pet them both. Message received. "I think maybe I can help. . . . I've been thinking it might be time for Jackpot to have a companion. I always feel so guilty leaving him alone. And they do seem to like each other."

"You mean you'll take her? Oh, Izzy, I would be so grateful! I will write you a check right now to pay for her room and board for the next ten years!"

"Don't be silly." Isabel crouched down and looked Corky straight in the eyes. She was a beauty, with a luxurious, speckled black-and-white coat, pretty brown eyes, and a sweet demeanor. "You've been through enough, little lady. You ready to give up farm life and move to the lake?" Corky wagged her stubby little tail and licked her face. Isabel laughed and stood up. "I think that was a yes. And Jackpot seems to approve, too. . . . Looks like you're coming home with us, Corky! Okay, I would love to stay but I have to get to the hardware and I need to drop these two off first and get her settled in."

"Oh, God." Meg's face sunk into a frown.

"What is it?" Isabel said in alarm.

"It's Earl's lady friend, and when I say 'lady' . . ." Isabel bent over slightly to look inside the car that was slowly pulling up to the house. Sure enough, there was Tammy Trudlow again, but now she was by herself and driving her usual junker. She drove around the circular drive slowly, like a prowler, then squeaked to a stop right next to them. She rolled down her window and flicked her cigarette ash out the window before taking another drag. "You seen Earl? He ain't answerin' his phone."

"Earl went up to Wellington," Meg said matter-of-factly.

"When'll he be back?" Tammy asked, taking another drag off her cigarette.

"I have no idea, Tammy. Not my day to watch him." Meg looked at Isabel and rolled her eyes.

Tammy looked over at Isabel and gave her a strange look. "Do I know you?"

"Probably not," was Isabel's curt response. Tammy stared at her a little longer, then turned back to Meg. Her cigarette now dangling off her thin lips. "Well, tell him I stopped by . . . *pleeeese*," she sneered as she rolled up her window, giving Isabel another odd, up and down glance before pulling out of the drive.

Meg exhaled and went limp, shaking her head slowly. "What is my brother *thinking*?"

"Well, sometimes good people make bad choices," Isabel said, trying her best to ease Meg's obvious discomfort.

"I mean my brother, God love him, is not the most eligible bachelor in the county, but Tammy Trudlow? We all know she's only looking for a meal ticket. Or bail money. I hope Earl sees the light before he does something crazy. If he marries that woman, I don't know what I'll do, Isabel. The boys can't stand her, either!" Meg was watching Tammy's car drive away, still unsettled by their brief encounter.

"Well, let's jump off that bridge when we get to it. I'm sure Earl will come to his senses soon enough. It's about time for Tammy to go back to jail anyway, isn't it?"

Meg chuckled and gave Isabel a hug. They walked over and said hello to Meg's nephews and had a little chat. They were such nice, well-mannered boys, Isabel thought.

"Listen, Meg, I really do have to run. Freddie's going to be wondering where I am."

Meg smiled and they walked back to Isabel's van with the boys following behind. "I just can't begin to thank you enough for taking Corky. This is such a relief. I know Daddy would be so thankful to know she was going to such a good home."

"I'm happy I could help out . . . she'll make a nice addition to the Puddles clan." She gave Meg a hug.

Then the sound of crackling gravel got their attention again. They looked up to see Earl pulling into the drive in his old Ford truck with Grady following close behind. Meg looked at Isabel. "Can you stay another minute, Iz? I'm just a wreck about this."

Isabel checked her watch. She'd be a little late for work, but she knew Freddie would understand. "Sure . . . I can stay for a little bit," she said, patting her on the arm.

Earl got out of his truck and the boys ran to greet him, while Grady walked over to say hello to Meg and Isabel. Earl came over and gave Isabel a slightly awkward hug, then turned back to the boys. "You guys go on in the house. Your Aunt Meg and I need to talk to the sheriff a minute."

Grady looked at Isabel, wondering with his eyes if she was planning to stay or not. Meg seemed to pick up on it, too. "I asked Izzy to stay, Sheriff. Shall we go up and sit on the porch?"

Grady agreed with a smile. "I passed Earl out on Mulberry Road, so I figured I'd just come on back now. I hope that's okay. I don't mean to be a pest. . . . I know this is a difficult time, and on behalf of myself and the sheriff's department I want to again offer condolences. Your father was a fine man . . . as fine as they come. This community was lucky to have both your father and mother for as long as we did."

"Thank you, Sheriff. That's very nice of you to say," Meg said softly. "He held you in very high regard, too. Thought you were doing a fine job as sheriff. And he had known a lot of them over the years." Earl Jr. nodded in agreement with his sister.

"I know you two would like to know what's going on here and why we decided we needed to involve the medical examiner in your father's death. . . . Without going into any details, which I am not at liberty to do until we get his report back, what I *can* tell you is this: Nothing is confirmed, but we have reason to believe that your father may not have died from natural causes." Meg took a gasp of air and grabbed Isabel's hand. Her brother furrowed his brow and looked confused. Isabel noticed Grady studying Earl's reaction. "Now, I know that's a lot to take in, but—"

Meg interrupted. "Sheriff Pemberton. Are you telling us that you think somebody may have killed my father?"

"Yes, Ms. Jonasson, I mean—I'm sorry, I've forgotten your married name."

"Blackburn. And please call me Meg."

"Yes, Meg, I'm afraid that is what I'm telling you. . . . Nothing is confirmed, which is why we needed to do the autopsy. We should know more very shortly."

"Oh, dear Lord . . ." Meg was stunned. Grady continued to watch her brother, who was slower than his sister in processing the information. Meg continued. "But how? I mean, who would want my father dead? Who murders an eighty-eight-year-old man?"

"That's what we'll need to investigate, *if* the medical examiner's report indicates this was murder. We can't rule out an accidental death yet, either, though. Let me ask you this, Earl, do you know if your father was involved in any sort of an accident on the day he passed? Maybe in his workshop or working around the house? I know he stayed pretty active right up to the end."

Earl nodded. "He surely was . . . Dad always had projects going on . . . but no accidents that I know of."

Meg was lost. "What kind of accident are you talking about, Sheriff?"

Grady's walkie-talkie suddenly came to life. "Grady, can you please call the office right away? On your cell phone . . . Over."

Isabel recognized Ginny's voice. "Copy that," Grady replied as he stood up. "If you'll excuse me just a minute, folks." Pulling out his flip phone, Grady stepped off the porch and out onto the lawn. Meg and Earl stared at each other as the shock of this news continued to sink in. Isabel was busy eavesdropping on Grady's call with Ginny.

"Hey, Gin, what's going on?" He listened for a moment. "That was fast. . . . Yes, go ahead and open it."

Knowing Ginny, Isabel was pretty sure whatever it was they were talking about was already open. Grady listened carefully for about a minute, then said, "That's all I need to know for now. Thanks . . . I'll see you a little later."

Grady closed his phone and put it back in his pocket, then walked slowly back onto the porch and sat down again. "Well, we got the medical examiner's report back sooner than I expected. Your father did not die of a stroke. I'm sorry to have to tell you this, I really am, but I'm afraid he died from a two-inch nail found embedded in his skull, which resulted in a cerebral hemorrhage. At first glance it must have looked like a stroke to Dr. Stratton . . . he signed the death certificate."

Meg immediately broke down in tears as this horrible news registered. Earl Jr. sat dumfounded and still. Isabel tried to comfort Meg as best she could, but she, too, was reeling from the news. Earl Jonasson's death was now officially a murder, and she was the one who had uncovered it. This wasn't the news Grady was hoping for, either. He was feeling slightly queasy about learning that he was now investigating the murder of Meg and Junior's father, but he had no other choice other than to immediately move into his official role as sheriff. "I know this must come as a terrible blow, but I'm going to need the two of you to come down and answer some questions for me." Grady got up to leave. "If you could come down tomorrow morning, I sure would appreciate it."

Meg was staring into the distance but finally managed a response. "Yes, of course . . . We'll be down first thing, Sheriff. Thank you for coming."

Grady's expression read *pensive* as he climbed back into his SUV and slowly pulled out of the drive. Isabel wondered what was going through his mind right now. She hated leaving Meg after hearing such awful news, but she needed to get to work or Freddie really would begin to worry. And she still had to get the dogs home. This was one of those occasions when Isabel could imagine a cell phone might be convenient.

Chapter 7

Isabel rushed into the hardware just as Freddie was finishing up with a customer. Otherwise the store was empty. "Sorry I'm late, Freddie." Her cousin peered at her over his glasses. "I'm docking your pay!" Isabel made a face at him as she walked behind the counter and grabbed the apron hanging behind the office door. When she came back to the counter, Freddie was holding up a single bolt, carefully inspecting it. "That'll be thirty-five cents plus tax, Lanny. You owe me thirty-eight cents. . . . Boy, if I keep raking it in like this, I should be able to retire by the time I'm . . . oh, I don't know . . . a hundred and two? You want a bag?"

"No, I'll just put it in my pocket, Fred," the man said quietly, slipping his purchase into the front pocket of his overalls. "Well, now I'm up another quarter of a cent! French Riviera, here I come!" Freddie laughed as his customer headed for the door. "You take good care now, Lanny. . . . Tell Margie hello for me."

Isabel finished tying up her apron and walked up to the counter. "Was that Lanny Beckwith? Boy, he's gotten old."

Freddie closed the drawer on the cash register. "Creeps up on all of us, Izzy . . . Although you never seem to age a bit.

You're just as pretty as you were when you were Pumpkin Queen."

Isabel looked at him and raised her eyebrows. "*Asparagus* Queen, thank you very much."

"Oh, that's right! Well you're the queen of every vegetable in this county, as far as I'm concerned, Cousin!"

Isabel smiled. "That's very sweet of you to lie like that, Freddie," she said as she began to straighten up the counter.

Freddie ducked into the office while Isabel continued organizing the counter. He reappeared moments later holding a new cardboard display case and placed it on the counter near the cash register.

"What do you have there, Freddie?"

"They just came in. Air horns. The rep made me a good deal. See, you pull the trigger here and it lets out a mighty blast . . . Want to hear?"

"Please don't. My nerves are already shot today. I hate those things. Carl used to have one he'd use to call the kids in off the lake. I always thought it was obnoxious. My father rang a bell . . . much more civilized."

"Here, I want you to have one," Freddie said as he handed her an air horn. "In case of emergency . . . Anybody comes at you, this will scare 'em off toot sweet!"

Isabel declined. "Don't be silly. Thank you anyway, but I'm not going to carry an air horn around with me."

"Why? You carry around everything but the kitchen sink in that purse of yours! I'd feel better if you had one. I'm taking one home to Carol, too. A woman can't be too safe these days, not even in sleepy little Kentwater County."

"Thank you anyway, Freddie. You're a doll. But I don't think I need to worry about my safety around here." No sooner had she said it than she remembered she had likely just uncovered a murder. Maybe she shouldn't be so sure.

Freddie took one of the horns out of the display and

walked back into the office. "I'm putting this in your purse. It's a gift, so you can't return it." He came back and took another for himself and disappeared down the lightbulb aisle, yelling back to her, "I'm going to go check on Frank . . . see if he's working or napping again! And if he's napping, I have just the thing to get his attention!"

Frank was the stock boy, a fortysomething-year-old stock boy who had worked for Freddie for twenty-plus years. His mother, Myna, whom he still lived with, worked there before him. Among Frank's long list of ailments, he also claimed to be narcoleptic, so he was often found napping in unlikely places around the store. Isabel wasn't sure she was buying the narcolepsy defense. She was pretty sure it was more likely just an excuse to nap wherever and whenever he liked. But she and Freddie were always patient with Frank. They knew he wasn't quite all there, or as Frances liked to say, "Frank's a couple drumsticks shy of a bucket."

Isabel was still straightening up when Mrs. Abernathy walked around the counter, talking to her and rubbing up against her leg. "Well, look who's here! I haven't seen *you* in a while! Has anybody fed you today?" She bent down to pet the big orange tabby, and the store's resident mouser. Mrs. Abernathy didn't care much for Freddie or Frank, but she loved Isabel. She immediately started purring, followed by more talking. "What's on your mind, Mrs. Abernathy? You're a very chatty catty today."

Frank suddenly came running up to the counter in a panic. "Isabel, we need you back here!" He turned and ran back down the aisle with Isabel racing behind him. Something must have happened to Freddie. She followed Frank into the farm supply department in back, where she saw Freddie slumped over a large galvanized water trough. "Freddie! What's wrong? What happened?"

Freddie slowly lifted his head and smiled. "Looks like

Mrs. Abernathy wasn't fixed after all." Isabel, flushed with relief, let out a heavy sigh and walked over to the trough. She looked down to see a litter of newborn kittens, then felt Mrs. Abernathy rubbing against her leg again.

"Oh, that's so sweet. . . . You wanted to show me your babies." The cat leaped into the trough where Isabel had made a bed for her months ago with an old blanket, then began bathing her kittens with her tongue.

Freddie and Frank had had enough kitten time, so they wandered off. Isabel watched the newborns enjoying a late lunch with their mom until she heard the front doorbell chime, her cue to head back to the front of the store. When she got to the counter she couldn't believe her eyes: standing in front of her, holding a brand-new shovel and a couple of blue plastic tarps still in their packages, was the sketchy-looking long-haired man she had seen with Tammy Trudlow at the Dog and Suds just a couple of hours before . . . but this time he was wearing his hat correctly and had taken his sunglasses off. The young man was probably in his mid- to late twenties, with blondish hair, bright blue eyes, and a smattering of reddish-blond whiskers on his face. Up close, he didn't look as sketchy as he did before. In fact, with a shave and a haircut he could pass for good-looking. But anybody who kept company with the likes of Tammy Trudlow was not somebody you could trust, so Isabel was already feeling nervous. Had they noticed her at the drive-in? Had Tammy sent him in to check her out after seeing her with Meg? Or was this pure coincidence? Isabel's mind was racing, but she remained calm. "Hello . . . May I help you?" she asked politely, walking around the counter and reaching down nonchalantly to ring the bell to summon assistance from the back, just in case.

"Yeah, I bought this shovel a few days back and these tarps. But I can't find the receipt. Anyway, it turns out I don't need 'em after all, so I'd like to get my money back."

Just then Freddie appeared at the counter, but he had already heard the young man's request as he came down the aisle. "Sorry, my friend, but we only offer store credit without a receipt."

The young man looked up at him and took a slightly imposing pause before continuing. "I don't want any store credit. I don't live here. These tarps are still in the package—brand new. And look here, this shovel has never even touched any dirt. Still has the price tag. I paid cash. You don't believe I bought this stuff here?"

Freddie forced a smile. "No, I know you did. I sold it to you. I certainly don't mind taking it all back and giving you a credit. It's just store policy that we don't give refunds without a receipt. Sorry." Freddie pointed to a big sign over the counter clearly stating that very policy. Of course Freddie always made exceptions for his regulars, but not for some out-of-town character like the one presently standing in front of him.

The young man turned back to Isabel, who then forced her own smile. "If you'll give me your name, I'll write you up a credit slip. You can use it whenever you like."

The young man hesitated, then Freddie jumped in. "The shovel is twenty-nine ninety-nine and the two tarps are four ninety-nine each, Iz. Just add the tax up. Didn't you buy some duct tape, too?" The young man looked back at Freddie with surprise.

"Good memory . . . I'll find a use for the duct tape." He hesitated slightly, then resigned himself to the store policy. "Name is Jason . . . Last name Swerley." Isabel noticed right away that he seemed to have a hard time making eye contact. His eyes were darting around as if he were following a fly around the store. Isabel never trusted people who didn't make eye contact. She also found his purchases very peculiar. A shovel? Tarps? Duct tape? What was a young man from out of town doing buying stuff like that? Out-of-towners usually stuck to BBQs or beach chairs and umbrellas. Then again, maybe she was overthinking this a little.

"Are you any relation to the Chicago Swerleys?" Isabel asked. She didn't know of any Chicago Swerleys, but she wanted to disarm him a bit and try to learn more about this person.

"No, ma'am . . . I'm from Jackson. Jackson, Michigan . . . I've been living there for a while anyway."

Isabel continued writing out his credit slip. "And what brings you to town so late in the season, Mr. Swerley? Did you come up to see the colors?"

He gave her a peculiar look. "The colors?"

Isabel looked up. "The leaves . . . They're going to be beautiful this year after this Indian summer we're having. Always makes the colors more vibrant."

Jason Swerley did not look like an autumn-color enthusiast. He was not comfortable answering questions, either. But given that he was talking to a harmless-looking middle-aged woman wearing a red hardware store apron, he obliged. "No, ma'am. I work construction. . . . came up here to do some work for a friend of mine."

Isabel stopped writing and looked up again. "Who's that? In this town we know just about everybody. Isn't that right, Freddie?"

Freddie was busy straightening packages of birdseed on a shelf nearby. "True enough . . . whether we want to know 'em or not."

The young man was getting impatient. "Can I just get my credit slip, please? I kind of need to be on my way."

Isabel tore off the slip and handed him his copy. The young man nodded a thank-you, then turned to leave. "Oh, wait . . . do we have your phone number?" she asked.

"Why would you need my phone number?" he replied suspiciously as he turned around.

86

M. V. Byrne

"Well, we're getting ready to draw names for our annual fall raffle. Any customer who makes a purchase between Labor Day and Thanksgiving is eligible to win a new riding lawn mower."

Freddie stopped what he was doing and looked at his cousin as if she had just lost her mind. She could see he was about to speak up so she reached down and rang the bell again. "Freddie, Frank needs you in back." Isabel smiled at her customer and continued, "So if we don't have a way to contact you, we can't tell you if you won or not. And I'll tell you what . . . with business being as slow as it has been this fall, your chances of owning a brand-new John Deere riding mower are pretty darn good! Comes with a trailer, too."

Freddie was completely in the dark on this raffle business but, knowing his cousin as he did, he decided not to chime in, having learned over the years that there was usually a method to her madness. Jason perked up a bit. "Well, okay." He recited his number while she wrote it down. "I guess if I win, it'll be worth a trip back up to get it. When's the drawing?"

"Oh . . . it's, uh, just after Thanksgiving. . . . Thank you, Mr. Swerley. We'll let you know if you win it. Keep your fingers crossed!"

Jason nodded, mumbled a thank-you, and walked out the door. Isabel waited two seconds and ran to the window, hiding behind a display of chain saws to get a look at him and who he might be with. He climbed into the same silver pickup she had seen earlier, which was now parked directly in front of the store. She grabbed the broom from the office and rushed out the door to sweep the sidewalk just as he pulled away, then, pulling a pen out of her apron, she wrote the tag number down on the palm of her hand. It was a temporary tag, so she couldn't tell whether or not it was from Michigan.

When she went back inside, Freddie was standing behind the front counter with his arms folded. Isabel didn't wait for him to ask what was going on. "I know you're probably wondering what that was all about, Freddie."

"I'm just hoping whatever it was about doesn't involve me having to give away a John Deere riding mower to some hippie from the other side of the state!"

Isabel chuckled. "Let's go back and look at Mrs. Abernathy's kittens again, shall we?" She promised to tell him more when she could, after assuring him there would be no lawn tractor giveaway. Freddie didn't have the longest attention span in the world, so he moved on pretty quickly. The conversation quickly turned to what they were going to do with Mrs. Abernathy's kittens. He agreed to keep one or two around the store to help their mother with her mousing duties, but the others would have to go. Unless she wanted to take on even more pets—and she didn't—adding "find homes for kittens" would be the next thing to go on her to-do list. Isabel loved cats, but she didn't want them in her house. Keeping up with the hair and the litter box was too much work. And where she lived, outdoor cats didn't have a very long life expectancy.

Before she knew it, it was almost six o'clock and time to close up shop. Freddie was on the phone with his wife, Carol, who invited her cousin-in-law to come home for dinner with him, but Isabel graciously declined. She had too much on her mind to be very good company, so she told Freddie to "thank her just the same" as she flipped the sign on the front door to CLOSED.

Just then, mid-flip, a handsome, well-dressed, studious-looking young man with wire-rim glasses and a mop of strawberry blond hair rushed up to the front door. He looked at his watch, then gave Isabel a pleading look with his doe-like eyes and flashed a bright smile. She smiled back and let him in.

"Thank you so much, ma'am. I promise I won't be a minute. I was hoping you might have a pair of rubber waders in a size twelve? I need them first thing tomorrow morning, before you open, or I wouldn't bother you with it now."

"Well, let me see if we can help you out." Isabel rang the bell and Freddie instantly appeared at the counter. He had already removed his red vest and had his jacket on. "Freddie, this gentleman is looking for a pair of waders in a size twelve."

Freddie was only too happy to oblige. A $119.99 sale for a pair of waders would be a nice way to end the day. "I believe I might be able to help you out, my friend. I'll just need to go down to the basement and check my stock."

"Thank you, sir. I sure appreciate it." The polite young man stood at the counter and looked around. Isabel couldn't help but think what a pleasant change he was from her earlier customer. "Very nice store you have here. . . . I've always loved hardware stores."

"It's my cousin Freddie's. My uncle Handy opened it in 1946. Been here ever since."

"Mom-and-pop stores like this are few and far between these days, thanks to Home De—"

Isabel held up her hand and stopped him. "We don't mention that name in here."

The young man stopped cold and got wide-eyed, fearful he had offended the nice lady who had just let him into her store at closing time. Isabel laughed. "I'm just kidding. Sure, there's a Home Depot up in Wellington. So, if you want to waste time driving forty minutes there and forty minutes back, plus the gas, just to pick up a lightbulb for eighty-nine cents cheaper than what we sell it for, well, that's your business. We offer sensible folks an alternative." The young man smiled, relieved he was in the clear. Isabel couldn't resist inquiring about his purchase. "You don't look like you're here to fish. Let me guess, you need to take your dock out of the water?"

"No, ma'am. They're for work."

She looked at him curiously.

He continued, "I'm an engineer. I'm here to survey some land. Well, I've already surveyed a lot of it, but now I need to have a look at some of the marshy areas tomorrow morning."

"I see. . . . What kind of engineer? If you don't mind my asking." Isabel was really not a nosy person, just curious by nature.

Freddie returned with a large box and dropped it on the counter. "Size twelves!"

"Oh, great!" The man helped Freddie take the waders out of the box and did a quick examination, then resumed answering Isabel's question. "I'm a wind engineer. I test wind velocities and wind behavior. I'm looking for the most ideal places to install turbines. This stretch along Lake Michigan is a very windy area. . . . But I probably don't need to tell you two that."

Freddie was quick to jump in. "It's windy, all right! I took my grandson out to the Big Lake to fly his kite last weekend. Haven't seen him since! I expect he's somewhere over Canada by now." All three of them laughed as Freddie continued. "Yes, come to think of it I heard some talk about that at the Rotary Club a few weeks back. Someone mentioned they wanted to put in some of those wind generators north of town. . . . Would you like to try these on?"

"No, that won't be necessary . . . as long as they're size twelves, they should be fine," the young man answered as he reached into his back pocket for his wallet.

Freddie repacked the waders. "Cash or credit?"

"Credit, please."

Isabel's curiosity was piqued. "Are you talking about those gigantic windmill things?"

The young man chuckled. "Well we refer to them as wind turbines, but yes."

"I saw something on TV about those . . . I certainly am a

believer in alternative energy, solar and such . . . I mean we can't suck oil out of the earth forever. But those things . . . well, no offense, they're terrible eyesores! Are you really planning to put those up in Kentwater County?"

"Well, *I'm* not, but the company that hired me is hoping to. . . . And I may be a little biased, but I think wind farms are beautiful," the wind engineer said with a smile as he laid his credit card on the counter.

"Wind farms? Is that what you call them?" Freddie asked as he picked up the credit card and ran it through his machine.

"Yes, sir. But instead of cherries or asparagus—which I know are both big around here—we're farming energy from the wind. Someday wind farming will be one of the greatest providers of natural energy in the world, if not *the* greatest."

"Well, that's bad news for the birds," Isabel quipped. She was not happy with where this conversation was going. "And just where do you plan to put these monstrosities? I'm sorry, I don't mean to be rude, but I'm afraid I don't share your aesthetic, Mr.—"

"Metcalf, Zander Metcalf . . . so, I gather you're not a fan?" Zander did his best impression of a rim shot. "Bu-dum-bum."

Freddie laughed and Isabel managed a smile as Zander reached out to shake her hand. She obliged. "I'm Isabel Puddles, and this is my cousin Freddie Peabody." Zander and Freddie shook hands. "So, back to my question . . . where exactly are you planning to put these, whatever you call them, Mr. Metcalf?"

"Well, the company I work for—it's called Wind-X—has a few places in mind along this stretch of the lake in the north part of your county. My job is to help them decide what locations are most viable."

"And then do you buy the land?" Freddie asked.

"Sometimes the company leases the land, other times they

buy it. It's more or less up to the landowner. But that's not really my department. I'm a private contractor. They hire me to survey the land and analyze the behavior of the wind. Then I recommend where they're going to get the most bang for their buck. They make the land deals."

"Well, I'm sorry, Mr. Metcalf, nothing personal, but I hope this company finds the most bang for their buck in some other county other than ours," Isabel said in a tone that was unusually curt for her.

"Progress, Cousin . . . I guess it's the old 'not in my backyard' conundrum, right, Mr. Metcalf? We've got a windy backyard, so what can you do? Would you like a bag?"

"Oh, no, thank you," the young man replied emphatically. "I use as few plastic bags as humanly possible."

"Well, that we can agree on," Isabel said. "Plastic shopping bags are a scourge."

"I couldn't agree more," Zander replied as he picked up his box of waders and tucked it under his arm.

Freddie began putting his jacket back on. "I think I heard they were looking to put those turbines up near the Three Sisters."

The "Three Sisters" were three hills that passed for mountains in this part of Michigan, huddled together just off the Big Lake. The locally famous trio was part of a large undeveloped parcel of land along the lakeshore owned mostly by the state. The land directly to the east of the Three Sisters was a combination of marsh and woods and, a little farther east, some of the most fertile farmland in the state.

"Oh, no . . . that's such a beautiful, unspoiled area," Isabel moaned. "But I would think the Sisters would block the wind, wouldn't they?" she asked, almost hopefully.

"Actually, the wind accelerates to get around those hills, then accelerates again into the valley as it narrows. That area just east of those three hills is about as perfect as it gets. Well, folks, I need to be on my way. It was a pleasure doing business with you. Maybe I'll see you around town. Looks like I'm here for a few weeks anyway. Bye for now."

"Thanks for coming in, Mr. Metcalf," Freddie said, shaking his hand again.

"Yes . . . come back and see us," Isabel added. She may not have liked the reason he came to town, but she couldn't help but like him. Such a nice young man. When the door closed, she turned directly to Freddie with both hands on her hips. "That's progress? Really, Freddie? You want our beautiful countryside ruined in the name of *progress* with those, those . . ."

"Wind turbines," Freddie said calmly.

Isabel objected. "No, they're giant sky fans that are going to be whirling above our heads and ruining our views! I think it's an awful idea!"

"Well, whatever they are, they just helped me make a hundred-twenty-dollar sale before they even started whirling!"

Isabel shook her head in disgust. "Like the ducks and geese around here don't have enough to worry about with all you rifle-happy hunters shooting them out of the sky. Now they've got to worry about being chopped to bits in midflight."

Freddie could see he was fighting a losing battle. "I'm late for dinner. Last chance for meat loaf."

"Thank you anyway, Freddie. I'm going home to hibernate." She took her apron off and hung it behind the door. "Wind turbines . . . what next?"

Isabel mulled over this latest technological affront to her community as she drove home. She still hadn't gotten over the cell phone tower they had recently put up outside the Gull Harbor village limits. *Just* outside. Yet another reason she never wanted to own a cell phone. The phone company's solution to residents' objections that it would create an eyesore was to cover it in artificial pine branches. So now, instead of looking like a cell phone tower, it looked like a cell phone tower covered in artificial pine branches. She bristled every time she drove by it.

Dusk had fallen by the time Isabel got back to Poplar Bluff. As soon as she got out of the van, she could tell their Indian summer was coming to an end. The temperature was now dropping to where you would expect it to be in Michigan in mid-October, and it was dropping fast. She also realized she had forgotten to stop for milk, so it was going to be black coffee *again* in the morning. Isabel just wasn't herself. She was distracted and worn out. The last two days had done her in. All she wanted to do was build a fire, relax on the sofa with her book, and get better acquainted with her new roommate, Corky.

Building that first fire on the first chilly day of autumn was one of Isabel's favorite rituals. From October through March, she had a fire most evenings, her reward for collecting wood and kindling all spring and summer. She kept it stacked on the side of the house until winter approached, when she had to move it all onto the porch. It was a task that was becoming more of a chore every year, but it was still well worth the effort. There was something about a fire that calmed Isabel's nerves and buoyed her spirit, especially a fire set in *her* fireplace. She had been sitting in front of that old stone fireplace since she was a little girl. Some of her fondest childhood memories were made right there, roasting marshmallows and making s'mores with her mom and dad, and emptying the stocking they hung on the mantel for her every Christmas. She still roasted the occasional marshmallow just for old times' sake. One year her dad brought home a popcorn popper with a long handle so you could hold it over the fire. That was fun for a while, but these days, she was happy to give modern technology a nod of approval by making her popcorn in the microwave.

Tonight, fire or no fire, Isabel's mind was still unsettled. She was anxious to talk to Grady about her encounter at the hardware store with Tammy Trudlow's friend, Jason Swerley. She also wanted to give him the phone number she was cleverly able to extract from him, as well as the tag number on the truck. She wasn't exactly sure what any of this new information might or might not mean, but she felt it needed to be reported. If she hadn't seen him with Tammy Trudlow, she wouldn't have given it any thought, but a shovel? Tarps? Duct tape? It all seemed pretty nefarious.

She went to pick up the phone to call Ginny, but then remembered her grandson had a football game that night, so she knew that's where she and Grady would be. Isabel put the phone down. There was no need to interrupt them with this right now. No sooner had she hung up than the phone rang, startling her as it always did, and making Jackpot bark. "Hello." It was Frances.

"Why do I get the feeling you're avoiding me, Isabel Puddles? I've been back from Buffalo for three days and I haven't heard boo from you!" Frances was what some people referred to as a "high-maintenance friend," but Isabel had been maintaining her for forty-plus years, so she knew what to do.

"Why don't you come on over for dinner? Isn't tonight Hank's bowling night? I've got some spaghetti sauce I can thaw out and I'll whip up a salad."

"Garlic bread, too?" Frances asked.

"Yes, garlic bread, too," Isabel assured her.

"I'll be right over. . . . Just need to stop and pick us up a box of wine."

Isabel hung up and got busy in the kitchen. She took the spaghetti sauce out of the freezer and popped it into the microwave, then went into the living room to lay the fire. After making a salad and converting a slightly stale baguette into garlic bread ready for the oven, she still had time before

Frances got there to make her to-do list for tomorrow, which now included finding homes for kittens and picking up candy for Halloween, which was coming up. Maybe if she got ambitious, she would put up a few decorations, or at least put out the old straw scarecrow she used to lean against the light post, just so the neighbors knew she was still a good sport. She didn't get many trick-or-treaters at Poplar Bluff anymore, but a few of her neighbors around the lake had kids or grandkids who would stop by to model their costumes for her before going out, so she liked to have candy on hand. And if a few leftover Reese's Peanut Butter Cups ended up in her fridge, well, she would just have to live with that.

When her kids were young, Isabel always did caramel apples for Halloween, but that practice ended long ago. If or when she ever became a grandmother, she planned to start doing all that fun grandma stuff again, but more and more she wondered if that would ever happen. Carly didn't appear to be in any hurry to have kids. Her career as a bank manager seemed to be her primary focus in life. She was still young, so there was plenty of time to have a family, but, children or no children, a husband would be a good start.

And she knew that having kids probably wasn't in the cards for Charlie, who was either too busy working or too busy traveling to think about a family. "Mom . . . I can't even keep houseplants alive. I killed a cactus. . . . You know how hard it is to kill a cactus?" Charlie said the last time his mother dropped a hint about starting a family. So, she accepted that her dream of becoming a caramel-apple-making super-grandma might never come true. But she never pressured either of her kids about it, other than the occasional good-humored hint. Isabel was very proud of both her children and their accomplishments, and she admired the adults they had become. They were smart, kindhearted, good-humored, conscientious citizens who were happy with the paths in life they had chosen. That's what should matter most for any mother, of course, but she would still love to be a grandmother someday. It just seemed to be part of the script everybody in her family had followed for generations, and now it was her turn to play the role, and hopefully play it as well as her beloved grandmothers did. But it was out of her control, and Isabel Puddles was a woman who tried hard not to worry too much about things that were out of her control. Of course the Earl Jonasson situation was *completely* out of her control, and she was up to her eyeballs in that, so that philosophy didn't always work out.

After her dinner prep was complete, she went back to her to-do list . . . *Kittens, Halloween candy, doggie bed for Corky, post office, dry cleaners. Weight Watchers* and *oil change* held their positions at the bottom of the list. Isabel tapped her pen and thought about what else she needed to do when she was suddenly interrupted by a knock at the door. "It's open," she yelled.

Isabel was expecting Frances, but instead looked up to find Grady and Ginny standing in the kitchen doorway wearing matching blue-and-gold Hartley Saxons sweatshirts. Their look was festive, but their expressions were glum. Isabel abandoned her list and got up to greet them. "Have you two had supper? I'm making spaghetti. Frances is on her way over."

Grady was the first to answer. "Thanks, Iz, we ate at the game."

"Who won?" Isabel asked.

"Shelbyville," Ginny answered with some disdain. "Well, how could they not with both refs in the tank for them? But my Kevin played very well, didn't he, Grady?"

"He did . . . Made an interception in the third quarter and ran a good thirty yards until—"

"Until he tripped," Ginny added. "He's growing so fast, he's still a little clumsy." Ginny sat down at the kitchen table and moved on to the topic on everybody's mind. "So, can you believe it, Iz? Can you *believe* we have a murder on our hands in our quiet little community?"

"It's not something I want to believe. I kept hoping there might be another explanation, but . . ." Isabel's voice trailed off.

"You've opened quite a hornet's nest, Izzy," Grady said with a half smile.

"What's so scary to me," Ginny continued, "is that there's a murderer out there somewhere, running around putting nails in people's heads!"

Grady sat down next to Ginny at the table. "I'm going to have to talk to the press in the morning, Iz. Well, what press there is around here. I haven't heard from the *New York Times*, but I've already received a few calls from the locals. Better to just get it out there. But I want you to know that I'm going to keep your name out of this for as long as I can. If or when we make an arrest and have a trial, you *will* need to testify, but that's likely way down the line."

"I'll do anything I can do to help, Grady. You know that. But thank you for keeping me out of it, at least for the time being." She got up to check her spaghetti sauce and give it a stir.

"I am going to need you to come down tomorrow and give us a statement," Grady added.

"Of course . . . Whatever you need." She turned the microwave back on before continuing. "I just can't stop thinking about poor Meg. She's so distraught. I've never seen her like that." Isabel got some plates and bowls out of the cupboard and some silverware out of the drawer, setting it all down on the tile counter with a clang. Finally she couldn't help herself. She had to ask. "Grady . . . you probably can't answer me, and I probably shouldn't even be asking, but I got the impression from the way you were looking at Junior that you think he might have had something to do with his father's murder?"

She ended by opening a can of mixed nuts and setting them down on the table.

Ginny wanted to change the subject. "He's just going to pick out the cashews. You watch . . . makes me crazy. I tell him the polite thing to do is just say, 'No, thank you. I don't care for mixed nuts,' but to just go in and scavenge for the cashews? I just don't think it's right."

Grady defiantly picked out a cashew, popped it into his mouth, and gave Ginny a look before turning to Isabel. "I guess I need to work on my poker face. . . . Well, what I *can* tell you is that nobody has been ruled out—not Meg, not her husband, not her nephews, not the farmhands who were around the place picking apples, and not Tammy Trudlow. Nobody. We'll just have to see where the investigation takes us. But—and you understand this does not leave this table—I do have some suspicions about Junior."

"Oh, dear . . . I just can't imagine he'd be capable. But I do think there may be somebody new you should be looking at." Just as she was about to fill Grady in on her encounter at the Dog and Suds with Tammy, and her friend who came into the hardware, Frances appeared in the kitchen. She took one look at the somber-looking threesome and slammed her box of wine down before grabbing a handful of mixed nuts.

"Who died?" Frances went for the kitchen cupboard. "I'm getting some wineglasses out. I've been here five seconds and you people are already bringing me down!"

Grady and Ginny got up to leave, offering their apologies for running off. Grady hardly knew Frances, but Ginny had known her for many years, and although she was always polite, she wasn't terribly fond of her cousin's best friend. Ginny was no wallflower, but she felt Frances was just a little too over the top. "She makes me nervous," she had said to Isabel more than once. "You just never know what's going to come out of her mouth." Isabel couldn't argue that position very convincingly, but Frances's unbridled honesty was one of the things she loved about her.

"All right, well, I won't take it personally, but between you two and my best friend here, I'm starting to get a complex! I used to be so popular!" Frances put two glasses on the table and dived into the mixed nuts again. "I love mixed nuts but I can't keep them around the house. Hank just picks out all the cashews. I tell him, 'Why can't you just buy yourself a can of cashews, for God's sake, and leave me the mixed nuts?!' You think he pays any attention? I might as well be asking my cat to do a crossword puzzle with me."

Grady and Ginny chuckled politely and headed for the door while Frances opened the box of wine like a pro. "Fran, I'm going to walk them out," Isabel said, getting up. "Pour us some wine if you would and get the water boiling for the spaghetti. I'll be right back."

"And now I've been relegated to kitchen help!" Frances pulled the box to the edge of the counter, opened the spigot, and poured herself a healthy glass of wine.

Once they got out to the driveway, Isabel told Grady and Ginny everything that had happened that day with Tammy Trudlow and Jason Swerley, and then gave Grady a slip of paper with both Jason's phone number and the tag number on the truck. Grady had been listening attentively, but he was staying tight-lipped. "Okay, well, thanks, Izzy . . . I'll make a record of all this." He and Ginny climbed into the SUV.

"What time do you want me to come in tomorrow?" Isabel asked Grady as he started the engine.

"Meg and Junior are coming first thing in the morning, so probably best if you come in sometime after lunch?"

"I'll be there. Good night, you two. Drive safely . . . I saw a couple deer on my way home tonight." Isabel waved good-bye as they pulled out and headed down the road. When she came back in, Frances was already on her second glass of wine and starting to get a little loopy.

"I was about to pour wine for the dogs, I was getting so lonely."

"Sorry . . . I had some business to discuss with Grady. Have you met Corky?"

"Yes, we met. Cute. Is she a permanent resident or another boarder?"

"Corky is Jackpot's new sister."

Frances looked over at the dogs cuddling on the sofa. "They seem a little chummy for brother and sister. . . . Where'd she come from?"

"She's Earl Jonasson's dog. Meg and the family couldn't take her in, so it was either here or the shelter. And after what she just went through, I couldn't let that happen."

"It's just a terrible thing . . . just terrible." Frances was fond of Meg, and they had known each other for years, but they were never close friends. "How's Meg doing? Must be very hard on her . . . It's hard enough to lose a parent, but to lose one to murder?"

Isabel began to nod in agreement, then stopped cold. "Wait a minute . . . Where did you get the idea Earl Jonasson was *murdered*?" she asked, trying to disguise her amazement that this news had already leaked.

"Honey, this is a small town. How long do you think it's going to take for something like that to get out? I've heard it from five different people today and with five different stories. But I have my suspicions. And, by the way, you don't seem very surprised. I'll bet Sheriff Pemberton told you all about it. And I'm guessing that's why he was here tonight and why you all looked so glum."

Isabel was still in shock that the gossip was already circulating and hoped she didn't get blamed for it getting out. But after Grady's press conference in the morning, it would all be out in the open anyway. "Please, by all means, tell me what you've heard," Isabel offered invitingly as she took a sip from her wine.

"Well the latest, according to—actually I shouldn't tell you who—let's just say a reliable source who heard it first-hand, is—"

"So the *latest*"—Isabel interrupted, inserting air quotes—"is a rumor now about to be *three* times removed?"

"Whatever you say, Iz . . . You know I don't do math. Anyway, this person claimed that he—or she—overheard Earl Sr. and Earl Jr. arguing just a week or two before Earl Sr. died. And the argument had something to do with land and money."

Isabel listened, somewhat skeptically, before jumping in. "That's it? That's all you've got? Fathers and sons argue all the time, Frances."

Frances was offended that her juicy piece of gossip didn't seem to be gaining any traction. "Okay, well, I also know this: Earl Sr. was having serious money problems. The bank was breathing down his neck. After Ruth got sick, he had to take out a loan against the farm to pay her medical bills, or whatever insurance wouldn't cover, which of course was most of it, with those criminals. Did you know they flew poor Ruth over to the Mayo Clinic in an air ambulance? Can you imagine what *that* cost?"

Isabel did know about that. She also remembered the news they got at Mayo wasn't good. Frances wasn't finished. But then Frances was never finished.

"They couldn't do anything for her, so back she came to, well, sadly, to die. And then she lingered . . . and lingered . . . and lingered."

Isabel was getting impatient. "Kind of like you're doing right now with this story?"

Of course Isabel knew all about Ruth's illness and the excellent, round-the-clock care she received at home, but she didn't know anything about any financial difficulties the

Jonasson family was having. That surprised her. But she was playing it cool, which only prompted Frances to keep going.

"And I happen to know something *else* that may figure into this."

"And what might that be?" Isabel asked nonchalantly as she dropped the pasta into the pot of boiling water and Frances went back to the wine box for a refill.

"Earl Jonasson had a sizable life insurance policy," Frances offered, as though it were some kind of a bombshell revelation. Isabel was not impressed.

"So? Most people have life insurance policies, Frances . . . But how would *you* know that?"

"Because my sister's husband's brother sold it to him," she answered with confidence.

Isabel was trying not to seem too invested, but she had to at least give this information some thought. "So that information is *four* times removed, but okay. . . . Now, getting back to this argument that somebody told somebody they allegedly overheard . . . were there any details beyond it being about land and money?"

Frances took another swig of her wine. "Well, I guess he, I mean this *person*, couldn't hear the whole conversation. . . . Just bits and pieces. But they did hear Earl Jr. swear at his father and call him a 'stubborn son of a blankety-blank' and accused him of 'destroying the family.' Doesn't sound to me like they were on very good father-son terms."

"So, what you're saying here is that there's now a rumor going around—one you're now helping to spread, by the way—that Junior killed his father because he was angry with him over something having to do with land and money, or a life insurance policy?"

Frances needed to clarify. "Well, for the record, I didn't start any such rumor. This information came to me unsolicited. I'm merely relaying that information."

"Then how did he do it, exactly? I had been led to understand that Earl died of a stroke."

"There are things you can do to make somebody look like they died of natural causes when they were actually murdered. And who's going to be suspicious when an eighty-eight-year-old man dies? Haven't you ever watched *CSI*?"

"You know I don't watch those shows."

"You did the poor old man's hair and makeup, Izzy. . . . Did *you* notice anything suspicious?"

"I'm not at liberty to say." Isabel was ready to change the subject, but she was very troubled to hear about the fact pattern developing . . . one that did seem to be implicating Earl Jr. "I'm getting peckish, aren't you? Do me a favor and toss that salad. I'll put the garlic bread in."

Frances shot her a suspicious look. "Hmmm . . . well, it looks to me like somebody might know just a little bit more about all this than she's letting on."

Isabel ignored her and poured more salt into the pot of boiling pasta. "Do you salt your pasta water?"

"Honey, I salt everything." Frances knew when to give up. When Isabel Puddles decided to be tight-lipped, she knew there was no prying them open.

Frances had been just a little bit overserved, so she called Hank to come and pick her up after bowling, which meant Isabel would have to go pick her up in the morning. But it was a routine she was used to. Frances loved her boxed wine and, some nights, she loved it a little too much. After she left, Isabel sat on the sofa in front of the fire knitting with Jackpot curled up against her on one side, and Corky on the other. Knitting was not only something she loved to do but it had become a form of meditation. It concentrated her mind. But tonight, what her mind was inescapably concentrated on was the tragedy that had befallen the Jonasson family. She stared into the fire and thought more about what Frances had told her, and wondered whether or not any of it was true. If it was, Earl Jr. had motive for days if there was bad blood developing over looming financial problems, and if there was a life insurance policy he wanted to get his hands on. Frances loved to gossip, there was no doubt about that, but she was also, as a rule, pretty reliable, and not one for spreading completely unfounded rumors. There was usually fire behind the smoke. She made a mental note to bring all this up to Grady. If there had been an argument between father and son days before the father was murdered, that was nothing to ignore. Of course the way gossip flew around this county, there was a good chance Grady had already heard about it.

After dozing off on the sofa with her knitting collapsed in her lap, Isabel woke up to Jackpot and Corky barking at something outside. They probably spotted a raccoon. Hopefully not a skunk. She'd been down that road more than once and it was not pleasant. She called the dogs in and started to get ready for bed. Given the swirl of thoughts in her head, and knowing Grady was going to go public with Earl Jonasson's murder in the morning, she knew she was probably looking at another restless night.

After climbing into bed, Jackpot jumped up and took his usual place, but Corky curled up on the hardwood by the door. She had obviously been trained not to jump up on beds. Isabel got up and went to the kitchen, where she grabbed Jack's daybed and brought it back into the bedroom, laying it on the floor next to her. Corky licked her hand as she laid it down as if to say thank you, then cozied up in it. She let out a deep sigh, and closed her eyes. Isabel wondered if she was missing Earl. Poor girl.

After another failed attempt to read her book, and after staring at the ceiling for an hour or so, Isabel was suddenly struck with a flash of insight. She sat bolt upright in bed and snapped on the lamp. Officially wide awake at 2:10 a.m., she

reached into her bedside table drawer and pulled out the yellow
legal pad and pen she always kept handy in case she thought of
anything she was afraid she might forget when morning rolled
around. These were usually things that had to do with mun-
dane household stuff, or sometimes a strange dream, but this
time it was because she was determined to keep track of anything that might be useful for Grady's murder investigation.
Isabel had just remembered that while driving back from her
visit with Meg at the farm today, driving west, she saw the
Three Sisters off in the distance. And that got her thinking
about the wind engineer, Zander Metcalf, who had come in to
buy waders. And *that* triggered a childhood memory of her and
Meg, Gil Cook, and Elliot Crowder, who, one summer during
junior high school, all went canoeing through a marsh on the
Jonasson land, hunting for bullfrogs to enter in the annual frog-
jumping contest at the fairgrounds. Could that be the land the
wind engineer was talking about as being so ideal for his wind
turbines? Was his company, Wind-X, trying to make a land
deal with Earl Jonasson? And could *that* be the reason he and
his son were arguing over land and money? It sure sounded like
a plausible theory, but also very sad if it were true.

It was no secret that most of the farmers in the county had
suffered over the past several years. There had been a drought
one year, followed by an infestation of aphids and Japanese
beetles that attacked many of the county's fruit orchards the
next. Corn rootworms wreaked havoc on the sweet corn crop
for two seasons in a row after that. She could see the stress on
the faces of the farmers coming into the hardware, and she
often heard them complaining that they were barely making
ends meet. Savings were being drained, parcels of land were
being sold off, and farms and homes refinanced—anything to
keep the banks off their backs. Clive Barrow, who had spent
thirty years growing some of the best Honeycrisp apples in
the world, connected a hose from the exhaust pipe on his

tractor, ran it into a garden shed, and killed himself after his orchards were completely wiped out by aphids.

The Jonassons had been lucky through these rough times. They had water on their land that was spring fed, and they had sprayed their crops early at the first sign of any pest problems. The tragedy that had befallen their family wasn't losing their crops, it was losing Ruth, their matriarch.

If the Jonasson farm was in danger of being lost to the bank, Earl Jr. certainly would have wanted to do whatever he could to stop that from happening. And if his father had been offered a substantial sum of money either to sell or lease his land to that power company so that they could install their wind turbines, he probably would have encouraged him to do it. But Isabel had a hunch that Earl Sr.—being a proud fourth- or maybe fifth-generation farmer, and the custodian of a large and very valuable tract of land that, to him, represented an even more valuable family tradition—probably wouldn't be interested in having that land turned into something resembling an amusement park. But if his son saw this opportunity as the only way to avoid impending financial ruin, it was certainly something that could provoke an argument, and it was also within the realm of possibility, however terrible, that he decided to take action before the deal went away, namely, to murder his father. It was not the most original story in the world, but unfortunately it was the one that made the most sense right now. The only part of this scenario that didn't make any sense to Isabel was that she still couldn't imagine Earl Jr. having it in him to kill his father, no matter how dire the situation . . . unless he had some help, or at least some encouragement from, say, his fiancée?

After writing down all her notes, Isabel got out of bed and went to the kitchen to make some tea. She was fighting the impulse to call Frances and demand she tell her who told *her* about this alleged argument. Sitting down at the kitchen counter for a moment, she took a sip of her tea and reached for the phone. Her impulse won the fight. Frances picked up on the second ring. Isabel began with an apology. "I'm sorry to call you at such an ungodly hour, Frances."

"Isabel, what's wrong? Are you okay? Who's dead?" Frances answered drowsily.

"I'm fine . . . and nobody died, well, other than Earl Jonasson . . . But, Frances, I have a very, very important question to ask." She heard Frances telling Hank to go back to sleep. In that moment she realized that telling Frances the truth at this hour of the night was probably a safe bet. It was also the best way to get the information out of her she wanted. By the time she got up and around the next morning and got the rumor mill churning again, Grady would have already announced that the murder investigation was under way.

"It's two forty-five in the morning, Iz. What could possibly be so important that it couldn't wait for breakfast?"

"Frances . . . Earl Jonasson *was* murdered. I don't know how or if it relates to what you heard, but I know for a fact that he was murdered. Grady is going to make an announcement to the press first thing in the morning. Now, I need to know how you found out about this argument he had with Junior. It could be the key to figuring out who's responsible for killing that poor old man." Isabel's pitch was met with silence, until finally . . .

"Okay . . . now, you didn't hear this from me, but it was Julie Welker—Rock and Brenda Welker's daughter—she's dating that cute new sheriff's deputy."

"The one who gave me the ticket?"

"Yes, that's the one. I'd let him write me a ticket any day of the week. Anyway, I ran into Julie yesterday at Hobson's— by the way, do you think his cinnamon buns are as good as they used to be? I don't think they're as flavorful. And the texture is—"

"Frances, can we please stay on the subject here?" Isabel was already losing patience.

"Well, Julie told me—and, by the way, she doesn't think they're as good anymore, either. We both agreed they're just not as chewy. You know Bobby Hobson still asks about you."

Isabel took a deep breath. Given that she might be on the cusp of getting the information she wanted, she decided to just wait for Frances to get back on track. "Anyway, Julie told me that she was sitting in her car waiting for Deputy What's His Name to get back from patrol so they could go to Grand Rapids to see a movie—I forget what she said they were going to see—anyway, that skinny old drunk who's always out washing the patrol cars in his jail clothes. What's his name?"

"Roger."

"Roger! So Roger offered to wash Julie's car while she waited for her date. It was pretty dirty, so she let him have at it. Why not? Oh! Brad Pitt! It was that new Brad Pitt movie they were going to see. . . . He's not as good as he used to be, either, if you ask me. . . . Anyway, she got out and stood there while he was washing her car, and he started telling her about how sad he was about old Earl's death. Then he told her about how Earl had pulled an old travel trailer he owned into a stand of trees behind the barn and let him live in it over the summer in exchange for doing some work around the farm. So he was in the trailer one morning when he heard both the Earls arguing. He figured they must have thought he was gone because he had taken his bicycle inside the trailer the night before. Oh, and get this. You want to know why he took his bicycle in that night?" Frances didn't bother waiting for an answer. "Well, I'll tell you . . . because he had seen a bear on TV riding a bicycle once—must have been watching a circus, I suppose—and since he had just heard there had been a black bear spotted in the area, he brought his bike inside because he didn't want the bear riding off with it. So, he's a drunk *and* he's a dimwit. But Julie said he did a very good job on her car. Of course he's had plenty of practice, hasn't he?" Even woken from a sound sleep at 2:45 in the morning, Frances Spitler loved to talk.

"Go back to sleep. Thank you. I'm sorry to wake you at this hour, but I had to know. And please do not say anything about any of this until Grady makes it official in the morning, okay?"

Frances yawned. "Okay. Good night . . . see you at breakfast?"

"I'll be there at eight thirty. Good night, Frances." Isabel hung up the phone. Finding a few more pieces of the puzzle helped put her mind to rest, but it was not a very pretty picture. If everything Frances was telling her was true, and this land the wind engineer was surveying was indeed Jonasson land—as she was now pretty certain it was—it would appear Earl Jr. would have had plenty of motive to get rid of his father. But she needed more information. Maybe Zander Metcalf could shed some light on how deals like these were made, and what kind of money was involved. He did say it "wasn't his department," but he must know *something*. Tracking the wind engineer down after breakfast was now moving to the top of tomorrow's to-do list.

After she settled back into bed, Isabel's mind drifted back to her great uncle Maynard and a land deal he'd made way back in the 1950s . . . One day a Detroit businessman approached Uncle Maynard and offered to lease a small swath of his land so that he could erect a billboard to promote his new diner down the road. Uncle Maynard agreed to the twenty dollars a month the man offered. They signed a one-year lease agreement, and a week later his billboard went up. But after six months, the owner of the Harmony Diner stopped paying his rent. Five more months went by and no rent payments. When Uncle Maynard, a very quiet, polite, non-confrontational man, went down to the diner and asked the owner nicely to pay his back rent, he told him business was slow and he couldn't afford to make the payments. But the parking lot was always full whenever Uncle Maynard drove by, so that didn't square with him at all. So he left the diner without his rent money. Obviously this deadbeat businessman thought he had found an easy mark. The next month, after the man missed his sixth rent payment in a row, Uncle Maynard decided the time had come to take matters into his own hands—along with a paintbrush, a bucket of paint, and a ladder. He then proceeded to settle the score in his own creative way. The diner billboard originally read as follows:

HARMONY DINER
HOMEMADE PICKLES AND BRATWURST
BEST FOOD IN THE COUNTY
GUARANTEED TO MAKE
YOU SING!

But it read something else entirely when Uncle Maynard finished with it:

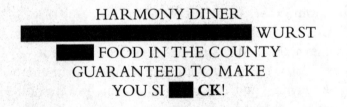

The irate business owner showed up at Uncle Maynard's house with his billboard painter the very next day and handed him a check for $120, along with a few choice words. Uncle Maynard handed the check back and told him to come back later . . . with cash. When the man returned with the money, Uncle Maynard accepted it with a thank-you, but then had to share some unfortunate news: their twelve-month lease agreement had expired. So if he wanted to renew, it would now be twenty-five dollars a month for twelve more months, payable up front . . . in cash. In an apoplectic rage, the man told Uncle Maynard he was going to sue or, better yet, go home, get an ax, and chop the sign down himself. Uncle Maynard then informed him that he had grown fond of the sign and had decided to leave it up for a while, following up with fair warning that he would personally shoot any trespassers who came onto his land without permission. So the man was left with two choices: Take the matter to court while the sign stayed in place and mocked his business for who knows how long or he could pay up. The man came back the next morning with three hundred dollars cash for the next year's rent, and Uncle Maynard gave him his blessing to repaint his sign. The story had become part of Kentwater County folklore.

Chapter 8

Isabel and Frances were still buttering their toast when Chet came rushing out of the kitchen and flipped on the TV, an old Zenith that sat on top of a cherry crate at the end of the breakfast counter. "Just heard on the radio Sheriff Pemberton was making some announcement about Earl Jonasson!" Chet yelled to the room.

The place was full of regulars who were immediately riveted by seeing their own Sheriff Pemberton on the local news standing on the Hartley courthouse steps and announcing that they had just opened an investigation into the murder of Earl Jonasson. Grady took some questions from the small gaggle of reporters who, along with a couple of local news crews, were joined by folks from town who were curious about such an unusual commotion at the courthouse. None of the questions about the investigation were ones he could answer, but he was able to inform the group in a blanket statement that "there was nobody currently in custody" but they did have a "person of interest" and they were looking into "possible motives." Grady then thanked everybody for coming and wrapped things up.

Chet turned off the TV and Kayla made a beeline for Isabel and Frances, now digging into their cold eggs. "So, who do you think did it? You really think Earl Jr. killed his daddy? I've heard people whispering about that. He sure doesn't seem the murdering type, but then I guess you never can tell."

After listening to twenty minutes of wild conjecture among the Land's End staff and customers about the who and how behind Earl's murder—including a theory floated by the county conspiracy theorist, Clem Haskil, who proclaimed that it was most likely a mob hit—Isabel was through with all this mindless banter and addressed the room. "I think we all need to stop speculating about this and just let Grady do his job. The truth will come out soon enough." She finished her hash browns and passed on more coffee when Kayla came back to the table. "No, I'm good, thank you. I've got a busy day. I need to get going."

"Me, too," Frances said, reaching for her purse. "I'm going to Wellington to get my hair done and I'm stopping at the More-For-Less. You need anything?"

"Frances, how many times are you going to ask me that? You know how I feel about those big discount stores," Isabel said, finishing the last of her coffee and dabbing her mouth with her napkin.

"And I know how you feel about saving money, too, so I keep thinking maybe you'll get with the program one of these days," Frances cracked as she began digging through her purse.

Isabel was unmoved. "I'm happy to spend an extra forty-two cents on peanut butter, or an extra dollar for batteries if it will help keep the Kroger and Freddie's hardware store in business. You won't catch me dead in one of those places. It's un-American!" Isabel laid nine one-dollar bills and four quarters on the table to cover her breakfast.

Frances followed suit. "Honey, I think maybe your high horse could use some hay. And it's a *lot* cheaper at the More-For-Less!" Isabel ignored the jab. Frances continued. "All I know is they've got four-packs of paper towels on sale for a dollar-eighty-nine this week, so if that makes me a Communist, well, I guess I'll have to live with that."

Kayla looked at Isabel and hesitated briefly before caving in. "I do my best to support our local merchants, I really do, Isabel, but that's a *very* good price. And the way my family goes through paper towels?" She turned to Frances, "Can you pick up four four-packs for me? Here's ten dollars."

"I'll be happy to," Frances replied, taking two fives from Kayla and smiling at Isabel, who shook her head and waved good-bye over her head as she left.

Isabel had a couple hours to kill before she had to meet with Grady, so she figured this would be a good time to try to find Zander Metcalf. He might already be at work in the marsh, and although she had found her waders in the garage before leaving for breakfast, after she threw them in the van she had to stop and ask herself: Was she really going to wade into a marsh to talk to him? How would she explain that away as a coincidence? She was a bit old to be hunting bullfrogs. A more sensible strategy was to find out where he was staying, and then *accidentally* run into him there.

There weren't many options as far as nice hotels in the county. There were lots of quaint old bed-and-breakfast establishments, and some kitschy old motor hotels scattered around, but what passed for the nicest hotel in the county—the sort of place Isabel imagined where a wind engineer might stay—was the Michigander Lodge, just off the freeway. She knew the manager, not well, but she was pretty sure she could get the information she wanted from him.

The Michigander Lodge was at one time a Howard Johnson Motor Lodge but the orange roof shingles had been removed many years ago, and the fried clam strips Isabel loved as a kid were now a distant memory. The place sat abandoned for a long time, but after an extensive renovation, the hotel was back, and now with a north woods rustic charm, complete with a moose head in the lobby. The indoor pool, strangely enough—given the overall decorative theme—included a tiki bar, intended to attract off-season travelers and serve as a party venue for the more adventurous locals.

Isabel quickly learned her instincts about where to find Zander Metcalf were right. At the very moment she pulled into the motel parking lot, he was pulling out in a big white SUV with the Wind-X company logo on the driver's-side door. He didn't see her, and for a split second she thought about trying to wave him down, but then thought maybe it was a better idea to just follow him and see exactly where he was headed. That way she would know for certain if she was right about the land he was surveying being Jonasson land. She turned around sharply in the parking lot, her loyal old van groaning and screeching, reminding her that she was probably in need of power-steering fluid, too, along with that overdue oil change. She looked both ways and made another of her Michigan stops before speeding off in hot pursuit of Zander, now heading north on the freeway. Once she got a few car-lengths behind him, she reached into the glove box to retrieve her sunglasses, just in case he happened to glance into his rearview mirror and wonder why the lady from the hardware store was tailing him.

About five miles north of town she looked to the west and saw the Three Sisters huddled together, watching over the valley to the east, and the Big Lake to the west. It was a view she had seen countless times in her life, but one that now took on new significance. To her right, a few hundred yards off in the distance, was the marshy area where she remembered hunting bullfrogs before the new freeway was built. Skeletal remains of dozens of long-dead trees poked up through the brackish water, creating a peaceful but eerie-looking landscape.

Just as she anticipated, Zander signaled right as he approached the Monroe Road exit. Many of the country roads in the county were, for whatever reason, named after more obscure US presidents: Monroe, Buchanan, Polk, Tyler. Isabel followed him down the off-ramp, slowing a bit so she wouldn't be right on his bumper when he came to the stop sign. He turned right and headed east a bit until his blinker went on again, then turned north onto a dirt road. Isabel followed, pulling slowly off to the side to think of a strategy for casually running in to him on a remote country road.

After the dust settled, Isabel noticed a large black car parked off to the side. She couldn't tell what kind it was, but it looked expensive. Zander pulled up slowly behind it and stopped. She kept her distance and watched as he got out of his SUV at the same time that a silver-haired man dressed casually in khakis and a light blue cardigan sweater got out of his imposing black sedan. She had never seen him before, but he wasn't a local, of that she was certain. The two shook hands and exchanged what appeared to be a friendly greeting, then got back into Zander's SUV and headed down the road a few hundred yards before turning abruptly into a wide-open field, bouncing across the terrain until coming to a stop square in the middle.

Isabel remembered she had an old pair of binoculars under the seat that she had taken the last time Ginny dragged her to a football game. She watched as Zander popped open the back hatch and removed several large black cases. He then began doing what she assumed was wind-engineering stuff: setting up tall tripods with fans attached at the top, with wires attached to metal boxes sitting at the base.

The silver-haired stranger, who she had by now surmised was Zander's boss from the power company, seemed to be supervising, walking with him around the field and taking notes as Zander planted each of the tripods in the ground and then raised them like periscopes, ten feet or more in the air, each of them with flags attached; some red, some yellow, some green. This went on for a while, and because it was a windy day, the fans were spinning fiercely, and the flags all flapping wildly. Zander appeared to be taking readings and making his own notes. All things considered, it was a strange sight to behold in the middle of a country field.

Under these conditions, Isabel realized, there was no way a "chance" meeting could take place. She looked at her watch. She had to meet Grady in an hour, so it was time to head back into town anyway. What struck her as peculiar, though, as she turned around and headed back to the main road, was that this was obviously not the marshy area Zander was talking about the day before and preparing to survey. He didn't need waders for this. And although she couldn't be certain, she was pretty sure the land he was on now was not Jonasson land. It was too far north. She was certain the Jonasson land was all south of Monroe Road.

As she drove back down the dirt road, she recognized an old abandoned farmhouse with a dilapidated barn and a rusty silo covered in ivy, mostly hidden from view by a sea of dead corn stalks. The ruins had been there for decades. As kids they used to sneak into it through the storm cellar doors, despite being warned by Mr. Jonasson to stay away from it. Isabel could still picture the interior of that house—one they assumed was haunted, of course—with pieces of old furniture, dust-encrusted dishes in the kitchen cabinets, tattered lace curtains, and a tarnished brass bed frame upstairs. But what she remembered most was a family portrait hanging above a crumbling brick fireplace: a photograph of a stern-looking old farmer, his dour-looking wife, and their four kids, each of them looking unhappier than the next. She didn't remember the backstory on the old farm or the family, but she did remember it was not on Jonasson land, which was why they were not allowed to go in. She would have to remember to ask Frances or Ginny the history behind it. . . . they would remember.

Chapter 9

Isabel had never seen the Kentwater County sheriff's office so busy. It usually had more of a Mayberry feeling, with Sheriff Taylor at his desk, eating a ham salad sandwich Aunt Bea made for him, and Barney napping off in the corner, but today it was a beehive of activity. Deputies in uniform were huddled about, deep in conversation, while a half dozen other men and women dressed in business attire—whom she had never seen in her life—were typing furiously on laptop computers, talking on their cell phones, or both. And in the middle of it all was a frazzled-looking Ginny manning the office phones, which were ringing incessantly. She looked up at her cousin with a pleading expression, then quickly waved at a man across the room to get his attention. When she did, she pointed to Isabel and gave him the thumbs-up. The man made his way over to Isabel right away with a smile. "Hello, are you Mrs. Puddles?"

"I am," Isabel said, slightly curious about what was happening, or what was about to. The man extended his hand.

"Very nice to meet you. I'm Detective Zakarian from the Michigan State Police."

Isabel cautiously shook his hand. "Nice to meet you, too . . . I think."

Detective Zakarian was probably in his late-thirties and handsome, with dark features, and wearing a tie and a sport coat. He reminded her of one of her favorite detectives as a kid—Joe Mannix.

"I know the sheriff was planning to take your statement, but as you can see, it's a bit crazy around here right now and he's still tied up. And since I'm leading the forensic side of things, he thought it made sense that I take your statement anyway. Would you mind following me into the conference room?"

"Certainly Detective Zakarian. Lead the way," Isabel replied graciously. She could see Grady in his office, sitting at the desk as she passed by. Although the door was closed and the shades partially drawn, she could still make out Meg and Earl Jr. sitting in front of him with their backs to the outer office.

As they approached the conference room down the hall, Isabel made an attempt at small talk to calm her nerves a little. She had never been interviewed by a detective. "Has anybody ever told you that you look like Joe Mannix?"

"No, they haven't," Detective Zakarian replied as he opened the door for her. "Who's Joe Mannix?"

"Never mind," she answered, knowing that explaining it would just make her feel even older. After they sat down, Detective Zakarian took out a handheld device and laid it on the table. Isabel looked at it suspiciously. "Is that a phone or a tape recorder?"

"Both," he answered as he pulled a notebook from a backpack on the floor next to his chair, then a pen from his shirt pocket. "I'm going to record our conversation, but I still like to take notes. I'm old-school that way."

"Joe Mannix was old school, too. . . . So, is that one of those cell phones that takes pictures?"

"Yes, it does. . . . I think they all do now, though, don't they?"

"I wouldn't know. I don't own a cell phone," Isabel declared with some measure of pride as she shifted in her chair.

"Well, you might want to consider it, Mrs. Puddles. I finally convinced my mother to get one. She loves it now. They're very convenient."

"So I've heard." She chose to ignore the fact that he had just drawn a parallel between herself and his mother.

Detective Zakarian picked up the device and busied himself with it for a moment, then turned it back to Isabel. "Is this who you're referring to?"

Isabel squinted, then took out her reading glasses and looked again. "Joe Mannix! That's him!"

Detective Zakarian studied the image a little more closely. "I guess I do see a resemblance. . . . He looks Armenian. So am I."

She looked at the image of Mannix again and smiled. She hadn't seen his face in years. "Handsome as ever . . . you know, I always thought he and Peggy had something going." She looked up at a befuddled Detective Zakarian. "Well, you wouldn't know. That show was probably canceled before you were even born. Anyway, how did you do that?"

"Well, this phone is also a handheld computer, with a connection to the Internet. I just did a quick Google search."

"I've heard of the Google. Everybody's googling! But I'm afraid I wouldn't know a Google from a gaggle. I don't even own a computer, Detective. I'm just a country girl at heart! Still getting used to electricity. I have to admit, though, that I do love the indoor plumbing."

Detective Zakarian laughed. He didn't meet many folks like Isabel Puddles in suburban Detroit. He laid his magical device on the table, tapped something, and then cleared his throat, "Now, Mrs. Puddles, let's begin with how you came to be the person tasked with doing the body preparation of Mr. Jonasson."

Body preparation? That sounds so clinical, Isabel thought. She much preferred Gil Cook's *fixing up.* But since he asked, she started from the beginning, going all the way back to Gladys DeLong.

Almost an hour later, Isabel came out of the conference room and back into the same frenetic atmosphere. Grady was still in his office, but he was now alone with Earl Jr. Meg was nowhere to be found. She noticed Gil Cook sitting next to Ginny's desk. He stood up and saluted as he walked toward her. "Hey there, Izzy. Can you believe all this?"

"No, I can't. And I'd like *not* to believe it." She noticed the detective following behind her. "Gil, this is Detective Zakarian."

The detective extended his hand. "Michigan State Police. Are you Gil Cook?"

"I am," Gil replied as they shook hands.

"Nice to meet you, Mr. Cook." He turned to Isabel. "Mrs. Puddles, it was a pleasure to meet you. Thank you so much for your time and your cooperation. I will be in touch if I have any more questions. Mr. Cook, if you would come with me, please?"

Gil looked at Isabel and arched his eyebrows. He was rarely at a loss for some smart remark, no matter how silly, but this was not a situation in which anybody was feeling very silly, not even Gil. Ginny was still trapped on the phone, so Isabel headed for the door, anxious to get away from all the activity.

"Izzy, I'll call you later tonight!" Ginny yelled from across the room. Isabel gave her a finger wave and disappeared out the back door.

As soon as she walked out into the parking lot, she spotted Roger coming around the corner wearing his yellow jump-suit and dragging a rake. What he wasn't wearing was his usual smile.

"Hello, Mrs. Puddles," he said in a low voice.

"Hello there, Roger . . . I guess the leaves are going to be keeping you busy for a while now."

"Yes, ma'am, it's that time'a year," Roger replied with a nod.

Isabel seized the opportunity to see if there was any truth to what she had heard from Frances about an argument. "So, Roger, I hear you were doing some work out at the Jonasson farm?"

"I did this past summer, yes, ma'am. . . . That Mr. Jonasson sure was a nice man. . . . I sure did like him. Just can't believe anybody would want to kill a nice old man like that."

"I know it's hard to believe. I've known the Jonassons my whole life, practically. A nicer couple you'd never want to meet."

Roger nodded in agreement "I never knew the missus, but Mr. J. talked about her an awful lot."

"So, you were living in a trailer in back of the barn, I heard?" Isabel inquired with a smile. "That was very nice of Earl. . . . But that's the kind of man he was."

Roger stared off into the distance. "Yes, ma'am. He set me up in a nice old trailer. Fed me, too. And he still paid me for the work. Just a nice old man . . . Sure is a shame."

Isabel nodded back in agreement. "Roger . . . I was just curious if you ever heard Mr. Jonasson and his son arguing, or talking about wind turbines?"

Roger looked at her suspiciously. "Wind what?"

"Turbines . . . wind turbines," she repeated slowly.

Roger looked like he might be on the verge of answering when he stopped himself. "Mrs. Puddles, I'm sorry, but I ain't s'posed to talk about any of this with nobody. Sheriff Pemberton told me I wasn't allowed."

She stared at him for a beat, trying to decipher what she could from his facial expression. "Well, I'm just curious about these wind turbines I've been hearing about. I like to keep up with technology, you know? I thought I heard they were putting some in on a piece of Jonasson land. I think it would be all right if you told me about *that*, don't you?"

Roger stared at the ground and kicked at a pebble. She was pretty sure he knew something but she wasn't going to force it "Okay, well, don't you worry about it, Roger . . . we don't want to go against the sheriff." She patted him on the shoulder. "I'll let you get back to work. You take care now."

"Yes, ma'am." Roger nodded as he continued across the parking lot dragging his rake.

Isabel decided to head across the street to the courthouse and pay a visit to an old acquaintance, Phoebe Farnsworth, who for the past twenty years had been the county registrar of deeds. Phoebe had been a year ahead of Isabel in high school, but they were varsity cheerleaders together for a year. She had never been the friendliest person in the world, but for some reason she always liked Isabel. Phoebe would be able to tell her for certain if it was Jonasson land that Zander Metcalf had been talking about surveying for his wind turbines and whose land she had seen him surveying earlier in the day.

Phoebe was happy to see Isabel walk into her office. After a few minutes of chitchat, which of course included the latest on the Earl Jonasson case, she got out her maps and they began to scour the land parcels in the northwest corner of the county. After some checking and cross-checking, Phoebe had an answer. She turned the map toward Isabel and began tracing the borders with her index finger as she explained. "Well, the marshy area you're talking about near the freeway here is

the very western edge of the Jonasson land. On the other side
of the freeway is the state-owned land surrounding the Three
Sisters."

Isabel took out her reading glasses again and went in for
a closer look. "And what about this land here?" she asked,
pointing to the parcel of land where she had seen Zander.

"Well, it looks to me like . . . let's see . . . yes, that land
across Monroe Road, just to the north used to be Suggs land,
but when Myrtle Suggs finally died—I think she was just shy
of a hundred and mean as dirt—her kids sold that property to
Beryl Vanderhoff. . . . Well, it belongs to his widow, Marlene,
now. Beryl died about six months ago."

"Vanderhoff . . . I don't know that name. Should I?" Isabel
asked curiously.

"Probably not. Chicago summer people. It was just a
hobby farm for Beryl. He was a very nice man. Her? A little
snooty for my taste. My husband and I got to know them
a little out at Heritage Hills. We took up golf . . . we're at
that age, you know. Beryl was a big, handsome man. Good
golfer . . . dropped dead after putting in for a birdie on the
eighteenth hole. Poor man . . . But a nice way to go if you're
a golfer, I suppose."

Isabel suddenly remembered to ask about the old farmhouse. "I forgot the story about that old farmhouse that sits
on that land. We used to sneak in there when we were kids.
Spooky old place."

"That's the old Trudlow place," Phoebe replied.

Isabel wasn't sure she heard her right. "Did you say the
Trudlow place?"

Phoebe smiled. "There aren't many of 'em left. You probably wouldn't know that family. Certainly not people the
MacGregors or the Peabodys would have had anything to do
with. The only one I know is Tammy Trudlow. She's not very
popular around town . . . well, except with the bail bonds-

man . . . and maybe last call at the Black Bear Tavern. And she has a brother . . . apparently he's in prison. I've never met him. I'd like to keep it that way, too. Not exactly the crème de la crème of Kentwater County society."

"I've heard of the Trudlows. I just never knew they owned any land. . . . And I'm happy to say I don't know Tammy Trudlow personally, but I do know *of* her." Isabel added an eye roll.

Phoebe continued with the Trudlow family bio. "I guess it would have been her great-grandparents who originally owned that place. The old man wasn't much of a farmer. Couldn't quite make it work, I guess. Hanged himself in the barn one winter. Most of that land Earl Jonasson's dad bought from the Trudlow widow way back, but she kept the farmhouse and a small parcel, maybe five acres surrounding it." Phoebe pointed to the map. "But you see it's landlocked, so it's pretty much worthless today."

"I don't think I ever heard that story. Or if I did, I forgot it. We always thought the place was haunted. Now I know why." Isabel flashed back to that haunting photograph of Tammy's ancestors hanging in the old farmhouse. "Phoebe . . . what do you mean by landlocked exactly?"

"Well, after the county reconnoitered the roads back forty, fifty years ago, the boundaries on all that land had to be adjusted. Barney Trudlow—that would be Tammy's grandfather—raised a big stink with the county about it. Sued and lost. Then the state came in a few years later to build the freeway and made what I'm sure was a fair enough offer for his land, but the old cur wouldn't sell. So they took it anyway, claiming eminent domain. He sued again, and lost again. So the Trudlows were left high and dry. To get to their land, they'd have to trespass through land owned by the state, the Jonassons, or the Suggses—now owned by the Vanderhoffs. So, unless they could parachute in, they were out of luck.

And there that property still sits. Tammy and her brother still own it, and they still pay taxes on it, which don't amount to anything. But they must have some idea that they're going to be able to reclaim it someday."

"Well, that's quite a story," Isabel said as her wheels started turning. According to the map, that land where she saw the wind engineer belonged to this Vanderhoff woman now.

Phoebe leaned over the counter and spoke in a hushed tone. "Between you and me, I think Tammy Trudlow went after Earl Jr. so she could somehow get her hands on that property again. And you didn't hear this from me, but I wouldn't be a bit surprised if she put him up to killing his daddy just to move things along a little faster. *Or* she did it herself . . . what do you think?"

"I don't know what to think anymore, Phoebe," Isabel answered quietly. "It's all such a mess . . . just a sad, terrible mess. I've known Earl Jr. almost my whole life. I just can't imagine he would ever—" Isabel stopped talking when the office door flew open. It was Phoebe's deputy registrar, Melvin Akins, a sweet, delicate young man who spoke with a lisp. Melvin was practically breathless.

"They juth arrethted Earl Joneathon!"

"Whaaaaaat?!" Isabel blurted out.

Phoebe offered a translation. "He said 'they just arrested Earl Jonasson'!"

"I know what he *said*, Phoebe! I just can't believe it! They *arrested* him? Already?"

Isabel quickly thanked Phoebe for the information and rushed out of the registrar of deeds office. She stood on the sidewalk in front of the courthouse for a moment in a state of disbelief. She was dying to go back across the street and get the scoop from Ginny. Maybe it wasn't true. . . . Maybe Melvin was unknowingly spreading a rumor. But just then she saw Grady pulling around the corner in his SUV. And, hunched over in the backseat, staring at her through the window as they passed-by, was Earl Jr., looking pale and stricken. But there was something about the look on his face that wasn't right. He didn't look like a man who was guilty of a horrible crime . . . he just looked like a man who was scared to death.

Isabel finally remembered to stop at the Kroger on her way home to get milk, and also got an earful from Wanda Wagers—the head checker, and one of Hartley's biggest gossips. Of course she was all atwitter about Earl Jr.'s arrest. It hadn't been even thirty minutes since the news broke, but Wanda was already adding her usual flourish. Grady had not released the medical examiner's report or any other information about the murder weapon, but, according to Wanda, Earl Sr. had been shot point-blank, square between the eyes, with a hunting rifle by an inebriated Earl Jr. after an argument over a tractor he wanted to buy, but his father wouldn't let him. Isabel's first instinct was to scold her for spreading such a hurtful rumor—not to mention a wildly inaccurate one—but Wanda was like a stray dog whose temperament you couldn't quite trust. And nobody believed anything she said anyway.

After pulling into her driveway, Isabel was greeted at the front gate by Jackpot and Corky, who were both thrilled to see her. She took a moment to reflect on how the dogs throughout her life—whether it was Ernie, Pepper, Jackpot, and now Corky—had always served as constant reminders of what was right with the world. Whenever she was troubled about her own life, worried about family or friends, or just overwhelmed with the injustice of the universe, her dogs reminded her there was still more love and loyalty in the world than there was hatred and deception. That kind of goodness might not always be seen in the two-legged form, but she had always been able to count on it from the four-legged set. Isabel was always surprised to meet people who didn't like dogs. She felt sorry for them. In her mind they were missing out on one of the great joys in life.

Once inside, Isabel gave Jackpot and Corky each a treat, made a cup of tea, and then walked out onto her deck. The fall colors were on full display now, and the lake was surrounded by a wreath of vivid reds and oranges. Lost in thought, she went from planter to planter, sipping her tea and picking out dead geraniums, while the dogs ran onto the dock. Jackpot had already introduced Corky to one of his favorite pastimes—stalking minnows—and she took to it right away. It was a nice break for the squirrels. Isabel's geraniums hadn't done so well that summer, but she realized she hadn't given them the attention they needed, either. Her vegetable garden had suffered even more over the summer. There just wasn't enough time in the day to attend to all of it. When the deer finally broke through the garden fence she had built, she decided it was time to surrender. Since then, at various times of the day, she could look out her kitchen window or pull into her driveway to find a whole family of deer enjoying lunch or an early dinner as her guests. The deer always looked up politely as if to say thank you, then carried on with their meal. The raccoons were another story. They preferred a late supper. Whenever Isabel flicked on the floodlights in the yard, there would usually be two or three of the furry little bandits gorging on berries or squash or whatever they were in the mood for that night. But instead of a polite nod to the generosity of their hostess, she got dirty looks as they rose on their haunches and impatiently waited for her to turn off the lights. After twenty-odd years of devoted vegetable gardening, Isabel was retiring. Let the neighbors feed the wildlife. She was done.

Stepping down from her deck and onto the stone path leading down to the dock, she noticed the steps she *thought* she had recently repaired were even more wobbly now. Before she or somebody broke their neck, she decided it was probably time to call her handyman, Toby Hallstrom. Toby was a tall blond boy of Nordic descent and the son of Joyce Hallstrom, another old friend of Isabel since high school. After recently graduating from college, Toby realized he was a small-town boy at heart and decided to move back home. He started his own business providing handyman services, property management, a landscaping service in the spring and summer, and a leaf- and snow-removal service in the fall and winter. He was also quite an accomplished carpenter, so he had a side business building decks. Toby had more work than he knew what to do with, especially in the summer, so he had begun hiring seasonal employees to help manage his workload. But for local regulars, and family friends like Isabel, he always tried to do the work himself, and usually at a discount.

Toby was as loyal and trustworthy as they came, and although she knew he wouldn't charge her any more than he needed to, it was always hard for Isabel to part with money for repairs she thought she should be able to take care of herself. She gave the railing another little shake and pushed on the top step again with her foot. Before she made the call to Toby, she wanted to take another look and see if maybe she could make the repairs herself, after all. Absentmindedly, she leaned against the opposite railing, which then completely collapsed. As she instinctively grabbed for something, anything, to try to catch herself, her mug, still filled with tea, went flying into the lake. She tried desperately to grab onto the other railing to keep from falling but missed, then went careening down the sloped lawn toward the water. By the time she finally regained her balance, she was about two feet away from taking a header right into the water. Jackpot and Corky, both of them still out on the dock, froze and pricked up their ears, looking back at her in bewilderment. She had to laugh at herself, but she was hoping none of the neighbors had witnessed her clumsiness. Isabel walked back up to the house. She'd go look for her mug in the morning.

"Hello, Toby? It's Isabel Puddles calling. . . . I'm fine. . . . how are *you* doing? Well, good . . . listen, I know you're a busy man, but I wonder if you might come by and have a look at my deck?"

Toby arrived at Poplar Bluff about an hour later in his grandfather's vintage pickup truck, which he had lovingly restored. He jumped out with a wave and a big smile, followed by his faithful German shepherd, Kaiser, who was immediately greeted by his old friend Jackpot. Isabel had been at the shelter the day Kaiser came in a few years before. He was just a puppy that somebody found abandoned at a rest area. Isabel could never quite wrap her head around how people could abandon puppies or kittens like that, but it happened all the time.

About a week before the puppy arrived, Isabel had run into Toby's mother at the Kroger. Joyce told her that Toby was finally home from school, but he was still heartbroken about the death of his old golden retriever, Madge, who had died just before he graduated. Isabel Puddles was not a woman prone to being overly emotional, and certainly not in public, but stories about beloved pets crossing over the Rainbow Bridge absolutely wrecked her. As she listened to Joyce tell the story, she was doing her best not to come unglued in the frozen foods section.

Joyce continued. "Madge was getting worse—cancer— and in a lot of pain, so when Dr. Peterson said it was time to put her down, I called Toby at school and gave him the bad news. He was crushed, but he told me if they had to do it, he wanted to be with her. So he drove all night from Columbus, stopped and picked his dad and me up at home, and we went straight to see her at the vet's in the morning. She'd been there a couple days by then so they could control her pain, poor thing. She had been so out of it . . . just lying there on her side. But the minute Toby walked in, her tail started thumping on the table. And when he leaned down to talk to her, she lifted her head just a little and gave him a kiss, then closed her eyes again. I was a mess. Jerry was worse. Even Dr. Peterson had tears in her eyes. Toby asked the doctor if he could take her to her favorite spot at the Big Lake where they spent most of their time in the summers. She would chase tennis balls into the water and up and down the beach for hours on end. That dog was so devoted to him." Isabel was about to lose it. She had just come in for a loaf of bread and now she was on the verge of an emotional breakdown. Joyce went on. "So, Dr. Peterson gave him a syringe and told him how to administer the drug. Then Toby—he was so brave—he picked her up, put her in his truck, and they drove to the beach, just the two of them. Jerry and I get emotional watching Hallmark commercials, so you can imagine the state we were in by then. While he was gone, I went out and dug a hole under the tree where Madge used to lay in the shade when it got too hot, and Jerry went out to his workshop and built a nice wooden box. Toby came home a few hours later with Madge wrapped up in a blanket. Then his dad took over. He got her out of the truck and put her in the box while Toby and I sat on the couch together in the living room and he cried his eyes out. Last time he cried like that was when his grandfather Tobias died. He was crying, I was crying. I know Jerry was out there bawling, too. . . . Well we finally all said our good-byes to that sweet old dog. Toby put a tennis ball in the box with her, and we buried her. Then he turned around and drove back to school."

"She waited for him," Isabel said softly.

"Yes, I believe she did. And do you know that in that

same spot where we buried her, every spring, when they were never there before, ever—my hand to God—a whole clump of daffodils comes up."

By then both of them had tears running down their cheeks and Joyce was doling out tissues. They gave each other a hug just as Wanda Wagers walked past them, coming back from her break. She would have a field day coming up with a story about that. But before they said good-bye, they had both decided that a new puppy might be just the thing Toby needed, so Isabel promised to keep an eye out.

And then in came this adorable little puppy, and Isabel knew immediately that he was the one. She called Joyce, who brought Toby down to the shelter that afternoon. It was love at first sight for both of them. He took him home that day, and the two had been inseparable ever since. To this day, whenever Kaiser saw her, he always came up wagging his tail to say hello. In her mind, he was saying thank you.

The last time she ran into Joyce, this time at the bank, she told her that over the summer Toby had been dating a girl who didn't like dogs, especially big dogs, and she objected to Kaiser coming with them on dates to the beach or on hiking trips. Apparently Toby obliged and left Kaiser at home a few times. But not only did he miss having his dog with him, he was overwhelmed with guilt. So he finally decided something had to give or some*one* had to go. So someone did go, and it wasn't Kaiser.

Toby grabbed his toolbox from the bed of his truck while Jackpot and Kaiser wrestled on the grass. Isabel had taken care of Kaiser for a week while Toby and the rest of the Hallstrom family took a trip to Florida, so the two were old friends. Corky sat quietly on the front stoop, trying to figure out who this enormous German invader was.

"Hey there, Mrs. Puddles!" Toby yelled to her from the driveway.

"Hi, Toby . . . Kaiser has gotten so big and handsome!" The same could be said for Toby, but Isabel wasn't going to be the one to say it.

"He's a big boy! Hard to believe I used to hold him up with one hand." Toby walked up and gave Isabel a hug while Kaiser broke away to say his usual hello to her, too.

"Let's walk around to the deck and I'll show you what my problem is." The two headed around the house with Jackpot and Kaiser, while Corky cautiously brought up the rear.

"I'm afraid my deck is disintegrating, Toby. But my husband put it in twenty years ago, so I can't say as I'm surprised." Toby began to assess the situation. He jumped up onto the deck, avoiding what was left of the stairs, and stomped around to check out its condition, then jumped back down onto the grass. Corky finally felt comfortable enough to come over to greet him with her tail wagging. "This is the newest member of the Puddles family. Corky, say hello to Toby."

"What a pretty girl," Toby said as he crouched down to pet her. "I'm surprised Kaiser hasn't been over here to flirt with you yet." He then stood up and got down to business. "So, I think the deck itself feels petty sturdy. But the stairs and these railings are all rotted out, so they should be completely replaced." Toby gave the remaining railing a little tug. It was barely hanging on. "This is pretty dangerous."

Without sharing her earlier experience, Isabel concurred. "Well, let's do it, then. But let's try not to break the bank. Better that than breaking my neck, though, I guess."

Toby laughed. "I can build you a whole new set of steps with new railings for probably a hundred and fifty dollars? Maybe less. But I can't get to it right away. I've got a big job going on right now over on the Big Lake that I have to finish before the snow flies. I've got a couple guys helping me, but we're still under the gun. . . . But here's what I'll do. I'll take the measurements now and build it back at my shop—steps, railings the whole shebang. Then I can come back and attach it, or I'll have one of my guys come and do it."

"That sounds fine, but there's no hurry. Just get to it when you can." Toby tested the remaining railing again and kicked a couple of the steps. "Let's see what I can do here so you can at least get up and down safely in the meantime. I'll be right back." He headed up to his truck while Isabel watched Jackpot and Kaiser standing lakeside at full alert as a group of kayakers paddled by and waved. Isabel waved back, although she had no idea who they were.

Toby returned carrying a power tool she had never seen before. "What do you have there, Toby?"

He leaned down, straightened out the first step, held the contraption to it, and *bam!* The noise startled Isabel as well as the dogs, who both immediately turned their attention from the kayakers to the deck. *Bam.* "It's a nail gun, Mrs. Puddles. A real time saver." Toby proceeded to go to town on the steps. *Bam, bam, bam* . . . In no time flat he had reattached the loose steps as well as the surviving railing. He tested for strength, then proceeded to add a few more nails, just to be safe. *Bam, bam, bam.*

"That thing scares me!" Isabel was wincing in anticipation of the next firing of the nail gun. *Bam, bam, bam.* Toby stood back up. "It's loud, that's for sure. But it gets the job done. I still enjoy pounding nails by hand, it's very therapeutic, but sometimes you just have to go for speed!" Toby decided the railing needed a little more help. *Bam, bam, bam.* "There . . . That should take care of it until we can get this replaced. But you still need to be careful." He whistled for Kaiser, who came running, and they all walked back up to the driveway.

"Okay, well, I'll see you soon, Mrs. Puddles." Toby

opened the door to his truck. "Let's go, boy!" Kaiser jumped in obediently and Toby pulled out of the drive with a parting wave and a friendly honk, his copilot looking back smiling with his head out the window.

Isabel walked back down to the deck and cautiously tested out the steps, followed by Jackpot . . . but Corky was nowhere to be found. She called her name, but still no Corky. She went inside to look for her, and finally into the bedroom, where she found her curled up in a ball in her bed, shaking. That nail gun must have frightened her, poor girl. Well, it frightened Isabel, too, so she wasn't surprised.

Corky stayed curled up in her bed for hours after Toby left. This was the first indication Isabel had that maybe Corky was a little high strung, something not uncommon for cocker spaniels, or a few people she knew, including her best friend, Frances. She tried to coax her out of her bed with a doggie treat but with no success. She then began to repeatedly squeeze her new squeaky toy, a plastic chipmunk she had been obsessed with the day before, but today it seemed to frighten her, too. Isabel got down on the floor next to her and began to pet her gently until something suddenly dawned on her. . . . Maybe there was a good reason that Corky was traumatized by hearing that nail gun. Maybe it was a *nail gun* that killed Earl. And Corky would have been right there to witness it.

She got up off the floor and went straight to the kitchen to call Grady. She finally pried his cell phone number out of Ginny, so she could reach him anytime now. Maybe there *was* something to the convenience of cell phones, at least when other people had them. When Grady answered, Isabel cut right to the chase. "Grady, I believe I know how that nail ended up in Earl's skull."

Grady calmly replied, "A nail gun?"

"Yes! How did you know that's what I was going to say?"

"Well, I talked with the woman at the state police forensic

lab working this case. She said it most likely *was* a nail gun. She said it was the only way a nail could be driven into some-body's skull that deep without blood. There were also skull fractures surrounding the entry site. I had a hunch that was it from the beginning. I mean nobody's going to stand still while somebody pounds a nail into their head."

Isabel was feeling a little foolish. She thought she had a hot scoop. "Oh . . . well, I guess that's good. I mean, it's good to know what the murder weapon was, right? Poor Earl . . . probably never knew what hit him."

"Iz, have you talked to Ginny? She said she was going to call you. I think she was a little frazzled with all the activity in the office today." At that moment she looked out the kitchen window and saw Ginny pulling into the driveway. "She just pulled in, Grady."

"Good. Keep her company for me, will you, please? I'm going to be here late tonight."

"I'll do my best."

Ginny came in the front door and walked straight into the kitchen. "Any more wine left in that box?"

Isabel smiled. "Hi, Gin . . . rough day?" She reached into the fridge, pulled out the box of red wine, and plopped it on the kitchen counter. "It's either half-full or half-empty—you decide."

Ginny looked relieved. "I don't care, as long as it's wine. Do I need to bother with a glass, or can I just hold my mouth open under the spigot?"

Isabel laughed. "Let's go with glasses." She poured the wine and joined Ginny at the kitchen table with some saltines and cheese. They toasted to Ginny's surviving a stressful day and engaged in some idle chatter, avoiding what was front and center on both their minds. Isabel didn't want Ginny to feel pressured into divulging any information she wasn't supposed to share but was dying for some details. Thankfully, halfway through her second glass of wine, Ginny was ready to talk turkey.

"Okay . . . I know by now you've heard that Earl Jr. was arrested. By the way, we need to turn on the six o'clock news. What time is it?"

"It's five forty-five," Isabel answered with her mouth full of cheese and cracker.

"Now, I'm swearing you to secrecy, Izzy. You promise you won't breathe a word?"

"Did I ever tell anybody about you climbing out your bedroom window and sneaking off to the Shelbyville prom with David Finnie?"

"My poor mother," Ginny lamented with *her* mouth full of cheese and cracker this time. "I think she went to her grave believing my story that I'd been kidnapped by Gypsies." She began to get reflective until Isabel snapped her back to the present.

"Ginny! What is it?" Isabel pleaded.

"Iz, I really think he did it. I think he's guilty . . . I think Earl Jr. killed his father."

Isabel mulled things over for a moment as she cut off another piece of Gouda and married it with a cracker. "Okay . . . may I ask what kind of evidence has led you to this epiphany?" Isabel popped the cracker and cheese into her mouth and waited for a response while Ginny took another long slug of wine, then reached over and picked up the box and gave it a little shake, just to make sure they were in good supply.

"Turns out his alibi didn't check out. The coroner determined the time of death to be between two and four in the afternoon. Junior said he took the boys to the movies . . . a two-fifteen show. That part is true. But the youngest told Grady that after their father bought them their tickets and got them their popcorn and sodas in the lobby, he left and said he would be waiting for them when they got out."

"And was he?" Isabel asked.

Ginny nodded. "He was."

"So, what's the big deal? He didn't want to sit through a kids' movie. Where did he say he went?"

"He said he went to Mickey's Roadhouse for some wings and a beer."

"Well?" Isabel said, implying that this seemed very plausible.

Ginny was more circumspect. "Well, maybe he did, maybe he didn't. He said he paid cash, so he doesn't have a receipt, but nobody there remembers seeing him. So, *maybe* he went home, nail-gunned his father in the head—which by the way they have determined was the murder weapon—and then drove back to the theater to pick up his boys. He would have had plenty of time to make the round trip."

"Okay, well, I'll admit that's not much of an alibi," Isabel conceded.

Ginny continued. "Not exactly airtight, is it? But there's more: He said he didn't own a nail gun. But the oldest boy had already told Grady he remembered his father using a nail gun to repair their chicken coop a few months back. So, when Grady brought it up again, Earl Jr. suddenly remembered his father *did* own a nail gun, but he said he hadn't used it since he fixed the chicken coop. When Grady asked him where it was, Junior said he had no idea."

Isabel was letting this information sink in. Things were not looking good for Junior.

Ginny continued. "The only missing piece to the puzzle now is a motive. Why would he do it? But I think Grady and these state police detectives are close to having that figured out, too . . . if they haven't already. Oh, it's six! Let's turn on the news."

They went into the living room and Isabel flipped on the TV. After slogging through a few minutes of live coverage about an overturned milk truck on the freeway, the pretty blond anchor woman came back on camera. "Kentwater County reeling after the brutal murder of an eighty-eight-year-old farmer, beloved in his community, and today, the arrest of his son for his murder . . . That story when we come back."

When they came back from the commercial, the lacquer-haired male anchor was now on camera. "Kentwater County is known to most of us for its windswept sand dunes and its miles of unspoiled Lake Michigan coastline—a Midwest vacation paradise. But this week, in the picturesque town of Hartley, the county seat, it became known instead for the murder of a wealthy eighty-eight-year-old farmer named Earl Jonasson." They cut away to a twenty-year-old photo of a smiling Earl Sr. sitting on a new tractor. "Now, his son and namesake, Earl Jonasson Jr., stands accused of his father's brutal murder, leaving the county in shock." They cut to Earl Jr.'s mug shot. "Our own Winnie Sutherland was in Hartley today and is here now with the latest. Winnie?"

Winnie's live shot, with picturesque Hartley Lake in the background, reiterated what the anchor said in his intro. "That's right, Chuck. Sand dunes, miles of gorgeous Lake Michigan shoreline . . . and now murder in the first degree." But before she cut to her taped package, Winnie added a flourish. "The residents of this quiet, bucolic town are still in shock after the murder of a fifth-generation cherry and asparagus farmer, eighty-eight-year-old Earl Jonasson, found dead in his rocking chair, a nail driven into his skull, and with his loyal cocker spaniel lying in his dead master's lap. Now his son, Earl Jonasson Jr., the father of the victim's four grandsons, is in jail tonight for his murder."

"Oh, for God's sake, Winnie, get to it!" Isabel yelled. Then, turning to Ginny, "Boy, these people love to hear themselves talk, don't they?"

They cut back to Earl Jr.'s mug shot again, wearing the same pained expression Isabel saw him with in the back of Grady's SUV. That look still troubled her. She had seen plenty of mug shots, and she liked to think—thanks to her keen intuition—that she could determine if they were guilty or not just by the look in their eyes. And Earl Jr.'s eyes didn't show guilt, they showed only sadness and fear. But Isabel also had to remind herself that she was not exactly in a position to be objective, since she had known him practically all his life. On the other hand, in this case her subjectivity may have mattered more.

Winnie Sutherland's taped piece included a clip from Grady's press conference with a sound bite of him announcing the murder investigation, followed by a shot of Earl Jr. in the back of the SUV on his way to jail. The rest consisted of Winnie doing man-on-the-street interviews with some Hartley locals.

Myron Turner, president of the Rotary Club, had this to say: "It's just hard to believe anybody would want to harm Earl Jonasson. He was the nicest man you'd ever want to meet. And murdered by his son? I don't know. We'll have to see. A man's still innocent until proven guilty, last I heard."

Roy Ebert, owner of Ebert's Glass Shop, wasn't thrilled about being on camera or being asked about the case by a strange woman with a microphone and a cameraman standing behind her. "It's a shame. . . . But what can you do?"

Now Ginny was annoyed. "Well, you can start by not shooting your father in the head with a nail gun, Roy! How 'bout that?"

They were both stopped cold when Frances Spitler suddenly popped up on the screen. Isabel yelled out, "Frances! I thought you were going to get your hair done!" Then she realized her hair was freshly cut and colored. Frances, true to form, was only too happy to share her opinion with Winnie.

"Well, what I hear is that Mr. Jonasson was in serious debt and on the verge of losing the family farm to the bank. The only thing that could save the day was a hefty life insurance policy Earl Sr. had, and with his son as the benefactor. Next thing you know, he ends up with a nail in his head. I don't think we need to bring Matlock in on this."

Ginny turned to Isabel with a stunned expression and her mouth wide open. "What is *wrong* with that woman? She has got the biggest mouth in this county! How would she know about any life insurance policy? And why would she talk about it on the news!"

Isabel was as shocked as Ginny, but she instinctively went into damage control to try to protect her bigmouthed best friend. "She did tell me last night that she knew about the insurance policy, because her brother-in-law's brother sold it to him. But that still doesn't make Junior guilty, and she certainly had no business speculating about it on the news."

"Grady's going to be furious," Ginny said, shaking her head.

"Well, I guess I wouldn't blame him," Isabel agreed.

Just then Ginny's cell phone rang. "And there he is right now . . . oh, boy." Ginny answered her phone, already wincing. "Hi . . . yes, I just saw her. . . . I don't know what's wrong with her. But plenty is!"

Isabel's phone then rang, so she left Ginny and went to the kitchen to answer it . . . and it was, who else? "Did you see me on the six o'clock news?!"

"As a matter of fact I did, Frances. Now, can you please explain to me why in the world—"

Frances was on a roll. "Well, how did I look? I'm so glad I ran into that reporter on my way *back* from the beauty parlor instead of on my way *there*! And lucky enough I was wearing green, which I really do think is my best color."

"Are you out of your ever-loving *mind*, Frances Spitler?!

Why would you *say* something like that on the six o'clock news? What if poor Earl Jr. is innocent? And, by the way, until he's proven guilty, he is presumed to be! You want to help send an innocent man to prison?"

"Honey, please . . . Maybe O.J.'s innocent, too. Junior killed his daddy and everybody in the county knows it."

"Well, so much for him ever getting a fair trial now, thanks to thinking like that!" Isabel scolded.

Ginny walked into the kitchen. "Is that Frances? Tell her Grady wants her in his office first thing in the morning. And if she's not there, he'll be happy to send a deputy to pick her up."

"Did you hear that? Grady is *not* happy. He wants you in his office—"

"I heard, I heard."

"You really stepped in it this time, Frances." Isabel was well beyond annoyed, but Ginny was approaching irate, yelling into the phone, "And you did it on the local news! Nice job, Frances!"

Frances was either trying to put on a brave front or she really didn't see what the big deal was. "Tell your cousin she better let those bees out of her bonnet before she gets stung. And she can tell the sheriff that I'll come and talk to him tomorrow morning at my leisure. I'm sure he'd like to know more about what *I* know about that insurance policy, too." Frances was off the subject. "Anyway, you didn't answer my question. How did I look? I've never been on TV before!"

Isabel was done. "Good night, Frances."

Ginny was, as their grandmother used to say, *madder than a wet hen.* "Grady says Frances has tainted the county's entire jury pool. I don't remember ever hearing him so angry."

Isabel never stayed mad at Frances for very long, and this, too, would pass, but Ginny was another story. She was always friendly and polite to Frances, but she put up with her only because she was Isabel's friend. Frances shouldn't have said what she said, and especially not on the six o'clock news, but it wasn't the end of the world. She had only gossiped about what everybody was already gossiping about anyway. Isabel was anxious to put this episode aside and calm her cousin down. She emptied the box of wine into Ginny's glass, fed the dogs, and then went into the kitchen to make them some supper: dill-pickle-and-grilled-cheese sandwiches with mustard—a Peabody family tradition—and then opened a can of tomato soup. It was the comfort food they both needed about now.

After dinner, Ginny was still feeling the wine, so she wasn't ready to drive home. Isabel built a fire and they sat with the dogs and watched *Wheel of Fortune*. Isabel played whenever she remembered to turn it on, and she was pretty good, too. Carly and Charlie tried to convince her to audition when the show came to Chicago, but their mother made it clear there was no way that was ever happening. But tonight, Isabel decided to concentrate on her knitting and let her cousin solve the puzzles, hoping it might keep her mind off how angry she was at Frances. It nearly killed her, though, when Ginny couldn't get "Chocolate Cream Pie" with ten out of seventeen letters called, including all three Cs *and* P, I and E! She dropped a few stiches during that puzzle and bit her lip in two places.

Ginny finally decided it was time to go. "Do we know when Earl's funeral is?" she asked, putting on her coat.

Isabel shook her head, adding, "Meg told me she was planning it with Gil, but that was before Junior was arrested. So, who knows now?" Isabel took a deep breath and exhaled. "What a mess."

"Yes, it is . . . and it gets messier every day, thanks to Frances Spitler," Ginny added as she aggressively zipped up her coat.

144   M. V. Byrne

"I'm sorry about Frances. I don't know what she was thinking," Isabel said as she stood up to walk Ginny out.

"Not your fault . . . Just the Big Mouth on the Big Lake flappin' her jib again!"

Isabel shook her head and shrugged. "Well, keeping secrets is not one of her virtues. Frances does like to talk. But she's a good egg. I don't know what I'd do without her."

Ginny gave her cousin a look that indicated she didn't agree with her assessment. Isabel opened the door and gave Ginny a good-bye hug. "By the way, Aunt Millie knew all about you and David Finnie going to the Shelbyville prom. I remember overhearing her say to my mother, 'What kind of Gypsies would kidnap a fourteen-year-old girl wearing a Hall and Oates nightshirt and bring her back wearing a formal gown and a wrist corsage?' But I promise I never breathed a word."

Ginny laughed as she opened the door. "Couldn't put much over on my mother."

"That was *my* Hall and Oates nightshirt, too, by the way," Isabel yelled as Ginny headed down the driveway. "You borrowed it for a sleepover and I never got it back!"

Ginny yelled back as she opened her car door, "Talk to the Gypsies!"

Chapter 10

"What do you mean you're in jail!" Isabel yelled into the phone. She had just come in from raking leaves and was wearing a knit cap pulled over her ears, so she wasn't sure she was hearing Frances correctly.

"I *mean*, I'm sitting in the drunk tank in the Kentwater County Sheriff's Office!" Frances snapped back.

"Have you been drinking, Frances? At this hour?!"

"Don't be ridiculous! Of course I haven't been drinking! Your cousin's future husband put me in jail for talking to that reporter on the news!"

Isabel was confused. "Can he do that, Frances?"

"Well, I guess the answer to that is yes! Because here I sit in the slammer like a common criminal!"

"How long have you been there?" Isabel asked, still trying to process the information.

"Well, let's see. . . . I came in, as requested, at a little after nine thirty a.m. And by nine thirty-five I was sitting in here. So almost a half hour. Thankfully they let me keep my purse and my cell phone."

"Well, that's not exactly hard time. Have you called Hank?"

"Why would I call Hank? He'd be happy to leave me here until he gets out of work and needs someone to make him his dinner!"

"I'll be right there." Isabel hung up and started to dial Ginny but decided against it. Better to get to the bottom of this in person. She understood that Grady was upset, but throwing Frances in jail seemed just a tad bit extreme.

Isabel walked into the office to find even more activity than the day before. Ginny was on the phone again. She forced a smile and a little wave, but she was looking particularly irritated. Grady was in his office talking to a woman she didn't recognize. She was pretty, middle-aged, with short blonde hair and wearing a smart navy-blue pantsuit. She was a petite woman, but even from a distance, managed to look imposing. Now she understood why Ginny was irritated. Grady waved Isabel into his office. She stopped at the door before entering and gave him a stern look. "Grady . . . I understand you're upset with Frances, but was it really necessary to lock her up? She's a grandmother, for the love of God."

The strange woman, who was beginning to look vaguely familiar, stood up and extended her hand to Isabel. "Hello, Isabel. I've heard a lot about you. I'm Beverly Atwater. I'm Earl Jonasson Jr.'s attorney."

Isabel shook her hand, just as she realized who she was meeting. "Nice to meet you, Ms. Atwater." It wasn't, but Isabel Puddles always believed in being polite. Anybody who followed high-profile crimes, murders mostly, in the state of Michigan knew who Beverly Atwater was, and most did not hold her in very high regard, Isabel included.

"Please . . . call me Beverly," she said, sitting back down.

Among the notorious defendants Beverly Atwater had been associated with was a man named Malcolm Metz, a successful Detroit businessman accused of murdering his brother-in-law, who "went missing" on a fishing trip they took on Lake Superior. Coincidentally, Metz owed him a large sum of money and the promissory note was coming due the following month. Metz claimed his brother-in-law fell overboard when he made a sharp turn with the boat, and by the time he turned around to fish him out, he was gone. It was later discovered that the promissory note Metz had signed had gone missing, too. The brother-in-law's remains washed up on shore with two bullet wounds in his back, six months after Metz was acquitted for the murder, thanks to Beverly Atwater's defense. And double jeopardy laws prevented him from being tried again. Thankfully, justice was served when he got twenty years for wire fraud, mail fraud, and tax evasion, after his wife, the victim's sister, turned him in. The man was almost seventy, so it amounted to a life sentence.

"You're a friend of Meg's, I understand," Beverly said as she crossed her legs and smiled.

"Since second grade, yes." At the moment, Isabel was more interested in getting Frances out of jail than she was in getting acquainted with Beverly Atwater, so she turned her attention back to Grady. "Grady, has Frances been arrested? And if she has, then I'd like to post her bail."

Grady picked up the phone. He could tell Isabel was not going to let this go. "Ginny, ask Deputy Clark to let Mrs. Spitler out of the holding tank and bring her in here please." He hung up the phone and smiled at Isabel. "I just wanted to give Frances a little time to think about what she did. Making those statements to a news reporter of all people was stupid and reckless. And it has made Beverly's job a lot more difficult."

Beverly was dying to jump in. "She has tainted the prospective jury pool, so now if we do end up going to trial, we may require a change of venue. I happen to believe that before we ever see the inside of a courtroom we will have found the real murderer, but this just makes our climb that much steeper. You see—"

Isabel was not about to be lectured by Beverly Atwater. "Sorry to interrupt," she said, putting her hand up toward Beverly but keeping her eyes on Grady, "but isn't it a little unorthodox for a defense attorney and the sheriff to be talking about a pending case together?"

Grady smiled. "Beverly and I go way back. You may not know this, Iz, but I did a year of law school before I decided I wanted to become a police officer instead. Bev and I were in the same class at U of M." Of course Isabel immediately began to wonder if they had ever dated, which was something Ginny either knew or was wondering about herself right now.

"It was the bar's loss and Kentwater County's gain," Beverly offered.

"I guess I didn't know you had gone to law school, Grady. God knows the world can get by with one less lawyer, so I think you made the right choice. No offense, Beverly."

Beverly chuckled. "None taken . . . Anyway, to help mitigate any further instances of local residents sharing uninformed and prejudiced opinions about the case, I have asked District Judge Meyer to issue a gag order for anybody directly or indirectly involved in the case, which he has now granted. I'm here to make sure the sheriff's department and the state police are aware that we're now playing by new rules. This gag order applies to you as well, Mrs. Puddles, since you are the one who made the initial discovery of the nail and the subsequent revelation that a murder had been committed. And since your friend has admitted she received confidential information from a family member regarding this alleged life insurance policy, if she decides to do another impromptu TV interview, she will be faced with *real* jail time. Not merely a time-out, along with a substantial fine."

Isabel was still processing this directive when a deputy delivered Frances to Grady's office. Isabel gave her a hug. "You okay?"

Frances was being stoic. "I'm *just* fine . . . or I will be, unless the sheriff here decides to send me to the electric chair for speaking my mind freely in a free country!"

"Michigan doesn't have the death penalty, Frances," Grady reminded her.

"Then I guess it's just life without parole for me!" Frances threw Beverly Atwater a look that was less than friendly.

Beverly was already not a fan of Frances's. "Mrs. Spitler, as I was telling Mrs. Puddles, there is now a gag order in place. That means that anybody who speaks about this case publicly will be facing serious fines and jail time. Your thirty minutes in a holding tank was just a taste of things to come if you decide to speak your mind freely again to the press—"

Frances was officially indignant. "*Who*, may I ask, are *you*?"

Grady jumped in, trying to keep the peace. "Frances, this is Beverly Atwater. She's Earl Jr.'s attorney."

Beverly put her hand out. Frances ignored it. "Well, that and seventy-five cents buys me a Baby Ruth bar. I don't care if she's the Queen of Sheba, I don't like her tone. And I'm not going to defend myself to her *or* to you, Grady Pemberton. Now, am I free to go or were you planning to waterboard me?"

Beverly couldn't resist punctuating her position. "Mrs. Spitler. The American judicial system depends on the premise that those accused of committing a crime are innocent until proven guilty for one, and secondly, that they are able to plead their case before a fair and impartial judge and jury. Your little stunt on the news last night has made it that much more difficult to seat a jury in this county that can be impartial, since you have now erroneously planted a seed for motive."

"You can spare me the civics lecture, lady," Frances responded with a sour expression and her voice beginning to rise.

"Frances, calm down. You're just making things worse," Isabel scolded her mildly.

"This *is* me being calm, Isabel. And now that the lawyers have been let loose on us like a pack of jackals, *you*, Grady, can expect to hear from mine!"

And with that, Frances stormed out of the office, only to return a few seconds later with some parting words for Beverly Atwater. "And, by the way . . . everybody in the state of Michigan with an IQ higher than room temperature knew Malcolm Metz killed his brother-in-law from the get-go. And that *includes* you! So don't get high and mighty with me. *You* put a murderer back on the streets and then cashed a fat paycheck for doing it! So, *your* idea of what constitutes justice and mine are very different. So, put that in your pipe and smoke it!" With that, Frances turned on her heels and disappeared.

An awkward silence followed until Beverly stood up to leave. "Well, I think that went well."

Isabel was not at all happy about what she had just witnessed, and she was going to speak her mind, too, before leaving to catch up with Frances. "Well, I know I feel safer knowing Frances Spitler was off the streets for thirty minutes. I think you both made your point. You managed to simultaneously frighten and humiliate her. Well done. Now, if you'll excuse me, I'm going to go check on my best friend—who, for the record, has never been anything but loyal and honest *and* a model citizen—and I'm going to make sure she's okay." Isabel left with her own parting shot directed at Grady. "I guess I'm lucky I didn't get thrown in the hoosegow for my rolling stop!" She walked briskly through the office saying nothing to Ginny, but the expression on Isabel's face said everything her cousin needed to know.

Frances was already gone by the time Isabel reached the parking lot, so she got in her van and instinctively drove right over to Frances's house. As she pulled into the driveway of the Spitler family's well-kept ranch home on the outskirts of town, she could see Frances through the kitchen window. Isabel knew what she was most likely doing to deal with the morning's unfortunate events. When Frances got angry or stressed, she baked bread. Not only because the kneading process gave her a chance to work out her aggression or angst but because she could later stress-eat away whatever remaining anxiety she was feeling. She had a hunch there might be more than a few loaves coming out of her kitchen today.

She gave a little knock before quietly opening the door and coming in. Frances, wearing the Kiss My Grits apron Isabel had gotten her years ago, already had her mixer out and was opening a large bag of flour. "How are you doing?"

"Super!" Frances replied, overselling just a bit. "You in the mood for whole wheat or rye?"

"I do love your rye bread," Isabel offered.

"Rye it is. You working at the hardware today?"

"Two to six."

"I'll bring a couple loaves down to you before you close up shop."

"That would be great! But I've still got a couple hours to kill. You want some help?"

"Isabel, you know I love you more than my next breath, but I think I just want to be alone. I'm afraid I wouldn't be very good company." Frances took out a measuring cup and began filling her mixing bowl with flour, aggressively enough so that she became almost lost in a billowing cloud of flour dust. She then suddenly stopped, dropped her measuring cup into the bowl, put both hands on the counter, and looked over at Isabel. "I know I shouldn't have said what I said. But I've never talked to a television reporter before and I wasn't think-ing about ending up on the six o'clock news!" She fished out her measuring cup and then stopped again. "But I *do* think Earl Jr. killed his father! I'm sorry, but I do . . . I just should have kept my opinion to myself, is all."

"Then lesson learned, I guess. I wouldn't fret about it. As long as we keep our opinions to ourselves from now on, we—"

"We can avoid the penitentiary? Well, that would be nice. I'd hate for my grandchildren to have to visit Nana in the big house."

Isabel chuckled and gave her a pat on the back. "I'm going to leave you to your baking. I'll see you a little later."

Isabel had skipped breakfast again, so when she saw Gil Cook's car in the Copper Kettle parking lot, she decided to stop in for a quick bite. Gil was at the counter, eating by himself and reading the newspaper, when she walked in and plopped down beside him. "Hello there, Gil."

Gil put the paper down and smiled. "Hello there, Iz," he replied with a mouth half-full of turkey club. Brittney was the waitress on duty. She was somewhere in her mid-twenties— a cute, plus-sized redhead with a tattoo of Betty Boop on her arm and a gap in her front teeth. Brittney was sweet, but she could get a little surly from time to time, giving the impression she was not all that happy with her job or her life. Her number one goal seemed to be meeting a man who would take her away from Hartley, Michigan, and to anyplace other than Hartley, Michigan. Isabel knew a little bit about her family background, so she couldn't say as she blamed her. Brittney said hello and set a menu down in front of her, even though she knew Isabel always ordered the same thing. Gil started right in. "So, is Frances still behind bars?"

"Boy, this must be the most gossipy town in America! No, she's out. And I'm so mad at Grady, I could just—"

"What was she thinking, Iz? I mean, she shouldn't have—"

"Well, wouldn't it be a wonderful world if none of us ever

did what we shouldn't do? She made a mistake, Gil. And she's sorry. But to put her in jail? I don't care if it was only for a half hour, it was mean and it was unnecessary. Now, can we please not talk about this?"

Brittney, not known for her speed, finally managed to drift over with a glass of water and take Isabel's order. "I'll have the turkey club."

"Mayo on the side?" Brittney asked with a snap of her gum, as though she had been sent from central casting to play the role of a disgruntled waitress.

"Mayo on the side," Isabel replied with a smile.

Gil made another attempt at friendly engagement. "Meg called me this morning to schedule Earl's funeral. Day after tomorrow at two p.m."

"Well, good . . . So, there's that to look forward to," Isabel replied as she polished her utensils with her napkin.

"Boy, you're in a mood, " Gil said with a half laugh.

"Yes, I am in a mood. I haven't had a decent night's sleep in days. I close my eyes at night and all I see is poor Earl lying on that gurney. And when I finally do fall asleep, I dream about the whole thing. It's awful. Oh, and by the way, Gil? I quit. Please do not ask me to *fix up* anybody else ever again. I'll go out and collect cans if I have to, but consider me retired from your hair and makeup department."

Gil laughed. "I don't know how Roger's going to feel about having competition. He's had the market cornered on can collecting for a while now."

Isabel finally found her sense of humor and chuckled. "Well, he can have Hartley and I'll take Gull Harbor." She reached over and patted Gil's arm. "I'm sorry to be such a grump, but this whole situation has just turned me into a nervous wreck."

Gil was quick to show his understanding. "I get it, Iz. . . . I know it's been hard on you, given how close you are to Meg."

"It's killing me that I can't tell her that I'm the one that discovered that nail. I just hope that when she does find out, she'll forgive me."

Gil finished chewing his last bite. "I think she'll be thankful that you were the one who helped ensure that her father's murderer was brought to justice."

Isabel wasn't so sure. "Or resent me because I helped ensure her brother was sent to prison for life."

Gil motioned to Brittney for his check. "Well, if her brother committed the murder, then that's where he belongs."

Isabel was processing this depressing dilemma when she heard a familiar voice over her shoulder.

"Excuse me . . . do you have carry-out?"

"Yes, sir, we do," Brittney answered in a flirty tone. "Here's a menu if you'd like to take a look." She gave the menu a quick wipe with her towel and handed it across the counter. Isabel followed it with her eyes to its recipient, who just happened to be her favorite wind engineer, Zander Metcalf. He recognized her immediately.

"Oh, hello . . . you're the lady from the hardware store."

"I am . . . and you're the man the wind blew in." Isabel was turning on the charm. Gil was taken aback by his friend's sudden change in disposition. She introduced the two and explained how they were acquainted. Gil was late for an appointment, so he politely excused himself after paying his check and said his good-byes. Meanwhile, Isabel couldn't believe her luck. "Hey, did I see you out on Monroe Road yesterday? I happened to be driving by and thought I saw somebody out there in a field setting up a bunch of strange-looking whirligigs."

Zander laughed. "Whirligigs . . . I love that word! Yes, that was me." He signaled to Brittney that he was ready to order. "I'll just have a cheeseburger and fries."

"And you want that to go?" she asked with a furtive smile.

What she was already clearly hoping for was that he would take *her* to go.

"Well, I was going to take it back to my hotel because I hate to eat alone in a restaurant." Then, turning to Isabel, "But if you don't mind company I'll go ahead and have my lunch right here."

"I don't mind in the least. Who wants to eat cold, soggy french fries in a hotel room anyway?"

Zander sat down where Gil had been sitting, then turned to his new lunch companion. "I'm so sorry, but I've forgotten your name. . . . I'm terrible with names."

"Isabel . . . Isabel Puddles." They shook hands again.

"Isabel . . . That's right." Then to Brittney, "May I please have an iced tea as well?"

"You certainly may," she replied, turning up the flirty dial even higher.

"And you're Zander Metcalf. I'm very good with names. So how did those waders work out?"

"Actually I never used them. In fact, I was hoping maybe I could return them?"

"Of course! Not a problem. I'll be there from two to six today if you want to come by." Isabel would have to get Freddie on board with this later. She needed to stay in Zander's good graces until she got the information she was after. "So, how is it you ended up not needing the waders?"

"Well, the parcel of land the company I'm working for was originally looking at, which had the marshy area I needed the waders for? Unfortunately, that all fell through. They had been trying to negotiate a deal for a while but couldn't close the deal. So, I had to start surveying their second choice, which is the land where you saw me. Shame, really. That other parcel is so ideal—some of the strongest, most consistent wind velocities I've seen along this coast. But you can't make people do something they don't want to do."

Isabel perked up. "I'm not sure what you mean."

"The guy who works in the company's land acquisitions department said there was a rich old farmer who owned the land they wanted, but he just resisted and resisted—wouldn't budge. He wanted nothing to do with wind turbines or wind farming. So, finally they gave up. Then all of a sudden it looked like maybe he was getting ready to change his mind, so they drew up all the papers and sent me back here a few days ago to do a secondary survey and start plotting out locations for the actual turbines. And then, sadly, he died . . . in fact, he died the day before he was supposed to sign the contracts. You probably know him . . . but I forget his name." Zander obviously hadn't heard anything about the suspicious nature of that rich old farmer's death, but he was probably too focused on his work to follow local goings-on.

Isabel decided to play dumb and move on. "So I noticed another gentleman out there with you. I figured he must be your boss?"

"No, that was the man who owns the new land we're looking at. He wanted to come out and see what I was doing."

"I thought that land was owned by the Vanderhoffs."

"I don't recall his name . . . but, no, I'm pretty sure that wasn't it."

"I'm beginning to think you aren't real good with names."

Zander laughed. "I can rattle off dynamic-pressure equations for days, but I couldn't tell you the name of my dentist."

"He didn't look like a local to me. Where's he from?"

"I'm not sure he mentioned where he was from. Ohio, maybe?"

Phoebe must have either given her a bum steer, or the Vanderhoff widow had already sold off the land. She started thinking about her list. What else could Zander tell her that might be useful? Her wheels were turning when he filled the silence with a nonsequitur.

"Isabel, can you recommend a nice restaurant in the area for dinner?" Brittney was delivering their lunches at that very moment.

"We're open for dinner," she said as she put Isabel's turkey club down in front of her. Even her voice had a wink in it.

Zander smiled. "And I'm sure dinner is delicious. But my fiancé is coming up this weekend, so I was hoping for something maybe a little romantic."

Brittney plopped the plate down in front of him with a heavy sigh. "Ketchup?"

"Yes, please," Zander replied politely, unaware that he had just put his waitress's latest escape fantasy into a nose dive.

"The Old Cottage Inn would be perfect," Isabel suggested. "Charming old place over on the old channel. Order the duck. It's out of this world."

"Thank you, Mrs. Puddles. That sounds perfect." Zander lifted up his burger. "Bon appétit."

Isabel waited for him to get a few bites into his lunch before she continued her discreet interrogation.

"So, Zander . . . you say this rich old farmer had been resisting this deal, but that he had changed his mind just before he died?"

"That's how I understood it, yes. But I guess it makes no difference now. Can you please pass the salt?"

Isabel's wheels were spinning. If this were true, then Earl Jr. wouldn't have had any motive for murder. Why would he be in such a hurry to get his hands on that life insurance policy if his father had decided to go through with a lucrative land deal, after all? What she wanted to know now was *how* lucrative a deal like that might be?

"Just out of curiosity . . . what would a deal like that rake in? Let's say I had—oh, I don't know—a hundred acres of land in a very windy location near the lake. What could I expect to sell it for?"

"Well, there are sales, and then lease deals. There are a lot of factors and variables involved, but it really comes down to how many turbines we can put on the land and how much power they can generate. Coming up with that equation isn't really part of my job. But we're usually talking a few hundred thousand, sometimes more than a million."

"Dollars?" Isabel was shocked.

"Well, that is the currency of choice, yes," Zander replied as he doused another french fry with ketchup and popped it into his mouth.

"Wow . . . that's a lot of money," she said taking another bite of her sandwich.

"This new deal, assuming it goes through, will cost the company more because we'll need more turbines to get the same output we would have gotten with *fewer* turbines on the other property. That's another reason they were holding out and hoping the old farmer would change his mind. But by the time he did, the clock had run out."

Isabel was bowled over by these numbers. "So, it looks like whoever this gentleman is who owns the other parcel of land got very lucky."

Brittney appeared behind the counter again with a look of resignation, as if she had just seen a glimpse of herself ten years into the future, still working the lunch shift at the Copper Kettle. "Can I get you anything else?" she asked, giving new meaning to the word *blasé*.

"Just the check," Zander replied cheerfully. "And I'd like to take care of both of them."

"Thank you, Zander, but you don't need to do that," Isabel said, reaching for her purse.

"I'd like to. I was happy to have such charming company. And to show my appreciation for taking back those waders."

"Well, that's very nice of you." She really liked this young man, so, being the consummate hostess, and knowing he didn't know anybody in town, she had an idea. "You know I'm having a few people over for Sunday dinner, which I do most Sundays . . . just a few friends and family. I'd love it if you and your fiancée could join us. Might be interesting to meet some of the locals and have a nice home-cooked meal, enjoy some Kentwater County hospitality. I'm making pot roast."

Brittney slapped Zander's check down in front of him so hard, it startled him. "I love pot roast! Thank you. We'll be happy to come," Zander said, taking a twenty and then a ten out of his wallet. He put both on top of the check and slid it across the counter to Brittney with a smile. "The rest is for you."

Brittney finally managed a smile. Twelve-dollar tips were not very common at the Copper Kettle lunch counter. "Thank you very much, sir. Please come back and see us."

Isabel reached into her purse and pulled out a pen. She flipped over her place mat and wrote down her address and phone number. "Now I'm going to draw you a map."

"No need," Zander said, standing up and putting on his coat. "As long as I have the address, I can GPS it."

Isabel had no idea what that meant, but, as with most things technical, she had learned not to ask because the answers never made much sense. She handed him the place mat with her Gull Lake address. "Okay, well, then, how about six o'clock?"

"Great. Can we bring anything?"

"I can't think of anything. Just yourselves."

"Thank you for the invitation, Isabel. Now, if you'll excuse me, I need to get back to my hotel room slash office and answer some e-mails." Zander folded up the place mat and put it in his pocket. "I'll try to come by with those waders later this afternoon. If you think of something you'd like me to bring, you can let me know then." Zander headed for the door. "Have a wonderful afternoon, ladies!"

Isabel was pleased with the information she had just gleaned from Zander. Now she felt bad for being so hard on him when they had first met. The man was just doing his job. She couldn't hold him responsible for introducing giant sky fans to her county, and it wasn't his fault they lived in a wind tunnel. She also felt a little guilty about being so sneaky in her questioning, but it was for the greater good. What she had just learned about this land deal may just put to rest any motive Earl Jr. had for killing his father. It would appear they were on the verge of making a small fortune, so he had far more incentive to keep his father alive than to kill him. Isabel was now convinced that whoever killed Earl Jonasson was still out there. She was also convinced that, to get to the bottom of this, it was time to venture down the oldest, most well-worn path there was . . . and follow the money.

She knew Grady didn't want her getting any more involved than she already was, but despite his lack of encouragement, Isabel was going to do what she thought was right. And that gag order didn't prevent her from quietly doing her own investigating, as long as she kept her mouth shut. After all, she was, as Gil pointed out, the one who got the proverbial ball rolling, so she was duty bound to follow that ball wherever it rolled. Isabel Puddles was now officially on the case.

Brittney appeared and began wiping down the counter as she finished up her sandwich. Isabel looked at her and smiled. "Such a nice young man . . . cute, smart, friendly."

Brittney scoffed, "Eh . . . not my type."

Anybody who knew her would agree that Brittney's "type" was anyone with a job, a pulse, and out-of-state plates, but Isabel played along.

"Well, you can afford to be discriminating, honey. With

that red hair and those pretty blue eyes, you'll find your Mr. Right one of these days. 'Every pot has a lid,' my grandmother used to say." Unfortunately, it looked to her like poor Brittney's pot was going to boil over if she didn't find a lid fast.

"You are too sweet, Mrs. Puddles. Can I offer you a scoop of cherry ice cream from the Amish dairy?"

It was the best ice cream on the planet. How could she say no? Actually she knew she couldn't, but she had to at least pretend that she could. "I don't know . . . I really shouldn't . . . I have a Weight Watchers weigh-in I've been putting off for days now. It's awfully tempting, though."

"Ice cream season is over and my manager said we need to make room in the freezer. So I'm just following instructions."

Isabel relented, "Well, I'd hate to go against Copper Kettle management."

Brittney got out a dish and then the ice cream scoop. "I don't know how Weight Watchers works, but I tried Jenny Craig once. Didn't work for me. Just try to get that lady on the phone when you're up to your elbow in a bag of kettle chips. You know I think I'll join you in a scoop or two. Why not? I'm a plus-sized girl and I'm always going to *be* a plus-sized girl."

Isabel laughed as Brittney dished them both out two big scoops. "Should we have some chocolate sauce?" Brittney asked after their first bite.

"How about we let that be our nod to moderation? This ice cream doesn't need a thing. The cherries, the cows, and the Amish did all the heavy lifting."

Brittney agreed. Isabel savored every bite. Those Amish sure did know their ice cream.

Chapter 11

"Fred's Hardware . . . Isabel speaking." It was Ginny.

"Hi, Iz . . . So, Grady wanted me to invite you to dinner tonight. Will you come?" Grady had moved pretty quickly into damage control, but Isabel was not quite ready to make nice.

"No, thanks, Gin. I've made other plans."

An awkward pause followed, until Ginny resumed. "I gather you're still mad about Frances?"

"Not mad. Just disappointed . . . and surprised. I think it was a mean-spirited thing to do."

"Well, I can tell you for a fact it was that Beverly Atwater woman who planted the idea in his head. But I have to be honest, Iz. I support what Grady did. Frances needed to be taught a lesson."

"There are other ways to teach a person a lesson without humiliating them, Gin."

Awkward pause number two . . .

"Well, I guess we'll just have to agree to disagree on this," Ginny offered.

"Or we can just disagree," Isabel offered in return.

Ginny wanted to end the conversation on a friendly note. "Well, okay, Isabel, suit yourself. I guess I'll see you Sunday?"

"I have a pretty busy Sunday. We'll see. I'll talk to you later."

Although Isabel was peeved with Grady, and that Atwater woman, she couldn't help being annoyed with Ginny, too, for being so quick to approve of the stunt. Isabel didn't hold on to things for very long, so she'd get over it. She just needed a little time. Freddie walked up with a box of outdoor thermometers and set them down on the counter. "Freddie, are you and Carol free for dinner Sunday night?"

"I'll call and ask her."

"I'm making pot roast," she added.

"In that case I'll call and *tell* her. You make the best pot roast in the state of Michigan. Not gonna miss that!"

Isabel enjoyed throwing dinner parties for family and friends, especially when things got a little too quiet around Poplar Bluff. And she especially loved doing Sunday dinners the way her mother and her grandmother always did. She began putting the rest of the guest list together in her head. Normally Grady and Ginny would be at the top of the Sunday-dinner guest list, but not this time. Frances and Hank would come (Hank never passed up a free meal). Zander and his fiancée, Freddie and Carolyn made six, and she would make seven. She preferred an even number, but this time odd would have to do.

Isabel was in back with Mrs. Abernathy and watching the kittens as closing time approached. She heard the front door chime and got to the front counter to find Frances standing there with a shopping bag, chatting with Freddie and looking a lot less stressed than she did a few hours before.

"Brought you some rye bread, Izzy."

Freddie was holding a loaf himself. "Thank you for the bread, Frances. Now, if you ladies will excuse me, I've got some shelves to finish stocking." Freddie disappeared down the electrical aisle.

"You feeling better now?" Isabel asked.

"Indeed I am! Bread therapy did the trick again. So, listen, I've decided this would be a good time for me to go to Milwaukee and see my daughter and my grandchildren. I don't want anything more to do with any of this Jonasson business. And I'm afraid if my lips get loose again, I'm going to wind up in stripes . . . so I'm taking the Badger over first thing Monday morning. I'll probably be gone a couple of weeks."

The Badger was an old ferry boat that had been running on the Big Lake between Michigan and Wisconsin for more than fifty years.

"What about Hank?" Isabel seemed a little surprised. "Two weeks is a long time to be without your wife."

Frances snorted. "What *about* Hank? He's working overtime now with this apple crop, so I hardly see him anyway . . . and the man's fifty-two years old. If he can't figure out how to keep himself fed for two weeks, well, like I told him, 'the good Lord helps those who help themselves,' but I'm sure the Lord will be happy to help him find his way to the freezer section at the Kroger, or the KFC drive-through."

Isabel laughed. "Well, I'll miss you to pieces, but I think it would be nice for you to spend some time with Lori and the kids. But can you come to dinner Sunday night? It'll be your bon voyage. I'm making pot roast."

"It depends . . . Who else is coming?" Frances was quick to inquire.

"Grady and Ginny are not invited."

"What time would you like us?"

"Six o'clock."

"We'll be there. Okay, I have to run. I've got more dough rising in my kitchen right now than Sara Lee." Frances plopped the shopping bag onto the counter. "Here are a couple loaves of rye bread for you. I'll bring another to dinner."

Frances waved good-bye and closed the door behind her just as the phone rang. "Fred's Hardware . . . Isabel speaking."

It was Meg. "Hey there, Izzy. I just tried you at home, so I hoped maybe I'd catch you at Fred's. Anyway, I just wanted to check and make sure you knew Dad's funeral is the day after tomorrow at two p.m. . . . at Cook's. Will you be able to make it?"

"Of course I will."

"There's going to be a little reception afterward at Byron and Doris Fletcher's house over on the lake."

"That sounds nice. How are you holding up?"

"Well, just barely . . . I hired a lawyer for my brother . . . Beverly Atwater. She's supposed to be the best. But the judge has denied him bail, pending a pretrial hearing next week. So that's the latest."

Isabel wanted to be upbeat so she changed the subject. "Well, I'll have you know Corky and Jackpot are getting along famously. She's doing just fine. If you want to come by the house later and see her, I'll be done here at six."

"Thanks, Iz, but I'm actually on my way to Kalamazoo right now. I have a meeting there later this afternoon and I won't be back until late. I'll plan to stop by tomorrow, though, and say hello. By the way, I didn't see it myself, but I heard about what Frances Spitler said on the news."

"She feels awful about it, Meg. You know how she is. She just speaks without thinking sometimes. But I do think she learned her lesson this time about spreading gossip—especially on the local news. "

"Well, the damage is done. But I know everybody thinks the same thing anyway. And I've got too much going on to be angry at Frances. I know my brother's innocent and we're going to prove it. But I will leave you with this for what it's worth. . . . Frances was right about the life insurance policy, but my nephews are the beneficiaries. Not one penny goes to my brother or to me. It's going straight into a trust fund that I'll manage, and it will be just enough to send four boys through four years of college. My brother couldn't touch it even if he wanted to."

That was even more proof that Earl Jr. had no motive to kill his father. "Well, see? There you go. I want you to know that I'm with you, Meg. I don't believe for a second that Junior would kill your father."

"Thank you, Iz. That means a lot to me," Meg replied quietly. Isabel could tell the stress of all this was taking its toll on her old friend. She thought it best not to dwell on it right now, so she moved the conversation along.

"Listen, I hear we're supposed to get some weather tonight off the lake, so you be careful driving."

"Okay, Iz, I will. Bye now."

Isabel still felt terribly guilty she wasn't able to tell Meg just how directly she was involved in this mess. This gag order had her feeling very anxious, so she was not about to talk about it to anybody. But that didn't mean she couldn't *think* about it. And this new information about the life insurance policy, and the fact that the wind farm deal was supposed to go through, after all, gave Earl Jr. zero motive for murdering his father.

But if Earl Jr. didn't do it, then who did? Who would have had any motive to kill a sweet old man like Earl Jonasson? And forget about motive. Who would be that evil? It didn't take much effort to arrive at one simple conclusion . . . Isabel just knew that somehow, some way, Tammy Trudlow had to be up to her neck tattoo in this.

Chapter 12

After racking up so many sleepless nights in a row, it looked like Isabel might finally be getting her first good night's sleep. The heavy rains that rolled in off the Big Lake that night had helped. Thunderstorms, as long as they were not accompanied by lightning, always lulled her into a state of calm. So, along with Jackpot and Corky, they were a trio of snug, deep-sleep snorers by ten p.m. But that blissful slumber was short-lived.

Just after midnight the phone rang. After realizing the ringing was not an unwelcome addition to a dream, Isabel managed to get to the kitchen in the dark, stubbing her toe somewhere along the way. Grimacing in pain, she answered on the fourth ring.

"Hello. This is Isabel." She was groggy. Of course this was Isabel. Who else would be answering her phone at midnight?

"Isabel Puddles?"

"Yes . . . Who's calling, please?" She felt a wave of dread wash over her and instinctively sat down at the kitchen counter to brace herself. This wasn't going to be good news, not at this hour.

"I'm Nurse Billings. I'm calling from the Mercy General Emergency Room."

"Oh, no . . . what's happened?" Isabel's heart was racing, but she was also relieved that if it was Mercy General, this wasn't about one of her kids. She took a deep breath.

"I'm calling about Meg Blackburn. I'm afraid she's been in a car accident."

"Oh, my God. Is she okay? How bad? Oh, please tell me she isn't . . . ?"

"She's very lucky is what she is. It could have been much, much worse. But she does have a broken wrist and some rib fractures. Her husband is away on business, so she was hoping you might be able to come down and pick her up. We can't seem to convince her to spend the night with us."

"Tell her I'm on my way. Thank you for calling." Isabel hung up without even saying good-bye. The rain had stopped, but it was still windy and cold, so she quickly changed into whatever warm clothes were within reach. The dogs were now awake and looking at her curiously, but they weren't curious enough to get up. She grabbed her waterproof parka, slipped into her duck boots, and flew out the door.

Isabel arrived at the hospital about thirty minutes later, relieved she hadn't had an accident herself after driving on slick roads with tires that should have been replaced quite some time ago. She rushed through the automatic doors of the emergency entrance and into the waiting room, where she found Meg sitting alone with a cast on her right hand and her arm in a sling. She was talking on her cell phone, but when she saw Isabel come in, she put it away and slowly stood up.

"Thank you so much for coming, Isabel. I felt terrible having to ask you."

Isabel walked over and gently rubbed her back. "Don't be ridiculous. Are you okay?"

"I'll be fine. Just still a little shaken up. That was Larry on the phone. He's driving up tonight from Chicago."

"Well, call him back and tell him to come straight to my

house. I'm taking you home and putting you to bed in my guest room. Who's with the boys?"

"My aunt Lorraine is down from Charlevoix for the funeral. Larry called her to tell her what happened. I'll have him let her know I'm staying with you tonight. I'm so sorry to bother you with this in the middle of the night."

"Stop apologizing. I would have been mad at you if you *hadn't* called me. Now, let's get you home. Corky will be very happy to see you."

Once they got safely onto the highway, it was time for Isabel to find out what happened. Meg began piecing together that evening's events for her. "Well, I was on the freeway. Only maybe thirty, forty minutes until I was home. I was sort of lost in thought, you know, thinking about the funeral and . . . well, everything, really. It was raining pretty hard, but there was no traffic to speak of . . . and then all of a sudden, this truck comes out of nowhere and flashes its brights. I was in the right-hand lane, and they just came up behind me and stayed for, oh, maybe a mile or two. And then all of a sudden, they start to pass me on the left, and when they got beside me they seemed to lose control. I put on my brakes and swerved to the right to avoid hitting them, and the next thing I knew I was fishtailing, and then a split second later I was heading down the embankment. All I could see was a stand of trees coming at me. I thought, well, this is it—game over. And then my car caught something—I have no idea what. That's when the airbags deployed, which is what broke my wrist, I guess. I rolled over once, maybe twice, and then came to a dead stop, upside down, not six feet away from those trees."

"My God, Meg! That's horrendous! You're lucky to be alive!" Isabel was quiet for a moment as she took it all in. "What about the truck? Did they stop to help?" Isabel asked.

"No. They just kept on going."

"Was it an eighteen-wheeler? They can be such bullies on the road."

"No, it was just a pickup truck. I couldn't make out who was driving. I could only see shadows. It was so dark and pouring rain, but it looked like there were two people in it. Thank God for my cell phone. I was able to call nine-one-one while I was still strapped in and hanging upside down. Then I called Larry. The state police and an ambulance were there within ten minutes."

"Were you able to get a license plate number on that truck? They could have killed you! And they didn't even stop?"

"It all happened in a blink. They were just behind me one second, and then on my left the next . . . and then I was rolling down the embankment."

"Did you get a description for the police? What color was this pickup?"

"Pretty sure it was gray or maybe silver . . . it looked like a fairly new one, too. I really think he was just a drunk driver. I don't think he even knew he ran me off the road. I guess I shouldn't assume it was a 'he,' right? I guess it could have been a drunk woman."

A *new* pickup? Gray or maybe silver? Like the one Tammy Trudlow was driving the other day? Isabel would have to cook on that one a little. The rest of the trip was spent with Meg mostly talking about the boys and how worried she was about them. Then there was some talk about which friends and family from out of town would be attending the funeral, and how nice it was of the Fletchers to offer to host the reception. Meg went on chatting, but all Isabel could think about was that pickup truck and who might have been driving it. She didn't have a clue as to why anybody would want to harm Meg, but it sure was coincidental. And she wouldn't put anything past that Tammy Trudlow. She was finally able to steer the conversation back to the accident to get some more crash details. "So, did they actually hit you, Meg?"

"I'm pretty sure the right rear of that truck clipped the front of my car . . . and that's when I braked and swerved right. I just can't remember for sure. Police said it looked like my car was totaled, so I guess we'll never know."

"Was it that pretty new white car of yours?"

Meg sighed. "Yes . . . wasn't even a year old. I loved that car. Oh, well . . . I guess that's what insurance is for. . . ." Meg trailed off and went silent for a few minutes, then started to doze off. Isabel let her sleep until they pulled into the driveway at Poplar Bluff, then woke her up gently and helped her into the house.

"Let's find you a nightgown and get you tucked into bed. My guest room has a feather bed and a big cozy comforter. You'll sleep like a baby."

Meg was a little groggy. "That sounds delightful. I'm not sure when Larry will get here. I hate him driving all night. I wish he had just flown into Grand Rapids tomorrow as planned. He's such a worrywart."

"Well, his wife was run off the road and nearly killed. I'd be worried if he *wasn't* worried."

Meg pulled out her phone with her good hand. "Oh, he sent me a text. He just left Chicago."

"I'm guessing he'll be in around six, then. I'll make sure I'm up and have some coffee going. You sleep in just as long as you want."

Corky was ecstatic to see Meg. After Isabel found a spare nightgown and got her settled into bed, she went to the kitchen to get a glass of water for her bedside. When she returned, Corky was on the bed with her head resting on Meg's chest. "Sorry, Izzy, I can't convince her to get down."

"She's fine. That's where she wants to be. Here's some

water in case you need your pain medication in the night."
She gave the little plastic pill bottle the nurse had given her a
shake. "I'll put them right here. Good night, Meg. I'm so glad
you're safe and sound."

"I can't thank you enough, Isabel. You're a lifesaver." Her
father's beloved cocker spaniel snuggled up even closer and
sighed. Meg started fighting back tears as she stroked Corky's
head. Isabel wanted them to have their moment, so she slowly
closed the door. A good cry would probably do her good.

Isabel was exhausted. She couldn't wait to get back into
bed. Unfortunately, regardless of what her body was telling
her, her brain was not ready to sleep. She couldn't get that
pickup truck out of her head. There were plenty of pickup
trucks in this part of Michigan, and plenty of them were gray
or silver, but, based on what Meg told her, unless the driver
was just blind drunk, it sounded as if she had been deliberately
run off the road. Was it pure coincidence that Tammy and her
"friend" Jason had been tooling around town in a mysterious
new silver pickup truck? It definitely required looking into.
At least now she had something to go on. If she could find that
silver pickup truck, and if it had a dent or a scrape with white
paint, that would be some pretty incriminating evidence, and
nothing Grady or the state police investigators could ignore.
But whatever evidence there might be, the pressing question
was why they would be trying to hurt or possibly even kill
Meg? Might it have been a warning? Or could there be some
kind of mysterious plot under way to eliminate the whole
Jonasson family?

Chapter 13

Once again, Isabel woke up to the phone ringing. Her first thought: *This has got to stop.* She had forgotten to set her alarm before she drifted off to sleep, as she was still weaving together murder plots and conspiracy theories in her head. She had no idea what time it was, but the sun was already up. She got to the phone just as her answering machine was picking up. It was Larry. She turned off the machine. "Hi, Larry, it's Isabel." She went on to explain that Meg was a little banged up but fine, and that she was still sleeping. Larry told her not to wake her and that he'd be there within the hour.

It was almost seven, so Isabel put on the coffee and decided to make some breakfast. Fifteen minutes later, Meg appeared in the kitchen, lured in by the smell of frying bacon.

"Good morning. How are you feeling? You in any pain?" Isabel asked as she got a coffee cup out of the cupboard for Meg.

"Only hurts when I breathe. Did I hear you talking to Larry earlier?"

"Yes. He'll be here soon. I'm getting breakfast. Coffee?"

Meg slowly eased herself into a chair at the kitchen table.

"That sounds wonderful. Corky cuddled with me all night. I can tell she misses Daddy."

"I'm sure she does, but she's found a good friend here with Jackpot . . . and with me. We've been very happy to welcome her to the Puddles family." Isabel sat down and they drank their coffee together and chatted awhile, looking out the window as the sun brightened up the lake. Before they knew it, Larry was pulling into the drive.

Meg rehashed the previous night's events with her husband over breakfast, but she was anxious to get back to the farm and see the boys. Larry helped clear the table, then helped his wife up from the table. She smiled at Isabel. "Izzy, I don't know what I would have done without you. Thank you again."

Larry concurred. "You're a good friend, Isabel. We owe you one."

Isabel pooh-poohed the remark. "You don't owe me a thing. I know you'd do the same for me. I'm just glad I was here to help. I'll see you tomorrow at Cook's." Isabel walked them to the door and out to Larry's car, where they said their good-byes.

Once back inside, she thought about going back to bed, but she also knew she would probably not be able to get back to sleep, so she decided to go out and do a little raking instead. Isabel found raking leaves, like knitting, to be a meditative endeavor, so she bundled up and went outside into the bracing autumn morning.

She was pushing a wheelbarrow full of dead maple leaves to the side lot when she heard Frances roaring down the road, leaving a wake of billowing leaves, and as usual, pulling into the driveway at warp speed. She climbed out of her car but left the engine running.

"Who's chasing you?" Isabel asked, parking her wheelbarrow.

"Well, there's no telling these days! Grady Pemberton? Beverly Atwater? The FBI? I'm a woman with a record now!"

Isabel chuckled. "Don't be so dramatic, Frances."

"I was just driving by and thought I'd stop to let you know I will not be attending Earl Jonasson's funeral tomorrow. Don't want to risk being tarred and feathered!"

Isabel removed her work gloves and smiled. "Well for what it's worth, Meg's not angry. She knows you were just repeating what most folks around here are thinking or saying anyway."

"Well, I'm still not going. Hank's not going, either. He says the only way he's ever going into Cook's again is on a gurney. I heard they cremated Earl, is that right?"

"I understand those were his wishes, yes," Isabel answered.

Frances was quiet for a moment.

"You know my daddy was cremated. But in those days of course the Church forbid it. And the Catholic cemetery wouldn't allow you to bury cremated remains."

Oh, Lord, Isabel thought to herself. *Here we go with Daddy's cremation story again.* She'd heard it at least two dozen times, but Frances carried on.

"If you'll remember, Daddy died on a business trip, so he was cremated in Tennessee, and then my brother Tommy drove down and picked him up. On his way back . . ."

Isabel picked up the story in her head. *He forgot Daddy in his room at a Holiday Inn back in Indianapolis and he was in Fort Wayne before he realized it. So he had to drive all the way back and pick him up at the front desk.* Isabel knew the story almost word for word. But there was more. . . .

"Naturally Mama wanted to hold his service at the church, but Father Mac wouldn't allow Daddy's ashes inside. He told Mama they could have a memorial, but no ashes. Can you imagine? Poor man couldn't attend his own funeral? So Tommy and me and Uncle Albert, we hatched a plan: We put Daddy's ashes in the urn Mama had picked out for him, and on the day of the funeral, which was at ten a.m., we went to the church at eight a.m. sharp when we knew the rectory housekeeper opened up to clean. So while Uncle Al and I distracted her and asked her about seating and where to put the flowers, et cetera, Tommy snuck in and hid Daddy's ashes under the altar. We didn't tell Mama until we all sat down. She told us later that it was wrong to go against Father Mac's wishes, but she was glad we did."

Isabel knew there was still one last beat to this story.

"Mama made it very clear she had no interest in being cremated. She wanted to be buried in the Catholic cemetery where *her* people were. But of course she kept telling us she wanted to be with Daddy. We took the hint. So, after she died, we took Daddy's urn to Cook's, and Gil's father, God love him, took the urn and tucked it right under Mama's arm and closed the lid. He was a Lutheran. What did he care? We had a closed casket and Father Mac never had a clue, and now Mama and Daddy are together for all eternity."

"So, what about you, Frances?" Isabel asked as she put her gloves back on and resumed raking. "Have you decided what's to become of you when the time comes?"

Frances scoffed. "Makes no difference to me! But if I go before Hank does, I know it'll be whatever's cheapest! Probably end up on a burn pile out back and my ashes put into a Tupperware."

Isabel laughed out loud. Frances had been making her laugh for forty years. She didn't care if she was nosy and a gossip and a pot stirrer—she was the closest thing to a sister she had ever had. Not even Ginny was as close to her as Frances was. "You are a character, Frances Spitler."

Frances got back in her car and threw it into reverse. "I'll see you here Sunday at six! I can almost taste your pot roast,

Izzy! Have fun at the funeral tomorrow!" And with that, Frances backed out, then shot down the road, disappearing in another billowing cloud of leaves and dust.

Isabel woke up the next morning feeling like she had finally had a good night's sleep. What a relief. The funeral would be difficult enough to get through without her being sleep deprived. After having her coffee, it was time to start getting ready. She already knew what she was going to wear. It was an outfit she had put together a while back that had been designated specifically for funerals. Somber, but not *too* somber, it consisted of a navy-and-white checked knee-length skirt, a navy jacket, and a white blouse. She kept the whole outfit hanging together in the guest room closet, as opposed to her own, because whenever she saw it, she got depressed. She wondered if, like Gladys DeLong, she would one day attach a note to it for her kids with instructions to bury her in it. No . . . she'd go with something a little more festive. Maybe a colorful caftan. But, whatever the case, she wasn't planning to shop for it anytime soon.

Isabel arrived at Cook's a little early. Gil was in the main reception area setting up some chairs when she walked in. The hit parade of hymns was already playing. "There's that music again," she remarked to him as she checked her hair in the hallway mirror. "Haven't you got anything a little more uplifting?"

"Well, we tried show tunes for a while, Iz, but that didn't go over well. My dance numbers were not well received. We don't get a lot of requests, although Jack Farrell did request Sinatra. 'My Way' on a loop . . . which was ironic, because if you'll remember, *Jack's* way was going the *wrong* way down a *one* way . . . and then into a cement truck. I haven't had any special requests since. So I just stick with the standards."

Isabel took off her coat and went to hang it up in the cloakroom. When she stepped inside, there was J.T. lurking again. "Hello, Mrs. Puddles."

She was only slightly startled this time. She took off her coat and handed it to him. "Hello, J.T. I think I'm going to talk to Gil about attaching a bell around your neck."

Isabel went to freshen up in the ladies' room, and by the time she came out, the place was beginning to fill up. She looked over and saw Meg placing a handsome mahogany box on a small table next to the podium. She took out a handkerchief and gave it a quick polish, then reached into her purse and took out a framed picture of her parents, one taken for their fiftieth wedding anniversary, and put it on top of the box. She wiped away some tears, then turned to see Isabel watching her, and smiled. The boys were already seated in the front row with Larry, who was sitting next to a sweet-looking old woman she presumed to be Aunt Lorraine.

Meg made her way into the reception area and began to shake hands and share hugs with a steady stream of guests. After about twenty minutes of chatting and mingling, the music stopped, and like some morbid game of musical chairs, people began to take their seats. Meg waved Isabel over and introduced her to her aunt. Then Isabel said hello to the boys: Kyle, Kevin, Kenny, and Kade, leaning over and giving each of them a kiss on the cheek and commenting on how handsome they looked. She sat down in the row behind the family and patted Meg on the shoulder to let her know she was there.

Just as Pastor Gregory from the Hartley First Baptist Church approached the podium, Bible in hand, there was a commotion in the reception area, followed by a series of gasps and whispers. Both Meg and Isabel looked back to see Earl Jr. standing there in a suit and tie, with Grady at his side. Beverly Atwater and two deputies were standing on his other side. What wasn't immediately apparent to most was that Junior was handcuffed to one of the deputies. When the boys looked back and saw their father, they all simultaneously jumped out of their chairs and ran back to him. One deputy stepped in front of Earl to prevent contact, but Grady waved him off. "Let them hug their dad, Deputy." Meg followed and joined in for an emotional group hug.

Isabel got up and walked back toward Grady, who gave her a cautious smile. "Hey there, Iz."

"You're a good man, Grady Pemberton. . . . I know you didn't have to do this," she said quietly.

Grady shrugged. "Well, I guess a man who's still presumed innocent has the right to attend his own father's funeral, bail or no bail."

J.T. went up and rearranged the chairs in the front row so that Junior and his deputy chaperone could sit with the family. Kade, the youngest boy, moved over and sat next to his dad, putting both arms around him and leaning his head on his shoulder, at which point Isabel and a few other women in the room started to sniffle. Beverly Atwater even looked a little emotional, and everybody knew what a tough nut she was to crack.

It was a simple, but beautiful service. Meg said a few words as did Aunt Lorraine. The boys—all of them except Kade, who wouldn't leave his father's side—got up and talked about what a wonderful grandfather Earl had been to them, and shared some of their happy memories. And they all mentioned how glad they were that Granddad and Nana were together again. Earl Jr. was stoic. He smiled when his sons talked about their grandfather—he was obviously a proud father and a proud son. Isabel never took her eyes off him, trying to read his behavior and body language. Now more than ever she was convinced he was an innocent man. Then something dawned on her. Where was Tammy Trudlow? It was a blessing she wasn't there, as far as Isabel was concerned. She couldn't imagine what kind of inappropriate getup she'd show up in. Maybe she had a special black tube top she wore to funerals? But to Isabel, her absence was very telling. She may not have known her potential fiancé was being allowed to attend his father's funeral, but if she had been a halfway decent person, wouldn't she have shown up to lend support to the family anyway? Or at least make an appearance?

After the service, about half of those attending headed over to the Fletchers' home on Hartley Lake for a late lunch reception, except poor Earl Jr., who was carted back off to jail. Watching those boys say good-bye to their father was one of the saddest things Isabel had ever witnessed, and as she drove over to the Fletchers, it was an image she was having a hard time shaking.

Byron and Doris Fletcher were a lovely old couple, both well into their seventies, who had lived in their beautiful old brick home on Hartley Lake for as long as Isabel could remember. They were snowbirds now, and spent most of the year in Florida playing golf, so they were perpetually tanned. Doris was a Farnsworth, which made her Phoebe Farnsworth's aunt, so Phoebe would be front and center at this gathering, despite being neither a friend of Meg's nor of the Jonasson family. But Phoebe wasn't one to miss a party, no matter how depressing the theme.

Isabel said a few hellos as she came in, then spotted Doris, Phoebe, and Meg standing near the large picture window overlooking the lake. She took off her coat, put it on the pile in the English hunt club–themed den, and walked back out to join them. After some friendly conversation, Doris turned to Meg as though a light had just gone on. "Oh! I played golf with one of your neighbors recently, during that delightful Indian summer we had."

Meg was perplexed. "Louise Hobart? She was playing golf up here?"

"No . . . Well, I guess she would have been your *father's* neighbor. She and her husband bought the old Suggs property off Monroe Road. Marlene Vanderhoff. Nice woman . . . A little *nose in the air,* but not as bad as some of the summer people we've golfed with. Byron and I met Marlene and her late husband last spring . . . I've forgotten his name . . . Help me out, Phoebe."

"Beryl. Like Milton Berle. No relation," Phoebe offered.

Doris continued. "Beryl . . . That's right. Good golfer. Big, strapping man . . . Picture of health. Byron and I were shocked when we heard he passed so suddenly. We saw them having lunch in the grill almost every day."

Phoebe huffed. "Well, that may have been what did him in." Their faces all registered surprise that she would say such a thing. "I'm just saying the food in there isn't to die *for,* it's to die *from.*"

They all chuckled a little under their breath, but Doris had to concur. "I'll admit, the food is, well, it's—"

"Awful, Aunt Doris? Is that the word you're looking for?"

Doris chuckled again and turned to Isabel. "Byron and I stick to their cocktails. It's hard to do too much damage to a scotch and soda."

"I haven't seen Marlene since Beryl died. How is she doing?" Phoebe asked her aunt.

"Well . . . ," Doris began, as though she were about to spill state secrets, "I saw her just the other day. She was on her way to the driving range when we asked her to fill in last minute for our foursome and she agreed. Candice Fluke broke her thumb loading her clubs into the trunk, poor thing. Of course she's always been clumsy . . . so, anyway, it was myself, Judy Langley, Lilly Dykstra, and Marlene. As I said, I knew her a little already, and the girls liked her fine. Pretty woman. No Dinah Shore, but not a bad golfer. So, after we finished, we were all going into the clubhouse for our usual lemon daiquiris, but Marlene begged off. Seems she had a gentleman waiting for her. He was a handsome fellow with silver hair. She didn't introduce us or mention who he was, which we all thought a little rude, but you know city people just have a different way of doing things. He took her clubs and put them in the trunk and off they went."

Phoebe's face registered disapproval. "She certainly didn't waste any time, did she? Her husband's been gone barely six months and she's already dating?"

"Well, Phoebe, it could have been her brother for all we know," Doris was quick to point out, but without much conviction. "We don't want to feed the gossip mill and stir up any trouble, do we? Which reminds me, Isabel . . . where's Frances? I thought she'd be here."

"She couldn't make it. She's off to see her daughter in Milwaukee." Isabel excused herself before Frances became the next topic. She walked around to say a few more hellos and poke around the buffet a little until Meg came up to her with a look of exasperation.

"Izzy, I've had about all the condolences I can take. And if I have to explain to one more person how I broke my wrist, I'm going to lose my mind."

"Here, this will make you feel better." Isabel popped a chocolate-raspberry tartlet into her mouth. Meg looked back in surprise as she chewed.

"You know, you're right. I do feel better." She reached for two more herself, handing one to Isabel and popping another into her mouth. She then looked over at her nephews lovingly, all sitting like little gentlemen on the sofa with their Uncle Larry. "Those poor guys . . . they're just so confused about all this."

"They're such well-behaved young men. They sure have been through a lot. It's hard to imagine any mother leaving four little boys behind like that. Then losing Ruth, and now your dad." Isabel shook her head, popped another tartlet, and slipped another to Meg.

"Kade was not even a year old when that woman left. Kyle wasn't yet six. He barely remembers her. But they're much better off without her. No mother is better than a bad mother, if you ask me." Meg looked over at Larry and got his attention, giving him the signal that she was ready to go.

"Lucky for them, they've got their adoring Aunt Meg and Uncle Larry." Isabel stopped for a moment before continuing. "Meg, what happens if . . . I mean, would you take—"

"I can't even think about that, Izzy. How would we ever manage raising four boys?! But of course we would do it. Larry loves those boys, too. But they need to be with their dad. So we just need to make sure he isn't sent to prison for something he didn't do."

Isabel nodded and looked around the room. "Where's Beverly Atwater? I thought she would be here."

Meg rolled her eyes slightly. "She left to go back to Detroit for a couple days."

Isabel had picked up on the eye roll. "Do you like her?"

Meg wasted no time responding. "Not particularly. She is not exactly a warm and fuzzy gal. And she's . . . well, as Doris said about that woman at the golf course, 'a little nose in the air.' But I didn't hire her to be my friend. I hired her because she's supposed to be the best criminal defense attorney in the state." Meg reached for another tartlet. "If I don't step away from these right now, people are going to start talking."

"I think people are too busy talking about Phoebe's husband. I heard he was a drinker, but the man has almost stumbled into the buffet twice." Meg laughed. It was the first time Isabel had heard her laugh in a while. She grabbed two more tartlets and quickly wrapped them in a napkin, then slipped them into Meg's pocket. She gave her a wink. "Let 'em talk."

Meg and Larry rounded up the boys and they said their good-byes, with Isabel right behind them. On her drive back to Poplar Bluff, her mind went back to that image of those boys saying good-bye to their dad. What a tragedy it would be for them if he were sent away to prison, even if he *was* guilty. But if he was innocent, as she was now convinced he was, it would be unspeakable.

Chapter 14

On Sunday morning, Isabel made coffee and started getting ready for church. She had originally planned to skip it, just to remind Ginny that she was not happy about Frances being thrown into the slammer like a common criminal. But Grady had redeemed himself by bringing Earl to his father's funeral, and she knew that Ginny was loyal above all else, so supporting her fiancé was the natural thing for her to do. And she never stayed mad at Ginny for very long anyway.

Reverend Willard had already begun his sermon when Isabel slid into the family pew. He gave her a friendly nod seasoned with just a hint of disapproval. She grabbed Ginny's hand and they exchanged smiles. After the sermon, they shared a cup of coffee in the church basement and split one of Mabel Matthison's pumpkin-raisin muffins. Ginny asked about the funeral and explained that when she heard Grady was bringing Earl Jr. in handcuffs, the whole thing made her so nervous she just couldn't go. Isabel assured her that she understood. She would have been a nervous wreck, too, if she had known what was happening, but she was glad to have been there to witness it. Seeing Earl Jr. with his boys not only cemented her belief that Earl was not guilty of this horrific crime, she told Ginny, but renewed her determination to figure out who *was* guilty. If the state attorney's office—which had jurisdiction over this case—was content to end his murder investigation with Earl Jr.'s arrest, either out of arrogance or laziness or ineptitude, Isabel was not going to rest until she proved them wrong.

With a dinner party to prepare for and grocery shopping still on her to-do list, Isabel was looking to make a discreet exit that wouldn't have any of her fellow Congregationalists wagging their tongues and accusing her of being too busy for God. When she saw an opportunity to bolt, she took it and started to get up, but Ginny grabbed her arm and pulled her back down. She reached into her purse and pulled out a piece of paper folded in half. "Now, you didn't get this from me, but I know you thought this information might be useful. Grady wasn't sold, but I tend to trust your hunches, Iz. It's about that boy who came into the hardware store, and the tag number on that truck he was driving. I found your note buried on Grady's desk. I'd know your handwriting anywhere. Anyway, I ran *him* and I ran the tag. The information is all right here. But, Iz . . . I want you to be careful. He's a pretty shady character."

Isabel took the paper and slipped it into her purse. "You're the best. Thank you." She made her way to the door, taking another muffin as she passed the refreshment table and ignoring the disapproving look from Eleanor Sullivan, who was in her Weight Watchers group.

After climbing into her van, she started the engine to get the heat going, then pulled out the slip of paper. Jason Swerley was indeed a resident of Jackson, Michigan, just as he had told her. What he left out was the part about his residence being Jackson State Prison, where he had recently been released after serving four years for burglary. He had also served time as a juvenile for vandalism, shoplifting, and auto theft. Not exactly a Boy Scout, but then Isabel wasn't surprised, given the company he kept. The truck was registered to Parker and Associates LLC in Akron, Ohio. Ginny had done some additional research and written down some information about the company and the owner, which wasn't much to go on. *Business: A construction consulting firm. Owner's name: Lou Parker . . . no criminal record. Two speeding tickets, five years apart. Fifty-eight years old. No civil suits. Ten-year-old, uncontested divorce decree.*

No warning bells there. And Jason Swerley did say he was doing a construction project for a friend, so driving that truck made sense if Lou Parker was the friend he was referring to. But how did a jailbird like him end up working for a legitimate businessman from Akron? And what was Tammy Trudlow doing driving that truck? Of course the simple conclusion was that Jason Swerley and Tammy Trudlow were carrying on some kind of a romance behind Earl Jr.'s back. They made a lot more sense as a couple . . . but maybe it was more sinister than that.

On her way home, Isabel stopped to do her shopping for dinner. Thankfully, Wanda was off, so she didn't have to listen to *her* latest harebrained gossip while she checked out. She arrived back at Poplar Bluff to a crisp, sunny autumn afternoon, with a mild breeze coming from the south that animated the blazing leaves and created a ripple of white caps across the lake.

Isabel noticed the light blinking on her answering machine as she carried the groceries into the kitchen. She figured it was one of the kids who favored Sundays for checking in on Mom, since they were both so busy during the rest of the week. She pressed play on her recorder, expecting to hear the voice of either Charlie or Carly, but heard another friendly voice instead.

"Hi, Mrs. Puddles, it's Toby. Sorry to bother you on a Sunday but I wanted to let you know I built your steps here at my workshop, along with a new set of railings. They're all ready to go. But I'm tied up all next week, still on this big project, so I'm going to send one of my guys over to install everything. Probably Monday or Tuesday at the latest. Hope that works for you. Please call me if you have any questions. Thanks!"

Isabel had forgotten all about the steps, but it would be nice to have that finally taken care of. After changing into her cooking sweats, she got busy with dinner. There were potatoes, carrots, and parsnips to peel and chop, beef to cut, flour, and brown in her old Dutch oven, and, most important, there were her grandmother Hazel's tightly held secret ingredients to add before it all went into the oven: a cup of bourbon mixed with a tablespoon of brown sugar, a splash of apple cider vinegar, and a teaspoon of allspice. A few hours in the oven smothered in caramelized onions and the rest of the vegetables, and the concoction would be transformed into a dish the word *succulent* was created for.

As was the custom, when the pot roast was finished and her dinner guests had assembled, Isabel would arrange it all onto her great-grandmother Zelda's big English porcelain platter— chips, cracks, and all—and land it gently in the middle of the table, followed by a tableside flourish of gravy. It made for a very impressive presentation, and it was not unusual for guests to applaud. Although she was happy to take a bow, it was as easy for her to do as making a sandwich. But tonight she was making an extra effort for Zander Metcalf and his fiancée to give them a warm Kentwater County welcome. Although dinner rolls from Hobson's were the usual accompaniment to her pot roast dinners, tonight it would be Frances's homemade rye bread and fresh butter from the Amish. And for dessert, Honeycrisp apple buckle—one of her specialties—with vanilla ice cream, also compliments of the Amish. It was about as perfect a midwestern feast as anybody could ask for. Zander Metcalf would leave Poplar Bluff tonight not only full but also knowing that Kentwater County was more than just a windy land of nail gun–wielding maniacs murdering elderly farmers.

With her pot roast in the oven, she got dressed for dinner in a pair of bold black-and-white–print hostess pants Carly bought for her on a trip to Madrid, and a black blouse with a ruffled collar she bought at a clearance sale. Jewelry was not usually part of Isabel's repertoire, but this was a special occasion, so she accessorized with a chunky gold-and-jade pendant necklace with matching earrings that belonged to her mother. She stopped and looked at herself in the full-length mirror in the hallway. "Not bad for an old broad," she said to herself.

After feeding the dogs—who each got a splash of pot roast juice in their dishes—she turned on the TV to listen to the local news, this time from a small local station farther north. She was hoping they wouldn't be covering the Jonasson murder, but as luck would have it, they were. In fact, it was the lead story. So, of course, now she had to listen. There was *breaking news*—which on a normal day for this station might be a downed tree or a moose sighting in town—but this evening began with a young reporter wearing an ill-fitting suit looking into the camera earnestly and reciting what had become the usual descriptors of Kentwater County; sand dunes, unspoiled Lake Michigan shoreline, yada, yada. This young man was going for high drama, though. He continued, "But on this autumn day, when most folks here in Hartley are heading home from church to watch some football, or heading off to the pumpkin patch to get ready for Halloween, or maybe over to McGrady's Orchard to pick apples—"

"Come on already!" Isabel yelled at the television.

The cub reporter continued ". . . instead residents were reminded that all was not well in this picturesque community, when Assistant State's Attorney Tom Garrett held a rare Sunday-morning press conference to get residents up to speed on the latest developments in the sensational Jonasson murder case—a case that has cast a sinister pall over this otherwise sleepy little town."

"Oh, brother," Isabel muttered at the young reporter who looked like he was probably still collecting an allowance from his parents. *Sensational?* Isabel said to herself. You would have thought Jack the Ripper had come to town. And then there was Tom Garrett, standing on the steps of the courthouse. He was new to the area, and Isabel had never seen him, but she'd heard his name a lot in the past few days. The man had intense, rodentlike eyes, tight lips, and a wispy gray comb-over that evoked a pang of sympathy for a man so desperate to deny his baldness. He possessed a somewhat robotic demeanor, almost intentionally devoid of personality, and an overall air of unpleasantness. But then prosecutors were not generally known for their bubbly personalities.

"Thank you all for coming," he said solemnly. The camera panned the crowd, which had stopped to gather outside the courthouse on a Sunday, perhaps on the way to the pumpkin patch. The "crowd" consisted of about four reporters, a couple of cameramen, and a handful of looky-loos, including Ava Milford, who lived across the street from the courthouse and was wearing her bathrobe, slippers, a Detroit Tigers cap on sideways, and holding her Siamese cat, named Piewacket.

Tom Garrett continued, "After receiving the official report last night from the Michigan State forensics lab, it has been determined that the murder weapon used to fire the fatal shot into Mr. Jonasson's skull was the same nail gun retrieved from the garage of the victim's son, Earl Jonasson Jr. It has further been determined that nails found in the garage, along with the weapon, also match the nail recovered from the victim. Finally, fingerprints and DNA found on the murder weapon have been determined to be that of the suspect now in custody. We feel the evidence is conclusive, and the state believes they have the perpetrator in custody. We hope to proceed to trial very soon."

A reporter yelled off camera, "Have you set a trial date?" To which Mr. Garrett replied, "A speedy trial is not only in keeping with the tenets of American jurisprudence, but we feel it is in the best interest of the community to resolve this case sooner than later. I will be talking to Mr. Jonasson's defense attorney, Beverly Atwater, tomorrow morning, when we meet with Judge Meyer, who will be trying this case, and we hope he will set a date satisfactory to both sides."

The eager cub reporter came back on camera. "Jonasson's lawyer, famed defense attorney Beverly Atwater, spoke to reporters about the implications of the nail gun found in her client's garage with his DNA, and had this to say."

They cut to Beverly and Meg outside the sheriff's office, where Beverly stopped to share her take on the forensics, and to taunt Tom Garrett. "If the nail gun seized from my client's garage is indeed the same nail gun used to murder his father, Mr. Jonasson, it is nothing close to being conclusive"—air quotes inserted—"evidence of my client's guilt. This was not a locked garage, the nail gun was not hidden, in fact it was lying out in plain sight . . . and there were many people who had access to it. And if they found Mr. Jonasson's fingerprints and DNA on it, well, that shouldn't come as any surprise, because it was his father's nail gun and he has now acknowledged that he had used it at some point to make repairs on the farm. What would be surprising is if we *did not* find his fingerprints and DNA on it."

Another reporter yelled a question at Meg as they turned to leave. "Do you think your brother murdered your father?"

Meg stopped, turned to the reporter, and said emphatically. "No, I do not. My brother is not a killer."

Another reporter chimed in. "Is it true you're discussing a plea deal with the state?"

Beverly whirled around and shot the reporter a steely-eyed look. "Do you work for the *National Enquirer*? I don't know where you're getting your information, but, no, that is absolutely false. Innocent men do not need to make plea deals, and my client is an innocent man."

Beverly and Meg began to walk away, but the reporter was not backing down. "Didn't you claim Malcolm Metz was an innocent man, too, Ms. Atwater?"

Beverly whipped her head back to the reporter and stared him down, saying nothing. But if looks could kill, Beverly Atwater would have been the next person to be charged with murder in Kentwater County.

Isabel's mind drifted back to Meg's accident, and whether it was an accident at all. Could Tammy Trudlow and Jason Swerley have been behind it? She knew Tammy and Jason had some kind of a connection, most likely a romantic one, and they both had a connection to a new silver pickup like the one that ran Meg off the road. They also both had criminal histories. These two seemed far more capable of murder than Earl Jr. did. But none of it seemed to matter much to Grady, the Michigan State Police, or Tom Garrett from the state attorney's office, who all appeared to be convinced they had their man.

Isabel's guests would be arriving soon. She turned off the TV and lit the fire, along with a few candles, then turned on some dinner party music from a CD she bought, aptly titled *Dinner Party Music*. The doorbell rang just as she put her apple buckle into the oven. Perfect timing. She went to the door knowing it had to be Zander and his fiancée because her other guests wouldn't think to ring the doorbell. She opened the door with a smile, apologizing for the barking dogs, to find

Zander on the stoop, also smiling, and standing next to a tall, very handsome, dark-featured man about Zander's age. Both were wearing sport coats and looking very dapper, especially for this neck of the woods. Zander was holding a bouquet of yellow Gerber daisies, while his companion held a bottle of expensive-looking wine in each hand.

"Hello, Isabel." Zander held out his hand and she pulled him in for a hug. "I'm a hugger. Welcome to Poplar Bluff, Zander."

"Thank you. What a beautiful spot," Zander offered as he handed the flowers to Isabel.

"Thank you . . . these are just lovely. So Zander where's your—"

Zander was quick to interrupt. "Isabel, this is Josh."

Isabel's head was suddenly spinning faster than a wind turbine in a Lake Michigan squall. . . . *Oh!* But the squall moved through just as quickly as it had appeared. Isabel didn't skip a beat. "Josh! It's lovely to meet you. Please come in." *One shouldn't just assume anymore*, she told herself as she closed the door behind them. *It's a different world.*

"Very nice to meet *you*, Isabel. Zander's told me a lot about you. And who are these guys?" He handed the wine bottles to Isabel and bent down to greet the dogs, who took to him immediately.

"The little guy is Jackpot, and Corky is the newest member of the family."

"Hi, guys! Nice to meet you, too." He gave them both scratches behind their ears, then stood up and took the bottles back. "Hope you like California Cabernets."

"Well, most of the wine that comes through this door comes in a box, so I'm sure I'm going to love it! And, Zander, how did you know Gerber daisies were one of my very favorites! You boys are so thoughtful. Please come in!"

They walked through the house and toward the kitchen, stopping in the living room to take in the view of the lake. "Your home is lovely, Isabel," Josh said as he looked around. "And the view is stunning. . . . Wow!"

Isabel was thinking the same of Josh. She was pretty sure he was about the best-looking man ever to walk into her home.

"Just amazing," offered Zander.

"Well, thank you both. I do love it here. Now what can I get you to drink? I have beer, scotch, Canadian whiskey . . . or we can open the wine you brought."

"A beer would be great. Let's save the wine for dinner," Josh suggested as he plopped the bottles down in the center of Isabel's impeccably set table. "I hear you're making pot roast. Actually I can *smell* you're making pot roast. This Cab will pair perfectly." Josh's manners were as polished as he was.

"Beer works for me, too," Zander added. "I can't get over this *view*, Isabel. How long have you been here?"

Isabel presented the boys with two bottles of imported beer Charlie had left in the fridge. "Almost my entire life. We moved here when I was just a little girl, and I raised my own children here," she said, pouring herself a light Canadian Club and water. They toasted, and she led her guests out onto the deck. "It's chilly, but the view from the deck is even better. Let's go out for a minute, at least."

After giving them as concise a history of her family, Poplar Bluff, and her kids as she was able to, they started back inside just as Frances appeared at the slider and stepped out onto the deck. She wasted no time introducing herself, in as embarrassing a fashion as Isabel expected.

"You two look like you just stepped out of a catalog! Hello, I'm Frances Spitler. Isabel's best friend since kindergarten. And I'm sorry to disappoint you boys, but I'm a married woman."

Isabel rolled her eyes and the boys laughed. "And where *is* your husband?" Isabel asked.

Frances threw her a look. "Sick. And the only reason I know he's not faking it is because he would never miss your pot roast." She turned back to Zander and Josh. "Do you know this woman will still not tell me the secret recipe for her pot roast? I guess she plans to take it to the grave. Okay, now, who are you two and what are you doing *here*?"

Zander and Josh were already finding Frances entertaining. They introduced themselves before Isabel could do the honors.

"You're the windmill fella," Frances said to Zander.

"I am the wind *turbine* fella, yes," he replied with a chuckle. "And this is Josh, my—"

At that moment Freddie pulled open the slider and stuck his head out. "Who do I need to know to get a drink around here?"

"You know where the bar is, Freddie!" Then, turning to her guests: "Come on, let's go in. I've got a fire all ready to go."

Frances was not done ogling the handsome newcomers. "Well, it's a pleasure to meet you both. You certainly have prettied up this dinner party."

Isabel shook her head. "Stop making a spectacle of yourself, Frances . . . for the love of God."

Once inside, and after Zander and Josh had been introduced to Freddie and Carol, Isabel put out her usual spread of appetizers: saltine crackers, cheese, summer sausage, smoked almonds, her famous bread-and-butter pickles—and because she had special guests—a dish of her pickled asparagus. Sitting by the crackling fire, they immediately fell into a friendly back-and-forth, drinking, eating, laughing, and getting acquainted. Carol was quiet as usual, while Freddie, also as usual, was anything but. He took a liking to the boys right away, and was thrilled to discover that Josh's father had been

a major in the 1st Marine Division at Camp Pendleton just
as he had been, although they had been several years apart.
But Isabel was getting nervous for some reason, and Frances
was picking up on it. When the timer went off for her apple
buckle, she excused herself to go to the kitchen. Frances followed. As she put on her oven mitts, Frances cut to the chase.
"So, are we going to talk about the elephant in the room?"

"What elephant?"

"The *pink* elephant?" Frances answered in an unusually
hushed tone.

Isabel pulled her apple buckle out of the oven and placed it
on a cooling rack. "I had no idea. He said his fiancé was coming up. I just assumed . . . It's a new world, Frances."

"And a pretty world. Those boys are the cutest pair I've
seen since Kenny Rogers and Dolly Parton went on tour.
Shame they can't have babies."

Isabel's jaw dropped. "What a thing to say! Please tell me
you don't plan to say or do something embarrassing."

"Oh, hush. Don't be ridiculous. You know my nephew
Bryce is as gay as a clutch bag and I love him to death. I knew
it before *he* did. I think they're adorable." Frances moved in
closer and lowered her voice even more. "So, does Freddie
know? Is that what you're worried about?"

"Well, they haven't made a formal announcement, but I
know Freddie to be a kind and decent man, so I can't imagine
he'd have any issue with this if it comes up. But it might not
come up at all, so let's just leave it alone. Don't stir the pot,
Frances . . . for once . . . Please?"

They walked back into the living room together just as
Freddie asked Josh what he did for a living. "I'm an assistant professor of biological physics at University of Michigan.
I'm thinking about going to medical school"—then, turning
to Zander and patting him on the leg—"but we'll see how

that works out. We have to decide if we want to stay in Ann Arbor."

Carol reached for a smoked almond. "And how do you two know each other?" she asked innocently before popping it into her mouth. Now it was Zander's turn to tiptoe around what was becoming increasingly obvious.

"We met at Michigan as undergrads . . . we were in the same fraternity."

Josh smiled. "And we're still in the same fraternity." He winked at Zander. With that, even Carol, who was not known for ever being ahead of the curve, was starting to pick up on the social cues . . . but not Freddie.

"So, Josh, did you ever think about joining the Marines? It must be in your blood."

Josh laughed. "My dad was all for it, but my mom was *completely* against it. I was on the fence, although I did love the uniforms. I thought I wanted to be a pilot for a while, so I joined the ROTC thinking I might go into the Air Force. *That,* Mom was okay with . . . but in the end, it didn't work out."

"What happened?" Freddie asked.

Carol scolded him. "Freddie, don't be so nosy!"

"No, it's fine," Josh said as he sliced off a piece of cheese and put it on a cracker, then handed it to Zander. "Turns out I'm afraid to fly." There was a brief pause before everybody laughed. "No, actually it was pretty straightforward, no pun intended. This was quite a few years ago, mind you, but, well, *they* asked, and *I* told."

Freddie's eyebrows furled as his gears slowly began to click into place, until finally . . . "Oh! Oh, I see . . . well, that's a shame. . . . I mean, it's not a shame that you're . . ." Freddie was on the ropes. "I mean it's a shame you had to leave the ROTC."

Frances leaned over and whispered to Isabel, "If he were a boxer, this is where they'd be pulling out the smelling salts." Isabel ignored her while Freddie stuttered on.

"All I mean is that it's too bad you weren't able to pursue what you—"

Josh came to Freddie's rescue. "No, it was all for the best. I met this guy instead . . . so as they say, all's well that ends well." Josh smiled at Zander, who was looking a bit tentative. Isabel reached for the cheese tray and began to pass it in an effort to avoid what she feared could become an excruciatingly awkward pause.

"How do you like this cheese, Zander? It's from the Amish dairy. Have you been?"

"No, I haven't, but I'd love to go. It's delicious."

Josh tried a piece and nodded in agreement. "It's good. I like cheese, but Zander *loves* cheese. He's very lactose tolerant."

"We'll have to go when you have some time," Isabel suggested. "And their ice cream is the best you've ever had. We'll be having some with dessert."

Poor Freddie was still struggling a bit to get his bearings. Isabel didn't know what else to say, while Frances sat back with a smile, enjoying the show. Carol finally chimed in to do her part to normalize the situation.

"Izzy, the smell of that pot roast could raise the dead." The whole room agreed in chorus.

Freddie finally found his way back into the conversation, starting with the dogs, "Must be torture for you two!"

Isabel laughed. "They're waiting patiently for scraps. Now, if you folks will excuse me, I'm going to get that roast out of the oven and we'll be sitting down in just a few minutes. Frances, could I get you to fix the table, please? It's still set for seven. And, Josh, would you mind coming in and opening those beautiful bottles of wine you brought?"

"Not at all." Josh jumped up. Frances joined him and

wasted no time tucking her arm under his as they headed for the kitchen. While Josh opened the wine and went around the table pouring, Frances excused herself to go "powder her nose." Finally Josh couldn't resist asking. "Zander didn't tell you he and I were engaged, did he? Or if he told you he was engaged, I'm guessing he didn't tell you *he* was engaged to a *he*."

Isabel was busy preparing her gravy, which gave her something to focus on. "Well, he said he had a fiancé who was coming up for the weekend, and he asked about a romantic place to have dinner. That's all. I didn't pry. I didn't *think* to pry, to be honest. By the way, did you go to the Old Cottage Inn?"

"We did. And the duck was out of this world."

"Good. I'm glad you enjoyed it. Anyway . . . it wasn't like he *avoided* telling me. We just didn't have much time to talk."

"Zander's not always as comfortable as I'd like for him to be with all of it. For his sake, not mine. It's his upbringing. His parents are not exactly supportive. In fact, they have yet to decide if they'll be attending the wedding."

"That's terrible," Isabel said as she seasoned her gravy with a few pinches of salt. Josh grabbed a glass of wine off the table for the hostess and one for himself. They clinked.

"*They're* terrible . . . but I'll deny I said that. *Salud!*" Josh raised his glass.

Isabel raised her glass and took a sip. "Oh, my goodness, that's the most delicious wine I have ever tasted."

Josh nodded in agreement. "It's my favorite. I grew up in the Napa Valley, so I've tried a Cabernet or two in my day."

Isabel took another sip. "Just delicious . . . How will I ever go back to the box now? So, Josh, do you mind if I ask how *your* parents feel about your marriage?"

"I've been very lucky. My parents—especially my big macho Marine dad—are just as excited as we are about the wedding, if not more so. Same with my brother and sister. They all love Zander. In fact, if his parents don't come—and I secretly hope they don't, because, as I mentioned, they're terrible—my dad and my sister will stand up for me, and my mom and my brother will stand up for Zander."

Isabel was touched. "They sound like lovely people. Well, I think it's wonderful you're getting married, and that you're finally *able* to. I never understood why people were so against it. Like my grandmother used to say, 'People need to spend six months of the year minding their own business, and the other six months staying out of *other* people's business.' "

Josh laughed and they clinked again. "Wise words indeed. I like your grandmother. And I like *you*, Isabel."

"I like you, too, Josh—*and* your fiancé. Okay, my gravy is ready. Will you please tell the others to come to the table?" Josh went into the living room, and Frances appeared in the kitchen looking impish. "Isn't that something?"

"What?" Isabel asked as she carefully assembled the beef and vegetables on the platter.

"I didn't want to interrupt . . . so I listened from the foyer."

"Try to keep it off the six o'clock news, will you, please?"

Josh and Carol appeared at the table first, followed by Freddie, who had his arm around Zander's shoulder, laughing and chatting him up. Isabel smiled, proud that she could always count on her family to be the kind and accepting people all good Congregationalists should be. She felt bad for Zander that he didn't have that with his own parents.

Isabel's dinner party was a thundering success. The pot roast was, as usual, a hit, as was Frances's rye bread, and Josh's wine. Freddie regaled everybody with a litany of bad jokes and his usual yarns about some of Kentwater County's more eccentric citizens—stories she had heard a hundred times but still enjoyed. A few glasses of wine into dinner, he admitted he was a little taken aback when he learned Zander and Josh were engaged.

Frances laughed. "Watching you figure it out, Freddie, was like watching a roulette ball bouncing around the wheel in slow motion."

"And then landing on *gay!*" Josh added.

The table erupted in laughter, with nobody laughing harder than Freddie. Soon the topic of Zander and Josh's impending summer wedding in Saugatuck came up. Saugatuck was a town about two hours down the Big Lake, a charming old artists' colony with shops, galleries, and restaurants, surrounded by beautiful old homes and cottages, all meticulously preserved. It was to the Midwest what Provincetown was to the East Coast. The boys talked about the old cottage they bought and had spent the last three years refurbishing, and how much they were looking forward to having their wedding in their own backyard.

Isabel toasted to the happy couple, and after a few more jokes and local stories, compliments of Freddie—along with some brandy they had with their coffee and apple buckle—Freddie had a confession to make. He admitted he wasn't all that gung ho about gay marriage, at least not at first, but he had come around on the topic a while ago. "I finally decided, why not let the gays suffer, too!" Freddie howled. The boys had heard that joke a million times, but, coming from Freddie, it somehow seemed fresh and funny.

Carol smacked him in the arm, and then with a comment completely out of character for her, got her husband back. "I'd gay marry Ellen in a minute if she'd have me . . . I think she's adorable."

The boys barely avoided tandem spit takes of their brandy, while Freddie pounded his hand on the table. "By God! I married a lesbian!"

The laughter must have been ringing across the lake. Isabel could not have been more pleased with how much everybody enjoyed one another's company. When they realized it was almost eleven o'clock and time to go, there was a lot of talk about getting together again, and Zander and Josh invited everybody to their wedding. Then, on their way out the door, after lots of good-night hugs, Isabel reminded Zander about bringing back the waders. "I'll be at the store tomorrow. Don't forget!"

Zander stopped and turned around. "You know it looks like I need them, after all. Apparently the original land deal is going through. The old farmer's executor just signed the contracts. So, I've got get to get out in that marsh first thing in the morning. Good night, Isabel. Thank you again for a wonderful evening, and for that amazing pot roast!"

She waved good-bye. "You are more than welcome. So glad you could make it." Isabel closed the door slowly.

Well, *that* was an interesting development. The deal was back on? Frances was at the sink rinsing dishes and putting them into the dishwasher when she walked into the kitchen. "Well, you outdid yourself tonight," Frances said.

"It was a fun evening," Isabel agreed. "And we could do with a little more fun these days. I'm going to make myself a cup of tea. Join me?"

Frances wiped her hands with a dish towel and hung it over the side of the sink. "I'd rather have another brandy, but I guess tea will have to do if I'm going to make it home alive."

Isabel filled up the teakettle as Frances sat down at the kitchen counter. "By the way, I heard about Meg's accident. Is she okay?"

"Where did you hear about that?" Isabel asked as she dropped a couple chamomile tea bags into their cups.

"There isn't much that gets past me, Iz. I ran into Dorothy Osborne at the post office. She's in my bridge club. Her brother has a tow company out near the freeway. Triple A called him to go pull Meg's car out of the ditch. He said it was a mangled mess. Said he couldn't believe she wasn't killed."

The teakettle slowly started to whistle. "It was pretty bad," Isabel concurred. "Poor Meg . . . as if she hasn't been through enough already," she said as she filled their tea mugs. "Let's sit down in the living room and enjoy what's left of the fire." Isabel launched into some small talk to steer Frances away from anything else Jonasson-related. "So, what time do you catch the Badger tomorrow?"

Frances took a sip and then dunked her tea bag a few times. "I'm on the ten a.m. crossing." She took another sip, this one intended to punctuate the end of that conversation and begin a new one. "Now, Izzy, I know I'm not supposed to say anything about anything, but unless Grady Pemberton, or Beverly Atwater, or that Tom Garrett are hiding in your broom closet, I should be okay. So, let me ask you this . . . If Earl Jr. didn't kill his father—and you know my feelings about that—then who in the world do you think did it?"

Isabel didn't skip a beat. "Tammy Trudlow."

"Tammy Trudlow? What makes you think *she* did it? She doesn't have the sense God gave a goat." Frances laughed.

"I have my reasons," Isabel said matter-of-factly. "And, by the way, murder isn't rocket science."

"But it makes no sense . . . she was already going to marry Earl Jr.—at least that was the rumor—and her father-in-law to be was eighty-eight years old. So, if she was after the money, she wasn't going to have to wait very long to get her hands on it."

"Well, like you said, she's no brain trust . . . and Earl's father lived to be ninety-eight and died chopping wood. So, the Jonassons are pretty solid stock. Ten years is a long time to wait if you're greedy."

"What if I told you it would have been impossible for Tammy Trudlow to murder Earl Jonasson?" Frances took a long sip of her tea for a dramatic pause.

"And how would *you* know that?" Isabel asked, daring her to offer a theory.

"Because I happen to know she was in jail the day Earl was murdered."

Isabel shot her a look. "What do you mean she was in jail?"

"Well we didn't do time *together*, but Wanda from the Kroger told me Tammy got arrested at the Gas n' Go in Shelbyville for shoplifting a couple packs of Twizzlers and a handful of Slim Jims. Shoved them right down her brassiere. Apparently she was wearing one for a change. Happened just a day or two before Earl turned up dead. Junior bailed her out the morning they were supposed to have that first viewing at Cook's."

"I wouldn't say Wanda Wagers is exactly a dependable source," Isabel scoffed.

"Normally no. But Wanda's brother just happens to be Barry, from Barry's Bail Bonds in Shelbyville. He wrote her bond."

Isabel could almost hear her own brakes squeaking to a stop. Why was she just now hearing about this? If this was true, it would explain why Grady didn't seem very interested in looking into Tammy's possible involvement in Earl's murder. It definitely changed the equation a little, but just because Tammy was in jail, it didn't mean she couldn't have put somebody else up to it . . . somebody like her friend Jason Swerley, maybe? There was no reason to go into this with Frances right now, though. "Well, I guess that's that. Maybe he *did* do it. I don't know anymore. But that's what trials are for, so I guess we'll have to see."

Frances looked at her suspiciously. She seemed to be acquiescing a little too quickly, and that wasn't like Isabel Puddles. But Frances was happy to move on, regardless. She'd had quite enough of the Jonasson murder case. "Well, Iz, I better get going. I need to get up early and pack. Thank you for another fabulous dinner. And I'm so excited for our first gay wedding next summer! Aren't you? What do you wear to a gay wedding?"

Isabel chuckled. "Well, I would think the same thing you wear to an un-gay wedding."

Frances put on her coat and gloves. "Oh, no! Have you never watched *Project Runway*? What if Tim Gunn's there?" Isabel had no clue what or who that was. "We're going to have to step up our game for this affair. We'll start shopping when I get back. The gays don't do dowdy. If we show up in chiffon, or some off-the-rack, mother-of-the-bride number, we won't even get in the door!"

Chapter 15

Bam, bam, bam . . . Isabel was in the bathroom brushing her teeth when she started hearing the obnoxious sound reverberating through her house. *Bam, bam, bam.* It took her a minute, but then she remembered Toby's message about sending someone over to install the new stairs for the deck. *Bam, bam, bam* . . . Jackpot was already at the glass slider, barking, while Corky, once again, was cowering in her bed. Isabel looked at the clock. It was eight a.m., a little early to be under a nail gun attack, but she would be glad to have the job finished. She put on her robe, went to the kitchen, and got a pot of coffee going. *Bam, bam, bam* . . . She pulled back the drape and peeked out to see a heavyset young man with red hair in a ponytail and a scraggly red beard working out on the deck. He looked oddly familiar, but she figured he was probably just someone she had seen around town. After finishing her first cup of coffee, she decided to get dressed and go out to offer the young man a cup. She slid open the door. "Good morning!"

"Mornin'!" the young man yelled back. "You must be Mrs. Puddles!"

He seemed pleasant enough. "I am . . . and you are . . . ?"

"Glen!" he yelled back. *Bam, bam, bam.*

"You're working awfully early, Glen. Can I bring you a cup of coffee?"

"Oh, no, I don't drink coffee, ma'am. Upsets my stomach. I'm sorry about the noise. I won't be long. The stairs match up just right. All I have to do is attach these railings and you'll be good to go!" *Bam, bam, bam.* Isabel gave him a wave and closed the door. She would be happy to be rid of Glen and his nail gun, but not as happy as Corky would be . . . poor girl. Isabel sat down with her coffee just as the phone started to ring. It was Freddie. "Hey, Izzy! What a great time we had last night! Spectacular dinner party—and your pot roast was one for the record books."

Isabel was on to him. "You didn't call to talk about my pot roast, Freddie. What's up?"

"Well, I have to ask a favor. Frank has to leave after lunch today. His great-aunt over in Gaylord took a spill, so he needs to drive over and check on her. And I've got an appointment with Dr. Miller at one o'clock. So, do you think you could come in for a couple hours?" *Bam, bam, bam.* "What's that sound?" Freddie asked.

"Oh, I've got a man with a nail gun out there fixing my deck. Sure, Freddie. What time do you want me to come in?" *Bam, bam, bam.*

"Those things scare the holy heck out of me," Freddie said. "You know I heard about a man over in—"

Isabel stopped him cold. "Freddie, whatever nail gun–related story you're about to share with me, I do not want to hear."

Freddie laughed. "If you could be here at twelve thirty, that would be terrific."

"I'll see you at twelve thirty." Isabel had to go into Hartley anyway and run some errands, so it was no trouble to put in a couple of extra hours at the hardware. *Bam, bam, bam.* She went in to check again on Corky, who was still in her bed, shaking like a leaf. She couldn't resist picking her up to try to comfort her. Taking her into the living room, she sat down on the sofa and bundled her up with a throw blanket. *Bam, bam, bam.* "He's got to be almost done, sweetheart. I know it's very scary. I hate it, too." *Bam, bam, bam.* They sat a little while longer until the noise finally abated, followed by a knock on the slider. She put Corky down on the sofa and went to the door to find Glen. She slid the door open with a smile. "All done?"

He was blowing into his hands to warm them up. "Yes, ma'am . . . but Toby wanted me to make sure you approved the job before I left."

She put her coffee down on the kitchen table. "Let's go have a look." Jackpot led the way, running out onto the deck, then continuing down the new steps to the dock for morning minnow patrol. She first tested the railings, then walked down and back up the steps. "Perfect! Nice and sturdy. Good work Glen. Do you have a bill for me?"

Glen started wrapping the cord around his nail gun. "Toby didn't say nothin' to me about—" His eyes suddenly locked on the partially open glass slider. Isabel's eyes followed him, where she saw Corky slowly coming through the door.

"That's Corky coming to say hello now that the coast is clear. That nail gun of yours nearly scared her to death." But something wasn't right. . . . Isabel immediately noticed Corky had a strange demeanor about her. She stopped in the middle of the deck and hunched down, her eyes fixed on Glen, before she bolted straight for him, snarling and barking, in a streak of black-and-white rage.

Glen leaped toward the steps, but before he could take his next step to escape, Corky lunged at him and bit ferociously into the calf of his right leg. Isabel was mortified. "Corky! Stop it! Corky! No!" She tried to swat her off Glen's leg, but she was not letting go. After swatting at Corky a few more times, Isabel finally got her to release Glen's leg, but only long enough to get a better grip, this time on his ankle. The enraged cocker spaniel held on as Glen swung wildly at her with his arms and tried to kick her with his free leg, missing Corky, but coming close to Isabel a few times as she desperately tried to pull her off. Jackpot was now on the scene, too, barking and circling the commotion, doing his part to end the assault. Corky's growling and snarling, Jackpot's barking, Isabel's yelling, and Glen's swearing, combined with his anguished screams of pain, must have been quite a wake-up call for her neighbors around the lake. Struggling to free his leg, Glen made a futile attempt to climb over the deck railing, happy to risk the six-foot drop to the ground if only he could shake this possessed dog off his leg. But Corky kept pulling him back down. His jeans were now ripped at the ankle and Isabel could see blood soaking into Glen's white socks. She managed to get her hand under Corky's collar and tugged as hard as she could. Finally, in the split second when the dog let loose to readjust her bite, Isabel was able to yank her away, then fell backward onto her behind, clutching a still thrashing Corky. Glen wrenched his injured leg away so fast, he fell over the side of the deck with a scream, followed by a thud, followed by a grunt.

"Oh, my Lord, Glen, are you all right? I'm so sorry! I don't know what got into her!" No reply. *Oh, God*, she thought for a split second, *Corky's killed the handyman*. All of a sudden, Glen popped his head up like a terrorized puppet, wide-eyed and hyperventilating. He turned in a panic and made a break for it, up the sloping lawn toward the driveway, half running, half limping. Corky was still wrestling with Isabel to get loose. But as hard as she tried to hang on to her, Isabel was no match. Corky broke free and ran down the steps in pursuit of her prey. Isabel followed, rounding the deck and chasing her as she tore up the lawn and gained ground on Glen, who was running for his life. Now just a few feet away, Corky was getting ready to pounce and sink her teeth into him again, but the terrified handyman reached his truck just in time. He threw open the door and tumbled inside to safety, slamming the door behind him. Corky jumped up and scratched against the door, still barking and growling, while Isabel chugged up the hill after her. Before she could reach him, Glen started the engine with a roar, slammed the truck into reverse, and backed out of the driveway, his rear wheels spinning backward in the gravel until he hit the road. He then threw the truck into drive and sped away, with Corky still in hot pursuit, until finally giving up after about a couple hundred feet down the road.

Isabel was stunned. She had never seen behavior like this from any dog in her life, and she certainly didn't expect it from *this* dog. Corky slowly dragged herself back up the drive, winded, drooling, and with her head hanging so low her ears were skimming the ground. She sat down in the driveway, several feet in front of Isabel, and stared at her with the strangest expression. Jackpot slowly approached her, then cautiously rubbed his head against hers, licked her ear, and then sat down next to her. Isabel wasn't quite sure what to do, but her first instinct was to make sure Glen was okay. She left Corky and Jackpot in the driveway and ran into the kitchen to call Toby. Thankfully he answered right away. "Toby, it's Isabel Puddles. I'm so glad I got you. I'm afraid something terrible has happened."

"You don't like the stairs?" Toby asked with alarm.

"The stairs are fine . . . perfect . . . but Glen may not be. I'm afraid Corky—remember my new dog you met?—well, she bit him pretty hard, and more than once. He took off before I could see how bad it was. But I'm very concerned. He probably needs to go have it looked at. I'll pay for the doctor's bill, of course. I just feel terrible, Toby. I don't know what got into her." She looked through the kitchen window to see Corky now lying down in the drive on her belly, still half-dazed, with Jackpot at her side.

"Please calm down, Mrs. Puddles, I'm sure it's not that bad. Let me call Glen and see what's going on. He's supposed to be coming back to the job site after he left you. Hang on just a second, please." Isabel heard Toby yelling out. "Jason, do you have Glen's cell phone number?"

Isabel heard someone faintly reply, "Who?"

"Glen Trudlow! Do you have his cell phone number?"

Toby was back. "Sorry, Mrs. Puddles. I'll talk to him ASAP and let you know if it's anything serious, okay? I'm sure he's fine. He's a pretty sturdy guy."

Isabel went quiet.

"Mrs. Puddles? Are you still there?"

"Yes, I'm here . . . sorry, Toby. Did I hear you say Glen *Trudlow*?"

"Yeah, he's one of the guys I hired to help me on this project, and his buddy Jason."

"Is he any relation to *Tammy* Trudlow?"

"I think he did mention he had a sister," Toby replied. "Hey, what's Glen's sister's name?" Back to Isabel. "Yep, Tammy . . . you know her?"

"I know *of* her. I was just curious, is all."

"I really have to run, Mrs. Puddles, I'm working on a big deck project over here on the Big Lake. There's still a lot to do and we're racing against the first snow. I'll let you know what's going on with Glen as soon as he calls me back. If it's anything to worry about, that is. Otherwise, please don't concern yourself. I'm sure he'll survive a little dog bite. He better, because I need him on this job! Talk to you later, Mrs. Puddles!" With that, Toby hung up.

Isabel's mind began to race. Those eyes . . . Of course! Those were Trudlow eyes! Beady, slightly crossed . . . She *knew* she somehow recognized him! According to Phoebe, he had been in prison, but he had obviously been sprung. And the Jason that Toby was talking to had to be Jason Swerley. Could Toby be the friend he said he had come up to work for? But that made no sense at all. How would a nice boy like Toby be friends with the likes of these two jailbirds? What did make sense, though, was that Glen was the friend Jason had come up to work for. They were probably prison buddies.

Isabel rushed back out to check on Corky, who was still lying in the driveway and wearing the same strange expression. She sat down on the front stoop and called her over. Corky got up and walked toward her, her floppy ears swinging side to side. She pulled her close and wrapped her arms around her. And then, like snowflakes in a snow globe slowly settling on a winter landscape, everything started to become crystal clear. She hugged Corky closer. "You poor girl. No wonder. That was *him*, wasn't it?" Corky looked her right in the eyes, then licked her face. She could have sworn this dog understood what she had just said to her. Isabel picked her up and carried her inside, sitting down on the sofa where a still very alarmed Jackpot immediately joined them.

Isabel stroked Corky's head and stared out at the lake, trying to piece things together in her mind, or as much of it as she could. Obviously Tammy couldn't have committed the actual murder because she was in jail. But maybe she got herself arrested for shoplifting on purpose, just so she would have an alibi, and then put her brother and his friend up to murdering Earl Jonasson. But could Tammy Trudlow be such a criminal mastermind? Maybe the *original* plan was to murder Earl and make him disappear, which would explain why Jason was in the hardware buying a shovel and a tarp, but then for whatever reason they decided to go the nail gun route. Suddenly a lot of questions badly in need of answers were piling up.

Isabel got up to go get dressed. She needed to find Grady

and tell him she had an eyewitness to Earl Jonasson's murder. As she raced to get dressed, something else dawned on her . . . even more damning evidence. During all the commotion and panic, she hadn't even noticed the pickup truck Glen had raced off in . . . the *silver* pickup truck.

On her way into town, Isabel thought about how best to bring all this up to Grady without his thinking she was nuts. Suggesting to him that a cocker spaniel had just identified the real killer was a stretch, to say the least, but she knew to her core it was a fact. After a lifetime spent as a dog lover and dog owner, one thing she knew for sure, and that was that dog behavior was a lot easier to understand than human behavior. There was only one explanation for why an otherwise sweet and gentle dog would suddenly turn into Cujo, and that was because she knew Glen Trudlow was the man who had killed her master.

Turning onto State Street in Hartley, she spotted Grady and Ginny pulling out of the sheriff's department parking lot, most likely on their way to lunch for the fried perch special at the Copper Kettle, and those two never missed it. Isabel pulled a U-turn and began following them, but after a few blocks decided it was better to wait until after they had their lunch. Grady might be a little more amenable to what she had to tell him on a full stomach. She'd call them in a half hour. Thirty minutes wouldn't make any difference.

What Isabel didn't know was that right now, every second counted.

Chapter 16

Freddie was standing at the counter playing solitaire when Isabel came in. He could tell right away his cousin was upset about something. "Are you feeling okay, Iz? You don't look good. I can cancel Dr. Miller, if—"

"Don't be silly, Freddie. I'm fine. Just have a lot on my mind." Isabel grabbed her apron from behind the door and tied it on. "I'm worried about Meg, what with her dad, and her brother and the accident. Just a little stressed . . . Go to the doctor!"

"All right, well, I'm going to go have my lunch before I go. Carol made me a shepherd's pie with the leftover roast beef you sent home with us last night." Freddie headed to the back of the store just as the phone rang.

"Good afternoon, Fred's Hardware, Isabel speaking." It was Larry.

"Hey there, Iz. Sorry to bother you at work but I was just wondering if you've seen Meg?"

"Why, no, I haven't. Not since after the funeral at the Fletcher's house."

"Oh, I see . . . well, she went into town to get groceries and run some errands, but that was over three hours ago. She should have been home by now. I thought maybe she stopped to have lunch or coffee with you or something. I can't seem to reach her on her cell phone, either."

Larry was obviously concerned. Isabel didn't like the sound of this, either, but she didn't want to add to his worry. "I'm sure she just got sidetracked. If she comes into the store, I'll tell her to call you right away." But Isabel's concern was growing. It wasn't like Meg to disappear like this.

"I'll bet she just forgot to charge her phone again," Larry offered as a possibility, one Isabel was quick to accept.

"I'll bet that's it. Or maybe she stopped in to see Earl, or got held up at the grocery store. Mondays are busy, and there are lots of folks who would want to corral her. I wouldn't worry, Larry. It's hard to get into too much trouble in Hartley, Michigan!" She immediately realized what a dumb thing that was to say to someone whose father-in-law was just murdered and whose brother-in-law was now in jail for allegedly doing it.

"Okay, thanks, Isabel . . ." Larry drifted off without saying good-bye.

"Bye, Larry." Isabel hung up the phone and looked up to find Herb Coleman, a regular customer, standing at the counter with a rake. "Hello, Herb, how are you today?" Herb laid the rake down on the counter and pulled out his wallet.

"Well, I'm still on the right side of the grass, Isabel, so I guess I need to keep it raked!" Herb laughed at his joke and handed her a twenty-dollar bill. Isabel smiled and counted back his change. "Give my best to Lucille."

Herb headed for the door with his rake. "Will do, Isabel!" He opened the door and disappeared. Just as she was about to close the cash drawer, she noticed a loose piece of paper tucked inside that looked familiar. It was a credit slip filled out in her handwriting and stapled to a receipt for a shovel and two blue tarps. The same goods Jason Swerley had returned the week before. She assumed it was the old receipt at first, until she looked closer and saw that the cash register receipt was dated that same morning. "Freddie!"

Freddie came rushing back to the front of the store with his napkin still tucked into his shirt collar and his mouth still full of shepherd's pie. "What's wrong?"

"When did Jason Swerley come back and use this credit slip?"

Freddie looked at the slip. "Frank must have waited on him this morning before I got in."

"Has Frank left already?"

Freddie nodded. "Yes, he left around ten o'clock."

Isabel was beginning to panic. "And he picked up the same shovel and tarps . . . I'm sorry, Freddie, but I have to go. You're just going to have to close up while you're at the doctor. Or get Carol down here. I'll explain later!"

Before Freddie could even get his thoughts together, let alone speak, Isabel was out the door. A split second later she reappeared, untying her apron, tossing it on the counter, and then disappearing again. "Sorry, Freddie!"

Freddie looked down at the cat, who looked equally baffled by Isabel's unusual behavior. "Well, Mrs. Abernathy . . . I think that splash you just heard was my dear old cousin going off the deep end."

Isabel jumped into her van and raced over to the Copper Kettle to find Grady. She was pretty sure he was going to think she was crazy, but her only concern now was Meg. After Corky's attack on Glen Trudlow, and Jason Swerley coming back in for tarps and a shovel only a few days after Meg had been run off the road and nearly killed, she had to convince Grady that the Trudlows not only were involved in Earl Jonasson's murder but may well be plotting Meg's murder next or, worse, had already carried it out.

She had just pulled into the Copper Kettle's parking lot when she saw Grady rushing out. Something was very wrong. Isabel's stomach sank. "Grady, what's wrong?!" she yelled to him as he ran toward his SUV.

"Can't talk, Iz! Meg Blackburn's gone missing! Just found her car abandoned over by the Big Lake."

Isabel felt as if she had just been punched in the stomach. She parked and ran over to Grady's car as he started it up. "Does Larry know?"

"I just sent a deputy to get him! Gotta go!" Grady slammed his door and squealed out of the parking lot just as Ginny ran out to try to catch him.

"He left his walkie-talkie. Now how am I supposed to know what's going on?!" Ginny turned back to Isabel. "So you heard?"

Isabel nodded sadly, lost in a stare. "I did. This isn't good. Ginny, I have to go."

"Isabel, I know that look. . . . Where are you going?"

Isabel climbed into her van. "I think I might have this all figured out, Gin. But I gotta move fast!" With that, she slammed the door and started the engine with a roar.

"Izzy, you be careful!" Ginny called after her cousin as she peeled out of the parking lot.

Isabel needed to talk to Toby fast, but she didn't have his phone number with her. This marked the very first time she fully embraced how "convenient" a cell phone would be. She started to head home to make the call, then realized Toby's mother, Joyce, was closer to her than Poplar Bluff, so she decided to stop and see if she could reach him for her. Luckily, Joyce was in the front yard decorating for Halloween when Isabel pulled in. Toby's mother knew immediately that this was not a social call. "What's wrong, Isabel?"

Isabel hesitated. "I'm not sure, but I need to talk to Toby. Meg Blackburn's gone missing. I think she's been abducted!"

Joyce was dumbfounded. "What? Are you kidding me!"

Isabel shook her head, exasperated. "I wish I were, Joyce."

Joyce stared at her for a beat. "Well, what in the world does Toby have to do with it?"

"So far as I know, nothing. But I think a couple of his employees might know plenty."

"What do you mean 'so far as you know'?" Joyce was now a little on the defensive.

"I only mean I don't know what's going on, but I think Toby can help me figure it out!"

Joyce was now moving into panic mode. "I just tried to call him fifteen minutes ago to see if he wanted me to bring him some lunch, but I got his voice mail. He's trying to finish up a big project, so I know he's busy. Oh, my God, Isabel, is my son in any danger?"

"No, but Meg Blackburn is! Do you know where he's working?"

"It's a new house over on the Big Lake. I don't know the address, but I know how to get there."

Isabel reached over and opened the passenger-side door. "Get in! Let's go! I'll tell you what I can on the way."

After driving about ten minutes through the thick old-growth forest that bordered the Big Lake, Isabel had given Joyce a rundown of what was happening. Toby's mother was now officially panicked, too. After turning off the main road, and then driving way too fast down a sand-packed road for about a mile, Joyce pointed out an impressive-looking log cabin sitting on a bluff overlooking the lake. "That's it."

Isabel slowed down and pulled into the driveway and parked behind Toby's truck, but he was nowhere to be seen. They got out of the van and rushed around to the side of the house facing the lake, where they were happily greeted by Kaiser. Both of them were relieved to find Toby on the deck, wearing a pair of safety goggles and getting ready to start up his table saw. When he saw them, he stopped what he was doing and lifted up his goggles. "Well, hello, there ladies, this is certainly a surprise."

Toby's mom walked over and gave him a bigger hug than usual. "Thank God you're okay." Toby was confused. She hugged him again. "Toby, Isabel has some concerns about a couple of your employees. She told me some things on the way over that are very troubling."

Isabel wasted no time getting to the point. "Toby, is Jason's last name Swerley, by any chance?"

"Yes, ma'am, it is. Is he in some kind of trouble?"

"That remains to be seen. How do you know Jason, if you don't mind my asking?"

Toby was now even more confused. "Well, I kind of inherited him . . . along with Glen. They were both working for Mr. Parker, who's the owner of this build I'm working on here. They were finishing up another project for him when I was hired to build this deck. Mr. Parker knew I was shorthanded, so he suggested I hire them. They've been real good workers."

Parker. That name rang a bell. Then a synapse fired red hot in her brain. Lou Parker! He was the owner of the silver pickup truck—the businessman from Ohio Ginny checked out for her. Was this Parker character somehow involved in all this, too? "Do you know where they are now?"

"Is this about the dog bite, Mrs. Puddles?" Toby asked.

"No . . . well, not entirely," she answered, then pulling her cards a little closer to her chest, "but I would like to make sure Glen is okay."

"He came back here after he left your house. And, I'll be honest, he was kind of shaken up. He showed me the bites. They were pretty deep punctures, so I asked Jason to take him over to Dr. Miller's office and have him take a look. But that was a while ago. I expect they'll be back anytime now."

Isabel was about to continue her line of questioning when they heard a car pulling into the driveway. "That's probably them right now," Toby said as he walked to the end of the deck and poked his head around the house to check. "Nope . . . it's just Mr. Parker checking in on me. He's with his girlfriend. Nice lady . . . should I mention anything to him about all this?"

"No, let's keep this between us for now, Toby." Isabel was thinking on the fly. She didn't want to talk with Parker right now. "Joyce, let's leave Toby alone with his boss. Why don't we walk down to the beach and take in the view for a minute? I've always loved this stretch of beach."

Isabel and an increasingly perplexed Joyce left Toby and Kaiser on the deck and walked down the newly constructed stairs and through the grass-covered dunes leading to the beach. But before they had completely descended, Isabel peeked back through the tall grass to see Toby talking to an attractive, well-dressed older couple on the deck in what appeared to be a very friendly exchange. She was wearing a smart, expensive-looking plaid wool coat. The man, handsome with gray hair, was wearing a light blue cardigan sweater. From a distance, he looked familiar.

"Joyce . . . does your cell phone have a camera?"

Joyce nodded. "I think they all do these days, Izzy."

Isabel peeked again. "Good. Do you think you could snap a quick shot of that couple?"

Joyce was beginning to lose her patience. "What is going on here, Isabel Puddles?"

"I'm not sure. Have you ever met them?"

"No. All I know is that they're obviously rich. Toby told me this property was on the market last summer for one point four million dollars. This deck alone is costing them north of forty thousand. He says they seem very nice, though. I hope whatever is happening here is not going to jeopardize my son in any way, or this job. This is his biggest project yet. If you can promise me Toby is not going to be in any trouble here, I'll take your photo for you."

"Toby's done nothing wrong, Joyce. He's a dream. I just need to know if they're who I think they might be."

"Well, I'm going to trust you, Iz." Joyce turned around, held her phone up, and discreetly snapped a picture of the deck, which included Toby and the couple. "There you go." She showed Isabel the photo.

"Super. Now, you can send that right from your phone, can't you?"

"Yes, I can."

"Good. I need Phoebe Farnsworth to look at it. She'll be able to tell me if my hunch is right. You must have Phoebe's number." Phoebe and Joyce had been best friends since high school. Joyce punched a button, looking at Isabel suspiciously until her call was answered. "Pheebs, it's Joyce. I'm here with Isabel Puddles over at Toby's job site. I'm about to send you a photo. She wants to know if you know the couple Toby's talking to on the deck. Stand by." Joyce fiddled with her phone, waited a few seconds, then held it back to her ear. "Did you get it? Okay, hang on." She handed her phone to Isabel. "She wants to talk to you."

Phoebe wasted no time. "That's Marlene Vanderhoff. I have no idea who *he* is. But if you'll recall, my aunt Doris mentioned she had a handsome gentleman friend with silver hair who picked her up at the club that day. This one fits the bill. Izzy, why are you so interested in Marlene and her boyfriend?"

"I can't talk right now, Phoebe. I'll explain later." Isabel really had no explanation for her nagging suspicion that Parker and his girlfriend might somehow be involved in this mess, but she knew something wasn't adding up . . . or maybe it *was* adding up. She was just handing the phone back to Joyce when she heard Phoebe's voice again.

"Isabel, you've heard about Meg Blackburn, I assume?"

Isabel felt another punch in the stomach as she held the phone back to her ear. "I know she's missing. And they found her car. . . . Is there more?" Isabel winced as she waited for Phoebe's reply.

"Now they've found her purse and her phone. That's the latest around the courthouse, anyway. I guess they have police tape up all around Culpepper Cove right now."

Culpepper Cove was a small, rocky inlet a few miles down the lake from where they were standing, a place only the locals knew about, especially teenage locals. It was there at the cove, sitting in the front seat of a Plymouth Duster over-looking Lake Michigan, that Carl Puddles first kissed Isabel Peabody.

"Oh, no . . . Oh, no . . . This is terrible." Her hand was trembling as she gave the phone back to Joyce without saying good-bye to Phoebe. "We have to go." The deck was empty when they climbed back up the steps. Isabel ran over and poked her head around the corner of the house to see Toby waving good-bye to the couple as they were backing out of the drive in a black luxury sedan. As soon as the car was out of sight, Isabel rushed down the driveway with Joyce trailing be-hind and went straight to her van. "Toby, thank you for your help!" She could see Joyce hesitating as she opened her door.

"Iz, I think I'm going to stay here with Toby." She was obviously worried about her son. "I'll have his dad come and get me in a little bit. Keep us posted about Meg, will you please?"

"Will do!" Isabel yelled as she started up the van. She put it into reverse, and as she checked behind her before pulling out, her heart skipped a beat when she saw a silver pickup truck pulling in, with Glen and Jason inside. After they climbed out, Isabel took a deep breath and put the van back into park, turned off the engine, and got out again, instinctively turning on the charm so that neither of them would suspect she was on to them.

"Glen! I've been looking all over for you! Are you okay? How's your leg?" Glen was more than a little surprised to see this Puddles woman again. He looked around to make sure his four-legged attacker was not with her. Jason was on his cell phone, but after staring at Isabel for a beat, he climbed back into the driver's side of the truck.

"I'm okay . . . just a little sore." He then turned to Toby who had joined them. "Sorry it took so long, boss."

"Did you have Dr. Miller look at that leg?" Toby asked with genuine concern.

Glen hesitated. "Oh . . . no . . . he was out of the office today. I went to see another doctor my sister has over in Shelbyville. I forget his name. Anyway, he took a look and cleaned it out . . . put some bandages on for me." Glen lifted his pant leg to show his bandages. "He said I'll be fine."

Isabel jumped right in. "I want to pay for your doctor's visit, Glen. It's the least I can do. I feel terrible. Just tell me his name and I'll call and make the arrangements."

"No worries, ma'am. The doctor didn't charge me nothin'. Let's just forget it ever happened."

A few things struck Isabel about this exchange. First, the most obvious, was that Dr. Miller was *not* out of the office because Freddie had an appointment with him. Second, that bandage job was definitely not done by a medical professional. Or if it was, he should lose his license. And third, since when did doctors do anything for free?

"Well, all right, then . . . if you're sure. I have to run, folks. You take care of that leg, Glen. Toby, Joyce, it was lovely to see you."

Isabel started to make her way back to the van, but not before she took a quick detour around the back of the pickup. As she rounded the rear of the truck bed, there it was, plain as day, on the right rear quarter panel—a scrape, along with a dent about the size of a grapefruit . . . and it was embedded with white paint to match Meg's white car. Bingo. Isabel's heart was racing as she walked back up the drive. Before getting back into her van, she looked over and noticed Jason staring at her. She forced a smile and waved. "Pretty truck!" she yelled at him. After starting the engine, she backed out slowly, giving Jason—still staring at her—another wave as she cleared the driveway and took off down the road, heading straight for the sheriff's office.

Isabel rushed into the office, breathless from her mad dash across the parking lot. The office was empty except for a nervous-looking Ginny pacing the floor.

"Any word on Meg?!" Isabel yelled. Ginny stopped pacing and gave her a blank stare. Not a good sign. Isabel continued, "Is Grady still over at Culpepper Cove? I need to talk to him ASAP!"

"Everyone's still there . . . Grady, the state police, Larry Blackburn . . . they're all there." Ginny hesitated before sharing more news. "The Coast Guard is off the cove now, too, Iz."

"The Coast Guard? What in the world has the Coast Guard got to do with anything?"

Ginny got quiet for a moment before answering. "They're dragging the cove, Iz. They think Meg might have committed suicide."

Meg's friend Isabel was having none of that. "Absolutely not! Impossible! She's been abducted, Ginny. I'd bet my life on it! And I'd bet my life on knowing exactly who took her, too! I really need to talk to Grady. Can you get him for me?"

"He's not going to like it, Izzy." Isabel gave her cousin a look she had been familiar with since childhood. "Okay, I'll try him on his cell." She picked up the phone and dialed while Isabel stood by anxiously. "Hi, it's me. . . . I know you have your hands full, but I have Isabel here and she really needs to—" Ginny stared at Isabel as she listened to Grady, then nodded. "All right . . . all right, I'll tell her." She hung up the phone, not looking happy. "He says he can't talk to you right now. And he wants me to tell you that he doesn't want you to get any more involved in this than you already are. He wants you to go home and wait for word. It doesn't look good, Iz."

"So because they think Meg's killed herself—which is ridiculous—they're wasting time searching for a body in the lake that's not there instead of going after the people who abducted her and may be planning to kill her? If they haven't already! Well, Ginny, it looks like I have no choice *but* to get more involved." Isabel turned on her heels and rushed out the door as her cousin watched helplessly.

Chapter 17

Isabel was rushing into the parking lot of the sheriff's office just as Beverly Atwater was pulling in. Isabel ignored her, speed-walking right past her and getting into her van without so much as a glance. She had nothing to say right now to some high-priced, high-heel-wearing Detroit lawyer. Beverly jumped out of her car dressed in an outfit that Isabel would have had to work two months at the hardware and knit twenty-five scarves to pay for, and rushed over to the van. It was merely out of small-town politeness that she stopped and put her window down. Beverly, on the other hand, went with the big-city approach. "Where the hell is Culpepper Cove?"

"Well, hello, Beverly . . . I'm fine, thank you . . . and you?" Isabel was always surprised at how challenged city people were when it came to rudimentary good manners. "I'm afraid if this has anything to do with the Jonasson case, I am, as you know, not at liberty to talk. I suggest you go in and talk to Sheriff Pemberton's secretary. Maybe she can give you directions, although it's hard to find if you don't know the back roads."

Isabel put her van into drive and got ready to pull away, then locked eyes with Beverly. "But while the rest of you are out looking for Meg's *body* at the cove, I'm going to go look for *Meg* before it's too late. And, FYI, I'm pretty sure I know who has her."

With that, Beverly ran around to the passenger-side of the van and swung open the door. "They're nuts if they think Meg killed herself. Not a chance. I'm coming with you!"

Before Isabel could object to taking on a passenger, especially this one, Beverly was in the front seat, digging around for her seat belt. Isabel looked her over suspiciously, but quickly realized she might do well to have some backup, although Beverly Atwater would not have been her first choice.

With Beverly now strapped in, Isabel screeched out of the parking lot at breakneck speed, careening onto State Street and instantly unnerving her new copilot. "Whoa! Have you got a spare helmet?"

Isabel was in the zone. "No helmet, but don't worry. Your airbag still works. I think."

After safely clearing the city limits, Isabel turned west and headed back toward the Big Lake. "Okay, so what's this theory of yours, Isabel? Who do you think has Meg?" Beverly asked, keeping one eye on the road.

Isabel approached a slow-moving tractor ahead, pulling a hay wagon, passing it with a *swoosh* and blowing the cap right off the farmer's head. She noticed Beverly's foot was poised over her imaginary brake pedal. "Well, to start with, I'm convinced Tammy Trudlow is behind *all* of this. I know she was in jail the day it happened, but I think she recruited her brother, Glen, and maybe her boyfriend, Jason, to murder Meg's dad. And now, God forbid, maybe Meg, too."

Beverly nodded in agreement. "Well, I've been convinced from the start that Tammy Trudlow was somehow involved. Of course, *proving* it is another story. I do know about Glen Trudlow, and I'm familiar with his buddy Jason's story, too. They were cellmates at Jackson. Both dumb as rocks so they would have needed a ringleader, and Tammy fits the bill. But what makes you so sure it was one of them who fired that nail into Mr. Jonasson's skull?"

Isabel began explaining the source of her epiphany, relaying the events at Poplar Bluff that morning. "So, after Corky's meltdown, and after talking to Toby and learning that the man she had attacked was Tammy's brother, everything became clear as a bell. That otherwise sweet dog remembered Glen *and* the nail gun . . . so she attacked." She looked over at Beverly, but could tell she wasn't completely sold.

"It sounds like a good plot point for a Lassie movie, but I can't put a cocker spaniel on the witness stand, Isabel."

Smug and condescending were not two of Isabel's favorite personality traits but she wasn't planning on making friends with Beverly Atwater anyway, so she ignored the remark and continued. "Okay, well, let me tell you about how I first came to meet Jason Swerley." She then went on to tell Beverly about Jason returning the shovel and the two tarps last week, then coming back with his store credit and making the same purchase that morning.

Beverly raised her eyebrows. "Not a good sign, but circumstantial. Unless we find Meg's body buried and wrapped up in a blue tarp." Beverly was one tough cookie. But Isabel wasn't through.

"Well, then, how about this? Meg said she thought the silver pickup truck that ran her off the road might have clipped her first, right? And if it had, it would have been with the right rear of the truck, correct?"

Beverly's eyes were glued to another tractor ahead. She slammed on her imaginary brakes just before Isabel passed with another *swoosh*. *This* farmer was able to grab his cap before it blew off. Beverly exhaled. Isabel was unfazed as she continued.

"Well, just today I saw the silver pickup truck that Jason, Glen, and Tammy have been tooling around town in, and guess what? It has a dent and a scrape with white paint on the right rear. And what color was Meg's car? White."

Now Beverly was getting on board. "Well, if the paint matches up, then we have forensics, and the makings of a case, or at least a case for attempted murder."

Isabel veered off the road, throwing up some dirt and gravel. Beverly grabbed her armrests and braced herself until they were back on the pavement. "Sorry," Isabel said with a grimace.

"Okay, so where exactly are we going now?" Beverly asked tentatively, "I mean, if our luck holds up and we survive this trip."

"We're going back to the job site where Glen and Jason are working. Then we're going to hide somewhere close by. When they knock off work at five, we'll follow them, discreetly, and if my hunch is right, *hopefully* they'll lead us straight to Meg."

Beverly nodded as she thought this plan over, but she had another pressing question. "So, let's say these three stooges did conspire to murder Meg's father . . . why would they want to do Meg any harm?"

Isabel was only too happy to break it down for her. "Let me put myself in Tammy's shoes, or flip-flops, which is all I've ever seen her in, rain or shine. I have somehow convinced a gullible, lonely, middle-aged single father that I want to be his wife and the stepmother to his four boys. And that man also happens to be the son, and one of two heirs, to a sizable estate upon the death of the family patriarch. So, if I'm an impatient person, who also happens to be a sociopath, I decide I'm going to recruit a couple of flunkie ex-cons to arrange for the murder of that patriarch, which not only gets me closer to benefitting from his death but gets me there much faster. Now, there's only one impediment to my fiancé inheriting the entire estate . . ."

Beverly tied things up. "So getting Meg out of the picture, means my soon-to-be husband inherits *everything*."

Isabel nodded in agreement. "Exactly. But you know getting rid of Meg solves another problem for Miss Congeniality. Meg's already let her brother know she doesn't trust Tammy, nor does she approve of any marriage between the two. I know Meg, and I know she would do everything and anything in her power to keep her brother from marrying that woman. And Tammy knows it, too. Of course she didn't think anybody was going to find out Mr. Jonasson was murdered, or that Junior would be *charged* with that murder. So that had to change things up a little for her, because would she be able to cash in if her fiancé was in prison? But with Meg out of the picture, all she would need was a quickie jailhouse wedding before he was convicted and she would get it all. It's so diabolical, it's hard to believe that girl could come up with it."

Beverly could now see that Isabel's theory was holding water—at least partially. It also made her fear, if she was right, that they might have already made their move. "Isabel, we need to prepare ourselves for the possibility that if you're right about all this, we may be too late."

"Let's not even think about that! Besides, I don't see how they would have had the time today! Glen left my house at about eight forty-five this morning. Meg must have left the farm around nine because Larry called me at noon and said she had been gone three hours. Glen and Jason showed up back at Toby's job site just an hour or so ago . . . so I think they've stashed her somewhere until they can finish the job."

"I sure hope you're right about that, Isabel. The question is, can we find her in time?" Isabel swerved off the road again, kicking up more gravel and putting Beverly back into crash-preparation mode. After exhaling, she continued. "I'm going to be honest with you, Isabel, because, well . . . because I'm not sure I'm going to get out of this van alive, so why not? I thought Earl Jr. was guilty when I took on this case. He had plenty of motive, a shaky alibi, and the murder weapon with his prints and DNA on it was sitting on a shelf in his garage. I was pretty sure even Marcia Clark could get a conviction. I took the case anyway because that's my job. But after spending time with Earl, I became convinced in pretty short order that he was innocent. He just doesn't have it in him. Now we know Tammy couldn't have actually committed the murder because she was in jail. But everything you're telling me makes it more likely than not that she got her lowlife brother and this Jason Swerley character to do her dirty work for her."

Beverly had her eyes on an approaching curve, then felt a wave of relief as Isabel began to slow for it. "Now I know the brother has it in him because he served time for battery and assault with a deadly weapon. I also know that shortly after he was released from prison he went to work in the kitchen at some restaurant around here, and after he was fired for punching out the dishwasher, the owner was concerned enough about his violent nature that he took out a restraining order. So a choirboy he is not. Jason on the other hand is just a petty burglar. But he's not playing with a full deck, and these are just the type of people the likes of Tammy and Glen Trudlow can easily manipulate. I'll also bet if things had gone as planned, and you hadn't discovered that nail in Mr. Jonasson's head, phase two would have been getting rid of Earl Jr. after she finally got him to marry her. Probably Meg, too."

At that moment Isabel spotted a car careening straight toward them, and fast. She swerved onto the shoulder, fearful of a head-on collision . . . but not before she had time to identify the driver screaming into her cell phone. "Speak of the devil . . . and I do mean the devil! That was our friend

Tammy right there! And in quite a hurry as usual . . . That woman's been driving around town lately like she's in a demolition derby!"

Beverly opened her eyes and exhaled again. "Seems to be the norm around here," she said through gritted teeth. "Should we turn around and follow her?"

Just then, off to the right, Isabel noticed the dilapidated old Trudlow farmhouse sitting alone, creepily peeking up from the sea of dead corn stalks surrounding it. A light switched on. "I've got a better idea! Beverly, hang on!"

Isabel cranked the steering wheel to the right, screeching off the asphalt and onto a dirt road so sharply, her two left wheels lifted off the road slightly. Beverly raised both arms and pressed her hands against the roof, bracing for a rollover, as Isabel slammed on the brakes. They slid about twenty-five feet before coming to a stop, engulfed in a cloud of dust. Isabel's passenger stared straight ahead, slowly shaking her head. "Boy, if they don't get you with a nail gun in this county, they'll make sure to take care of you on the open road," Beverly mumbled to herself.

Isabel pointed through the windshield. "You see that broken-down old farmhouse over there? Nobody's lived there in about fifty years. And it's been landlocked for most of that time, so you can't get to it without trespassing. And you know who owns it? Believe it or not, Tammy and Glen Trudlow." Beverly looked puzzled. "I hadn't really thought of Tammy and Glen as part of the landed gentry."

Isabel threw the van into park and turned off the engine. "Come on. Let's go."

"Go where?" Beverly wasn't sure she liked where this was heading, but her partner was already out of the van. Isabel leaned back in.

"If you were going to hide somebody until you figured out how to get rid of them, and you also knew that local law

enforcement was going to be scouring the county looking for
them, an abandoned farmhouse with no roads leading to it
would be a pretty good place to do it, don't you think? And
is it pure coincidence that Tammy was racing away from this
direction two minutes ago?"

Beverly mulled things over for a second. "But we should
probably get a warrant."

"A *search* warrant? There's no time for that! If Meg is in
that farmhouse right now, and that gang has unfinished business to attend to, they'll be back here sooner than later. We
need to move now!"

Beverly opened her door. "You're right. Let's go. Wait!"
She looked down at her feet. "Any chance you have an extra
pair of shoes in here? These are Jimmy Choos . . . I'll destroy
them in that cornfield."

"Well, it's good to see you've got your priorities in order,
Beverly." Isabel was beyond annoyed, but Beverly defended
her position. "I just bought these yesterday! They were three
hundred dollars! On sale!"

Isabel was slightly disgusted. "I haven't spent three hundred dollars on shoes *total* in my entire life! Hold on a minute." She climbed back into the van, pulled out her waders,
and presented them to Beverly.

"What am I supposed to do with these? Fly-fish?" Beverly
said, furrowing her perfectly tweezed eyebrows.

"It's the best I can do. Or else you can go barefoot and
deal with the pain." Isabel held up the waders for her. "Now,
kick off your Johnny *Whatevers* and step in. I'll adjust the sus-
penders for you."

Beverly thought it over for a second, then tossed her shoes
back into the van. It took a minute, but she was finally suited
up in the waders and ready to go. The meticulously coiffed
Beverly Atwater now looked like Martha Stewart posing for
the cover of *Field & Stream*.

The two women began cutting through the dead corn-stalks with only the rusty dome of the grain silo to guide them. Minutes later they came to a clearing of overgrown grass that surrounded the old farmhouse. It was just as creepy as Isabel remembered from childhood. There was no sign of life, but there were what looked like fresh tire tracks circling around the grass and disappearing down a narrow tractor trail that led out to the main road. Isabel's spirits were buoyed.

The two crept up to the house slowly and stealthily, but they did not see any signs of life. They cautiously stepped up onto the porch, and Isabel tiptoed over to what she re-membered to be the kitchen window to peek through. The kitchen also looked exactly as she had remembered it. The only thing out of place was what appeared to be a large fast-food beverage cup sitting on the old kitchen table. That was unusual. Isabel tiptoed back and carefully pushed open the kitchen door just enough to slip in, signaling Beverly, who awkwardly followed behind in her waders. Isabel carefully picked up the cup and held it up for Beverly to see. It was from Arby's. She gave it a little shake. Their eyes widened in disbelief. There were still ice cubes inside! Now they knew they were on to something. The improbable detective team sprang into action, instinctively splitting up, with Isabel run-ning upstairs, while Beverly waddled through the downstairs, checking out each room. A minute later they met back in the kitchen shaking their heads. Nothing.

"Let's check the cellar," Isabel whispered.

"Why are we whispering?" Beverly whispered back.

"I don't know. . . . It just feels like we should be whisper-ing." Isabel reached over and opened the same cellar door she remembered going through as a kid, and with the same trepi-dation. They looked at each other, took a deep breath, and began to inch their way down the creaky stairs and into the pitch-black basement, until Beverly remembered she had a fix for that. Reaching through the top of her waders and into her jacket pocket, she pulled out her phone, and, presto, they had a flashlight. "Where did that come from?" Isabel whispered in wonder.

"I forgot; it's an app I have on my phone," Beverly replied.

Isabel shook her head, unable to process such advanced technology. "Who knew? I really might have to consider getting one of those," she said.

"They're very convenient," Beverly offered.

When they reached the bottom of the stairs, they found the spooky, icy cold basement, empty, except for some old wooden cherry crates stacked in haphazard piles in one corner, and an old hand-crank washtub in another, all covered in cobwebs. Beverly carefully scanned the cellar with her phone flashlight until the eerie silence was broken by a tremendous crash. The two women grabbed each other and simultaneously screamed. Frozen in terror, they almost collapsed in relief when they saw a frightened cat race across the dirt floor. Desperate to escape the intruders, the cat zigzagged across the floor until it finally slipped out between the two cellar doors that led outside, shooting a welcome sliver of light across the basement.

After catching their breath and checking their heartbeats, Beverly picked her phone up from the floor and reengaged the flashlight when, to their horror, half-hidden behind the cherry crates, they spotted a blue tarp lying in a heap. "Oh, God . . . Oh, please, no . . . Please, no," Isabel said softly. She was paralyzed for a split second before running over to the blue tarp. "We're too late! Beverly . . . we're too late."

Isabel dropped to her knees onto the dirt floor beside the tarp-covered heap, while Beverly stood behind her, shaking so badly she could barely hold her phone. Isabel took a breath and ripped back the tarp to find that their greatest fear was realized. There was Meg, curled up, motionless, her arms bound together behind her back with duct tape, and her legs bound at the ankles. She was blindfolded with an old handkerchief and a piece of duct tape was covering her mouth.

"They murdered her. . . . Those animals murdered her," Beverly said as she knelt down reverently next to Meg. The two took a moment, then Isabel gently pulled off the blindfold—and to their amazement, there was Meg, staring back at them. The two women gasped. "Oh, thank God! Meg, you're alive! You're alive! Beverly, call nine-one-one!"

Beverly immediately began fumbling with her phone, while Isabel yanked the duct tape from Meg's mouth and heard her first, barely audible word. "Ouch."

"Sorry! Meg, you're alive!"

Meg stared back at her. "Am I? Are you sure?" Isabel lifted her up slightly and held her. "You found me, Isabel." Meg's eyes began to flood with tears as she looked over Isabel's shoulder and spotted her accomplice. "Beverly, you're here, too."

"Yes, we're both here and we're going to get you *out* of here pronto!" Isabel assured her. Both she and Beverly began undoing the tape from Meg's hands and wrists, complicated by the fact that Meg's right wrist was still in a cast. "Beverly, you work on her legs. I don't suppose that phone of yours has a scissors, does it?"

Beverly got busy unraveling the tape from around Meg's ankles. Having been tied up for several hours by now, Isabel knew she had to be suffering, her pain compounded by her injuries from her accident just a few days before. "What kind of monsters would do something like this to another human being?" Isabel asked Beverly and the universe.

"The same kind of monsters who would shoot an old man in the head with a nail gun," Beverly replied.

At the very moment they were able to free her, Meg

started getting faint and going limp. "Come on, Meg. We can do this!" Isabel coached.

Meg started to come to a little. "Iz . . . I need some water . . . please . . . I'm so . . ." Her voice trailed off again.

Isabel was at a loss. "Meg, you're in the old Trudlow farmhouse. There's no water here." Then a light went on. "Wait! Beverly! Go grab that Arby's cup upstairs. It still has ice in it!"

Beverly got up rather inelegantly, thanks to her waders, and made her way to the stairs. "Have you called nine-one-one?" Isabel yelled after her.

"I can't get a signal!" Beverly yelled back as she wobbled up the stairs to retrieve the Arby's cup. "Maybe I can get one upstairs!"

Isabel watched helplessly as Meg went from faint and limp to sobbing uncontrollably. She did her best to comfort her, but there was no time for a nervous breakdown. "We need to get you out of here, Meg! You need to pull it together! You're going to be fine. But those people who took you are going to be back here any minute."

That did the trick. Meg managed to get to her feet just as Beverly showed up with the Arby's cup. She removed the lid and handed it to Meg, who got as much water out of it as she could, then started to chew the ice.

"Come on, let's get going," Isabel said, pulling her by the arm.

No sooner had the three begun to move toward the stairs than they heard a car door slam, then another. Isabel whispered, "It's them. It's Glen and Jason."

Meg was confused. "Who are Glen and Jason? Are they the ones who brought me here?" she asked, trying to keep her emotions under control.

"Most likely," Beverly added.

"Glen *Trudlow*? Tammy's brother?" Meg asked.

"Yes. The Donny and Marie of Kentwater County," Isabel quipped—inappropriately, given the situation.

Muted voices coming from outside trailed down into the basement, followed by the sound of the kitchen door squeaking open, then heavy footsteps clopping across the floor above them. Beverly was still fidgeting with her phone.

"Damnit! Why can't I get a signal? Crap!"

Meg had the answer. "This is a dead zone. You won't get a signal here."

Isabel was done with the 911 plan. And the next time somebody told her how convenient cell phones were, she would certainly have a story to tell. "Let's see if we can get out through those cellar doors where that cat escaped."

"Where will we go, Iz? What if they come after us? They'll kill us." Meg knew better than anyone how evil these people were.

"What's the difference if they kill us in the basement or in a cornfield?" Beverly offered.

Isabel knew she had a point, but Beverly's lack of a winning spirit wasn't exactly helpful. Right now she needed Meg to keep it together. "Meg, you just have to follow us. My van is parked over on that little dirt road, the one that leads to Jonasson Pond."

Meg started getting emotional again. "I remember when we used to ice skate on—"

Isabel cut her off and patted her on the back. "We'll reminisce later. Now all you have to do is make it through that cornfield and into my van and you're home free. You can do this."

Isabel was coming off as a pillar of confidence, but inside she was more like a wobbly bowl of Jell-O. She knew this was a risky move, but what choice did they have?

Dusk was beginning to settle outside. This was good. It got dark fast this time of year, so if they could make a break for it without being seen by the two goons upstairs, they could make their way back to the van pretty quickly—assuming the cellar doors were not chained or somehow locked. But that cat had made an easy exit, so Isabel was feeling optimistic. The three women joined hands and moved closer to the doors, helped along with more team confidence building from Beverly. "What if they're locked? Just because the cat got out doesn't mean we can. We'll be trapped like rats. Dead rats."

Isabel turned to her. "You were never a cheerleader, were you, Beverly."

If the doors were locked, Isabel knew, the only plan remaining would be for them to hide behind those cherry crates, and when Meg's captors came downstairs, three middle-aged women, one of them injured, would have to overpower two young men, both ex-cons. Not terrific odds.

"Please don't let them be locked," Beverly mumbled as they made their way to the stone steps leading to the cellar doors.

Meg offered a shred of optimism. "I think that's how they got me down here . . . but I was pretty out of it."

"Let's hope you're right," Isabel whispered as she crept up the steps, took a deep breath, and slowly pushed up on the right door with her right shoulder. When she had raised it about a foot, they all breathed a sigh of relief. Isabel lowered the door softly and turned to her teammates to share the game plan. "Okay. Now, on three, I'm going to push this side open again, climb out, and hold the door while you two slip out. Beverly, you come out after me and help Meg out. Then make a break for the cornfield." She knew this was a pretty big ask for a woman with a broken wrist and fractured ribs who had been hog-tied for several hours, and another one in waist-high waders. "Then I want you to head toward the sunset and you'll run straight into the road where we left the van. I'll follow right behind you. Got it?" Beverly and Meg nodded.

"Okay, on three . . . One, two, three." Isabel carefully pushed open the door again, poking her head up like a meerkat to make sure the coast was clear. She quickly signaled Beverly, who climbed through the doorway, then reached back down to grab Meg's good hand, pulling her up as instructed. They both looked back at Isabel who mouthed a very emphatic *go*.

Beverly kept a tight grip on Meg as they made their way across the clearing. It wasn't ballet, but they managed to make it across and disappear into the cornfield. So far, so good. Isabel cautiously began to lower the door when, out of nowhere, there was a flash of movement. She looked down to see another cat leaping out of the darkened basement and up the steps, grazing her leg before it tore across the grass clearing toward the barn. Isabel was so startled she lost her grip on the cellar door. She winced and pulled up her shoulders as she waited for it to slam shut. When it did, and with quite a bang, she knew she was in trouble. Spotting an old overgrown shrub along the side of the house just a few feet away, she dived behind it. Once hidden, she realized she was right under the kitchen window, and could hear Glen and Jason inside.

"What the hell was that?" Glen asked Jason, who seemed to shrug his answer.

"Wind? A ghost? Maybe one'a your ancestors makin' themselfs known."

"Are you sure you taped her up good?" Glen asked.

Jason scoffed. "Ain't no way that lady's gettin' herself free until we decide to *let* her free," he proclaimed with confidence.

"What do you mean until we *let her free*?" Glen asked his partner in crime.

"Tammy said after this deal was squared away we would let her go." Jason's reply was met with an evil cackle.

"Tammy sold you a bill'a goods. We're gonna let her go,

all right. Let her go right into a hole we're gonna dig in one'a these cornfields."

Jason was angry now. "You two already got me involved with one murder I didn't plan on gettin' involved with. I ain't lettin' you get me involved in another one!"

Glen did his best to placate his friend, apparently not realizing until now how anti-murder his prison buddy was. "Well, you can take it up with Tammy. But in the meantime let's go down and check on her. Wait . . . let me get my gun."

Isabel could hear them heading for the stairs. That was her chance to make a run for it. She burst out from behind the shrub and raced across the clearing, charging into the darkening cornfield. Fifty feet in, she almost stumbled over Meg and Beverly, who were hunkered down together. "Please tell me nobody fell and sprained their ankle," she asked, hoping they had not somehow been transported into an escape scene from a Lifetime movie.

"We couldn't make out which way is west. The sun's already set!" Beverly said frantically.

Isabel looked up and around. She couldn't tell where they were now, either. "Well, we just need to run in any direction other than the one we came from. They have guns!"

Beverly gave her a look. "They're murderers! Of course they have guns!" Isabel jumped up to see if she could see over the cornstalks. No luck. Then she had an idea. Reaching into her pocket, she pulled out her car keys and began to push the lock button, hoping to hear that familiar chirp indicating the doors were already locked. And, lo and behold, there it was. Without speaking, they all understood what to do next. Isabel continued pushing the button every few seconds, and the three escapees followed each chirp until they finally had the van in sight. Looking in both directions before leaving the cover of the cornfield, they made a break for it. Then, just as they began to scamper into the van, they heard a spooky, singsongy voice in the distance. "Missus Blaaaackbuuuurn!" The voice was too close for comfort. "We're here to help you, Missus Blackburn. We're with the sheriff's department. We're here to rescue you!"

"Let's add impersonating an officer to your murder and kidnapping charges, you dirtbags!" Beverly mumbled as she slid the side door closed. "Okay, where's the seat belt back here?"

Isabel looked back. "You're kidding me, right?" With that she started the engine and slammed the van into drive, fishtailing onto the dirt road at the very moment Jason and Glen sprang out of the cornfield. Glen was wielding a gun and still limping from his dog bite. Isabel instinctively swerved to miss them both and sped past.

"You should have just hit them!" Beverly yelled from the backseat as the van sped down the road, leaving their assailants in a cloud of dust.

"Oh, my God, Isabel! We did it! We got away!" Meg was ecstatic.

"We're not in the clear yet! Beverly, maybe you can get your cell phone to work *now*?" Isabel implored.

Beverly remained silent until she finally fessed up. "I think I dropped my phone back in that cellar."

Isabel looked back over her shoulder, then again a couple more times just to get the full picture. There in the backseat of her van was Michigan's best-known criminal defense attorney, sitting there helplessly and swimming up to her chest in a pair of rubber waders. Her expensive cream-colored designer pantsuit—whatever could be seen of it above her waders—was now more of a creamy mud color. Her once stylish blonde hair was now hanging over her face and tangled with dried corn silk. She was missing her left earring, part of her right sleeve, and all of her dignity. Beverly Atwater was just too pitiful a sight right now to be reprimanded, so Isabel focused her attention back on the road. "I guess it won't work here, anyway. I'm just going to drive us straight to Culpepper Cove."

"That's where they took me after they grabbed me in the IGA parking lot. The one with the red hair and the ponytail was hiding in the backseat of Larry's car. When I got in, he put a gun to the back of my head and ordered me to drive. The other one was waiting at the cove. Then they blindfolded me, tied me up, or duct-taped me, I guess, and put me into the back of a pickup truck."

"Well, that's what you get for shopping at the IGA, Meg. Those kinds of things don't happen at the Kroger," Isabel scolded.

"They had a sale on frozen pizzas. The boys love frozen pizza. Why are we going back to the cove, Isabel?"

Isabel was focused on the rearview mirror now, making sure they weren't being chased. "Last we knew, Grady, Larry, and the state police were there looking for you."

"And the Coast Guard," Beverly added. "They were dragging the lake, looking for your body."

Meg was distraught. "Oh, no! Larry and the boys think I'm dead?"

Evidently determined to make matters worse at every possible turn, Beverly chimed in again. "Not only *that*. They think you killed yourself."

Before that breaking news could even sink in for Meg, Isabel looked to her right as they roared into a dirt road intersection and was suddenly blinded by headlights. A car was coming straight at them and was about to hit them broadside. Meg turned and saw the car racing at them, too, but she remained silent and stoic. Given what she had been through in the past seventy-two hours, Meg Blackburn had the look of a woman who had just come to a very clear realization that the universe wanted her dead. Beverly, on the other hand, began screaming like a wild banshee.

Isabel cranked the wheel hard to the left, hoping that would give the other car enough room to swerve around them instead of T-boning them. They all squeezed their eyes and braced for impact, with Beverly still screaming at the top of her lungs. And then suddenly . . . nothing, only silence. Miraculously the car had gotten around them. When Isabel opened her eyes, all she could see were thick clouds of dust in her headlights. They had miraculously avoided a collision that very likely would have killed them all.

Beverly pulled herself up off the floor and back into her seat, adjusting her waders and shaking her head, mumbling something about the humiliation of being discovered dead in a minivan, wearing a pair of waders. But before they could even get their bearings again, a man in a baseball cap came running up to the passenger side and opened Meg's door. "Is everybody all right?"

"We're fine. But we need your help," Isabel pleaded.

Beverly leaned forward to address the man, trying to regain some composure and assert her authority, which was a tricky thing to pull off in her present condition. "My name is Beverly Atwater. I'm an attorney. You may have heard of me."

"No, ma'am, I don't believe I have."

Beverly waved him off. "Doesn't matter. Now, please listen very carefully. I need you to call the Kentwater Sheriff's Department right away and tell them that I'm with Meg Blackburn and Isabel Puddles, and that we're, well, we're wherever we are right now. You have a cell phone, I presume?"

"Doesn't everybody these days, Ms. Atwater? But I'm afraid mine is out of juice at the moment. Always seems to happen when it's least convenient, doesn't it?" the man replied to Beverly while smiling strangely first at Meg, then over at Isabel.

"Well, that's just terrific!" Beverly said, throwing her arms up. "You know, if you're going to race around the backroads like some bootlegger on the run from the feds, it might be a good idea to have ready access to nine-one-one!"

The man smiled. "This is a dead zone anyway, ma'am. You need to drive a few miles east to get any cell reception."

Isabel kept staring at the man. Why did he look so familiar? She looked over at the dust-coated black sedan parked several feet away, then looked back at the man just as he lifted and adjusted his Cleveland Indians baseball cap, uncovering a head of thick gray hair. This time he was wearing a menacing smirk. And then it hit her . . . It was Parker! He *was* somehow in on this, just as she suspected! Isabel threw the van into drive and stepped on the gas. Meg almost tumbled out her open door before Isabel reached over and grabbed her by her jacket and yanked her back inside.

Beverly screamed. "Oh my gaaaaaaaaaawd," she moaned. "Here we go again! What are you doing, Isabel!"

"He's with them!" Isabel screamed back.

"Who's with who?" Beverly yelled from the backseat.

"Parker!" Isabel yelled back. "He's the one with the silver pickup . . . the man Glen and Jason have been working for!"

They were now racing down the road as fast as a fourteen-year-old Chrysler Town & Country with 182,000 miles on it could take them, and heading back toward the main road. And then they heard the gunshot. Isabel instantly felt one of her rear tires blow. "They hit us!" she yelled as she began to lose control of the van, fishtailing back and forth until finally careening off the road and into a drainage ditch, coming to an abrupt stop, almost exactly where they had been parked in the first place. This escape was not going well at all.

Chapter 18

Beverly was back on the floor muttering to herself again as the dust settled and the van began to list slightly to one side. Meg remained in a quasi-catatonic state.

"Is everybody okay?" Isabel asked as she tried to catch her breath. But before anybody could answer, there was Glen Trudlow again, tapping on the driver's-side window with his gun. Isabel looked away and into the rearview mirror, where she saw Lou Parker racing up behind them in his car and then skidding to a halt. He climbed out, slammed his door, and came straight toward the right side of the van with a tire iron in his hand, and in one rage-fueled stroke smashed open the large side window where Beverly was sitting. Shattered glass flew through the interior. By the time they lifted their heads, Parker had already slid open the door and was holding a gun to Beverly's head.

"Well, I'm sorry it's come down to this, ladies, but it looks like we have a problem on our hands. And I'm afraid I see only one way of solving it."

Beverly and Meg were frozen in terror, but Isabel found her tongue. "You don't really think you're going to get away with this, do you, Mr. Parker?" He was clearly unnerved to discover she knew his name, but he tried to conceal it. "The sheriff's department, the state police, and the FBI are all looking for Meg as we speak. Once they discover Beverly and I are missing—if they haven't already—they're going to be swarming all over this county looking for us, too. You and the rest of your motley crew won't stand a chance." Isabel threw in the FBI reference in an attempt to shake him up. Apparently it didn't work.

Parker smiled. "Well, then, I guess we'll just have to make sure we hide you somewhere they'll never think to look. And when I say hide *you*, I mean your *bodies*." Brandishing his own gun, he ordered Isabel and Meg into the backseat with Beverly as he climbed back out of the van and waved Glen over. "You have more duct tape?"

"Yes, boss," Glen answered like a Marine reporting for duty. All that was missing was a salute. "But it's back at the house." He stared at Parker blankly.

"Well, go get it, you idiot!" Parker screamed. "And is that barn door unlocked!"

"I think so, boss," Glen replied, his voice wavering.

"We've already established that *thinking* isn't really your thing, is it, Glen? Make *sure* it is! We're going to stash this van with them in it until I can figure out what to do!"

Glen limped off as fast as he could until Parker whistled and stopped him in his tracks. "Wait! Get back here! We need to get this van out of sight before someone comes along. We'll tape 'em up in the barn. Jason! You get over here, too!"

Jason appeared at his boss's side in a flash. "You get behind the wheel," he ordered. Then, back to Glen, "You're going to help me push."

Jason ran around the back of the van and climbed into the driver's seat. The engine was still running, so he slipped it into reverse as Glen and Parker began pushing from the front. After some rocking back and forth they were finally able to get the van out of the ditch and back onto the dirt road. Jason shut off the engine to await his marching orders. The brief silence was interrupted by the sound of another car approaching, one with a bad muffler. For a moment Isabel thought this was good news, but when she looked over her shoulder, she saw a familiar old rust bucket: it was Tammy. "Well, it looks like the gang's all here," she told her seatmates.

Tammy parked several feet in front of the van. Parker looked up and cursed under his breath, then yelled at Jason. "Keep an eye on them. I need to go talk to Tammy. Looks like she's about to have another one of her fits." He turned back to his three captives. "And if you ladies try to make a break for it, I'll shoot you like rabbits."

"You say the cutest things," Isabel replied calmly, stealing a line from an old movie. She couldn't remember which one, but this wasn't the time to polish up her *Jeopardy!* skills. They watched Parker tuck his gun into his pants and approach Tammy cautiously, as one might a wounded wildebeest. She was already leaning against the side of her car smoking, looking as if she had a lot on her mind, and none of it good. The two immediately got into a heated exchange, with Glen standing next to them, silent and slack-jawed. Jason looked on through the windshield, leaning over the steering wheel and wearing an expression that fell somewhere between concerned and afraid. Nobody could hear exactly what was being said, but after a couple of minutes of intense arguing, Parker's voice suddenly rang out. "Tammy, you need to calm down!"

Jason kept his eyes peeled on the scene unfolding in the middle of the road. "You'd need a tranquilizer gun to calm that one down. She scares the bejesus out of me. I never met anybody on the inside any meaner than that woman." Then, turning back to his hostages, "And I was on a cell block with a serial killer!" Isabel was surprised Jason had decided to talk to them out of the blue like this, so she decided to take the opportunity to try to engage him. She remembered reading an article somewhere about how to survive a hostage situation. It said that if you remained calm and talked to your captors, you had a much better chance of surviving. The point being to humanize yourself *and* them, making it less likely they would want to harm you. Of course she had no idea this was information that would ever become useful to a middle-aged Michigan woman who was the president of her knitting circle. "How'd you get mixed up with these people, anyway, Jason?" Isabel asked him. "You seem like a pretty sensible young man. I don't know much about Parker, but these Trudlows come from a long line of—"

"Criminals and lowlifes!" Meg was back, and with a vengeance. "Which one of you deranged animals killed my father?" Meg had apparently not read the same article Isabel had. "Do you know my brother is sitting in a jail cell right now, facing a life sentence for a murder he didn't commit! And my four nephews are facing a life sentence without their father! How do you people live with that?"

Jason slowly turned back to Meg. "I had nothin' to do with killin' your daddy, ma'am. That was Tammy's idea, but they was in this together. And it was Glen that did him in. I had nothin' to do with it—nothin'! I only just learned how that all went down when Glen got drunk on sloe gin and Mountain Dew the other night and told me everything. Boy, I wish I never agreed to come up here. I should'a known Tammy was up to no good. And her brother does anything she tells him to do. He's afraid of her, too."

Meg managed to get her temper under control. "My poor brother is sitting in jail, accused of killing his own father, and he still refuses to believe Tammy could have had anything to do with it. He still thinks she loves him."

"Well, your brother is lucky he *is* in jail, because I'd bet my life that after she got him to marry her, he was gonna be the very next one on her hit list!"

"So, murdering Mr. Jonasson was all about Tammy getting her hands on Junior's money?" Isabel asked, reaching over and grabbing Meg's arm, knowing this conversation had to be heartbreaking for her.

"Of course it was," Jason replied. "She smelled money, and once she was on that scent, she was gonna get to it, no matter what it took. Tammy would crawl over her dead grandpa to steal her grandma's purse. She's as stone cold as they get." Jason turned his attention back to the argument between Parker and Tammy, then shook his head. Isabel distracted him again.

"How did this plan come about, Jason?" He kept his eye on the argument, but still seemed surprisingly eager to talk.

"I don't have no idea what the plan was. I didn't plan the plan. There was one plan, and then when this Parker come along, there was another plan."

"Why is Parker involved? What's in it for him?" Isabel asked.

"All I know is it has to do with a whole lot of money, and there's some kind'a deal where Glen and Tammy would get their old family farm back. Don't know why anybody would care about that spooky old house and a few acres of land, but Tammy is determined to get that farm back."

Isabel was quick to follow up again. "But how did you and the Trudlows get together with Parker?"

"Glen met him when he was workin' in the kitchen at the golf course after he got released. That's how Glen and me got to be friends—we was on kitchen duty at Jackson. Anyway, Parker was carryin' on with some married woman at the club and Glen caught 'em together, you know, alone in the banquet room. Parker paid him to keep quiet about it. Then he offered Glen a job after he got fired for whatever he got fired for. I forget."

"And that married woman Glen caught Parker with was Marlene Vanderhoff," Isabel surmised.

"Marlene, yeah. I never met her, but I seen her. I guess her husband died not long after that happened, so her and her boyfriend ended up gettin' engaged. Don't know nothin' more about her 'cept she's a rich widow. So then Parker hired Glen to help out with some stuff while him and Marlene finished building that big old house over on the lake. Well, you seen it today. That place must'a cost a million bucks. Anyway, Glen called me a couple weeks ago to come up and help him build a deck. I was a carpenter apprentice before I went in, and he knew I was flat broke. And Parker was payin' good money."

Isabel kept talking to him calmly and politely. "So, how did you end up working for Toby?" she asked, hoping against all hope that Toby wasn't somehow mixed up with this band of criminals.

"Parker said he didn't think we could handle building the deck on our own, but by then I think he had another job in mind, if you know what I mean." He looked at Meg sheepishly. "But I ain't gonna go into that. Anyway, he hired that local kid, Toby, and then asked him to hire us to help *him* out, but like I said, I think it was all just a cover. That Toby's a real good carpenter. I'm okay . . . Glen couldn't build a birdhouse . . . well, not one any bird would wanna live in." A bolt of anger suddenly struck Jason. "I just came up here to work! I needed the money! I didn't plan to get involved in any murder or any kidnapping!" Jason got quiet. "I was tryin' to turn over a new leaf!" He looked back at Meg. "I'm very sorry about your daddy, ma'am, and your brother. I truly am. I didn't have nothin' to do with any of that. And I didn't have no idea when he told me to meet him over by the lake this morning that he was gonna show up there with you holdin' a gun at your head. But what could I do? I don't have no gun! Glen wouldn't think nothing about shootin' me if I didn't cooperate. I watched him nearly choke a man to death for stealing a bag'a Skittles outta his cell. Those Trudlows have killin' in their blood, I'm tellin' ya!"

Isabel wanted to keep him talking. "So, what was this plan to kidnap Meg all about?"

Jason slowly shook his head. "I really don't know. After we got her to the farm, Tammy said we was just gonna keep her stashed for a bit . . . something about gettin' her outta the way until some contract got signed." He turned to Meg again. "She didn't say nothin' about killin' you! I would not have gone along with that! I promise I wouldn't." Jason's face was expressing more and more remorse. "When I got out, I swore I was never gonna do nothin' that would get me sent back to prison."

"And yet here you are, Jason," Beverly offered. "At minimum you'll be charged with accessory to murder, and now three counts of kidnapping. That's a life sentence."

Why didn't this woman know when to shut up? Isabel thought.

Jason was suddenly rattled. "There ain't no way I'm goin' back in! No way!" He looked back at his partners, who were still standing in the road, yelling at each other. "What the hell are they still arguing about?"

"Why were you buying tarps and a shovel at the hardware?" Isabel asked, trying to get him back to the story and play on his guilt.

"That's where I know you from! You're the lady from the hardware! I don't s'pose I won that lawn tractor, did I?"

Isabel almost felt bad for him now. "No. I'm sorry."

Jason continued. "No, I didn't expect to. I ain't never won nothin' in my life, not even a scratcher ticket. Anyway, Glen gave me a whole list of stuff to buy that day. I had no idea what it was for. Come to find out they had planned to use it to get rid of . . ." He looked at Meg again, who turned her head away. "Well, it turned out they didn't need it, after all. When I brought that stuff back, I was just lookin' to put a few dollars in my pocket. I'm still flat broke. They ain't paid me a nickel yet! That's why I didn't want no store credit. You know I don't really want to talk about this anymore in front of . . ." He motioned to Meg with his head.

Meg laughed one of those laughs that had nothing to do with funny. "Well, this is an interesting time to become sensitive to my feelings! Go ahead, Jason. I'm mostly numb by now."

"Well, all right. This is how I heard it, anyway. Tammy sent Glen out to your daddy's farm. Glen said he was just plannin' to snatch him and bring him back to the old farmhouse. He was hunkered down in the brush, watchin' him for a while. He said the old man, Mr. Jonasson, I mean, had been doing some work on his porch before he sat down."

"And had Mr. Jonasson been using a nail gun?" Isabel asked.

"I guess so. Glen said there was one just layin' there on the porch. So he decided it would be best to just walk up and tell him some story about his truck breakin' down, and then pull out his gun and make him go with him. He had his pickup parked just outta sight."

"Parker's silver pickup?" Isabel confirmed.

"Yes, ma'am. But when he pulled his gun out, Mr. Jonasson got up and tried to wrestle it away from him, and he did. I guess he knocked it off the porch. So Glen said he shoved him back into his chair and grabbed that nail gun and was gonna just knock him out, but then the thing fired on accident." He turned to Meg in a bizarre attempt to comfort her. "He probably didn't feel a thing, ma'am. I bet he ever knew what hit him."

Meg responded with a look of contained rage that almost took his breath away. Jason turned away as if he'd just seen a ghost, then refocused his attention on Isabel. "Glen said he was about to cart his body off to the truck when this dog appeared outta nowhere and came straight for him. He made a break for a ladder that was leaning there against the house and climbed up on the roof. He was afraid to come down for a good while, but finally he jumped off the back porch and snuck back to the truck."

As Jason continued, Isabel felt a pang of pride for Corky. "Tammy was in jail for shopliftin', which a'course now I know she done on purpose so she couldn't be fingered for nothin'. I figured that out on my own. Then your brother went and bailed her out the next day and told her your daddy died of a stroke. So her and Glen thought they had got away with the perfect crime. But then I guess somebody at the funeral home found the nail."

Isabel stared blankly at Jason, while Beverly gave her a quick, knowing glance.

"When Tammy found out they was gonna do this autopsy, she called and read Glen the riot act up one side and down the other. So then he thinks he better come up with a plan to cover his tracks."

Isabel was finally putting this all together "And that was to go back and hide that nail gun in Earl Jr's garage, to make it look like *he* killed his father."

"Yep. He went back the next day. Thought he was bein' smart, but when he told Tammy what he done, she went ballistic on him again. She wasn't very happy about her boyfriend maybe goin' to prison on account of her plan was to marry him. He was her ticket to easy street. And when Tammy ain't happy, well . . ." Jason got lost in thought for a moment before continuing. "When I heard about all this, that's when I knew it didn't matter if I had nothin' to do with it or not. As long as I was an ex-con hangin' around with these two, I was goin' down with 'em, sure as day."

"Why didn't you just go to the police?" Isabel asked.

Jason forced a smile. "Well, ma'am, I don't have what you would call a real good relationship with the police. But I did think about it. And I think Tammy thought I might do just that, so she warned me if they got caught, she'd tell 'em I did it, and not Glen. That woman is pure evil."

"So, when they asked you to come back to the hardware this morning to pick up the shovel and the tarps again, it was because they planned to murder Meg and bury her body?" Isabel asked as she grabbed Meg's arm again.

Jason looked puzzled. "I didn't go back in there today."

Isabel looked at him suspiciously. "But I found the credit slip I wrote you the other day in the cash drawer just this morning."

Jason shook his head. "Must'a been Glen that came in. I gave him that credit slip. I wasn't gonna use it. But, yeah, I guess that's what they was plannin' to do, same as they was plannin' to do with . . ." He looked at Meg with a sympathetic smile. She shot daggers back.

Just when Isabel was feeling confident that she was making some headway in her effort to peel Jason from the herd, another gunshot rang out. They all jumped in their seats and then looked up the road, but nobody was standing there anymore. Then another shot rang out. A terrified-looking Jason immediately started up the van and threw it into drive. Seconds later they were wobbling back down the dirt road toward the Trudlow farmhouse and going at a pretty good clip, despite the blown-out back tire.

"What are you doing?" Beverly yelled at him.

Jason cranked the wheel hard, and suddenly they were bouncing wildly through the cornfield. "I'm drivin' us into that barn 'til I know what's goin' on! Don't know about you three, but I'd rather not get shot if I can help it!"

Moments later they were inside the barn, surrounded in darkness. Jason jumped out of the van and closed the doors behind them, then climbed back inside. "Now we're just gonna wait here until we know what happened back there."

They all took a moment to compose themselves until Beverly spoke up. "You might want to turn the engine off unless succumbing to carbon monoxide poisoning is more attractive to you than a gunshot wound."

Jason turned off the engine, and seconds later, the barn lit up. Everyone swiveled their heads to look out the rear window to see the barn doors swinging open and a pair of headlights shining in.

Then they heard Glen yelling, "Jason! Get out here and help us!"

Jason hesitated, took a deep breath, then jumped out of the van and stopped cold. "Holy crap! You shot him?! Is he dead?"

Then for the first time they heard Tammy's voice. "I hope so! He ought to be. I shot him twice. And he stopped breathin'. That's usually a pretty good sign. Yes, he's dead, you moron! Now, help us out here!"

Isabel was able to lift her head just far enough to see Glen dragging Lou Parker into the barn by his feet and dropping him at the side of the van. She whispered to the girls, "They killed Parker." Neither of them reacted. Nothing could surprise them at this point.

"Now we need to figure out what to do with him," Tammy said as she sat down on a nearby bale of hay, presumably to think.

"Hey, what happened to his baseball cap?" Glen asked in earnest. "I liked that cap."

"Shut up, Glen," Tammy barked. "You want to wear the cap of a dead guy? What are you, sick?" said the woman with two murders now under her belt.

Glen got quiet. "I just thought it was a nice cap, is all. No point of it going to waste. There wasn't no blood on it."

"I swear, Glen. Sometimes I wonder if you've got sense enough to pound sand." She took a moment and turned to her second cohort, "Jason, why are you starin' at me?"

"Why'd you have to go and shoot him, Tammy? Don't we have enough trouble on our hands here already?"

"I shot him because I figured out he was plannin' to screw us over. I found out he couldn't get us that easement to our land we need like he promised. You know why? 'Cuz it turns out he don't own that land, the dirty liar. That girlfriend, Marlene, she owns it. He says she don't know nothin' about any of this and he planned to keep it that way. I told him the only reason we done what we done was to get our family's land back so we could make our own windmill deal. He said we should just be happy with the five grand he gave us up front, and if we weren't, well, tough luck, because he had proof we did the old man in. So that's when I shot him— twice. The second time was just for fun."

Glen fully supported his sister's decision. "He just wanted us to do his dirty work for him, that's all. He got what he asked for! Okay, I'm gonna go get his car and pull it in here. Is that still what you want to do, Tam?"

"I just thought of a better idea," Tammy said. "How 'bout you put him in the trunk and take that car and drive it to Jonasson Pond. It ain't more than a mile or so down the road. I remember there's a trail runs straight down the hill and right to the edge of that pond. Just put it in neutral, and let her go. That's a deep pond. Nobody'll ever find it—or him. Two birds, know what I mean? Should'a sunk the old man in there, too. Then we wouldn't be in this mess. A'course you botched that job up."

"You know what that car is worth, Tammy? That's a brand-new Mercedes-Benz! We'd be crazy to sink that car in a pond. We should stash it in here for a while." Glen had stopped focusing on the dead guy's baseball cap and had in- stead adopted an appreciation for German engineering.

"What? You want to put it on Craigslist, Glen?" Tammy snapped.

"We could just keep it here in the barn until things cool down!" Glen snapped back.

"And what do you think would happen if the cops found Parker's car stashed in our barn after he's gone missin'? Glen, we're gonna have all the money we need when this is all over. You can buy your own Mercedes-Benz," Tammy declared with confidence.

Glen wasn't convinced. "How do you figure? You just shot the golden goose twice in the chest!"

Tammy laughed. "Here's how I figure . . . Marlene is gonna give us the fifty grand her boyfriend owes us, *and* she's gonna give us that easement we need to get back to our property—the property the Jonassons locked us outta!" That last bit seemed to be directed to Meg. She continued, "Then, like I said, we're gonna make our own deal with those windmill people."

Jason finally got involved. "What makes you so sure she's gonna cooperate with that plan?" he asked.

"Because *she* knows *we* know everything."

Glen still wasn't feeling reassured. "Yeah but *she* knows everything, too, Tammy, don't she?"

Tammy lowered her voice. "Glen, it don't matter if you was the one that done the old man in—*or* that other one. If we was to get caught, she's goin' down with us. It was *her* boyfriend who was behind all this. I don't care what he said, Marlene had to know the plan all along. And even if she didn't, we'll say she did. And that's called bein' an accessory or somethin' like that. Anyway, we got our hands full with this predicament right now, so let's get this one in the trunk of his car and get rid of him. Jason, you help Glen out, then I want you to stay here with them three. You got them taped up or tied up or somethin'?"

"Not yet," answered Jason.

She slapped her hand against the van, startling its occupants. "Well, what are you waitin' for? Get it done! If they make a run for it, we can't catch all three of 'em! And we only got two guns!"

"What are we gonna do with them? The cops are gonna be all over this county lookin' for 'em if they ain't already." Jason was sounding more and more panicked. "Please tell me you ain't plannin' on . . . ?"

"On what?" Tammy paused. "You got a better idea?! A'course I am! I just ain't figured out how to do it yet. But we gotta take care of this one first! And his car! Now, Glen, are you gonna handle it or do I have to do it?"

Glen let out a heavy sigh. "I'll go do it. But it's a waste of a good Mercedes-Benz."

"Now I gotta get into town so people see me around and nobody gets suspicious," Tammy announced. "Glen, you got any of them Arby's coupons left?"

There was a dead pause. "I only got one left. I was savin' it for—"

"Just give it to me! I'm low on cash. You can buy all the Arby's you want when we finish cleanin' up this mess. Take your new Mercedes right through the drive-through and load up."

Glen reached into his pocket and begrudgingly handed over his wrinkled Arby's coupon as if it were the last Willy Wonka Golden Ticket.

"Thank you. Okay, now, I want that car took care of by the time I get back, Glen. And, Jason, I want them three tied, taped up, or whatever. And do a better job than you did last time!"

After Tammy left the barn, things immediately got quiet, like the silence that follows an explosion. Once he heard her car start up and chug away, Jason figured it was safe to speak. "What kind'a woman shoots a man twice and then goes off to Arby's for a roast beef?"

Glen wasn't happy, either. "And she didn't even ask us if

we wanted nothin'. That was my last two-for-one coupon. I'll tell you what, sometimes that sister of mine . . ." Glen stopped himself and redirected his energy. "Okay, I'm gonna go ditch this car. You better get these ladies secure. There's a couple more rolls of duct tape over there. I'll be a while, 'cuz I gotta walk back from the pond." He then yelled into the van, "With a sore leg, thanks to that damn dog!"

Glen closed the barn doors behind him and Jason climbed back into the van. He collapsed over the steering wheel and let out a groan born out of dire frustration. Isabel let him have his moment before launching her new strategy. He was obviously feeling trapped, so she wanted to offer him a way out. "You know, Jason, if you were to just let us go, I know Sheriff Pemberton will be fair with you. He's engaged to my cousin, you know, and he's a very fair man." She let that float for a moment until Beverly jumped in.

"You haven't killed anybody, Jason . . . yet. But Glen and your girlfriend are now two for two. And if they killed this Marlene woman's husband, which seems highly likely, that makes three."

Jason lifted his head and looked at Isabel. "You think they killed *him, too?*" Isabel lifted her eyebrows and shrugged in response. Jason went on. "And, by the way, Tammy ain't my girlfriend. Not no more. No, thank you. I'd be afraid to close my eyes at night."

Beverly ignored his romantic angst and went on. "Now, if they get rid of us, then they're six for six. You'll go to prison just for being associated with them. Just for knowing their *names*, they'll put you away for life."

Meg then added her two cents. "That is, if they don't kill you, too."

"Why would they bother killing me *now?*"

Meg looked at him almost sympathetically. "Why *wouldn't* they? You know way too much. And do you really think they plan to share whatever money they're able to get their grubby hands on with *you*?"

Isabel and Beverly nodded their approval of Meg's tactic. Jason was beginning to think things over.

"You really think they killed that lady's husband, too? The man from the golf club?" Jason asked in earnest.

Meg was annoyed. "Why would that come as any shock to you? I guess you haven't been paying very close attention, have you, Jason?"

"I think there's a pretty good chance they *did* kill Marlene's husband. There does seem to be a pattern," Isabel said in a calm, almost motherly voice. "And like Meg says, you may well be next on the list. After they convince you to kill us, that is."

Now it was time for Beverly to turn on her trademark charm. "You're already a dead man walking. I can't imagine a scenario where they *didn't* kill you."

"I ain't never killed anybody in my life and I do not intend to *start* killin' people. *And*, I don't intend to start lettin' people kill *me*!" Jason was becoming increasingly emotional. He let out a heavy sigh and shook his head. "I don't understand my life. I really don't." He collapsed on the steering wheel again.

Beverly recalibrated her approach and decided to try out *her* motherly voice. It was a stretch. "Jason, we all make bad choices in life. But that doesn't mean we shouldn't correct them when we have the chance. If you let us go, we will all make sure the authorities know you were not involved in these murders and that you alone spared our lives. You might just walk away from this whole mess with nothing but a bad taste in your mouth." Beverly knew that was a crock. He would definitely be going back to prison, but right now she needed to convince him otherwise.

Isabel was impressed with Beverly's new angle, so she picked up where she left off. "Beverly, you'll take on Jason's case won't you?" Then to Jason, "You know, she's the best defense attorney in the state, Jason. Maybe the whole country."

Beverly pretended to blush as Meg took the reins. "Why do you think we hired her for my brother? She'll have you coming out of this a hero."

Isabel went back in to try to close the deal. "All you have to do is back this van out of this barn, drive us to the sheriff's office, and this whole dreary affair will be over."

Jason lifted his head off the steering wheel and stared straight ahead into the darkness for a moment or two. He then straightened up in his seat and clutched the steering wheel, brimming with resolve. "I just don't think I can do it. This van has a flat tire. I ain't never fixed a flat tire before."

All three women sighed with relief. Isabel gave him a friendly tap on the shoulder with the back of her hand. "I can have that tire changed in five minutes!"

Jason stared back into the darkness. "So, what you're tellin' me is that if I let you three go, you'll see to it that they cut me some kind'a deal?"

Beverly was doubling down. "Jason, I know you did not ever expect to find yourself in a situation like this with the likes of the Trudlows. Like you said, you were trying to turn over a new leaf. But unfortunately those two scorpions were under it. Tammy and Glen have sucked you, unwillingly, into an evil murder plot. As far as I'm concerned, you are an innocent bystander . . . so far, anyway. But I promise you on my sacred oath as a lawyer, and as an officer of the court for the great state of Michigan, that if you back this van out right now and drive us to the sheriff's department, you will not spend *one* day in prison."

Isabel and Meg both looked at Jason, promoting Beverly's offer with the kindest expressions they could muster. Meg went a step further.

"Jason, I'm convinced you didn't have anything to do with

my father's murder. Your going back to prison doesn't bring *him* back to life, or bring my family any peace. But if you spare our lives, and you can help us prove Glen and Tammy were behind all this, well, that will save my brother's life, and the lives of my four precious nephews—innocent young boys who need their father. So, I'm asking you, begging you, to do the right thing here while you still have a chance to save us, save my brother, save yourself, and save your *soul*."

Meg's words sent chills down Isabel's spine. Beverly was amply impressed, too, and decided to rest her case. Meg just made a better closing argument than she could make here. Isabel looked over and noticed a tear running down Jason's right cheek. In a sudden rush of determination, he pushed open his door. "Okay, ladies, let's get this tire changed!"

Isabel was right behind him and took full control of the operation. "I've got a flashlight here in the glove box. Beverly, Meg, you go stand watch outside. Jason, I'm going to need you to hold the flashlight for me."

In less than two minutes Isabel had the spare tire and the jack out of the back of the van and was jacking up the back bumper. She had changed plenty of flat tires in her day, and at least twice on this van—once in the pouring rain. This was nothing, especially when their lives depended on it! Grabbing the lug wrench as effortlessly as she would pick up a soup spoon, Isabel got to work. A couple of stubborn lug nuts took some extra elbow grease and some help from Jason, but in under ten minutes, from start to finish, she had the tire off and the spare tire on, tightening the lug nuts like a pit stop mechanic at the Indy 500. She lowered the van, threw the jack and the lug wrench into the back with a clang, and clapped her hands together. "Okay, let's get out of here! Jason, you drive. I'm a nervous wreck."

Beverly and Meg climbed back in through the side door, and Isabel jumped into the passenger side. They were mak-

ing their escape—again! Jason took the wheel, started up the
van, dropped it into reverse, and gunned it out of the barn
into the darkened clearing . . . and right smack into the side
of Tammy's car. "What the—!" Jason turned around to check
on his passengers. "You ladies okay?" They were too rattled
and crestfallen to answer.

Then out of the darkness, like creatures from a horror
film, Glen and Tammy appeared on each side of the van, both
wearing evil smirks. Glen was on the driver's side, holding
his gun and pointing it directly at Jason. Tammy was on the
passenger side, holding an Arby's cup. Jason threw it back
into drive, hit the gas, and turned the van around sharply
in the clearing . . . and then suddenly a shot rang out. The
driver's-side window shattered, the women screamed, and
Jason slumped over the wheel.

A frightening silence followed as the van crept slowly back
across the clearing and came to rest against the old grain silo.
The women hunkered down in their seats, waiting for more
gunshots. Hearing none, they raised their heads to find Glen
glaring at them through the blasted-out driver's-side window.
Jason's body slowly began leaning sideways toward Isabel. She
could see the blood soaking into his denim jacket where the
bullet had torn into him. Glen leaned in and poked him with
his gun until he fell into a lifeless heap onto the floor between
the seats. Tammy rushed over to the van, breathless, but still
taking time to slurp the rest of her soda through her straw
before speaking. "Is he dead?"

Glen opened the door and leaned in. He reached down
and grabbed Jason's wrist. Beverly and Meg clung to each
other in the back while Isabel watched in stunned silence
from the passenger seat. Glen looked up at his sister. "He ain't
got no pulse, so I guess so."

"Well, good," Tammy declared as she tossed her cup to
the ground. "Saves us the trouble'a doin' him in later. I knew

from the start he was too much of a wimp to go through with this. Looks like it's just you and me now, brother."

Glen said nothing as he stared down blankly at Jason. Isabel thought she detected a hint of sadness over killing his prison buddy. "I just remembered he owes me twenty bucks." So much for that.

Tammy ignored him. "Okay, now we need to get rid of these three, and fast. There was state police all over town. Sooner we disappear them, the sooner we can get our money and get outta town. I think our best bet is to go with the pond again."

"That Mercedes disappeared in a hurry. Sure was a sad sight to see though," Glen said to his sister as he looked back into the van and gave his captors a heartless once-over.

"I swear, if you bring up that damn car again, I am gonna shoot you dead. Okay now, let's just tape 'em up and send 'em for a swim. They've been nothin' but trouble. By the way, here's your Arby's coupon back. I decided to try that chicken thing instead."

"I could eat a horse. How was it?" Glen asked.

"Well, a horse would probably be tastier," Tammy replied. "It was awful. I need to just stick with what I know, and what I know is the roast beef and cheddar."

Now back in possession of his two-for-one coupon, and with roast beef on the brain, Glen moved into high gear. "Let's get this done so we can get back there 'fore they close. I think I'm gonna get me a Frosty, too."

"That's Wendy's, fool, but Arby's got some shakes, and that apple turnover I like. Better than McDonald's, I think."

Inside the van, the women couldn't believe their ears, telegraphing their disgust to one another with their eyes. Their friend was lying dead in a heap and they were on the verge of committing a triple homicide, but all these psychopaths could think about was fast-food dessert menus.

"It's gettin' late! You better get a move on!" Tammy snapped. "They close at eleven. I'll hold the gun while you tape 'em up." Tammy purposely raised her voice so it would carry into the van. "Any of 'em cause any trouble or try to make a run for it, it'll be my pleasure to shoot 'em dead in their tracks."

"This is like *Jerry Springer* and *The Sopranos* had a baby," Beverly mumbled as she stared out the shattered side window into the pitch-black cornfield. Isabel sensed that Beverly and Meg had given up any hope that they would get out of this situation alive. Things were indeed looking pretty grim, but Isabel Puddles was a half-full kind of woman, so she was still holding out for a miracle. Still, her mind drifted to her kids, to Frances, to Ginny and Grady, to Gil Cook, to her cousin Freddie, Carol. . . . They would all be devastated. And what's worse, they might never know what happened to her if they all ended up at the bottom of Jonasson Pond. Then she thought about what would happen to Jackpot and Corky. What would happen to Poplar Bluff? Who would take over as president of the Knit Wits? And for some inexplicable reason, she thought about what would happen to the leftover pot roast in her fridge. Glen snapped her back to attention when he jumped into the van wearing two rolls of duct tape around his wrist like bracelets and ordered her into the back, while Tammy stood outside, pointing the gun into the van and snapping her gum.

Stepping over Jason's body, still lying between the seats, gave Isabel chills. Despite the dire predicament they were in, she felt horrible about the death of a boy who had, in his last moments of life, tried to do the right thing.

Beverly was the shortest, but Meg was the skinniest, so she slid into the middle of the seat, and Isabel sat next to the side door. Glen ordered them to hold their wrists together while he taped each of them up before moving on to their ankles. Next he secured all three together by wrapping the tape around their waists and around the seat several times, humming to himself as he worked. *What kind of psycho hums to himself as he prepares to murder three innocent women?* Isabel asked herself. The answer was staring her in the face.

Glen finished up, slid open the side door, climbed out, and then slammed it shut. He poked his head back in and looked at Isabel. "I only have one regret. I just wish that nasty ol' dog of yours was in here with you."

Isabel glared at him until his sister beckoned for him again. "You done yet?"

"I'm done. They ain't goin' nowhere. And with these broken windows, this old van is gonna sink like the *Titanic*. You gonna follow me, Tammy? I ain't walkin' back here this time."

"Let's go," she answered coldly. Glen climbed back into the driver's side and started up the van. "Thanks for changin' the tire, ladies," he said with an evil chuckle. They heard Tammy's junker start up next, and they were off, slowly crawling through the cornfield toward the dirt road that would lead them to Jonasson Pond and their watery demise.

Chapter 19

Things were looking about as grim as possible as they headed down the dirt road toward Jonasson Pond. With a psycho killer behind the wheel, three innocent women duct-taped in the back facing imminent death by drowning, and a dead man already lying on the floor, this was not the stuff happy endings were made of. But Isabel Puddles was not ready to give up yet. She was formulating a plan.

A few weeks before, while cleaning out her van, she had reached under the front passenger seat to retrieve a loose Dr Pepper bottle and cut the top of her hand pretty badly. So she knew something under there was very sharp. If she could stick her feet under there far enough to find whatever it was, maybe she could slice through the duct tape wrapped around her ankles. It was certainly worth a try. She scooted her feet forward and discreetly began searching. She got a shot of adrenaline when almost immediately she felt whatever it was and began to scrape at the tape wrapped around her ankles. If she could have just a few minutes more to work on it, she might have her ankles free by the time they hit the water. What she hadn't yet thought through was how she was going to free herself and everybody else with her feet. She looked over at the smashed-out window next to her and had another idea. Once Glen sent them down the hill, she would have at least a few seconds to try to use the broken shards of glass still sticking out of the window frame to try to cut the tape from around her wrists. With her wrists and her ankles free, she could get to work on freeing Meg and Beverly. It was a long shot, but it was the only shot they had.

Isabel was still working on her ankles when the van began to slow down. Glen turned the wheel to the right, onto the dirt road and onto the trail that led down to the pond a few hundred feet below. Isabel could see the reflection of a harvest moon glistening on the pond's mirrorlike surface, framed by cattails and a cluster of weeping willows on the other side. It looked so tranquil. No one would ever guess there was now a dead man in the trunk of a Mercedes at the bottom . . . whom they were about to join. Glen put the van in neutral, turned off the lights, and then opened the door. But before climbing out, he left his victims with some parting words: "Bon voyage, ladies!"

The second he slammed the door, Isabel sprang into action. She leaned over and began scraping the tape around her wrists against the largest, sharpest shard of glass she could reach. The van crept forward slowly at first, then began to gain speed. Beverly and Meg both had their eyes closed. Beverly was grimacing, while Meg's face was the picture of acceptance. Isabel worked feverishly as the van began careening toward the water, but her wrists and ankles were still bound when they splashed into the pond. They skimmed across the surface for several feet before they came to a stop and began to float. The van rocked gently from side to side for a few moments, but then slowly started to take on water. Isabel was still nowhere close to freeing herself. *Well, I guess this is it*, she thought. *This is how it ends.* And then she heard a familiar voice.

"Holy *crap*, this water is cold!" Rising from the bloody denim heap between the seats was Jason!

"You're alive!" Isabel screamed. Beverly and Meg looked up in shock.

"I think so! He only hit me in the shoulder! But I knew playin' possum was our best bet to get outta this fix!" Despite the fact that he was obviously in pain, Jason was the next to spring into action, scrambling to free the same three women he had been holding hostage less than an hour ago. He reached up to flip on the van's overhead light, which luckily was still working. He then picked up a large glass shard sitting on the driver's-side seat and began scratching at the duct tape wrapped around Isabel's wrists. "Not playing favorites, ladies, but I gotta start with somebody!"

"Just get my wrists free and move on to Meg and Beverly," Isabel instructed. "I'll get my ankles first and then I'll get theirs."

"You think those two are gone or are they up there watchin' us sink?" Jason asked.

Beverly was back. "Are you kidding? Glen's traveling at the speed of sound by now! Curly fries wait for no man!"

The water was pouring in faster now and was almost covering the women's ankles. Jason stayed focused, but he was struggling, having the use of only one arm. His tongue was working fine, though. "I think Tammy's keepin' that place in business. I don't get it. I mean who eats at Arby's anymore? Especially when there's a McDonald's right down the street!"

Meg was back again, with a fury. "Do you think we could spend a little less time discussing fast food and a little more time getting us out of this death trap?"

Jason was trying to free Isabel's wrists when the van suddenly lurched to one side. Water came pouring in where once there was a window. Within seconds, the frigid water was almost knee high and rising fast. Jason was still struggling to get Isabel's wrists loose. "Boy, he did a good job taping you ladies up."

The van abruptly lurched to the other side and the women screamed. Even more water rushed in from the smashed-out driver's-side window. The mood in the van, having gone from hopeless to hopeful, was getting grim again. But Jason remained determined. "I'm not leaving you ladies here. I promise you!" He jumped over to the other side of the van to try to balance it out and began rocking it slightly. Unfortunately, his attempt to make things better only made things worse. Water was now gushing in again from the side window.

A few more horrifyingly tense minutes passed, and the freezing cold water continued to rise. Isabel was still working on her ankles while Jason tried to free her wrists. The gentle rocking of the half-floating, half-sinking van belied the desperation inside. At this point Isabel realized that they might die from hypothermia before drowning. Another glimmer of hope flickered as she yelled victoriously, "I got my ankles free! I can move my legs!"

Jason was almost floating himself, but he still worked feverishly to free Isabel's wrists. She was helping as best she could with what strength she could muster to pull her wrists apart, but the stress and the cold water were taking their toll. She could feel herself getting weak. Then, almost magically, as if she had willed it to happen, her wrists broke free.

"Get their wrists, Jason! I'm going to work on their ankles," Isabel yelled as she slipped out from under the duct tape Glen had used to strap them all to the seat. She reached up and grabbed another loose shard of glass off the front seat. Meg was to her immediate left, so she reached down to find her ankles but the water was already too deep. She lifted her head, took the deepest breath she could, and dived under the water. Isabel grabbed Meg's right leg and followed it down to her bound ankles and began slicing with the shard of glass. She came up for air, then dived down again. Isabel and Jason were working desperately to free Meg and Beverly, but now the water had risen to their chests. Things were not looking good. The two women remained stoic, staring straight ahead, their teeth chattering from the cold as they bravely prepared for what now seemed inevitable. Isabel knew they were thinking about all the people they loved who were going to be left behind, just as she had been. She shouted encouragement. "Don't you worry, girls! We are getting you out of here!"

Suddenly they felt something strange happening, something very strange. . . . The van stopped rocking. It seemed to stop sinking and leaned to one side, then stopped, before leaning to the other side. It felt as if they were settling on the bottom of the pond! Everybody looked at one another in collective amazement. Meg and Beverly were still not free, but they had stopped sinking and they were not taking on any more water! Nobody dared move or speak, fearful they may upset whatever miracle was in the process of happening. Before they could fully process *this* miracle, another presented itself, and Isabel let out a scream. "My purse!" The famous *Let's Make a Deal* bag, the bag of tricks everyone constantly teased her about, and her chiropractor warned her about, had come floating up from the back of the van where she had thrown it earlier in the day. Thankfully she had zipped it closed before she tossed it in, which had kept most of the water out and allowed it to remain buoyant. Isabel grabbed it, unzipped it, then reached in with a look of apprehension. "Hold tight, ladies! I may have just the thing!" she yelled as she began digging through her bag. An eclectic assortment of items began floating out; a small package of soggy tissues, a package of gum, a tennis ball she was bringing home for the dogs, half a waterlogged Hershey's bar, a loose glove, and a library book. *That* was going to cost her, she couldn't help thinking. After what seemed like an eternity of digging—especially for Meg and Beverly, who were still duct taped in place—Isabel smiled broadly and pulled out something she was grasping tightly in her fist. "Bingo!" It was a Swiss Army knife, a gift from Charlie one Christmas.

Isabel flipped open the pocketknife and within a minute she managed to cut loose both Meg and Beverly. Once they were all free, Jason tugged on the side door with his good arm until he was able to slide it open and pull himself through, and to his surprise, found himself able to stand. But it didn't feel like the bottom of a pond. He began to bounce up and down cautiously, then smiled. "Well, guess what, ladies? I think we just parked ourselves on top of a Mercedes-Benz."

They couldn't believe their luck. The fact that they were just a matter of feet above a dead guy in the trunk didn't even register. Jason reached back in and gently pulled Meg out through the side window. Once out, she stood on the roof of the Mercedes and held on to the side of the van. Jason reached back in. "Your turn now, Ms. Atwater."

Beverly slowly scooted across the seat toward him. But just as she took his hand, Isabel yelled, "Wait! Stop! We've got to get her out of those waders! She'll sink like a rock! Jason, you hang on to Meg. I'll get Beverly out!" She and Beverly were the only ones with two good arms, so they frantically went to work yanking at the waders until Isabel gave them a final tug and got them off—along with Beverly's pants. Out of respect, Jason turned his head away, but she had her Spanx on, so neither of them was completely traumatized. Once the waders were off, Beverly reached back into the water and grabbed her soaking-wet pants gathered at her ankles. After some aggressive wiggling, she managed to shimmy back into them. Adding insult to injury, Beverly then watched wistfully as one of her Jimmy Choos floated past her. Poor Beverly, Isabel thought. Little did Michigan's leading defense attorney know when she woke up this morning that she would end this day nearly dying in a pond with her pants around her ankles.

Jason grabbed Beverly firmly by the arm and helped her out of the van with Isabel following behind. The van was empty now, but the sudden shift of weight caused it to list, so it was now taking on water again. All four of them stood on the edge of the Mercedes' submerged roof and watched in awe as the van turned on its side and in a matter of seconds disappeared beneath the murky water. The four survivors looked at one another and silently acknowledged how incredibly lucky they had been. But there would be time to show gratitude to the universe later. They still had to make it to shore.

They were only about twenty-five feet from the bank of the pond, but it was still too deep to slog in. They had to swim it. With two injured parties unable to swim, Isabel, having spent two summers as a lifeguard, knew what to do. She grabbed Jason from behind with one arm while Beverly watched and did the same with Meg, then they all turned their backs to the shore and began kicking wildly toward dry land. As soon as they were able to touch bottom, they all stood up, barely, and dragged themselves onto shore, collapsing in a scrum of exhaustion. They had done it. They had actually done it. Through sheer grit, determination, and a lot of good luck in the eleventh hour, they had escaped a certain and horrible death. But their relief was quickly followed by uncontrollable shaking. The outside temperature couldn't have been more than fifty degrees, and the water was even colder, so unless they found a way to get warm, and fast, Isabel knew that hypothermia was still a serious and potentially deadly threat. After all they had just been through, that would be just too cruel a fate. She looked over at an exhausted Jason and remembered they had another pressing situation. "Jason, let me look at that shoulder." He grimaced as he slowly peeled off his soaking wet, bloodstained denim jacket. Isabel then tore his shirtsleeve off at the shoulder. The cold water had stopped the bleeding somewhat, but now it was starting again.

She finished ripping his shirt off, and in no time she had fashioned a bandage that would have impressed any army medic. With what was left of his shirt, she tied a tourniquet above the wound. Beverly and Meg sat on the bank of the pond, huddled together and trying to share their body heat. After she finished with Jason he joined them, but moments later, they all looked up to see Isabel wading back into the water.

"*What* are you doing, Isabel!" Beverly yelled at her.

"Getting my purse! I can see it floating right there!" For a tense couple of minutes, Beverly, Meg, and Jason watched incredulously as Isabel waded back out and swam a few strokes to retrieve her purse. When she got back to shore, and before anybody could scold her, she raised her hand preemptively. "I've had this bag for twenty years! And it may have saved your lives, so . . ." She reached inside. "And look! My wallet's still in here! Along with sixty dollars! A little soggy, but I'll take it! Okay, people, we better get walking. But we need to keep an eye out for those two in case they decide to come back to check their work."

The beaten but unbowed foursome began sloshing up the trail leading to the main road. But no sooner had they reached the top than they saw a pair of headlights coming toward them. They instinctively dived for the nearest clump of bushes and hunkered down. Tammy and Glen were coming back! There was no way they could make a break for it. All they could do was hope they were hidden well enough. As the car got closer, Isabel lifted her head up slightly to see how close they were. But thanks to that bright harvest moon, she could see it wasn't Tammy and Glen, after all, it was a large white SUV. She jumped up and ran out to the road, but not in time for whoever was driving by to see her running toward them. As the car passed her with a *swoosh*, she saw a familiar logo on the side door: Wind-X.

"It's Zander!" Isabel yelled. With her dripping-wet purse

still hanging off her shoulder, she ran out into the middle of the road and began waving and yelling frantically as the SUV proceeded down the road, giving no indication of stopping. Then a spark. She dug inside her trusty tote again and, lo and behold, pulled out the air horn Freddie had insisted she carry in case she was ever in danger. And now would be the time for it! She pulled the trigger and a blast of sound emanated from the device that left her ears ringing like Saint Patrick's on Easter morning . . . and then she saw brake lights. She blasted the horn once more, threw her purse down, and began jumping and waving her arms. She yelled back to her wet and no doubt confused posse of survivors still hiding in the bushes. "He's backing up! He's backing up!"

A few seconds later, Zander was putting his SUV into park and climbing out, looking completely bewildered. Isabel ran over to him. "I want to hug you but I'm soaking wet! What are you doing out here at this hour, Zander?"

Zander was still in a state of shock. "Isabel! What am *I* doing out here? What are *you* doing out here? And why are you soaking wet!"

"Well, it's kind of a long story. Oh, and I'm not alone. Come on out! It's my friend Zander! We're safe!"

Zander's mouth fell open when he saw three waterlogged strangers shuffle out from the bushes. Their heads swiveled this way and that and their teeth were chattering uncontrollably. One of them had a bloody bandage around his arm, another had her arm in a cast. They looked disoriented and scared, as if they had just crash-landed on another planet. Zander could see this did promise to be a long story, but there would be time for that later. Zander wasted no time and sprang into action.

"Okay, everybody, get in my car!" He opened the back door of the passenger side and guided Meg, Beverly, and Jason inside. None of them managed to say a word yet. All they could do was look at him with both relief and disbelief. He put Isabel in the front seat, then reached across her and blasted the heat as high as it would go. Next he ran around the back, popped the hatch, dug around a little, and within seconds he was back in the driver's seat with some packages in his lap. He tore the first one open and unfurled something shiny and silver; it looked like a tinfoil blanket. He threw it over his shoulder to the backseat. "Wrap up in this."

Isabel looked at him curiously as he unwrapped another. "What are . . . ?"

"Mylar blankets." Zander kept unwrapping. "I was a Boy Scout. Eagle Scout, actually. Be Prepared is still my motto!" He gave the next blanket to Isabel. "Wrap up, Isabel. Hypothermia is nothing to fool around with." He unwrapped two more blankets for the backseat to share, then looked around at his passengers. "Okay, let's get you guys out of here!" Zander put the car in drive and hit the gas, spinning around and kicking up gravel in his wake as he sped back toward the main road. A few moments of silence followed, with only the sound of the engine and the very welcome sound of the heater blowing hot air at them.

"I guess you better take us to the sheriff's office," Isabel said calmly as she adjusted her blanket around her neck.

Zander disagreed. "No way. I'm taking you to the hospital."

"Yes . . . better idea," Isabel agreed.

After they turned onto the main road, Zander pulled out his phone. "We've got a couple miles to get out of this dead zone. Should we call the sheriff then and have him meet us at the hospital?"

There was a slightly awkward pause as Isabel, Meg, and Beverly all turned their heads to look at Jason. Regardless of how they got there, Jason had saved their lives, and not even Meg seemed to feel right about just turning him over to the sheriff to be arrested. Maybe for the first time in his life, Jason had done the right thing, but now he had the look of a man prepared to meet his fate. He nodded slowly. "Yes . . . you better call the sheriff."

Isabel took the cell phone from Zander, looked at it, and handed it back to Beverly. "Let's call my cousin Ginny. She can get to Grady right away. Can you punch the numbers in, please?"

Isabel began reciting Ginny's number to Beverly, who cajoled her, "You are going to have to either join the Amish or the modern world, Isabel!" Beverly handed the phone back to her.

When Isabel heard Ginny's voice, she started to get emotional and couldn't talk. Beverly grabbed the phone again. She identified herself and explained the situation very matter-of-factly, telling her that they had Meg, she was safe, and asked her to have Grady meet them at the hospital ASAP. Then Meg chimed in softly, "And please ask her to call my husband."

The remainder of the ride to the hospital was spent with Isabel and Beverly intermittently explaining what they had all just been through, leaving out Jason's involvement so as not to make Zander uneasy. The story was muddled and a bit fractured, but he listened intently, shaking his head in disbelief through most of it. Jason sat quietly with his chin in his chest and holding his shoulder, while Meg stared out the window in silence. Zander obviously didn't know Jason, and he had never met Meg. He had no idea she had even gone missing, so that information threw him a little bit, too. And he had never even heard of Beverly Atwater, which threw Beverly more than a little bit. Then Isabel remembered to ask Zander her initial question of the night when she saw him: What was he doing out there at that hour?

"Well, part of my wind analysis is to check wind levels at all hours of the day and night. So, I was on my way out to check on some new equipment I installed. I wanted to get a read on wind activity after midnight on the parcel I still hadn't finished analyzing. And I wanted to check some of my other gear to see if the full moon had any effect on the wind patterns."

"So, you were checking down by the beaver dam?" Meg asked, as if she already knew the answer.

"Exactly," Zander replied.

Isabel was intrigued. "Since when do we have beavers around here? You never told me about any beaver dam, Meg."

Meg smiled. "It's a complicated story, Iz. I'll tell you all about it later."

After a few more moments of silence, Zander spoke up. "You know, there really was no wind to speak of tonight. I almost didn't come. But it was weird. Something told me I should come out and check on my equipment tonight."

There was an unspoken but very grateful consensus among his exhausted passengers that Zander had made the right choice.

Chapter 20

The emergency room at Kentwater Memorial Hospital hadn't seen so much activity since the Moose Lodge Pancake Breakfast disaster of nearly a decade before. It was standing room only in the ER that evening after Floyd Dobbins—the lodge member in charge of the pancake-and-sausage feast held every Saturday morning during the summers—accidentally left a few dozen boxes of sausage links in the trunk of his car overnight in the middle of a heat wave, but decided to fry them up the next morning anyway. About a quarter of those in attendance at the breakfast were sick enough to go to the hospital, which started filling up by late afternoon. Virtually everybody who ate that sausage got sick to one degree or another, and by Sunday morning there wasn't a bottle of Pepto Bismol to be found anywhere in the county. Isabel was one of those unfortunate breakfast goers, but she was lucky. All it cost her was a day in bed and her love of sausage. She hadn't touched a sausage link since.

The Moose Lodge immediately relieved Floyd of his breakfast duties after Joanne Slusser—the wife of a lodge member, and the woman who headed up the pancake department—ratted him out. After Floyd was named in the paper as the man responsible for poisoning half the county, he and his wife slinked out of town and never returned. Floyd wasn't terribly well liked to begin with, so the sausage debacle didn't do a lot to improve his popularity. The last Isabel heard, Floyd was living in a Moose Lodge trailer park in Florida and spearheading their monthly fried shrimp night. "What could go wrong?" was Frances's response to that bit of gossip. To this day, many of the locals referred to any stomach ailment as a bout of "Floyd's Flu."

Once their conditions had been assessed by emergency room staff, and after Grady had arrived and been debriefed on the events of the evening, Isabel, Meg, and Beverly were told they needed to be admitted to the hospital. Jason required immediate surgery to remove the bullet from his shoulder, so he had already been whisked away, but not before one of Grady's deputies quietly arrested him while he was still lying on the gurney, and read him his rights on his way to surgery.

Due to concerns that the latest trauma Meg had endured might have exacerbated her previous injuries, or caused new ones, she was next to be sent upstairs. Then the focus turned to Isabel and Beverly, who both lobbied hard to be released but failed to convince the attending physician. The polite young man told them in as kindly a manner as possible that going through an ordeal like the one they had just experienced *at their age* "could present medical difficulties that have yet to manifest." He insisted they stay overnight for observation, so they finally demurred and agreed to share a room.

Because Tammy and Glen were still on the loose, and Grady didn't yet know who else might be involved in Kentwater County's first murder syndicate, he placed deputies outside everybody's doors before heading back out to continue the search. "You might start at Arby's!" Isabel yelled to Grady as he left their room, holding the door for the nurse as she entered.

Isabel asked their nurse if Zander was still there. She told her he had gone home, but wanted them to know he would come back in the morning to check on them.

"Boy, what a charmer that one is! And cute!" said the fortyish nurse attending to them. "And I didn't see a ring. I'll tell you what. I'm no cougar, but if I was ten years younger, I'd be on him like white on rice!"

Beverly turned to Isabel after their nurse left the room. "Well, she's right. He is adorable. But I'm pretty good with these things, and I get the feeling their age difference wouldn't be her biggest hurdle." Isabel just raised her eyebrows and shrugged.

It was getting late, but Beverly got busy on the phone talking to "her people" in Detroit, while Isabel tried unsuccessfully to reach Ginny again to ask her to go check on Jackpot and Corky. She felt terrible that the two were home alone in the dark, no doubt confused about her whereabouts, not to mention the whereabouts of their dinner. She was just about to call Freddie and ask him to do it when Ginny burst through the door, going straight to Isabel's bedside and giving her a big hug. "You poor thing. I could hardly believe my ears when Grady told me everything that happened." She hugged her again, then looked over at her roommate. "Hello, Beverly." It was a hello lacking in warmth and fuzziness, but it was still a hello, and Beverly didn't seem to care.

Ginny was fighting back tears and sat on the side of Isabel's bed and took her hand. "You were right, Izzy. You were right all along. And Lord knows what would have happened to Meg or her brother if you *hadn't* been right—and then had the moxie to follow your hunch! I'm just so proud of you. And I can tell you right now, Grady feels awful that he ever doubted you."

Isabel waved off the sentiment. "Well, he shouldn't. Grady's the best sheriff this county has had in my lifetime. Everybody has a bad day now and again. But right now it doesn't matter who was right or wrong. Those Trudlows are still out there and they aren't going to stop killing people until somebody stops them."

No sooner had those words left her lips than Grady walked into the room with a big smile. "I've got some good news, ladies." Beverly hung up the phone, and to a rapt audience Grady announced that his deputies had just paid a visit to a trailer Glen Trudlow had recently rented outside town. There they found Tammy and Glen basking in self-satisfaction, apparently assuming all five of their victims for the day were resting quietly at the bottom of Jonasson Pond. The two were casually watching a zombie movie, drinking beer, and sharing a box of Little Debbie cakes. But their quiet brother-sister bonding evening at home came to an abrupt end when the deputies broke down their door with their guns drawn and, seconds later, had them both in handcuffs. Given his casual relationship with reality, Glen asked the deputies if they could wait until the end of the movie before they were carted off. Tammy, given her very serious relationship with junk food, asked if she could take the last package of Little Debbie cakes with her. Both requests were denied.

Two more deputies had gone to question Marlene Vanderhoff, who was sound asleep when they arrived. She claimed to be completely oblivious to any of the events that had occurred over the past several hours. According to the deputies, she was visibly shaken when she learned her boyfriend had been shot and killed. She also claimed to know nothing about Earl Jonasson's murder or Meg's abduction. But Tammy and Glen wasted no time throwing her under the bus. Before they even made it back to the jail, they named Marlene and her boyfriend as the kingpins behind this murder rampage, so Grady had her arrested her, too. Meanwhile, back at the pond, crews were pulling out Isabel's van, and then Parker's Mercedes, with him still in the trunk.

After taking in all the new developments, Isabel turned to

her cousin and calmly asked, "Gin, can you please go check on the dogs? They didn't get their dinner. And if you could grab a couple of my jogging suits so Beverly and I have something to change into in the morning when they let us out of here, I sure would appreciate it."

Beverly looked over at Isabel, astonished. "After all we just went through, you're worried that your dogs had to skip a meal?"

Isabel was equally astonished. "I don't see why Jackpot and Corky need to go hungry just because their mom nearly got herself murdered."

Beverly shrugged her shoulders. "Fair enough. Oh, and thank you anyway Isabel, but for the record, I don't really do jogging suits. No offense."

"None taken." Isabel turned back to Ginny. "Just get the one jogging suit for me, then, either the pink one or the orange one. I guess Beverly plans to wear her hospital gown out of here in the morning looking like she just escaped from a mental hospital."

Beverly quickly rethought her remark. "Good point. What other colors do you have?"

Ginny was already headed for the door. "We aren't divvying up a bag of M&M's, Beverly. I'll bring you whatever I find." She still wasn't sure Beverly Atwater didn't have designs on Grady, but even putting that aside, Ginny was not a fan of city people in general. Grady and Isabel were both left struggling not to laugh.

After Grady finished up with a few more details about the arrests, the subject turned to Jason. Like a good Congregationalist, Isabel made the best case she could for mercy and forgiveness, making sure Grady fully understood that, had it not been for Jason, they would all be dead. She questioned whether he should even be arrested at all. Although Beverly was with her in spirit, she was much more circumspect about what was ahead for Jason. Twenty-plus years of practicing law had taught her that when it came to murder, kidnapping, and criminal conspiracy, leniency was not usually a go-to for the courts.

"Well we had to arrest him, Iz," Grady said. "We had no choice in that."

Beverly nodded in agreement. "I promised to defend him, Isabel, and I will. And I'll do my best to get a favorable plea deal based on some pretty extraordinary extenuating circumstances. I mean, the boy redeemed himself before our very eyes, took a bullet for doing it, and *then* saved us all from drowning. But even under the best of circumstances, he'll still have to do some time."

Isabel was suddenly bowled over with sadness. "Poor kid . . . I know what he did was—"

"Criminal?" Grady interrupted. "Yes, it was. And he has to take responsibility for that."

She nodded a noncommittal yes, but she was not through making her point. "But didn't he also take responsibility when he decided to risk *his* life to save *ours*, and not let us all die a horrible death? I mean, he finally did the right thing, maybe for the first time in his life, and we're going to reward him for that by sending him back to prison? Is that justice?"

Grady shrugged his shoulders. "The system is what it is. I just do the arresting. I let judges and juries—and Beverly—handle the justice end of it." Grady started putting his coat back on. "I've got to run. I can't tell you ladies how thankful I am that you're both alive and well. I'm so sorry for what you had to go through. And that's where *I* need to take responsibility. Not only did I fail to protect you three, which is my number one job, I also helped put an innocent man in jail and accused him of murdering his own father. And if that weren't bad enough, I jumped to the very wrong conclusion that his sister had killed herself. I think I need to take a hard look at whether or not I'm in the right business."

"Don't be silly," Isabel scolded. "I forbid you to beat yourself up over this. Who could have imagined something like this ever happening in our little community? You did your best, Grady, under some very bizarre circumstances."

Grady opened the door, then turned back and smiled contritely. "You should both be very proud of yourselves for what you did, and for surviving such an ordeal."

Beverly scoffed and pointed to Isabel. "She did the lion's share. I just went along for the ride. And the bad news for Meg is that, as far as I'm concerned, those were all billable hours. And I'll be expensing my Jimmy Choos!"

Isabel laughed. "Well, it was a joint effort. And we had some outside help, too."

Grady nodded. "Jason may have saved your lives in the end, but if you two hadn't risked *yours* to rescue Meg, she'd be dead. End of story. Now, if you'll excuse me, I need to get down to the office and get acquainted with my new guests. We've got a full house tonight! Get some rest, you two! You've earned it!" Grady gave them a casual salute as he left.

Isabel was quiet for a moment, then lifted her head off her pillow and turned to Beverly. "What ever happened to you promising Jason he wouldn't spend *one* day in jail?"

Beverly rolled her head over to her. "Yes, I did. But I knew that even if he *did* help us escape, he would still end up spending a lot more than *one* day in jail. So, technically, I was telling the truth, but lying at the same time. It's a technique we learn in law school. But if it helped him decide not to kill us, well, that's a lie I can live with."

Isabel was still torn. "I just can't help but feel bad for him. I think the boy's got a good heart. Maybe he discovered that *himself* tonight. I for one am going to testify on his behalf, so you need to call me to the stand as a character witness."

Beverly was quick to make sure Isabel understood what was going to happen. "There isn't going to be any testifying, because there isn't going to be a trial. Jason can't very well plead 'not guilty.' Any competent jury hearing the evidence would be happy to send him away for life, whether he killed anybody or not. Three counts of kidnapping, three for attempted murder, two counts of accessory to murder, possibly three if we discover what's her name's husband was murdered, too. And that's just the prosecution warming up. They could end up pinning Jimmy Hoffa's disappearance on him before all is said and done. The best we can hope for is a plea deal that minimizes the time he'll get, and maybe where he serves it. But you can absolutely write a letter to the judge. I'll serve as a character witness myself. Meg, however, might be of a different mind."

Isabel thought that one over. "Yes . . . I can see where she might not be so forgiving."

Beverly sat up in bed and attempted to elevate the mood. "Isabel, how about we celebrate that we're *alive*! We were minutes away from being entombed underwater in a Dodge minivan! Not the most glamorous way to go!"

Isabel was not quite ready to celebrate. "My poor van—and it's a Chrysler *Town and Country*, thank you very much."

Just then the nurse walked back in, surprised to see them both still awake. "Well, hello there, Cagney and Lacey. What are you still doing up? I can imagine you must be pretty wound up, but you gals need to get some rest! I'm going to get you both a little something to relax your nerves."

Beverly dismissed the idea. "The only thing that will put me out is anesthesia. Or a baseball bat. No sleeping pill has ever worked for me."

Isabel agreed, explaining to the nurse that she was completely immune to sleeping aids of any kind.

"We'll see," were the nurse's parting words as she left the room.

Chapter 21

Isabel finally woke up or, more likely, came to the next morning just after eleven. Her body felt heavy and her head was throbbing. Groggy didn't begin to cover it. She imagined this was how an animal in the wild must feel after having been shot with a tranquilizer gun. *What did that nurse give me?* she wondered.

Beverly was still out cold, snoring so loudly the windows were practically shaking. Isabel sat up in bed, and as her eyes slowly began to focus, she saw someone sitting across the room . . . someone who looked blurrily familiar. "Frances? Is that you?"

"Well, it's about time you got up! Good Lord, woman!" Frances folded up her newspaper and walked over to Isabel's bedside. She grabbed her hand. "I leave you alone for a few days and look at the mess you get yourself into." She sat down on her bedside. "How are you feeling, Iddy Bell?"

Isabel smiled, comforted to have her best friend there. "You haven't called me Iddy Bell since high school. How did you hear about all this?"

"Gil Cook called me last night and told me everything. I thought he was making it up! I got the first flight out of Milwaukee this morning and came straight to the hospital."

Frances leaned down for a hug and they both got a little teary. "Must have been just horrible what you went through."

Isabel shook her head. "I've had better days. But poor Meg had it a lot worse than Beverly and I did."

Frances looked over at Beverly, still snoring away with her mouth wide open. "Oh, is that Beverly Atwater? By the sound of it, I thought they put you in here with a mountain gorilla."

Just then, Gil Cook burst into the room, hugging a huge bouquet of flowers. He went straight to Isabel's bed and gave her a big kiss on the cheek.

"Hello, lady," he said, dropping the flowers onto her chest. "I'm so sorry, Izzy. This is all my fault. If I hadn't—"

Isabel raised her hand, "You can stop right there, Gil." She slowly inched herself up in bed, then leaned back against the headboard. "If you *hadn't*, we would never have learned the truth about what happened to poor Earl Jonasson, and those Trudlow psychopaths would have gotten away with murder. I also have a hunch it will be *two* murders, if we can prove they did in Marlene Vanderhoff's husband. Oh, and I almost forgot about their boss! Couldn't have happened to a nicer guy, but it still counts! So three! Who *knows* how many people might have ended up dead?"

Frances leaned over and took Gil's flowers off Isabel's chest. "Let me put these in some water. Did you buy these, Gil, or swipe 'em from a customer?" she said, laughing, as she left the room.

No sooner had Frances left than in walked Freddie and Carol. After a heartfelt reunion of hugs and gratitude—and with Beverly still sawing logs in the next bed—Isabel shared the highlights of the previous day's events with them all. Next, Ginny came in, and two minutes after her, in walked Zander and Josh—Zander holding a vase full of orange Gerber daisies and Josh dropping a box of chocolates on her bedside table.

After the gang shared some laughs and enjoyed some friendly back and forth, Beverly finally came to. She lifted her head and surveyed the room with a blank stare, then leaned back and pulled the blankets up over her head. Seconds later the nurse walked in.

"What is this, a convention? How did you all get in here? You're only allowed two visitors at a time, Mrs. Puddles," she said with a wink. "I'm afraid morning visiting hours are over, folks. You can all come back at three if you like. This lady needs her rest."

"All I've been *doing* is resting! This lady needs to get home!" Isabel told the nurse.

"The doctor will be making her rounds shortly. That'll be up to her. Now, let's wrap it up, people," the nurse said, clapping her hands together. After saying their good-byes, everybody filtered out of the room except for Ginny, who was lingering with the door half-open, not wanting to leave her cousin alone.

Isabel smiled. "Honey, I'm fine. I'm sure they'll let me out of here today. I don't see why they wouldn't. Oh, Gin, did you . . . ?"

Ginny smiled and nodded. "I stopped and fed them on my way over. They're fine. But I could tell they miss their mom."

Isabel was relieved. "I miss them, too! Now, you go on. I'm sure they need you down at the sheriff's department today."

Ginny nodded. "It's been pretty hectic down there. And there are newspaper and TV reporters all over town. From Grand Rapids, Lansing, Detroit, even Chicago. You all have made quite a splash . . . oh . . . sorry." They both laughed. "I almost forgot to tell you, Iz. Grady released Earl Junior this morning."

Isabel smiled. "That's good news. That poor man's nightmare has finally come to an end."

"Well, we needed the room!" Ginny said with a chuckle.

"I think he and the boys are all upstairs with Meg and Larry right now."

A wave of relief crashed over Isabel. Ginny patted her on the arm. "I'll be back to check on you later." Ginny threw her a kiss and opened the door to leave, practically bumping into Frances, who was on her way back in, carrying Gil's flowers in a vase. The two shared polite hellos as they jockeyed around each other at the door.

"Where have you been?" Isabel asked Frances. Beverly poked her head out from under the covers again, but, seeing it was Frances, pulled them back up.

"Well, I went up to see Meg. I felt I owed her an apology. And then her brother came in. And I *knew* I owed *him* an apology. They were both very gracious. So, I stand chastened and rebuked. Lesson learned." She turned her head in Beverly's direction, "So hopefully I won't have to worry about being locked up in my own hometown for exercising my First Amendment right to free speech ever again!" There was no response. Just more snoring. Beverly was out cold again.

Beverly finally woke up at about two in the afternoon, and they were both discharged just as afternoon visiting hours got under way. Ginny had left two velour jogging suits at the nurses' station, one in orange, and one in canary yellow. Isabel preferred bright colors for her "jogging" attire, thinking if she got lost in the woods, she would be easier to find, and when she was walking along the roadside, easier to miss. Ginny had also brought tennis shoes, socks, and two knit caps to cover their crazy-looking hairdos.

After getting dressed and saying good-bye to their nurses, Isabel and Beverly headed upstairs to see Meg, looking like a couple of mall walkers in their jogging suits. But Isabel wanted to make a stop along the way.

"I'm sorry, ma'am, but the sheriff said no visitors," the deputy standing outside Jason's door told Isabel officiously.

Isabel looked him up and down. "Well I'll talk to Grady about that. In the meantime, can you get a message to Jason for me, please? Will you tell him that Ms. Atwater and Mrs. Puddles stopped by to check in on him?"

"Sheriff Pemberton said we are not to communicate with him at all until his attorney is present."

Isabel smiled. "Well, then, I'd like to introduce you to his attorney. Meet Beverly Atwater. Beverly, this is Deputy—wait—aren't you the one who gave me that ticket for a rolling stop?"

"Yes, ma'am, I am . . . and I have lived to regret it. You seem to be very popular in this county. I'd have gotten a lot less grief for giving Shirley Temple a ticket for public tap dancing. You can go on in," he said, opening the door, "but I'll need to come with you."

Jason was staring out the window at the fall foliage when they walked into the room. The first thing they noticed was that his good arm was handcuffed to the bed rail. When he saw them, his eyes immediately welled with tears. He tried to say something, but nothing came out.

Isabel spoke up instead. "How's that arm feeling, honey?"

Jason composed himself and smiled. "Sore. How is Mrs. Blackburn?" he asked.

Beverly joined in. "She's just fine. We're going up to see her right now. She's with her husband and her nephews. And her brother has been released from jail, so he's with her, too."

Jason nodded. "And you two?"

Isabel looked at Beverly. "You think a dunk in a cold pond is going to hurt a couple'a tough old broads like us? We're just happy to be alive and dry. And, thanks to you, we are."

Jason looked back out the window. "Yeah, but, thanks to me, you might just as easily not have been." Jason was getting reflective. "I should'a gone to the police when I figured out what them three was up to."

Beverly jumped in again. "Let's stay positive. I want my clients thinking half-full, not half-empty."

Jason turned his head back to her. "So, are you really going to be my lawyer?"

Beverly looked him in the eye. "I said I would, didn't I?"

Jason thought a minute. "You also said I wouldn't spend *one* day in jail." He looked over at Isabel and smiled. "But I knew that was a crock. Not my first time to the rodeo. . . . But I deserve to do some time for what I did. Or *didn't* do. I just hope it ain't *too* much. And I do plan to stay positive. I'm gonna take some school classes inside, get my GED—not sure what that is exactly, but I'm gonna get it—maybe even take some college classes. I just want to better myself so when I do get out, *if* I do get out, I can finally, maybe, make somethin'a my life."

Isabel and Beverly were moved. "Well, I'm going to talk to the state's attorney tomorrow and we're going to see what we can do," Beverly told him. "I'll be in touch as soon as I have some news for you."

Isabel reached over and brushed his hair off his forehead. "You take care and heal up fast. We're not going to forget about you, Jason, or what you did for us. We'll see you later, okay?"

Jason nodded. He was too choked up to say good-bye.

The deputy opened the door and held it open as Beverly and Isabel left the room. "Thank you, Deputy," Isabel said as they passed by, but as they turned down the hallway toward the elevator, he had something on his mind.

"I don't understand. This guy kidnapped you and was ready to murder all three of you. Why are you so concerned about what happens to *him*?"

Beverly proceeded to the elevator, while Isabel turned

and took a few steps back and smiled at the handsome young deputy. "It's important in this life to forgive, Deputy. Jason made some very bad choices, choices that might indeed have cost us our lives. But ultimately he made the *right* choice and he *saved* our lives. You, on the other hand, made a choice that cost me fifty-five bucks that I could ill afford to part with. But I forgive you, too." She patted him on the arm, then turned and walked away, leaving the deputy speechless as he watched the two women get into the elevator.

Meg was sitting up in bed when Isabel and Beverly walked in. They were happy to see she was looking and acting more like her old self again.

"You just missed Earl and the boys! Larry took everybody home. He's going to smuggle me in some dinner later. I told him anything but Arby's!"

Isabel and Beverly laughed and went to opposite sides of her bed. Isabel gave her a hug. Beverly gave her a handshake. "Are you still on the clock?" Meg asked her.

"No, we're done. Case closed."

A nurse popped her head in. "Ms. Atwater, there's a call for you at the nurses' station. A Mr. Hastings."

Beverly smiled. "One of my partners. Probably the only one at least somewhat happy to hear I'm still alive. If you'll excuse me, ladies."

Beverly left the room, leaving Isabel and Meg alone. They stared at each other for a few moments, smiling, until Meg spoke up. "I owe you my life, Isabel. So does my brother."

Isabel shook her head. "You don't owe me anything. I know you would have done the same for me. And can you believe our luck that Zander came along when he did? He's the real hero here. We might very well have succumbed to hypothermia or had another run-in with you know who."

"We certainly do owe him, too. How did you come to know Zander, anyway, Iz?"

"He came into Freddie's to buy some waders. Come to find out he needed them to survey your land, well, the marshy part of your land. Of course, I had no idea there was any connection then. How long had you known about this deal Zander's company was proposing for the windmills?"

"You mean the wind turbines?" Meg smiled and nodded. "It's kind of a long story. You better pull up a chair, Iz." Isabel dragged a chair over and sat down while Meg continued. "So, here's what happened. Wind-X approached my father and asked if they could survey a parcel of our land on the western boundary. Apparently it's one of the windiest spots on the west coast of Michigan. They explained that they were in the wind turbine business. Daddy wasn't the least bit interested. He had no idea what a wind turbine was nor did he care, but my brother was curious, so he told them to go ahead and send an engineer up. I guess that was Zander. So, a few weeks go by and they call again and make an offer to lease three hundred acres to install their turbines, with an option to lease a hundred more. Daddy turned them down without even asking what they were offering, but Earl wanted to know what kind of a deal we were passing up, so he called them back. Well, when he heard the offer he was bowled over, so he asked them to give him some time to talk to *me* about it. He thought maybe the two of us could convince Daddy to at least consider it."

Isabel was listening attentively. So far everything Meg was saying jibed with what Zander had told her from the get-go. Meg continued, "I happened to be coming up that weekend, so we all sat down, even the boys, and we had a family meeting about it. It was a very serious offer, and a serious amount of money. It would have solved a lot of problems for us, problems that might have meant our losing the farm. Daddy listened and said he'd think it over. Then, over Sunday dinner, he told us he had reached a decision . . . and that decision was no. Earl tried to get him to change his mind and so did I, but I knew we were fighting a losing battle, so I finally gave up. But my brother just wouldn't let it go. Of course he had a lot more at stake than I did. If we lost the farm, *he* lost his livelihood. And he's got a family to support. I know he must have had that moneygrubbing Tammy Trudlow pressuring him, too. She didn't give two hoots about my brother or my nephews. All she cared about was getting him to the altar and then getting her hands on that money. Anyway, Earl was angry, and I understood that. He called Wind-X again and asked for a little more time, and they agreed. But they also said they had their eye on another parcel of land close by, so the clock was ticking. It was pretty tense for a while. I had never seen my brother so angry. Unfortunately, what all this amounted to circumstantially, at least as far as the sheriff and the state's attorney were concerned, was plenty of motive for murder. That and finding the nail gun in his garage with his DNA on it didn't look very good. But I know my brother." Meg smiled and took a deep breath.

Isabel was thinking. "What about Junior's alibi not checking out, Meg? I know that raised the red flags for Grady right out of the gate."

"Oh, that? Beverly cleared that up the same week she took the case. Nobody had seen my brother at Mickey's Roadhouse having wings and a beer because Mickey's doesn't serve wings. He was next door at Guffman's, where they *do* have wings, and where it turned out the bartender *did* remember him. Junior just wasn't thinking straight when Grady started asking questions. Neither of us were. So he got confused. And as luck would have it, bad luck, it was that particular bartender's last day on the job the day Earl came in. So, by the time we figured it all out and Beverly tracked him down and took his statement, Junior had already been arrested. And as far as that awful Tom Garrett from the state's attorney's office was concerned, my brother was guilty. Convicting him was just a formality. He wouldn't even go over there and interview him!" Meg had to take a breath to keep calm. "Well, it's all over now. Water under the bridge, or under the beaver dam, you might say."

Isabel perked up. "Oh, that's right! Tell me about this beaver dam, Meg. I had no idea we had any beavers around here anymore."

"Well, that's because my mother and father kept it a secret." Isabel looked confused. Meg chuckled and continued. "Do you want to know the real reason Daddy wouldn't make the deal with Wind-X? It wasn't about the land. We had plenty of that to spare. He didn't love the idea of sitting on his porch and looking out at a bunch of giant fans whirling above him, but he knew it would be an easy remedy to what had become a pretty dire financial situation. No, the real reason Daddy didn't want the land disturbed, especially that parcel Wind-X wanted over by the Three Sisters, was because of a promise he made to my mother."

This was really getting good. Isabel was all ears. Meg straightened up in bed and continued. "You know what created that marsh? The marsh where we used to hunt bullfrogs back in the day? It was from a beaver dam hidden downstream, a huge beaver colony that's been there for maybe a hundred years or more, Daddy said."

Isabel was shocked. "No kidding? Why did I think all the beavers around here had disappeared?"

Meg continued, "There aren't many left anywhere in lower Michigan, but around here, we have the Jonassons to thank in large part for that, I'm sad to say."

"I'm not following you, Meg."

"Daddy's people came over from Denmark sometime in the 1800s. And how did they survive? They were trappers. And they were good at it. It was the money they made from trapping that eventually paid for a good chunk of the land we still own today."

"And this beaver dam is still on your land?" Isabel asked, still somewhat astonished.

Meg smiled. "It is. My father discovered it just after he and Mother were married. It thrilled her no end. She had names for all of them. I couldn't tell any of them apart, but she could. Daddy loved them, too. We used to take picnics out there and watch them work when Earl and I were just kids. But we were both sworn to secrecy. My parents didn't want word getting out that there were beavers on our property for fear some amateur trapper might come for them. Or people would come and disturb them. They were very protective of that beaver colony. Before Mama died, Daddy made a promise to her that he would take care of them. I also think part of it was that he felt a little guilty. I think he was trying to make up for the sins of his grandfather and his great-grandfathers in a way."

"Well, that's just about the sweetest thing I've ever heard," Isabel said softly.

"After Mama passed, Daddy would go out there by himself and just sit for hours in an old Adirondack chair and watch those beavers."

Meg got a little misty-eyed. "Daddy was such an animal lover. Any livestock we ever had on the farm stayed on the farm until they died. The chickens were only for eggs, we always had a milk cow, and the goats were just for clearing brush. And remember that old pig we had?"

Isabel racked her brain for a moment. "I guess I do remember a pig. Didn't you win a ribbon at the fair with it one summer? Gertrude, was it?"

"Gertrude, yes! As much as I loved that pig, Daddy loved

her even more. Gertie used to follow him all over the farm just like a dog would. I think she was the only pig in this county that ever died of old age. Daddy stopped eating bacon because of that pig. He came in from the barn one morning for breakfast and asked my mother to stop frying bacon in the future because he was certain he saw Gertrude crying when the smell reached them out in the barn." Meg and Isabel both laughed. "We never ate bacon or sausage in our house again. Daddy cried like a baby the day he found Gertie dead in the barn. It was the first time I ever saw him cry."

Isabel was both touched and amazed by what she was hearing. "So you're telling me your father wouldn't sell that land, and that he was willing to pass up all that money, because he didn't want to disturb a colony of beavers?"

"That's exactly what I'm telling you. It was a promise he made to my mother, and Daddy never broke a promise. Mama's illness really broke the bank. He had taken a second mortgage out on the farm and completely depleted his savings by the time she passed. My brother and I both knew that burden was going to fall to us sooner or later. But neither of us would have done anything differently when it came to taking care of Mama. She had the very best care we could give her. And if it meant one day losing the farm, well, so be it."

"We should all be so lucky to have a husband and children care for us the way you all did for Ruth. Nothing lucky about cancer, but she sure was lucky to have all of you." Meg got wistful again. Isabel handed her the bottle of water sitting on the bedside table to distract her and get her back to the story. "But, Meg, Zander said your dad ended up changing his mind about this land deal. How did that come about?"

Meg took a sip of water. "Because, believe it or not, I found an expert who could relocate the beavers."

"You found a beaver relocation expert?"

Meg laughed. "Who knew that was a thing, right? But,

yes, she's an animal control expert from Michigan State, and her specialty is relocating beavers. And because we've got a river and several streams running through our land, along with a few good-sized ponds, we found them another spot. Actually a much better spot, very protected, and with lots of trees to keep them busy. So she put together a plan to move the entire colony to this new spot and assured Daddy that beavers were very adaptable and that they would be just fine. Plus, they would be much closer to the house, so it would be easier for him to go watch them. So, he agreed to it. He even agreed to give the university access so they could study them. So, the university paid for it all. It was a win-win. That's all it took. My father had kept his promise to my mother, Earl was happy, I was happy, the boys were happy, and soon the beavers would be happy. I called the people at Wind-X myself and told them to draw up the contract."

Meg started getting emotional again. "Then Daddy died the day before he was supposed to sign the paperwork."

"That's it!" Isabel yelled. "That's *it*. After your dad initially passed on the deal, their second choice was the land owned by Marlene Vanderhoff!"

This wasn't tracking for Meg. "I'm not following, Izzy."

"Tammy didn't want your father dead because he *wouldn't* make the deal, it was because he had changed his mind and decided he *would* make the deal!"

"I'm still not following."

"I couldn't figure out how Parker—Marlene Vanderhoff's boyfriend slash fiancé—worked into this and how he got involved with Tammy. He must have met her through her brother, who was working for him. After your dad passed, Parker thought his fiancée's deal with Wind-X was all locked up, so he was seeing dollar signs. Then, when he found out the deal with your dad was going through, after all, he hired Tammy and Glen to murder him before he could sign that contract! And poor Jason got dragged into it, thinking he was up here just to do some carpentry work. Not only that, I heard Tammy say that she killed Parker because he had re-neged on his promise to pay them fifty thousand dollars and get them an easement to their old farm. Tammy must have been hoping Wind-X might lease or buy the old Trudlow land, too! Now, *that's* motive."

Now Meg was starting to see the light. She shook her head. "Well, what those idiots didn't know was that I'm Dad-dy's executor. That's the reason I drove to Kalamazoo the other day, to meet with them. They said I was just in time, because they had all the papers drawn up for this other deal— I guess with this Vanderhoff woman—and they were getting ready to meet with her to sign everything. So, we got back in right under the wire."

"And that's the last piece of the puzzle! I couldn't figure out why they would want to do you any harm, but one of them obviously ran you off the road because they knew you were about to make a deal that would leave them out in the cold, so they wanted *you* dead, too."

"You're right, Iz, it all makes sense now. It's just hard to wrap your head around the despicable lengths to which peo-ple will go purely out of greed."

They were both taking a moment to contemplate when Beverly burst back into the room.

"Well, I have a new client, ladies! Want to take a guess? Never mind, you'll never guess. Marlene Vanderhoff! Her brother lives in Detroit and just called my firm. She is stead-fastly denying she had anything to do with any of this."

Isabel was practically speechless. "You've got to be kid-ding me."

Beverly plopped down in the other chair. "Nope. He claims his sister knew nothing. In fact, he warned her about that Parker miscreant from the beginning. Told her he thought he was a con man. He even told her he suspected he had something to do with her husband's death."

Isabel thought it over for a minute. "I suppose it's feasible, depending on how gullible a woman she is. Just because she cheated on her husband doesn't mean she had a hand in murdering him. I suppose she could have been in the dark about all the rest of it, too. But Tammy and Glen told Grady that Marlene was in on it."

"Well, I think it's safe to say those two have a bit of a credibility problem. *Boy*, I would love to get those two knuckle-draggers on the stand and rip them to shreds. That's the stuff I live for!"

At that moment it became very clear to Isabel how and why Beverly Atwater had earned her reputation.

"So, what are you going to do?" Meg asked her.

Beverly shrugged her shoulders. "I'm going to go meet with her tomorrow and hear her out. She's been denied bond, but her brother just ponied up a quarter-million-dollar retainer."

Isabel and Meg were looking at her curiously, which Beverly interpreted as judgment. "You know, a lot of folks thought Earl was guilty, too, and I was one of them—at least at first. Obviously I couldn't have been more wrong. I had a little 'come to Jesus' moment when we were strapped in that van. I made a promise to Whoever might be listening that if I got out of this alive, I was not going to defend clients accused of serious crimes if I believed they were guilty. So, like I said, I'm going to hear her out."

Isabel took a deep breath. "You can color me skeptical about Marlene's involvment, but I'm sure you'll make the right choice."

"Isabel, are you going to tell Beverly what you figured out? We finally have a motive that makes sense, Beverly."

"So you had your *Columbo* moment, Isabel?" Isabel ignored her remark and proceeded to go back over all the highlights, with some help from Meg. Beverly listened to her attentively until she wrapped up.

"Well, circumstantially it all makes perfect sense. And now we have motive. Once they do the forensics on that pickup truck, well, that's game, set, and match. Isabel, your sleuthing skills and your talents of deduction are most impressive."

Beverly looked at them both and smiled. It seemed as if she was actually feeling a little emotional. "All right, well, I hate to leave you two but I need to get back to work. I've enjoyed our time together—minus the kidnapping and being left for dead in an ice-cold pond part—but other than that it's been nice getting to know you both." She smiled again and then got serious. "I have to say, even as jaded as I am, I think you are two of the most courageous women I have ever known." Meg and Isabel were touched. "I'm going back to the Michigander Inn now and I'm going to take a long, hot bath. Isabel, thank you for, well, for everything."

Isabel smiled. "My friends call me Iz or Izzy. Either one."

Now Beverly was touched. "I'll get this jogging suit back to you tomorrow, Izzy. You know I might just have to pick up one of these. Very comfy."

"You keep it. Canary yellow is a good color on you."

"Thank you. I will cherish it. Meg, you rest up. You'll need all your strength when you get my bill! Ciao for now, ladies!" Beverly threw them kisses and swept out the door.

Isabel looked at Meg. "Boy, if you told me yesterday morning that I would be calling Beverly Atwater my friend just twenty-four hours later, I would have said you were nuts."

Meg nodded. "I wasn't sure what to make of her at first, either. But she's a good egg."

"Just a little hard-boiled," Isabel added. They started giggling together just like they used to in grade school. "Well, Meg, I need to get home and see Jackpot and your sister, Corky! Any idea when they're going to let you out of here?"

"I'm hoping tomorrow morning. I'm just waiting for the doctor to give the thumbs-up."

"You need me to come and pick you up?" Isabel asked.

"You've done quite enough. I don't have the words to thank you for what you've done, Iz. You saved my brother's life and you saved mine. I just—"

Isabel interrupted. "You being alive and well is all the thanks I need." She headed for the door. "I'll call you in the morning."

Just as she reached for the door, in walked Frances and Ginny, arm in arm and almost giddy. "What's going on here?" Isabel asked suspiciously. These two hadn't had an encounter in the last twenty years that wasn't strained and uncomfortable.

"Well, we just spent the last twenty minutes stuck in the elevator together!" Ginny said, smiling at Frances, who was still laughing.

"I told her I hadn't been trapped in such a confined space since her boyfriend threw me in the slammer!"

Ginny laughed even louder. "There's nothing like being trapped in an elevator to bring two people together!" Ginny was still wide-eyed, looking as if she had just gotten off a wild roller-coaster ride. "You know how claustrophobic I am, Iz! I thought I was going to lose my mind! I started hyper-ventilating and sweating. I was absolutely panic stricken! But Frances got me through it! She just kept talking and talking to me the whole time, trying to keep me calm, making me take deep breaths . . . and it worked! And before I knew it we were out!"

"Finally my big mouth gets the appreciation it deserves!" Frances boasted. "Chatty Cathy saves the day!"

Ginny suddenly looked embarrassed. "I can't believe the

way I'm going on about being stuck in an elevator after what you two have just been through."

That registered for Frances, too. "Oh, right. Well, we're all free now! Meg, I hope we'll see each other again soon. Now, let's get you home, Iddy Bell. I've got a box of wine chilling in the trunk of my car. Ginny you're coming, too."

After saying their good-byes to Meg, the three walked out into the hallway, chattering away until Frances pressed the button for the elevator. Ginny went quiet and gave her a look. "Not in a million years. I'll take the stairs."

Ginny followed Frances and Isabel back to Poplar Bluff. When they pulled into the drive, Isabel's eyes welled with tears, remembering how sad she felt, thinking she would never see this place again. The yard could still use a good raking, but to her, it had never looked better. She rushed up the walkway, and when she opened her front door, Jackpot and Corky went completely berserk. She sat right down in the middle of the foyer to hug and scratch them while they showered her with kisses. Frances stepped through the madness, hugging her box of wine, followed by Ginny, who smiled as she watched the reunion. After her welcoming committee finally calmed down, Isabel got up and went to the laundry room to get them some treats, while Frances got busy opening the wine and Ginny got out the glasses.

Isabel was relieved to see that her two oldest, closest friends had finally moved on from barely speaking terms to what looked like a promising friendship. They toasted to a happy ending, then went into the living room and sat down next to the fireplace. Isabel lit a fire and sat down on the sofa. Jackpot and Corky snuggled up next to her. As she looked out over the lake, with the magic hour upon them—Isabel's favorite time of day—a sense of normalcy finally returned to Poplar Bluff.

Chapter 22

Isabel woke up the next morning with Jackpot in his usual spot at the foot of her bed, and for the first time, Corky was on the bed cuddled up with her, too. But she was feeling a little foggy. Between Frances, Ginny, and herself, they had killed an entire box of wine, although Frances and Ginny had outpaced her considerably. After her feet hit the floor and she slid into her fuzzy slippers, her first thought was, *How in the world did those two get home?* She put on her robe and went into the living room, relieved to find Frances asleep on the sofa and Ginny curled up in Isabel's favorite overstuffed chair. As the consummate hostess, she was happy to see that at some point she had managed to provide blankets and pillows for them both.

Isabel couldn't remember the last time she had had too much to drink. It was a very rare occurrence. And now, with the headache that was presenting itself, she was reminded why. She fed the dogs and put on the coffee, and by then Ginny and Frances were awake. "If I had known we were going to have a slumber party, I would have brought my Earth, Wind and Fire records!" Frances yelled into the kitchen.

Ginny laughed, then asked, "Does anybody remember if I called Grady last night?"

"Yes, you did!" Isabel yelled back. "But I don't remember if Frances called Hank!"

"Oh, please. Why would I bother?" Frances said as she got up from the sofa, still wrapped in her blanket. "I'll bet he never noticed I was gone! If I'm not setting a plate of food down in front of him or blocking the TV, he doesn't even know I'm there. But that's about to change, let me tell you!"

Isabel wasn't quite sure what to make of that comment, but it was a can of worms she was not going to open right now. She carried two cups of coffee into the living room, cream and sugar for Frances, black for Ginny. "You girls want to head down to the Land's End for some breakfast?"

Ginny managed to sit up to drink her coffee. "Sure, let's go."

Frances was game, too, but she issued a warning. "You know folks will have heard all about what happened by now, so you better be prepared Izzy." Isabel hadn't thought about that. She hated being the center of attention.

Now Ginny had more information to make her even more uncomfortable. "I must have gotten a couple dozen calls yesterday morning from people wanting to talk to you."

Isabel looked both surprised and troubled. "What people?"

Ginny took another sip of her coffee. "I told you, Iz. I had newspaper reporters calling from all over, and I think every TV station in Michigan called. I even got a call from a TV producer in New York City. She told me she heard about the story from the Associated Press. You're famous, Iz!"

Isabel was visibly shaken. She sat down on the sofa next to Frances. "Oh, dear Lord."

Although it was troubling for Isabel, it certainly was not for Frances. "What's wrong? This is terrific! You deserve some attention for doing what you did. You're a hero! Why not enjoy it?"

"I am *not* a hero, and I do not want, nor do I need, any attention—especially not from a bunch of newspaper or TV reporters. Or New York City TV producers!" She looked back at Ginny in earnest. "You didn't give them any of my information, did you, Gin?"

Ginny looked surprised her cousin would even ask. "Of course not! I would never do that without asking you. But you aren't exactly a needle in a haystack, Iz. Everybody in the county knows you, and most of them know where you live. So, once they start asking around . . ."

Isabel got up with a heavy sigh. "I need more coffee." Walking into the kitchen, she noticed the light blinking on the answering machine on the counter. She pressed the red button, and to her unpleasant surprise heard, "Your answering machine is full." How could that be? Her answering machine had never been full or even close to it. She hesitated before hitting the playback button. "You have twenty-five new messages." She quickly hit stop. "Oh, dear Lord," she repeated as she continued to the kitchen in a state of shock.

After pouring herself another cup, she heard a strange rustling sound outside the kitchen window. As she leaned over the sink to look outside, a bearded man's head suddenly popped up like a jack-in-the-box. Isabel screamed, dropping her cup into the sink with a crash. The dogs, followed by Ginny and Frances, came rushing into the kitchen. "What in the world!" Frances yelled.

Isabel stood frozen, staring out the kitchen window. "Look."

Ginny and Frances joined her at the window and looked outside. Parked on either side of the road, and stretching fifty yards or more in each direction, were a half dozen TV satellite trucks, and another ten or more cars and vans. At the foot of her driveway were at least two dozen people, some with cameras perched on their shoulders, some holding microphones, and all of them staring at Isabel's house.

Ginny was the first to speak. "I'm calling Grady and telling him to get over here right now."

Isabel was still stricken. She quickly yanked the kitchen curtains shut, then walked over and sat down at the kitchen counter. "I thought it was a Peeping Tom. He was right outside my window." Isabel was suddenly indignant. "Are they allowed to do that?"

Ginny was angry. "No, they most certainly are not! That's trespassing! We'll let Grady sort it out when he gets here."

Frances, not surprisingly, was enthralled, and was now standing at the front door, looking through the peephole. "You want me to go out and talk to them?"

"*No!*" Isabel and Ginny both yelled back simultaneously.

Isabel put her elbows on the kitchen counter and dropped her head into her hands. She knew that, as of this day, her life might never be the same, or at least wouldn't be for a while. She remembered one of her Grandfather Peabody's favorite expressions: "No good deed goes unpunished."

After rushing through the house, closing all the blinds and curtains and making sure all the doors and windows were locked, Isabel began to pace. Frances maintained her position at the peephole, monitoring the movements of the army of media outside, while Ginny remained on the phone with Grady, who was already on his way. When they finally heard the short blurts from his siren announcing his arrival to the unwelcome minions, Isabel and Ginny felt a huge sense of relief. Frances on the other hand was disappointed that the fun might now be over.

Two deputies who arrived with Grady got busy wrapping police tape around trees and fence posts to create a perimeter, then began herding people back. Grady ignored them all, despite their desperate attempts to get him to stop and talk. He made his way up the driveway and to the front door, where Ginny opened it just far enough for him to slip in. He found Isabel still sitting at the counter, in complete disbelief.

"Looks like you've got company, Iz," Grady said with a chuckle. "I haven't seen press like this around here since they found crop circles in Henry Pickens's asparagus field."

"Put there after Henry got drunk and took his tractor out for a midnight joy ride!" Frances yelled from her position back at the peephole.

Grady sat down next to Isabel. "So, can you give me a description of the man you saw at your kitchen window, Iz? I'll go out and arrest him right now."

Isabel slowly shook her head. "I don't want anybody arrested. I just want them gone."

Ginny was still wound up. "How about I go out there and take the garden hose to them?"

Grady stared at her deadpan. "Or I have a canister of tear gas in my truck."

Ginny gave him a look. "Can you do that?"

Grady returned the look. "No." He turned to Isabel. "There's no excuse for trespassing or peeking in your window. That's a crime. But the rest of them are just doing their jobs. You've got to admit, it's one helluva story."

Ginny put her arm around her cousin. "You want to just come home with us, Izzy? I can't believe they'd be stupid enough to follow the sheriff home."

Isabel shook her head. "Thank you, but no. I just got home and I want to stay home."

"I don't blame you," Grady said as he headed for the door. "I have an idea. I'll be back."

Isabel and Ginny ran to the kitchen to peek through the curtains, with Frances still at the peephole. All of them were anxious to see what Grady had in store for these interlopers.

With a deputy standing on either side, Grady addressed the group. After a few minutes of back-and-forth, they all began to disperse, although they didn't look happy about it. Grady and his deputies waited until they had all gotten into their cars and vans, and along with the convoy of satellite trucks, slowly made their way down the road and eventually out of sight, no doubt disappointed that the small-town hero they had come to meet clearly had no interest in meeting *them*.

Grady came back inside to find all three women and both dogs in the foyer waiting to hear how he had gotten them to disperse so quickly. "I told them they were on a private road and that they would all be arrested for trespassing if they did not disperse immediately."

Isabel corrected him. "That's a county road, Grady."

Grady reached down to pet the dogs. "I know that, but they don't. I also might have told them that they could look for you at the press conference Beverly has scheduled for tomorrow."

Isabel wasn't sure she heard correctly. "Did you say press conference? *What* press conference? Why would she want to have a press conference?"

Ginny was quick to respond. "Did you think she was going to let a publicity bonanza like this one get away? She's probably already got you both booked on *60 Minutes!*"

Grady laughed. "She's going to make an announcement about Marlene Vanderhoff. I think she may be thinking about representing her. I guess she just can't get enough of Kentwater County."

"Too bad the feeling isn't mutual," Ginny cracked.

Isabel was not happy. "Grady, why would you tell them that? I have no intention of going to any press conference. Not tomorrow and not ever."

Grady smiled and put his arm around Isabel. "All I said was that they could *look* for you at the press conference. I made no guarantees they'd *find* you there."

Isabel forced a polite laugh. "So, you took a page from Beverly Atwater's book. I forgot you went to law school. Fine by me! I just want to be left alone."

"You plan to become the Greta Garbo of Gull Harbor?" Frances asked.

"No, Frances. I plan to get back to my dull, ordinary, drama-free everyday life. Just how I like it. This much attention is embarrassing."

"It looks like you're about to get even more attention," Ginny said, looking out the kitchen window again. Isabel peered out to see Freddie and Carol walking up the driveway, both carrying casserole dishes, followed by Zander and Josh, both holding bottles of champagne. Gil Cook pulled up right behind them in his red Beetle and tooted his arrival as usual.

Ginny turned to Isabel with a big smile. "You didn't think we were going to forget your birthday, did you?"

Isabel's mouth fell open. "Oh. My. God! It *is* my birthday! And look at me! I'm a wreck! I need to go make myself presentable!"

Frances and Ginny were right behind her, running into the guest room, where they had secretly stashed their overnight bags. Isabel caught them unpacking. "So, you had this planned all along?"

Frances yelled from the bathroom, "You bet we did! It's not every day a girl turns twenty-nine!"

An hour later—with the birthday girl, Ginny, and Frances all looking gorgeous and dressed to the nines—they had a full house. Friends, neighbors, and family from all over the county had dropped in to wish their new local hero a happy birthday. Roberta from the Antique Barn was there, Frank from the hardware store, Phoebe Farnsworth, Doris and Byron Fletcher, Joyce and Toby, and every member of the Knit Wits. Thankfully, because it was Michigan, and it was what people did, everybody brought food, so there was plenty to eat. Kayla from Land's End came, too, along with Chet, delivering a birthday carrot cake, Isabel's favorite, baked especially for his old high school crush. Still more friends and neighbors continued to file in.

Just as Isabel blew out the candles—after a rousing version of "Happy Birthday"—June Clapper, who ran the animal shelter where Isabel volunteered, walked in, carrying an adorable Chihuahua puppy the size of a softball. She told Isabel she needed somebody to foster the little guy. He was too young to be left alone in the kennels. June knew Isabel was a soft touch. "I thought he might help take your mind off what you've just been through," June said, handing him off to her. Isabel knew she was being played, but she had never said no to fostering a puppy and never would. As far as she was concerned, puppies were one of the very best things in life.

Isabel snuggled with the puppy and looked around the house. It was a lovely gathering, but she noticed there were a few people missing. Where were Meg and Larry? And what about Beverly? At that very moment, in walked Beverly, dressed impeccably with her hair perfectly coiffed again, sweeping into the party as though it were being held in her honor. She made her way over to greet Isabel, nodding and saying hello to the other guests and carrying a beautiful gift bag. But before she even reached her, Beverly's eyes fixed on the puppy.

"Where did *that* come from? Is it real?" She traded Isabel the gift bag for the puppy, pulling it to her chest.

"He's a rescue," Isabel told her, surprised to discover Beverly was a dog lover. She was practically swooning.

"When I was a little girl, we had a Chihuahua named Diego. He looked just like this little"—she lifted the puppy up to peek under the chassis—"guy. Poor Diego got lost the summer I turned thirteen. My father said he escaped from the backyard somehow, but I still think he was stolen. I never got over it. I'm still not over it."

Isabel saw an opening and made her move. "He is adorable, isn't he? My mother had a Chihuahua . . . Guapo. I think they're a very misunderstood breed. I am so glad you could make it, Beverly. Now I need to make the rounds and check on my company. Would you mind hanging on to him for a while?" Then she sunk the hook. "You know, he's looking for a home. Just FYI. I can't handle a third dog, and I hate to think about him going back to that cold, lonely shelter."

Isabel left her alone with the puppy and headed into the kitchen wearing a big smile. Beverly went straight to the sofa and sat down with the puppy, joined by Jackpot and Corky, who were more than a little interested in the new arrival.

After so many days of stress and sadness, culminating in a kidnapping and a brush with death by drowning, Isabel Puddles could not have been happier to see her home filled with so many dear friends and family. She had forgotten all about the gang of reporters who had upset her earlier. She felt not only grateful to be alive but blessed to have so many people in her life who cared so much about her. Now she wished she hadn't discouraged Ginny from calling Carly and Charlie. They were all that was missing from the picture. But they were busy, and there was no need for them to drop everything and fly to Michigan. For what? She was fine. *All's well that ends well*, she told herself. Before she knew it, Christmas would be here and they'd both be home. She'd tell them all about it then.

The doorbell snapped Isabel to attention, and she went to the front door to join the dogs who were already barking and waiting to see who was coming in next. Standing there were Meg and Larry. "Well, look who's here! Come in! Come in!"

Larry took her by the hand and guided her down to the stoop. "First we'd like you to come with us."

Isabel looked a little suspicious. "Okaaaay."

Meg grabbed her other hand. "We have a surprise for you, Izzy." They walked out into the driveway just as Earl and the boys pulled into the driveway in a brand-spanking-new, cranberry red, Chrysler Town & Country. Earl got out, followed by the boys, who jumped out and excitedly ran over to hug Isabel. Earl walked over and handed her the keys with a big smile and a warm embrace. "It's for you, Isabel. Happy birthday."

She looked at him in disbelief, then at Meg, then at Larry, and then back at Earl. "Oh, no . . . I couldn't possibly let you—"

Meg stopped her cold. "Isabel, this falls squarely into it's-the-least-we-could-do category."

Then Larry jumped in. "And you happen to be minus a van now, in case you don't remember."

Isabel was in shock. "But this is . . . oh, come on. That old van of mine was on its last legs anyway. I just can't let you—"

Earl put his arm around her. "I'm afraid what you can't do is say no, because the title is already in your name."

She looked at them all again in disbelief, then back at the van.

"And the insurance is paid for the next year," Larry added.

Isabel stared at the van, shaking her head. "It's beautiful. But I've never had a brand-new car in my life. I'd be afraid to drive it."

Meg guided her closer to the van. "Well, you do now. And there is nobody in the world more deserving of this than you."

Isabel was still having a hard time processing. "Well, it's the prettiest van I've ever seen in my life. But does it float?"

After everybody stopped laughing, Meg took the keys out of Isabel's hand and pressed a button. "And look, everything is automatic." The side door slowly slid open.

"Well, how about that? I won't have to throw my shoulder out every time I slide the door open and shut now," Isabel said in amazement.

"Go have a closer look, Izzy. It's even prettier on the inside."

Isabel walked over and slowly peeked her head inside, then let out a scream. There, in the backseat, barely able to contain themselves, sat Carly and Charlie. They both piled out and grabbed their mother in a group hug. She pulled away and then grabbed their faces and kissed them both. Tears were running down everybody's cheeks.

"What are you two doing here? How in the world did you find out?"

They both laughed. "Aunt Ginny called us both yesterday," Carly told her.

"But I told her I didn't want her to bother you two with this."

Charlie wasn't having that. "And what exactly *would* you bother us with, Mom, if it weren't to tell us you'd been kidnapped and almost murdered?"

Isabel scoffed, "Oh, honey, it wasn't that big a deal." Isabel grabbed her kids in another hug. "I just can't believe you're here! *Both* of you!"

Applause suddenly rang out. Isabel looked back at the house to see all her guests standing outside, clapping. She knew then that everybody was in on this. Carly and Charlie waved back, and Jackpot and Corky ran out excitedly, jumping right into the van. Beverly came out, still holding the puppy, and carrying the gift bag again. She handed it to Isabel. "Open it, Izzy."

Isabel introduced Beverly to her kids, then began to peek inside the gift bag. "Beverly, you didn't have to do—"

Beverly stopped her. "Consider it a trade, because this little guy is going home with me! Now, open it."

Isabel unwrapped her gift and looked inside the box. First she smiled, then laughed as she pulled out a new cell phone. Beverly gave her a hug. "It's time, Isabel. They really are very convenient . . . well, most of the time."

"Hallelujah!" Frances yelled. "Finally! All we have to do now is ween her off her butter churn!" More laughter followed as everybody gathered in the driveway to say hello to Carly and Charlie.

Isabel smiled at Beverly. "Well, thank you, Beverly. I guess I'm officially a modern woman." She handed the box with her new cell phone over to Charlie. "You're going to have to teach me how to use this thing."

Charlie handed it off to Carly. "I am my mother's son. I lean Luddite, too. Carly's the tech guru in the family."

Isabel laughed. She looked back at her new friend Beverly, and then back at her children adoringly. She looked over at Meg and Larry and Earl Jr., all three of them with tears in their eyes. She saw Earl's boys playing with the dogs. Frances, Freddie and Carol, Zander and Josh, Ginny and Grady, and the rest of her friends, both old and new, surrounded her in the driveway with love and birthday well wishes. She took a deep breath, grabbed her kids' hands, and savored the moment. Isabel Puddles felt like she was the luckiest woman in the world.

Chapter 23

One year later

Jackpot and Corky were already on minnow patrol when Isabel walked out onto the dock with her morning coffee. Summer had quietly faded away and the leaves had already started to turn the glorious shades of amber and red that announced the arrival of autumn. Now it was time to unwind and prepare for the cold but cozy months ahead.

It had been another busy summer in Gull Harbor, but Isabel was too busy to pay much attention to the throngs of summer people. As the anniversary of Earl Jonasson's murder—or what she now referred to as "the incident"—approached, she was feeling reflective. It had been an eventful year, not only for her but for everybody who had in one way or another been involved.

Kentwater County had rid itself of Tammy and Glen Trudlow for good. And while they were on trial facing murder, kidnapping, attempted murder, and a handful of other charges, the state's attorney's office—thanks to Grady's lobbying efforts—had found enough probable cause to have Beryl Vanderhoff's body exhumed. Toxicology reports determined that his death was the result of ingesting small doses of anti-freeze over a period of time. When the kitchen manager at the golf club where Glen worked after his release from prison testified that he had found anti-freeze in Glen's locker—which he remembered thinking was very strange—and that Glen had been a cook during the time Beryl and his wife had been eating there almost daily, a third murder charge was added.

The jury took half a day to find Glen and Tammy guilty of every charge brought against them, and both were eventually sentenced to life without the possibility of parole. The headline of the *Hartley Journal* over their dual mug shots read TRUD-LOWLIFES GET LIFE! It wasn't the most elegant headline in journalistic history, but it was catchy, and it got the point across.

Beverly, who was busy preparing her defense of Marlene Vanderhoff during the Trudlows' trial, was true to her word when she promised Jason she would get him the best deal she could. To that end, she had worked out a deal with the state's attorney's office. Tom Garrett had agreed to grant Jason partial immunity for testifying against Glen and Tammy. He did, and a plea deal followed. Jason was sentenced to thirty-six months in a "special alternative incarceration facility" in the southern part of the state. It was too far for Isabel to visit, but Jason had written to her several times, excited to tell her that he had received his GED and that he had even begun to take some college classes. Isabel always wrote back, encouraging him in his studies and reaffirming the brave step forward he had made toward turning his life around.

Soon after the Trudlows were put away, Beverly took Marlene Vanderhoff's case to trial and managed to convince a jury she was not guilty; beyond a reasonable doubt, at least. Isabel wasn't completely convinced, but she was ready to put the whole awful chapter to rest, so she chose to believe Beverly when she told her she really was innocent.

The big house on the lake everybody thought Parker had built was actually the house Marlene and her husband, Beryl, had been building together when he was murdered. Marlene wanted nothing more to do with the place or with Kentwater County, so rather than pay Beverly's astronomical legal fees, she had made a deal to deed the property over to her if she could win her an acquittal. So legal eagle Beverly Atwater had now become a summer person, along with her constant companion, Diego, named after the Chihuahua she had lost as a girl. She now carried the little guy with her everywhere she went—other than the courtroom—in a two-thousand-dollar Louis Vuitton bag. Beverly had spent a lot of time that summer in her new home on the Big Lake, and if she wasn't there, she and Diego were usually at Poplar Bluff with Isabel. The two of them had become great friends over the course of the year, as had all three dogs. "The incident" had changed Beverly, and she was happy to admit it had changed her for the better.

Meg and Larry Blackburn were spending most weekends on the farm with Earl Jr. and the boys, and Earl's new wife, Briana—a plump, neck tattoo–less, rap sheet–free, sweet-as-she-could-be first-grade teacher, who said she fell in love with Earl the first time she saw his mug shot on the news. Briana claimed she knew by the look in his eyes that he was innocent, so she began to write letters of support to him while he was in jail. The boys loved her, Meg and Larry loved her, and Earl and Briana obviously loved each other. Isabel couldn't have been happier for all parties involved, and she was thrilled to be able to see more of Meg. Their land deal with Wind-X had been finalized, but the wind turbines had yet to be erected, which was fine by Isabel, although she had been preparing herself for the inevitable.

Isabel had been to three weddings that summer: Earl and Briana's in June—a huge event Meg and Larry threw for them on the farm and attended by half the county. In July, Grady and Ginny had a much smaller affair, taking their vows on a friend's vintage yacht while cruising along the lakeshore. Isabel served as Ginny's maid of honor, just as she had for her first marriage, but this time she knew her cousin had made the right choice. The first time, although she chose not to share her opinion at the time, she had a sneaking suspicion that Ralph would turn out to be a bum . . . and he didn't disappoint. And in August, Isabel, Meg, Beverly, Frances, Freddie and Carol all rented a house in Saugatuck for the weekend to attend Zander and Josh's wedding. A very touching ceremony held on the same Lake Michigan beach where they met was followed by an elegant reception in the backyard of their newly renovated summer cottage. Zander's parents would not attend the actual ceremony, but they did manage to set aside their judgment just long enough to attend at least some of the reception, looking displaced and afraid. Josh quipped to Isabel out of earshot that they looked as if "their car had just broken down in a wild animal park." But Josh's family more than made up for their lack of support and enthusiasm, making it very clear to Zander's parents that if *they* weren't able to appreciate the gift they had been given in their son, they were only too happy to welcome him into *their* family. Zander's parents—whom Josh's adorable mother kept referring to under her breath as "Buzz Kill One and Buzz Kill Two"—slipped out the side gate after a dozen tanned and gorgeous young men appeared poolside in matching Speedos, and on cue, dived into the pool and performed a synchronized-swimming routine in honor of the newlyweds. It was a spectacle that would have impressed Esther Williams.

After the grooms left for their honeymoon in the Greek islands, the Kentwater County crew, all of whom had been a big hit with the boys' friends, which included Team Speedo, insisted they go with them to a late-night cabaret show at a local club following the reception. There Freddie Peabody made his cabaret debut after being dragged onstage by a Liza Minelli impersonator, joining her in an impressive rendition of "New York, New York" and, unfortunately, throwing out his hip while attempting a series of high kicks.

And while three marriages floated away into wedded bliss, another one had been grounded due to foul weather. Frances had separated from her husband, Hank. After two months apart, he was miserable without her. And the more miserable Hank was, the more Frances liked it. She told Isabel she had every intention of getting back together with him, eventually, but not until she was convinced he had learned his lesson about taking her for granted, and, after he signed her list of demands. That list included going out to dinner twice a week, hiring a cleaning lady once a week, and telling her she was beautiful every day of the week. "If I can lie about liking his mother for twenty-five years, he can lie about that!" Frances announced after adding that item to the list.

During their separation Frances had naturally moved in with Isabel. She was a handful, and things around Poplar Bluff were not nearly as quiet as they usually were, but Isabel enjoyed the company.

By now the dogs had made it clear—by sitting down in front of her and staring at her—that it was past their breakfast time. She was getting peckish, too, so it was time to wake up Frances and head over to the Land's End. Just as she was standing up, her cell phone rang, something she couldn't get used to. The fact that it was now possible to carry on a telephone conversation while sitting on her dock was still a novelty. Unfortunately it was the same Hollywood producer who had already called several times over the past few months to try to convince her to sell the rights to her story. The producer, a chatty young woman named Ashley, wanted to make a movie about Isabel and "the incident." After finally telling her the last time she called that she would think about it—just to get her off the phone—she was ready to pull the plug on the idea altogether. Of course the money was tempting, because things were, as always, tight, but she was already uncomfortable with the attention she had been getting over the past year, so she wasn't anxious to make things any worse. But there was more to it than that. She just wouldn't feel right taking any money for what she did, and cashing in on such a terrible tragedy. Even the very generous gift of the beautiful new van Meg and Earl had bought for her didn't feel quite right, but she accepted it graciously and gratefully, knowing it came from the heart . . . and it *was* a beautiful van.

Ashley the Hollywood producer did not give up easily. Isabel was being held hostage on the phone by her own good manners. "Well, I do thank you for your interest, Ashley, but I guess I'll just keep my life story to myself for now. If I change my mind, you'll be the first person I'll call." That didn't do it, so she was forced to listen a little longer. Her next idea almost made Isabel do a spit take with her last sip of coffee. "Well, it's an interesting idea, but I don't really see how you could make a musical out of this." The dogs continued giving her the look while Ashley prattled on. "No, I don't think I'd be interested in an animated version, either. . . . Listen, thank you again for your interest, but if I don't get breakfast ready for my dogs, they'll never forgive me. You have a nice day, Ashley. Bye-bye now." The girl was still talking when Isabel hung up.

Frances was already up and in the kitchen pouring a cup of coffee when Isabel walked in. She didn't even notice Hank sitting at the kitchen table at first. "Hank! What are you doing here?"

Frances put the cup of coffee down in front of him, somewhat indelicately, then went back to pour herself a cup. "That's what *I* asked him," Frances said curtly.

Hank took a sip of his coffee. "I'm here to try to convince this woman to come home with me, where she belongs."

Frances turned back to him. "Where I *belong*?" Isabel didn't like where things were heading here. Frances's neck and upper chest were getting blotchy and red, and that was never a good sign. She was moving quickly from a simmer to a rolling boil. "Where I *belong*, Hank, is where somebody appreciates me and respects me—and where I'm not treated like a full-time waitress, cleaning lady, gardener, and cook. I've already raised three children and sent them out into the world. I have no desire to raise a husband."

Hank stared at his coffee cup for a moment while Frances stared at him, then looked up at her and asked, "Do you have any cream for this coffee?"

Frances calmly walked over to the table, took his coffee cup, carried it to the sink, and dumped it out. She turned around now, looking as if she were wearing a bright red dickie. "Get out."

Hank looked at his wife as if she were crazy. "What do you mean, 'get out'?"

Frances gave him a moment to decipher what she thought was a fairly straightforward request, but he didn't seem to be picking up on it. "I mean stand up from the table, walk over to the front door, open it, and then close it behind you when you leave. And don't let it hit you in the you-know-what on your way out!"

Hank stared at her defiantly. Frances shrugged her shoulders. "All right, then, *I'll* leave."

Frances marched out of the kitchen, leaving Isabel alone with Hank, and feeling very awkward. She would have loved to find the words to ease the tension that was lingering in the room, but she could not come up with a single thing to say. Hank finally scooted back in his chair, then slowly stood up and started putting on his coat. "I don't know what's gotten into her."

Isabel lifted her eyebrows and shrugged. At that moment Frances passed through the foyer fully dressed. "I'm going to go get some breakfast, Iz, if you want to meet me." Then, for Hank's benefit, "Someplace where people make you your breakfast, bring you your coffee *and* your cream, and then clean up after you! And get *paid* for it!" The door slammed behind her.

Isabel couldn't help but feel a little sorry for Hank. He was a good man who was just living in another era. "All I did was ask her for some cream," he said quietly as he buttoned up his coat.

Isabel recognized a teachable moment. "Honey, I'm afraid that may just be the problem. You *asked* for it. Did you ever think about just getting it yourself?"

Hank thought about it. "I guess if all it takes is putting my own cream in my coffee to get her back home, I could handle that."

"Well . . . baby steps," Isabel replied. *Bless his little heart,* she thought.

Isabel walked into the Land's End to find Frances sitting at a table with a very handsome, distinguished-looking older man with a beard. "There she is right now! Isabel Puddles come over here and meet Theodore Mansfield."

The man stood up and reached out his hand. "Well, it is a *pleasure* to meet you, Mrs. Puddles."

Frances was wearing a big smile. "Call her Isabel."

He smiled at Isabel. "May I?"

"May you what?"

"Call you Isabel?"

She smiled back at him. "Well, I guess it makes sense. It's my name. Or did you have another one in mind?"

Theodore laughed. "I sure have heard a lot about you. You're rather famous, you know."

"Don't remind me," Isabel replied, then realized they had stopped shaking hands and were now *holding* hands. She took back her hand and sat down, but not before Theodore had pulled her chair out for her. Frances was still smiling. "Such good manners. Theodore is a writer . . . from London. London, England."

"Oh, *that* London. Well, that would account for the accent," Isabel said, smoothing out her place mat and trying to figure out exactly what was going on.

Frances turned back to Theodore. "How many books did you say you've written?"

He was still staring at Isabel as he sat back down. "Well, I don't believe I did say, but I think I'm up to twenty-two now . . . give or take."

Frances shook her head. "Can you believe that, Izzy? I haven't *read* twenty-two books in my entire life, but this one reads that in a month."

Isabel shook her head. "Don't be silly. I wish I had the time. But I *am* a reader. Would I know your work, Mr. Mansfield?"

"Well, you might, but I work under a nom de plume."

Frances scrunched her nose. "A nom de what?"

Isabel jumped in. "A nom de plume. It means he writes under a different name, Frances." She turned back to Theodore, "And that name is . . . ?"

"Archie Cavendish," he answered shyly.

Isabel arched her eyebrows. "You write the Hampstead Street mystery series?"

"That I do . . . or I did."

"Well, I've read every one of them. I liked them very much. I love a good mystery, especially English mysteries. Murder just seems to be a more polite business over there."

Theodore laughed as Isabel took a sip of her coffee. She was more than a little impressed, but trying not to show it too much. "My old friend Gladys DeLong got me onto that series.

She'd be thrilled to know I was having breakfast with Archie Cavendish. Do I call you Archie or Theodore?"

Theodore smiled. "My friends call me Teddy. And I would be happy to meet your friend Gladys."

Isabel took another sip of her coffee. "Well, sadly, Gladys passed away last year."

Teddy expressed his condolences with his intense blue eyes, as Isabel continued. "She was my high school English teacher. Gladys taught me my love of reading."

What she wanted to ask him now was what in the world he was doing in Gull Harbor, but she went in a different direction instead. "So what are you working on now? I mean now that you've killed off Detective Waverly."

"Well, it was time, wasn't it? If you'll recall, I began the series soon after Waverly retired from Scotland Yard. Had I begun another novel in that series, he would have to have been just shy of a hundred." Isabel laughed as Teddy continued. "So I've begun work on a new series set here in the States, this time with a female protagonist . . . a character inspired by a story I read not long ago in the *Chicago Tribune*. My daughter and her family live there, you see, so I visit quite often. Anyway, I picked up the paper one morning and read this fascinating story about a lovely woman, a widow, from a small town in Michigan, who, with no criminal investigative background at all, solved two murders, saved a childhood friend from *being* murdered, saved an innocent man from going to prison for murder, and ensured that the two who *were* guilty were sent away for life. Oh, and she herself survived being kidnapped and nearly drowned in a pond."

Isabel's breakfast arrived. She was processing but at a loss for words as she reached for the salt and pepper. Frances was smiling like the Cheshire Cat. "He's talking about you, Isabel!"

Isabel stared at Frances for a beat. "Yes. I figured that out, Frances."

Teddy continued. "So, you can only imagine my surprise when my daughter told me that she and her husband had just purchased a summer home in the same town where this woman lives. When she suggested I come over to see the new house and witness the fall colors, I agreed, secretly hoping I might actually find a way to meet the indomitable and rather elusive Isabel Puddles. And here I am. And here *you* are."

Isabel folded up a piece of bacon into a slice of toast, dipped it into her egg yolk—her routine since childhood—and took a bite, saying nothing.

"I hope I haven't put you off or frightened you. I can assure you I'm not a stalker. It was just a happy coincidence that I came in for breakfast this morning, and when I mentioned your name to my waitress, well, the next thing I knew I was having breakfast with Frances here."

Isabel finished chewing and smiled. "No, you haven't put me off at all. In fact, I'm very flattered that somebody of your literary stature would be even remotely interested in me. It's just that I have declined every offer so far from folks who have offered to buy the rights to what everybody keeps calling *my story*. It's not *my* story. If it's anybody's story, it's Earl Jonasson's story, and the Jonasson family's story. I only played a part in it. I finally shook a Hollywood producer just this morning who has been after me about it for months. You want to talk about stalking. But I'm afraid I'm just not interested, Teddy. A sweet and kind old man was brutally murdered, some very dear people lost their father, and some precious young boys lost their grandfather. And another man I never knew, but who by all accounts was also a very nice man, was poisoned to death. All in the name of money . . . pure greed. For me to accept any money for what I did would be . . . well, it would be unseemly at best. So, I thank you anyway, but I'm afraid I'm just not interested."

Teddy looked over at a scowling Frances, then back at Isabel with a smile. "I'm afraid you've misunderstood me, Isabel.

I'm not offering to buy *your* story or anybody else's story. I'm a writer. I *create* stories, I don't buy them. That would take all the fun out of it. All I said was that you had *inspired* me and my new character. I read that article in the morning, and by that evening I had finished writing the first chapter of my newest book. My heroine is a former Chicago police detective who was injured in the line of duty and who is now a private investigator uncovering corruption in city government. And she's African American."

Isabel was trying to figure out the link here while Teddy continued.

"You see, Detective Waverly's character was inspired by an eccentric older man I met one afternoon in Kensington Gardens thirty years ago. He was out looking for his neighbor's lost cat and I joined in the search. After we found the elusive feline, we sat down and had a chat. Turns out he had just recently retired from Scotland Yard, and he told me about a few intriguing stories of cases he had worked on and I was off to the races. I dedicated my first book to him."

Isabel was now too embarrassed to speak, but Frances wasn't. She may have been disappointed to learn that Isabel was not on the cusp of literary stardom, but she was quick to identify another opportunity.

"So, are you married, Teddy?" Isabel shot her a look. Frances ignored her. "Just curious . . . I don't see a ring."

Teddy smiled. He reached into his shirt and pulled out a modest gold chain with two gold wedding bands attached. "My wife died twelve years ago." Frances and Isabel were moved. Frances plopped a ten-dollar bill down on the table and got up to leave. "Listen, kids, I've got to run. Teddy, it was a pleasure to meet you. I hope we'll see more of you around here. Izzy, I'll see you back at the house." Frances swept out the door with a wave to the dining room.

Isabel smiled at Teddy again, still somewhat embarrassed.

"She's staying with me for the time being. She's had a little kerfuffle with her husband."

At that moment she looked out the window and saw Hank getting out of his truck, holding a bouquet of yellow roses in one hand and a small carton of cream in the other. Something must have finally sunk in for Hank over coffee that morning. She watched as a smile appeared on Frances's face. He held out his arms and they hugged. Isabel laughed. "But it looks like I may be losing a roommate."

Teddy looked out the window. "Nothing like roses to smooth over a kerfuffle. Only pink would do with Fiona when I was in the doghouse."

The two locked eyes for a moment until Teddy broke the silence. "Isabel . . . I've heard about a lovely little spot off the lake. My daughter tells me the duck is out of this world." Then, thinking out loud, "Now, what did she say it was called?"

"The Old Cottage Inn," Isabel offered.

"That's it!" Teddy smiled, hesitating slightly before continuing, "I hope I'm not being too forward, but might you be free for dinner tomorrow evening?"

Isabel hadn't been asked out to dinner by a man since . . . actually, she had never been asked out to dinner by a man, unless her late husband Carl saying, "Hey, you feel like going to Pizza Hut tonight?" counted as being asked out to dinner. Isabel smiled as she watched Frances and Hank in the parking lot laughing together, with Hank leaning over the hood of his wife's car, pen in hand, and signing what must have been her list of demands.

"Well, Teddy, I do happen to be free for dinner tomorrow evening, and, yes, your daughter is right. The duck is out of this world."